Picasso Prince

R.O. Palmer

Cyndi,

To a fellow Dickinsonian
and old friend.
Enjoy the latest adventure
of your fellow
Cynthia.

R O Palmer

Cover photo by R.O. Palmer.

Dedicated to

Steve Palmer

who opened my eyes to the magic of color

Novels by R.O. Palmer

Picasso Prince

Darress Theatre

Queen of Diamonds

Patriot James

www.ropalmer.com

Acknowledgments

The author thanks:

Sarah Cypher, for focusing me on point-of-view.

My writing group, the HighlandScribes, for critiquing below the surface, and specifically to Joan Lisi, Debbie Patrucker, Mira Peck, and Wendy Vandame for reading the entire manuscript.

Meghan O'Hare, for honest editing.

Sharon Palmer, for telling me what I don't want to hear.

Steve Palmer, for sharing his wisdom about both writing and art.

Charlie Schultz, for an art insider's perspective.

Author's Notes

As a writer, I'm in an "arts" phase. My last book, *Darress Theatre*, revolved around local theatre. A book in progress, *Quartet*, gets inside the heads of four musicians. *Picasso Prince* deals with paintings, auctions, and beauty, both human and artistic.

In addition to writing about art, I've wanted to craft a mystery that wasn't a typical mystery and a romance that wasn't a typical romance. These ingredients came together, with a pinch of travelogue, to become *Picasso Prince*.

I like to cruise, so I set the story on an ocean liner. Although the ship in my story isn't real, its sights and sounds are based on personal experience (with one notable addition). If you've cruised, you might relive a past vacation. If not, perhaps this book will make you want to sail the Caribbean.

Picasso Prince is written in present tense to place the reader in the moment, seeing and sensing what the protagonist sees and senses. For spice, each secondary character gets one "guest point-of-view chapter." The result is that the reader knows a little more about what's going on than the protagonist. I hope you enjoy the result.

If you want to learn more about Cynthia James's past, read *Patriot James* and *Darress Theatre*.

Ars est celare artem

(Art lies in concealing art)

— Ovid

Picasso Prince

R.O. Palmer

Prologue

"I'll pay you…" Malcolm pants, "five… thousand… dollars."

"What?" she says. A quick inhalation brings on momentary dizziness—or is it confusion? The money would blot out the red ink that's drowning her business. Circling him, she raises, ever so slightly, the brow over one dark eye, assessing her student.

He recoils, shakes droplets of sweat from his chestnut hair. A trim mustache glistens. He rises into a half-sitting position and takes several more deep breaths. "Five thousand dollars," he says, louder. "Plus expenses—to be my bodyguard on a one-week Caribbean cruise."

She laughs—to make a show of disbelief—then, with her wristband, wipes perspiration from her forehead. "You're crazy. What's the catch?"

"No catch."

"There's always a catch." She snaps her fingers twice. "Now quit stalling and take me down, tough guy."

They bend forward, circling clockwise on wall-to-wall tumbling mats. He's taller; she's younger, more athletic; both are slim—physically, equal adversaries.

Malcolm shoots toward her thighs. She recedes like a matador's cape. Off-balance, he stumbles forward. She shoves his shoulder as he sprawls face-down.

Flat on the mat, he lies motionless.

She snatches a towel from a wall hook, looks over her shoulder. "You okay?"

"Yeah," he coughs. "I think."

"Serves you right for lunging. You know better." She tosses the towel onto the back of his neck. "Time's up for tonight."

Malcolm pushes himself onto his hands and knees with a grunt too deep for his wiry torso. He looks pathetic, just as he had when he begged her for self-defense lessons after claiming he'd been mugged.

"Quit faking," she says.

"What about my offer?"

She shakes her head. Malcolm Golden continues to surprise her—one reason she teaches him hand-to-hand combat long after he could take care of himself. Another reason: he's one of a handful of people who makes her smile. Looking a decade younger than his 45 years, he moves with a grace that convinces two out of three women that he's gay. She's undecided.

He may not be movie-star material, but neither does he have to pay for a date, whatever his sexual orientation. It's Malcolm's charisma that intrigues her. He has an easy-going charm that defies rules. Why else would she be working at 8:50 on a Sunday night?

"So what do you say, Cynthia?"

Her mind returns to the money. She's two months behind on rent and is paying perpetual interest on her Mastercard. Then she remembers why this is a pipedream. "I can't carry a gun," she says. "I'm a convicted felon." There. It's out. She shrugs, figuring that her criminal record is a deal breaker.

Watching her eyes, Malcolm says, "The Incas ruled half a continent for centuries without guns."

She shakes her head. "So?"

"Being of Peruvian descent, you must know all about the Incan civilization."

She squints; her neck tenses. "How do you know than I'm part Peruvian?"

"Lucky guess. You have a bit of a South American thing going on in your eyes."

"Only one-eighth…. And what do the Incas have to do with your offer?"

"Maybe nothing," he says, as if he means *something*.

"Go on."

"I want a non-threatening bodyguard, someone who doesn't look like muscle. And by the way, you couldn't smuggle a gun onto the *Persian Prince*, anyway. So, are you in?"

Her mind whirs through the math of desperation. If he's serious enough to offer five, he might go higher. "I'd have conditions," she says. "*Lots* of conditions."

He rises and faces her. At 5-7, she's two inches shorter; at 125, she gauges herself fifteen pounds lighter.

"What sort of conditions?" he says.

She presses her tongue into her cheek, conjuring advantageous terms. "I don't have anything to wear," she says, which is true; she hasn't bought clothes other than underwear for over a year. "So you'd have to buy me a wardrobe appropriate for a fancy cruise. Adjoining rooms, with balconies. No fooling around... of course."

"Of course," he says. "But I don't think people *fool around* anymore. Couples *hook up*." He smiles. "What else?"

She catches herself smiling back, which irks her. She should maintain a professional façade, but even as she thinks this, her smile spreads from her jaw to her neck to her shoulders. "Well," she says, "a gift allowance. You'd pay for *all* expenses— including electronics. And I wouldn't consider doing it for less than a thousand a day."

"What else?" he says without blinking.

Her face flushes. "This sounds *so bogus*. Why does an *art professor* need a bodyguard?"

"I'm also a serious collector, and... well, I received an anonymous warning—you might call it a death threat."

This bombshell gets her attention. *Should I demand more money?* She narrows her eyes, draping a towel around her shoulders and stretching her neck like a waking cat. "Keep talking."

"The voyage in question is a connoisseurs' art auction cruise. A newly discovered Picasso will be up for sale. I have to have it! But someone is trying to intimidate me."

"A Picasso? *You?*" She squints. "That's got to be the major leagues. Millions, right?"

"You can think of me as *nouveau riche*."

This statement makes her say "Hmmm." While sometimes she sees Malcolm as a member of the upper crust—where everyone in his family has a Roman numeral tacked on after the Golden—he's just as often unpredictable, a playful Malc.

"So, will you do it?"

"When did you say the cruise was?"

Malcolm grimaces, clutches his foot. "Damn! Another cramp." He hops on one foot, massaging the other. "It's okay. Lucky I got this one in time."

She watches him fight off the cramp, his second in three weeks.

He flexes his ankle before putting weight on his foot. "I'm fine…. The cruise is mid-February."

She pivots toward the office.

"So you'll think about it?" he says to her back.

"Maybe," she answers without turning around. Various angles come to mind. Written threats usually amount to nothing—when people want to hurt you, they don't give warnings. Winter business is awful. She's fed up with the cold, and it's only the first week of January. Maria, her business partner, wants to visit relatives in Puerto Rico, so they could close the studio, save on heat.

The next question: should she spend seven days at sea with a charming client? Malcolm is good company and apparently filthy rich, but if he's not gay, things might get complicated, separate cabins or not. Something about the whole scenario is odd, yet she can smell the money. Her attitude is all posturing now—she's a hooked fish swimming for a safe eddy.

Two strides from her office door, she halts and turns around.

"Don't stop," he says. "You have a beautiful walk— feminine without being decorative."

She purses her lips, feigning displeasure. "Flattery won't help. This is business."

"Don't worry. You're not… my type. I'm just being honest."

"Honest?"

"I'm always honest in my appraisals." He frames her, his arms straight out, thumbs at right angles to his fingers. "Hooked nose," he says sternly. "Latin eyes. Sweaty, honey-brown bob on the last years of sheen. A figure that belongs in a leotard…. Way too many frowns."

Against her will, she cracks another smile.

"Aesthetically pleasing enough," he adds, lowering his picture frame. "But that's not why I want you."

"*Want* me?"

"As a bodyguard. The packaging is a bonus; I want the expertise wrapped inside."

"Why me? I'm just a self-defense teacher."

He shakes his head. "We both know that's not true."

Again, she stretches her neck. "What makes you say that?"

"I heard it was you who saved a certain politician's bacon."

My secrets aren't so secret, she thinks. A hundred questions pop to mind. She asks the first: "Are you *really* serious—a grand a day, plus expenses?"

"Seven day cruise, plus a travel day and clothes. Let's make it an even ten thousand. Three in advance, seven more when I come home with the painting, in one piece."

"Are you kidding me?" slips out before she can suppress her surprise. She was about to settle for eight.

"I'm a man of my word." He flexes his cramping foot. "And of course, I'll pay for the cruise and air fare."

She's tired of being a self-righteous hypocrite. In a heartbeat, her imagination pays off all her debts. She anticipates the warmth of Caribbean sun.

"Try a heating pad on the foot," she says. "I'll have that list of conditions next week. And bring the death threat."

Day 1 — Saturday

Ft. Lauderdale

1

Persian Prince

Cynthia James sticks her head out the window of a moving taxicab and strains to see the top of the ocean liner *Persian Prince*, which towers fifteen stories above its Port Everglades pier. The ship is three football fields long, its bulk more functional than artistic. She stares at the Empire Lines' logo, a purple and gold crown painted high on a giant white housing bigger than a smoke stack.

"Tell me your impression; what do you see?" Malcolm asks, using his art professor's voice. "About the ship. Don't think— just give a lightning response."

Caught off guard, she looks sideways at him. Something is off, but it's not his casual travel clothes, no spiffier than her L.L. Bean blouse and pants. Then it hits her—he shaved his mustache. He looks "less gay." Cynthia feels stupid, having flown from Newark without noticing. She turns back toward *Persian Prince* and says, "The logo's too small for the size of the ship."

"That crown's seventy-five feet high."

So much for small, she thinks. For the next week, frames of reference will be skewed.

The cab rounds a curve and stops in front of the terminal. They leave their luggage with one of twenty purple-shirted porters before walking up three steps into an immense concrete building.

The Empire Lines' Fort Lauderdale terminal could be the hangar for an airplane squadron. While observing the snaking security lines inside the vast hall, Cynthia has an eerie thought: this is Ellis Island in reverse—thousands of people already living the American Dream, queued, waiting to board a ship that will take them across the sea to islands of poverty.

Malcolm bypasses the lines and leads her toward a sign reading: Gold Services—which Cynthia guesses is Empire Lines' version of first class—then on to the Gold Services counter. The woman who checks them in—Annette, by her nametag—speaks in a Dutch accent, is exceedingly thorough, and treats Malcolm like a VIP. Annette hands him four gold cruise-ID card keys. He passes two cards to Cynthia.

"One for each room," he says. "Just as you specified."

"I didn't know that art professors got treated like royalty."

"Normally, I wouldn't warrant such TLC, but I'm on the cruise as an officer of the International Picasso Society."

"The what? Why didn't you tell me?"

"I'll explain later. Let's go. We have priority boarding."

Peering through one of the terminal's giant picture windows, Cynthia gapes at a small portion of the *Persian Prince*—so massive that she senses its gravitational pull. She has never been on an ocean liner, but she's heard the clichés: floating hotel, floating resort, floating city. This cruise ship is all of those, she thinks, and more—a floating miracle of technology. And excess. It's hard for her to believe that people expend so much energy to build a mobile pleasure-palace.

A slim female photographer asks Malcolm and Cynthia to pose for a boarding shot. Cynthia glances behind at the backdrop, a mural of the ship, and stifles a laugh at posing for a photo in front of a *picture* when the real thing is right there. But of course, the ship is too big. She wants to keep moving, but Malcolm stops and smiles. So, against her will, she does the same. A *flash* blinds her. It happens too quickly to avoid, evidence of how difficult it will be to stop an attempt on his life, however improbable.

Cynthia and Malcolm cross the fiberglass-enclosed gangway. Just before they reach the ship itself, there is a narrow gap between tunnel and hull through which she can peek. Cynthia slows, cranes her neck both ways but can see neither end of the ship. This threshold is to another world. Two steps inside, a white-uniformed crewman asks for her ID card and tells her to look at the blue spot on what appears to be an arcade game. The man inserts her card into the machine, which *bings* as it flashes her picture. The process is repeated for Malcolm. Next is the security x-ray conveyor belt and portal. She holds her breath while her sunglasses case passes through the scanner.

They proceed into a breath-taking, three-story atrium of opulence. Two curving staircases frame a twenty-foot waterfall. Purple silk ribbons adorn the banisters. Intricately woven Persian carpets hang from the walls. Malcolm tells her that the *Persian Prince* carries 1,100 crew and 3,500 passengers, a population larger than her town's.

Others are equally awed. Passengers mill around the atrium, gaping, pointing, snapping pictures. Cynthia soaks in the palatial atmosphere until Malcolm says, "I have to make a pit stop."

She pulls him into a paneled rest-room alcove and squeezes his elbow. "Remember, we stay together, and I enter all doors first."

Malcolm's eyes twinkle. "Even the men's room?"

Cynthia relaxes her grip. "I'll wait outside." He has made her smile...again.

Two minutes later, Malcolm pops out. "Should I wait for *you*, now?"

"I'm fine," Cynthia says. "Show me around."

In the center of the lobby, a striking young woman wearing a Tahitian grass skirt offers deck-plan brochures to passengers. She brightens upon seeing Malcolm. "Welcome back, Monsieur Golden," she coos in a French-Polynesian accent. "You know your way, yes?"

Malcolm nods, takes a brochure, hands it to Cynthia. "Yes. Thank you, Liat. I'll see you around the ship."

Liat smiles toward the next passenger. Malcolm and Cynthia walk up one of the curving staircases. "Who was that?" Cynthia asks, as they step onto an oval landing. There, she comes face-to-face with a second greeter, this one wearing a silky beach skirt, flowered tiara, and a halter adorned with baubles of costume jewelry.

"Miranda!" Malcolm gushes. He and Miranda air-kiss like girlfriends. Cynthia figures that a full embrace against a chest-full of gems would scratch.

"Cynthia, this is Miranda, one of the ship's International Escorts."

"*Hola*, Cynthia. Please to meet you," Miranda rattles in a Spanish accent. She looks to be in her early twenties and showcases a warm smile on a round face.

Cynthia smiles back. Because of Malcolm's affectionate greeting, she gives the escort a thorough once-over. The woman's copper skin glistens like spray-tan. Her midriff puffs with a roll of baby fat, but there is nothing babyish about her breasts. Around her neck hangs a thin gold chain with a heart-shaped name tag: *Miranda, Dominican Republic.*

"*Hola*, Miranda," Cynthia says. "What do International Escorts *do*?"

Miranda beams like a proud child. "We make sure all passengers enjoy the cruise." She hands a deck map to a passing woman the size of a hippo. "You have questions, just ask any escort." Miranda is drawn into a hug by the obese woman's equally large husband—at least he has plenty of padding. With Miranda distracted, Malcolm and Cynthia make their escape up to the next level.

Cynthia squints at Malcolm. "International Escorts, huh?"

"Ten on board, dressed in photogenic costumes. You'll see them around, in the boutiques, spa, casino, lounges—answering questions, looking pretty, often with a photographer in tow. Most men can't resist getting their picture taken with a gorgeous woman."

Cynthia wonders about Malcolm.

At the top of the stairs, she sees another escort, a leggy blonde in Alpine togs more suitable for sunbathing than hiking. Cynthia thinks the escorts are provocatively under-dressed, but she says to Malcolm, "Nice costumes."

"All the better to encourage passengers to spend money."

Cynthia glances to see if he's checking out Heidi-girl's statuesque legs, but his head angles for the view one level below—of Miranda's cleavage. Cynthia rolls her eyes, thinking that he isn't gay—maybe bisexual, but *definitely* not gay.

Malcolm tells Cynthia that he has sailed on the *Persian Prince* five times, and he gives her a veteran's tour of the public spaces. The indoor entertainment areas take up three entire decks, numbers 5, 6, and 7. Here, she sees the theatre, Internet Café, cocktail lounges, restaurants, and gift shops.

"The boutiques are open all night," Malcolm says. "Helps give the ship a happening feel for jet-lagged insomniacs."

Higher up, three more decks, 15-17, comprise the outdoor recreation areas: pools, sunbathing patios, spa, gym, running track, rock-climbing wall, plus the 24-hour buffet. According to Malcolm, most cruise ships have similar deck plans. "Features vary," he says, "but the grouping of public space into two multi-deck layers, medium and high—with passenger decks in between—is the industry standard."

Malcolm explains that Empire's five ships are different from the competition in one important facility. "The Casbah Casino is unsurpassed," Malcolm says as they stroll through. "Twice the size of any other line's casino, and generating four times the gross. It's Empire Lines' ace in the hole to seduce high rollers whose families don't like land resorts. But this location, tucked aft, is such that Mommy and the kids can pretend the casino isn't here. They enjoy everything else on the ship—with less congestion."

Cynthia raises a questioning eyebrow.

"When the casino's packed," he says, "there's more room around the pools."

Walking through the cavernous Casbah is eerie, like being in Walmart with no customers. Glitzy slot machines stand back-to-back, hungry to be fed. Giant ceiling-fan blades revolve overhead, and ubiquitous Persian rugs adorn the upper walls. The pristine carpet underfoot appears never to have been walked on. Silence presses on Cynthia's ears, as it does when she listens for sounds that aren't there.

Malcolm reads her mind. "Once we get into international waters, this place'll be hopping like a humongous pinball machine. Do you like games of chance?"

"I'm not much of a gambler." Cynthia's statement is truthful as far as casino games are concerned, although she risked her life on several occasions.

Malcolm drops his chin—perhaps a hint of disappointment—but he presses on, pushing through swinging double-doors into a room bursting with energy. "This is the Casbah Café. Think 'cigar bar meets sports betting parlor.'"

"Sounds like a men's lounge," she says. "Am *I* allowed?"

"Let's just say that if you hang out here, you'll be in the minority." He talks about satellite configurations and betting statistics, but Cynthia focuses on something Malcolm omits in his narrative—a waitress's harem costume. Cynthia understands why men will gravitate to this particular lounge.

Malcolm provides alternative reasons. "No other ship has the satellite capacity to get so many sporting events on TV. You can bet on everything from Pakistani Field Hockey to the Westminster Dog Show."

There are 20 or 25 men biding time with cocktails, eager for the ship to leave port so they can bet on anything that moves. Cynthia will bet on nothing. She wonders if Malcolm likes to gamble. After observing his analysis of the tote board, she guesses that he does. She pegs him as the sort of man who knows the odds on any game *before* he bets.

Their tour moves up a flight. "Do you know why Empire ships have masculine names?" Malcolm asks. *"Egyptian Pharaoh, Roman Caesar, Persian Prince."*

She shakes her head.

"Most cruise ships are feminine—princess this, queen that—but Empire wants to attract families where *men* make the vacation decisions—a niche business. Gamblers like the masculine names, and the company's research shows that gambling families spend more money overall, when you add in drinks, clothes, gifts, shore tours, etcetera. Empire markets heavily to Europeans who like to gamble."

Cynthia examines glittering chandeliers that sparkle like diamonds. "The company seems to be doing okay."

They start up a double-wide staircase, which Malcolm says is near the stern. Cynthia, disoriented without windows, has no choice but to believe him. They pass a slim man whom Cynthia at first mistakes for a teenager. The man's intense eyes make her uncomfortable. She glances at Malcolm, but he's examining a painting on the landing while stretching his fingers. Odd, she thinks. Then, the man is gone.

Several flights up, she turns the wrong way. Malcolm grabs her hand and pulls in the proper direction. "In two days, you'll know the layout."

The tour takes another twenty minutes. Cynthia, constantly checking the deck plan, would be totally lost without him. Are they on the port or starboard side? Near the bow or stern? What lounge was that? Which pool? Every hanging rug on every landing of every staircase starts to look the same. Imitation Persian carpet sprawls up every endless hallway and down every bottomless stairwell. She shakes her head at the number of bars and lounges, which have enough smiling servers in purple waistcoats for every passenger to have a personal cocktail waiter.

Cynthia's favorite deck is the Lido, number 15, which has their cabins in the bow section, plus two pools and the Palace Buffet. It's past lunch time, and she's famished.

They sample the buffet luncheon—Italian Day. Friends warned her about over-eating on ocean cruises, so she doesn't go back for thirds. Just thinking about a week of gluttony makes her pants tighter. It will be difficult to fight off the calories, meal after all-you-can-eat meal. She and Malcolm agree to avoid elevators and stick to the stairs.

Knowing little about art history, Cynthia had never heard of Malcolm Golden, II, six months ago when he walked into her studio asking for self-defense lessons. Since she agreed to this job, she learned that his book, *Art for the Ages*, is the standard text for introductory college courses, and his Pulitzer Prize-winning six-volume masterpiece, *From the Renaissance to Tomorrow*, is a scholarly classic. Internet book review sites say any art text that doesn't refer to Golden is obsolete. She found an article which stated: "At Princeton University, Golden is a living legend. Students wait a year to get into his classes." But Cynthia is about to receive a one-on-one tutorial. After lunch, Malcolm takes her to the ship's art gallery, amidships on Deck 5.

2

Art Appreciation

"Here's what you do," Malcolm says. "Stand in front of each piece; study it for five seconds and feel how your body responds. If you get goose-bumps, it's for real." His eyes blaze like a religious pilgrim's—he's serious about the goose-bumps.

Cynthia stifles a smile. This is *work*, she reminds herself—humor the client. She stares down the gallery, a sixty-foot long, twenty-foot wide hall in the center of the ship—no windows. Framed paintings hang on both walls; other paintings sit on easels in the center along with sculptures, leaving two viewing aisles. Sixty or so pieces of art might as well be 600. She flounders. "What should I look for?"

"Let the *art* tell you. Don't look. *See*."

Mumbo-jumbo, she thinks, but she says, "Okay."

Cynthia studies the nearest piece, a large canvas with swirling spatters of gloppy paint. She counts to five—no goose-bumps. Next, a framed piece of sports memorabilia, Henry Aaron's #44 Milwaukee Braves jersey from the 1957 World Series—not what she would call *art*. The next piece, a vibrant print, is a burst of dolphins under the sea. She likes how the animals meld with the water but has no idea where to focus. It seems that the dolphins are staring back at her. "How'm I doing?" she whispers.

No answer from Malcolm, but she swears that the dolphins giggle.

And so, she works her way around the gallery in five-second

intervals that sometimes stretch to thirty. Several times she is conscious of Malcolm staring at her, but she doesn't react. The more pieces she looks at, the less silly the exercise becomes. By the twentieth painting, she's enjoying the experience.

She lingers longest in front of a naked woman seated in profile on a low stucco wall. Bathed in gold light, the woman, spell-bound by a fountain, is surrounded by a Spanish courtyard. Her damp head is positioned so that her face catches the spray. Hints of glitter highlight a scar running up one leg. Cynthia self-consciously slides a finger across the choker around her neck.

By the fortieth piece, she's worn out. Some pictures bombard her with primary colors; others are subtler, hanging back in muted tones. It takes fifteen minutes to study every piece in the gallery, which reminds Cynthia of a gauntlet—appropriate, since she feels exhausted.

"That's it," she says, back where she started at the swirling oil splatters. "What's next, professor?"

"I'll tell you which pieces you liked by how you observed. Your favorite was the fountain nude. Next, the dolphins. Honorable mention to the beached fishing boat and the wacky pool table." After a short pause, he says, "So, am I right?"

Cynthia nods, feeling naked herself. "Pretty much. How'd you do that?"

"First lesson, clichéd but true: beauty is in the eye of the beholder. If something speaks to you, you study it longer, exploring and absorbing emotional truth. What's *true* is up to the individual, of course. I saw receptive signs in your eyes—the way you moved them around the picture—and in your body language. Art is communication of the soul, artist to appreciator, through the medium."

Cynthia wants to call him on what sounds like total B.S., but a fuzzy part of her almost understands. "Which is *your* favorite?" she asks.

"This is mere commercial art, not where I find favorites."

"Come on," she teases, "fair is fair—suck it up and pick one."

He walks her over to a large piece that she studied for the five-second minimum. It appears to be little more than color and lines. "We aren't looking for the same things," he says. "Your perception is primarily visual—the way you relate to the physical world. Most people start out that way. My taste is more emotional, difficult to comprehend until you've experienced aesthetics on a higher plane. I'm more enthralled by modulation and ambiguity."

"Modulation?" she asks.

"You're not ready for that."

"Okay. So what makes great art?"

He scratches his chin, looking professorial, and leads her back to the fountain woman. "Tell me why you like this piece."

Cynthia memorizes the painting, noting its color, texture, shadow, and contrast—the artistic elements as she knows them. "It expresses something missing, like when film can't capture the magic of low, golden light. The color and lines are refreshing and soothing at the same time."

"And...?" Malcolm prompts.

"The woman is mysterious, because of the scar. And vulnerable, because of the, ah... skin, I guess."

"And can you see yourself in that woman's skin, soaking in the moisture, the sunset, the moment?"

"Uh-huh."

He snaps his fingers. "That's why it's your favorite, your perfect sunset. It connects with who you are, and, therefore, it makes you *feel* and *think*. That's the magic of the best art, whether painting, sculpture, dance, music, or literature. It makes people both feel and think."

The more she listens, the less it sounds like bullshit. She asks, "But the fountain woman isn't great art, is it?"

"Great? No, not really. But it's good for its genre."

"How much is it worth?"

"The original went for five thousand. This framed lithograph will sell for about five hundred."

"Lithograph?"

"A method of reproduction. There's also Dye Sublimation, Repligraph, *Giclée*—French for splash or spurt. That's continuous-tone, inkjet-to-canvas technology."

Cynthia's makes an exorcist's finger cross. "*Way* too much information."

He chuckles. "Don't worry about the methods. What should

be important to you is whether you really like a piece."

"I like the fountain woman. What keeps that one from true greatness?"

"Ah, that's the eighty million dollar question. The fact that you're asking is a sign that you're making progress. The answer is: consensus. If enough people are moved deeply and the *right* people notice, then something is deemed great. That's what I call *public* greatness, like Picasso. But here's the secret: if art connects to you, makes *you* feel and think, then it's great, even if it's only private greatness."

"But you just said—"

"When you were a child, did you have any pictures on your bedroom wall that you remember? Special favorites?"

"Sure."

"I'll bet none were the Mona Lisa."

"Wilbur, from *Charlotte's Web,* and Princess Aurora from *Sleeping Beauty.*"

"And at the time, those images moved you, pleased you. Do you still have those pictures in your bedroom?" He pauses. "No. You've moved on, but that doesn't negate the connection. Stuffy art critics can't take that away from anyone."

Cynthia nods. "Thanks for making me feel good about my limited taste." She glances back at Malcolm's favorite painting. "You know, your explanation seems too simple for a fancy-schmantzy art professor."

"I tailor my lesson to the audience. After all the complexities, art comes down to a simple question. Does it take your soul—the part that makes you *humane* as well as human—to a new place? If so, how can anyone argue that it isn't great?"

"You sound like a poet." She stretches her neck. "What if millions claim that Dogs Playing Poker is great art?"

He scrunches his nose. "I'd suggest that they read my books."

Cynthia smiles, pauses again to study the misty lines of the fountain woman.

"Most men would find it sensual," Malcolm says. "Do you?"

Caught by surprise, Cynthia colors. "Women can appreciate feminine beauty without it being sexual."

"I said *sensual,* not sexual." He smiles. "Perhaps you'd like the fountain woman for your home."

"Part of my gift allowance?"

"No, but I'll make sure Sophia includes it in tomorrow's auction."

Cynthia's neck warms under her choker; she's eager to change the subject. "Who's Sophia?"

"The auctioneer."

"Where's the Picasso?"

"It's in the climate-controlled vault. They'll only show it at the first and last auctions—for security reasons." Malcolm's eyes dance. "Can't leave irreplaceable art sitting out where anyone can draw on a moustache."

3

Security

Nine flights up, Cynthia spies the same slim man she saw earlier on the staircase. He's on the other side of the landing, darting around a corner toward the outdoor pools. The man is out of sight before she can get Malcolm's attention.

Malcolm's and Cynthia's adjoining cabins are far forward on the port side of the Lido Deck. Their luggage waits in the hall along with a rolled yoga mat—her special request. At room L105, there are a number of promotional flyers in a mail rack by the door. Cynthia inserts the gold card key that will also serve as her ID and charge card. "Remember, stay behind me."

"I'll enjoy the view."

Cynthia bristles. "This is serious. A thousand-a-day serious."

The door opens into a dressing alcove—with a bathroom and doorless closet—that flows into the main cabin where a queen bed, loveseat, desk, and chair fill most of the floor space. Glass sliders open to a small balcony. The decor and bedding—Persian rug motif—appear brand new.

"Cozy," she remarks. "Not as big as I expected for a VIP from the Picasso Society."

Malcolm answers from the alcove while maneuvering her huge rolling suitcase. "We were limited by your requirement for adjoining rooms. There're only a handful on the ship."

"I'm joking," she says. "It's very nice." She touches his elbow. "Wait here. Let me check things out." She removes an electronic gadget the size of a cell phone from her shoulder bag.

"Bug detector." She sweeps her room, holding the device out like a can of air-freshener.

"No live devices." She opens the connecting door to the right and repeats the process in Malcolm's room, L103. The next few seconds are critical. She has two spy microphones in the sunglasses case clipped on her belt; she must place both so neither Malcolm nor the room steward will find them. "Do me a favor," she says. "Look in the outer pouch of my carry-on for a little blue box."

"Alright." He walks back into her room.

Deftly, she strips an adhesive tab and sticks one microphone to the springs while looking under his bed. She attaches the other to the back of his desk—near the phone. It isn't that she doesn't trust Malcolm.... Call her thorough.

"All clear," she says.

"I can't find the blue box."

"Must have buried it deeper. Sorry. I'll get it later."

The two cabins are mirror images of each other, and everything in each room sparkles, including a plate of cookies and chilled bottle of Dom Perignon on Malcolm's desk.

"Who's it from?"

He opens the card and nods. "Julia Sotelo."

"An old flame?"

"She's not particularly old," he says, "but she's definitely *el fuego.*"

Cynthia considers smiling, but doesn't. "Remember," she says, "always go through my room to go in or out of the hall."

"Only when you're decent?"

She rolls her eyes.

"Sorry, Cynthia. I couldn't resist."

Cynthia still doubts that anyone will try to harm Malcolm. A more likely problem will be him making a pass. Cynthia's ego isn't inflated—that's just the way men treat her. If it happens, the pass will be respectful, and she'll be gracious in her refusal.

They make eye contact. He camouflages something behind a forced smile. What? Admiration? No. Too soon, she thinks.

"Let's go up on the Sun Deck," he suggests. "They have a sail-away party."

"Not until we clear the channel—could be snipers on shore."

"You're more thorough than I expected."

"Another joke. But you're paying me ten grand to be thorough, so I should at least pretend to earn it. We'll go up in a few minutes, but first, let's relax." She steps outside onto his small balcony, leans over the rail, and looks down—a sheer, ten-story drop to the water. Malcolm told her the ship's draught is less than thirty feet, which means the *Persian Prince* has five times more volume above water than below, appearing top heavy. How much force would flip it? She remembers seeing *The Poseidon Adventure,* with Shelley Winters floundering like a manatee. *Bad omen.*

Still leaning out, Cynthia examines the waist-high safety railing and blue-tinted Plexiglas. She is surprised to see a gutter at the base, then realizes that it must rain, at least occasionally, wherever the ship may sail.

She's about to sit when she hears *knock-knock-knock.* "Stay," Malcolm says. "I'll get it." But Cynthia touches his shoulder, then goes to the door—part of the job.

It's their trim, smiling, purple-vested cabin steward. "Miguel at your service," he says in clipped English. He's from the Philippines—she reads this on his nametag—and profusely polite while advising them to take great care with the finicky vacuum toilet. He backs out, saying, "Okay to call Miguel any time. Any time."

Cynthia waves to Miguel as he shuts the door.

"Out here," Malcolm says from his balcony. He has carried out the champagne and cookies. He pours two flutes of the bubbly. She clinks to *bon voyage* but sets down her glass after a token sip. They sit on white plastic patio chairs, the only budget furnishings she's seen onboard.

"Now that we have some time," she says, "tell me more about the big auction."

Malcolm resettles himself and sips champagne. "Empire Lines has regular art auctions for collector wannabes, but once a year they run a special connoisseur cruise. This particular voyage is once-in-a-lifetime. Thursday's auction will feature originals from famous artists. The plum is a new, authenticated Picasso canvas that—"

"That somebody doesn't want you to have."

"But I will."

"What makes you so sure?"

"Knowing the competition. There are three syndicates of museum trustees that can bid competitively on the Picasso, which will go for around eighty-five million."

"Whoa! How do you know that?"

"It's my business to know value and to know what the bidders will bid before *they* do. Call it my talent, a talent even more useful in tough times like these. A few years ago, this Picasso would have fetched well over a hundred million."

"So who heads up these bidding syndicates?"

"Julia Sotelo and—"

"Ah, the champagne flame."

"The very same. And John Poindexter. Plus the Countess LaCroix."

"A real countess?"

He smiles. "But of course."

"That figures." Cynthia flips open a notebook to enter the names. The fact that she didn't bother asking these questions on the plane is more evidence that she hasn't taken the death threat seriously. "What makes them contenders?"

"Deep personal pockets and loyalty to a major museum. A non-profit institution can't afford the huge sums necessary to win top-flight pieces, so the winners tend to be extremely rich private collectors—"

"Like you."

"…like me. Who affiliate with museums and agree to loan pieces to their chosen favorites. There's a lot of ego in the art-loaning business. The museums throw all sorts of perks at their patrons as encouragement. Julia Sotelo represents the Prado in Madrid."

The word *Prado* jogs a memory. Cynthia once toured the museum while on assignment. Jet-lag dulled her senses that day—she doesn't remember whether she saw any Picassos—but she recalls the haunting hatred in Goya's drawings about Spain's war with Napoleon. So much for escaping her past. She blinks herself back to the present. What has she missed?

"…and the countess is lead trustee for the Louvre. Poindexter, for MOMA, where he's also Head Curator."

"Moe-ma?"

"You *are* an art neophyte. M-O-M-A. The *Museum of Modern Art.*"

She squints.

"In New York City," he adds.

She suppresses the urge to blurt, "I knew that," which would only sound pathetic. "Okay," she says. "Be sure to point out the big three."

"We're having dinner with two of them in the Emperors' Room tonight at eight o'clock. Julia and the real live countess. It's not formal—call it 'extra smart, not-so-casual.' Oh, I almost forgot. Wait here. I have a present for you."

Cynthia grabs his wrist.

"Relax, Cynthia. Just to my closet." She lets go. Malcolm says, "Give me two unsupervised minutes," as he backs off the balcony.

"I'll use my bathroom," she says.

Once he's out of sight, rooting in his closet, she walks into her cabin. She grabs a roll of scotch tape from her bag and hurries into the hall. There, she places a piece of tape over the seam of Malcolm's door—she'll be able to tell if he leaves the room between Miguel's cleanings. While outside, she takes the promotional flyers from the mail racks by each door. She slips back through her room into his. She listens—Malcolm rattling coat hangers. Cynthia takes the flyers onto his balcony.

She's sitting there, flipping through promotions for the spa, gift shops, shore tours, etc. when Malcolm appears with a black cocktail dress draped over his forearm. Cynthia guesses that the slinky garment cost at least $600.

"A *bon voyage* gift," Malcolm says. "I asked Maria about your size. You can wear it tonight."

Cynthia moves her hand toward the silky fabric…but doesn't touch. "I-I can't accept this."

"Why not?"

"It's too… personal."

"You're supposed to be my date."

"To everyone else, yes. But you and I know that this is strictly business." Her words don't sound convincing.

"Consider it part of the clothing allowance."

"No. That's all taken care of. This is way too much."

He shrugs. "Maybe you'll change your mind later in the cruise. We'll forget about it for now." He drapes the dress over a chair then sits next to her.

"I'm throwing all this stuff out, okay?" She picks up her room's flyers. "I'll toss yours, too."

"Did you go through my things?" he says.

"What? No."

"There." He points to the second group of flyers. "That's the death threat. What's it doing—?" He pushes a spa flyer to the side, uncovering a white, number-ten envelope with "Malcolm Golden, Persian Prince, Room L103" printed in the center.

For a moment, they both stare at the envelope as if expecting it to do a somersault.

"I wasn't in your stuff," Cynthia says, "and that isn't the same envelope."

Malcolm rips it open. He unfolds the contents, one sheet of paper, eyes it, then hands it to Cynthia, who reads the single line of printed words: *"Dear Malcolm, Remember, do not bid on the Picasso."*

"That's all?" Cynthia asks.

Malcolm runs his fingers inside the empty envelope. "That's it."

They each read the newest threat again.

"What do you think?" Malcolm says.

"We should tell somebody in the ship's security department."

"No! I hired you as a low-visibility deterrent. This second note doesn't change my plan one iota."

"The truth is," Cynthia says, "I didn't view the first letter as high-level danger. But now…"

"Now you're actually worried about me?" He grins. "I'm touched."

She swats his wrist with a spa flyer. "Maybe mid-level."

"Look," he says. "The ship's pulling out. Let's enjoy the experience—from the relative safety of the balcony."

Cynthia peers across the harbor toward the ocean, afraid that she has forgotten something.

The parade of ocean liners is impressive. Seven giant ships

leave port in single file through the channel, *Persian Prince* number six in line. Up close, each is a behemoth, but as they sail to sea and separate on the open water, the ships become tiny against vastness stretching to the horizon. The lead ship is a dot on the Atlantic…then a mere speck. Witnessing the scope of nature makes Cynthia light-headed.

The giant ship rolls as it clears the channel.

"Rip tide," Malcolm says.

"Shit," Cynthia mutters. Her stomach churns with every swell. She has indeed forgotten something: to take motion-sickness pills. She staggers for the bathroom and vomits into the toilet.

4

Adversaries

Malcolm offers to cancel their dinner reservation, but Cynthia is determined to meet his competition. He retires to his cabin, saying he needs a nap, having arisen at 5:00 a.m. She chews Bonine tablets and clutches her spinning mattress. Eventually, after the ship levels on open seas, the bed slows to the rhythm of a lazy waltz and her stomach settles. She listens—through tiny speakers in her imitation pearl ear studs—to Malcolm snoring in the adjacent room.

A safety drill, required by maritime law, interrupts Malcolm's sleep. Carrying life jackets, he and Cynthia descend seven decks to their muster station, the Arabian Nights Lounge, along with two hundred other passengers. There, crew members instruct the passengers how to put on the life jackets and explain the unlikely need for "survival craft." Cynthia thinks, whatever happened to *life boats*?

Two hours later, she showers, dresses in her third-nicest outfit, and stares at the mirror. The green turtleneck accents the jaundiced tint on her face. She usually wears little make-up, but now she applies various cosmetics until her cheeks look less reptilian. The result is a tad cheap, but cheap is better than green.

Fingers flick through drying hair. The bouncy bob frames her narrow face nicely, but she sighs, missing her silky tresses, twirled and pinned in a myriad of styles. Long hair was her teenage identity—until her stepfather used it to drag her across the hall. She recalls the piercing pain in her scalp, the carpet burns on her back. That living nightmare cost her ten years of therapy before she allowed her hair to grow long again—hair for which several men literally died. Then came prison—no long hair allowed. Cynthia has been out for almost three years without letting it grow back. She tells herself that 35-year-old hair won't shine like it did at 27, but the decision has more to do with identity than appearance. The long-haired avenger must stay buried.

The eyes in the mirror are anxious, the mouth somber. Happiness is still work. She wishes she could absorb Malcolm's *joie de vivre*. Maybe that's why she accepted this cushy gig. Or is she simply cruising for cash? Cynthia shakes her head, yet here she is, cruising for something. Excitement? No; her past adventures make a Caribbean cruise seem like a pony ride. Romance? Even if Malcolm is straight, he's unlikely to want more from her than a good lay. Then why? Perhaps seasickness is the going price for passengers who don't know what the hell they're doing onboard.

Two knocks on the connecting door. "Ready, Cyn?"

Is this the first time he's called her Cyn? She tugs up the turtleneck—old habits. A deep breath. Time to face-off with the high rollers.

Malcolm's idea of "extra smart, not-so-casual" is a tailor-made cashmere sport coat and silk shirt—super sophisticated. Cynthia, wearing blended polyester the color of seawater, feels like flotsam.

Taking tentative steps, she holds Malcolm's elbow on the walk to the restaurant. True to her pledge, she insists on using the stairs—at least they're going down. One small step at a time, she reminds herself.

"Sure you're up to this?" he asks at the restaurant's regal entrance.

She nods. They walk in holding hands. His palm is warm; hers is moist. For a moment, she feels sixteen.

The crystal centerpieces in the Emperors' Room are museum quality. Servers outnumber patrons and, in tuxedos, are better dressed. The linen and china are delicately trimmed in purple—very imperial. Malcolm gives his name to a mustachioed restaurant captain, who leads them to a secluded corner. While wending between occupied tables, Cynthia glances at seafood pasta and rack of lamb. The air whispers of capers and garlic.

"Julia and the countess are upstairs twiddling their thumbs," Malcolm remarks after they sit at a table for four. "They'll stay in the countess's suite until the *maître d'* calls them. Countess LaCroix waits for no one."

Cynthia doesn't mind. She uses the time to check out the staff members' movements; they glide to the kitchen and back with purple and gold towels draping their forearms—perfect, she observes, for hiding a handgun. More old habits.

She feels obligated to start a conversation, so she uses a technique taught by her father. "Tell me about Julia and the countess in twenty-five words or less."

"Julia is a rich widow on the prowl for a husband wealthier than her last, who was wealthier than her first. The countess treats everyone like subjects, including her husband, who never travels with her, and trustees of the Picasso Society, who only do because we have to."

Cynthia pretends to count the words on her fingers. "Long-winded, but not bad."

He smiles, which pleases Cynthia. She wants to keep him talking, so she asks, "How did a countess get on the Picasso Society board of trustees?"

"She's a senior acquisitions advisor for the Louvre."

"Is that some honorary title?"

"Not in this case. She studied art history—her specialty is Picasso, of course—and she and the count loan priceless masterpieces to the Louvre, plus they donate hundreds of thousands of Euros."

"I guess there's nothing honorary about money, huh?"

"True. The Louvre doesn't want her money going to the rival Musee Picasso or Musee d'Orsay, so it made her an acquisitions advi—"

"*Senior* acquisitions advisor," she corrects.

He laughs. "In any event, her position is legitimate enough for the Picasso Society. She consults on how the Louvre spends LaCroix contributions, and she lobbies hard for prime presentation of Picassos."

"Interesting," Cynthia says. Then she looks up. "Speak of the

Devil. Devils. This has to be them, right?"

Malcolm rises for two women who approach the table. Cynthia is unsure of the proper etiquette—to be safe, she stands, also. Malcolm makes the introductions: "Countess LaCroix and Julia Sotelo, meet Cynthia James." The fact that he uses a title instead of the countess's first name is not lost on a Jersey girl with two first names.

They all sit. Julia engages Malcolm in idle conversation.

The countess observes with an icy scowl.

Cynthia gauges both women to be in their early fifties, but they're opposites in every other respect. The petite countess is needle thin and pale as skim milk. Her silver sequined gown (extra smart or not, it's a *gown*) is worth more than Cynthia's Toyota. The countess's short, straight, chocolate brown hair—dyed—is styled for a roaring twenties costume party. Her spine remains rigid, as if screwed to the seat of her chair. Cynthia muses that the countess's smile muscles are paralyzed—maybe from the weight of too much money.

Julia, on the other hand, is flamboyance exaggerated, the image of an opera diva. Wavy jet-black hair (also dyed) shouts: *look at me!* Her low-cut scarlet dress reveals a generous portion of a full figure. Personality radiates from an indefatigable smile. A Spanish accent perfectly complements her flashy clothes and mannerisms.

After two minutes of small-talk, Cynthia concludes that Julia's excess is less irritating than the countess's severity. Barely. Julia dominates the conversation, which starts about art and intensifies to *all* about art. She mentions several famous paintings that she bought for the Prado, including the eight figure price tags. She drops names to prove that she knows every famous living artist, some of them intimately. The countess speaks sparingly—and not at all to Cynthia—mentioning only one artist, Picasso himself, who once balanced an eight-year-old countess-to-be on his knee.

Through it all, Malcolm displays his own detached strain of art snobbism.

By the second course, Cynthia's stomach is in mid-cruise form. The food is delicious, the staff vigilant without hovering. In that regard, they are like her—while she watches for a suspicious bulge under clothing, the waiters scrutinize half-empty glasses.

After the soup, Cynthia is full. She shouldn't have eaten the entire spinach salad or a second seven-grain roll. Conversation continues about museums and auctions. Cynthia feels as useless as the untouched silverware, cleared after every course. Occasionally, Julia and the countess speak in French—condescending asides meant to humiliate an outsider—lyrical strings of "*zon-plu, cheri, mon-zon-ze-zon-zon.*"

When Julia takes a breath, Malcolm asks Cynthia, "How are you enjoying dinner?"

"The food's delicious," Cynthia says, "so I'm surprised this restaurant isn't full."

"Well," Julia says, "there *is* a substantial cover charge. Didn't Malcolm tell you?"

"No. How much is it?"

The countess's haughty indifference cracks into a frown.

"What, I can't ask about price?" Cynthia says, an edge to her voice. "You've been dropping art prices all evening."

"That's different," Julia says, eyeing the color of her Riesling.

The countess takes a flea-size sip of seafood bisque.

Malcolm sits back, smirking.

"How is that different?" Cynthia asks.

"You're serious, aren't you?" Julia glances at Malcolm, looking for help. "Where should I begin?"

He shakes his head. "You got yourself into this one, Julia. I'd like to hear your explanation."

Julia sets down her wineglass. "Art philanthropy is multi-faceted. Patrons do *so* much more than stock museums. We're advancing history, culture, *and* art."

The countess offers the faintest of nods.

Cynthia thinks: what a load of self-serving crap.

But Julia, her eyes dancing, is just getting started. "You can't put a price tag on such things. Advanced civilization thrives on the arts. When art is promoted, mankind flourishes. When art is suppressed, dark ages descend."

"A history professor might quibble," Cynthia says. "About cause and effect, I mean."

"But the intrinsic value of art!" The color deepens on Julia's cheeks.

"I don't question the intrinsic value," Cynthia replies. "I just have a problem with the relative price. What's the Picasso expected to bring? Tens of millions, right?"

Julia covers her mouth at Cynthia's breach of etiquette. More telling, the countess blinks.

"It's not like the money is *creating* the art," Cynthia says. "The painting's already there. How much food for the hungry could you buy with the same money?"

The countess sits absolutely still until everyone focuses on *her*. "Our class gives generously to charities. And the high price of truly outstanding art is an incentive for artists to *be creative*."

"How does that justify spending millions for the painting of a *dead* artist?"

"I never—"

"Cynthia," Julia interrupts, "I don't think the countess approves of your cheek."

Malcolm holds up his palm. "It's only important that *I* approve of her cheek... and I do." His smile breaks the tension. He kisses Cynthia's right cheek.

Cynthia flushes—against her will.

Julia beams. "She's delightful—a breath of fresh air. We can use a bit of comeuppance from commoners now and then."

"So, Malcolm," Cynthia says. "Am I to be your Eliza Doolittle?"

Everyone laughs—except the countess.

A cutlery steward replaces all the silverware. Two waiters swoop in to clear the china. Two more deliver the entrées as if they were priceless jewels. The wine steward pours what Cynthia guesses is obscenely expensive Bordeaux. She takes her first bite. The restaurant and company may be pretentious, but the rack of lamb is superb.

5

La Comtesse de LaCroix

Yvonne has a splitting headache. The lobby elevator is irritatingly slow to arrive, giving her time to feel miserable—and misunderstood. Others see her as cold and aloof, but she, descended from a minister to the court of Louis XIV, is merely upholding the family honor. Her husband, the current le Comte de LaCroix, is a lush. Her son, the future count, is a gambler. And her sister, who only counts money, is a tramp. All dismal failures. If Yvonne must compensate for their sins, so be it. Because of her philanthropy, the name LaCroix is still respected in the art world.

"What did you think of Malcolm's girlfriend?" Julia asks.

The speck of a person isn't worth an acknowledgment, but Julia has forced the subject. *What was the trollop's surname, anyway? Something common with no pedigree...*

"The James woman?" Julia prompts.

Ah yes, Yvonne thinks, the James woman—a rotten apple: shiny cover, exquisite shape, but disgusting core, and no taste. The wasteful glutton ordered full portions—which she couldn't finish—instead of the seven course sampler. The fact that Mademoiselle James has no fortune isn't deplorable; what *is* despicable is that she whores after Malcolm's.

"Well?" Julia says after the elevator door closes, bestowing absolute privacy. It is understood what her single word means— Yvonne knows that Julia always pushes the issue, wanting to dissect Malcolm's companions, whom Julia views as competition.

"You mean: besides the abrasively scratchy voice?" Yvonne frowns, then deftly turns the tables. "What did *you* think, Julia?"

"Overall, not his usual… distraction. Certainly not as busty as Lori or Sibyl. A touch of danger. Somewhere between call-girl and pit-bull."

"Perfect, Julia." Yvonne almost smiles. "You have such a way with words, although, I might say that at dinner you sounded almost enamored of the gold-digger."

"I thought it unfair to gang up on the poor girl. We want to keep Malcolm off guard. He still has no idea what we're up to."

"Are you certain?"

"Oh yes, of course." Julia flicks hair that flows back from her face as if blown by a fan. "If he had an inkling, he would have tried to seduce me."

"Ha! Malcolm hasn't looked twice at you in a decade." Yvonne glances at Julia as if looking over the top of reading glasses. "Not even your shameless cleavage. One thing the tart has all over you is her body. Yours is not only over the hill, but sliding down the far side."

Julia inhales an exaggerated breath. "Extra curves are better than none."

Yvonne huffs before saying, "Which of us refused an invitation to spend a weekend with Prince Agusto at the Hotel Excelsior in Capri?" This renders Julia temporarily speechless. They ride in silence until the elevator stops.

The door slides open. Julia steps out, looks around. They are still alone. "That was a decade ago. People hang onto memories when that's all they have. Goodnight, Yvonne."

La Comtesse de LaCroix allows herself an inner smile. She and Julia have been tweaking each other's noses for 25 years, one of Yvonne's few social pleasures.

When the door opens again, this time on her own deck, Yvonne doesn't get off. Instead, she pushes "16" and takes a ride to the Sun Deck.

The art auctioneer, Sophia Caporetto, is waiting, leaning on a rail one deck above the serene Persian Gulf Pool. She wears neither her crew uniform nor nametag, just a black hooded sweat-suit that hides half her face, but not her tension. Sophia turns her head only briefly to acknowledge her visitor.

"You're late," Sophia snaps, looking back down at the pool.

"You know the service in the Emperors' Room."

"But I wouldn't—can't afford it."

"A pity." Yvonne stands awkwardly, forced to address the hood. She has not leaned her forearms on anything in thirty years, not even a mattress. Bending at the waist is common, the resulting posture embarrassing—her derriere on display—but tonight, for the cause, she does. The railing that chills her through the sleeves of her gown probably has not been cleaned in days. Thank heavens it is dark, and there is no one around to witness her debasement.

"You should invite me to dine with you," Sophia says with overt cynicism.

"Enough small talk," Yvonne says. "About the auction. Julia Sotelo and I are a team. She may bid on her own—to mislead others—but in the endgame, look to me, not Ms. Sotelo. It's very important."

"How important?"

"Don't get greedy. Your percentage will be quite lucrative."

"About that percentage…"

"Ah, yes," la Comtesse says, "Julia passed on your new demands. If the price goes over eighty million—"

"Which it will."

Yvonne bristles at the interruption. "If the price goes over eighty million, you will get the requested premium—as long as we win, of course."

"Good," Sophia says, still looking down at the pool and its soft yellow lights.

From her limited experience in lesser society, la Comtesse expects that Sophia is waiting for reciprocation—an equally plebeian "Good"—but Yvonne refuses to say it.

Finally, Sophia taps the rail with long fingernails. "If that's all, I have another appointment."

"Then by all means, go… as long as we have an understanding."

Sophia nods before walking aft.

Yvonne doesn't trust the greedy Italian, wouldn't mind if she suffered an unfortunate accident—

Realizing her awkward pose, la Comtesse straightens. She

reflects that Sophia's avarice is the fault of selfish private collectors, like Malcolm Golden, who poison the art world. La Comtesse has learned that to keep art in the public domain, one has to play the scavengers' dirty game, no matter how revolting.

Yvonne considers lingering in the open air, but a breeze whips several strands of hair across her forehead. The elements are always such a nuisance. She walks stiffly toward the elevator. It is fortunate that she encounters no one who might see her creased sleeves, disheveled hair, and wind-burned cheeks.

Back in the safety of her suite, she dials Julia Sotelo's room, waits for an answering pick-up, then says, "It's done. Now, do your part."

Next, Yvonne calls room service and housekeeping. She requires a glass of sherry and some extra pillows for proper appreciation of the priceless masterpieces she has brought along—to mitigate the offense of her suite's common walls.

Once the intrusion is endured, she is left happily alone. Reclining, she admires her Monet canvas, her Raphael sketch, and her petite Picasso.

6

First Night

Cynthia watches the elevator door close on Julia Sotelo and Countess LaCroix.

"So what did you think of them?" Malcolm asks.

Cynthia doesn't answer, distracted by the slim man once again, this time slipping into the elevator car to the left of the one occupied by Julia and the countess. "Do you know that man?" she asks.

"What man?"

"He just got into the far elevator. Earlier, we passed him on the stairs. Twice."

Malcolm shakes his head. "Must have missed him."

During awkward silence, Cynthia checks her watch: 10:47 p.m. It feels like she's on a date.

"So what did you think of them?" Malcolm repeats, louder, breaking the tension.

"Longest dinner of my life."

He grins. "Don't sugar-coat it."

"The food was great, but your friends are pretentious snobs."

"They're not my friends."

"Okay," Cynthia says. "Your *enemies* are pretentious snobs."

He laughs. "I hope that judgment doesn't go for me, too?"

"If the shoe fits…" Cynthia raises an eyebrow. "Actually, I googled you before we sailed. You give money to charities that really help people. I wouldn't have taken this job if you didn't do some good with your wealth." This is a lie, but after enduring several hours with pompous philanthropists, Cynthia wants to project noble motives.

He beams. "So you investigated me. I'm flattered. What else did you learn?"

Cynthia glances around the lobby. "Let's go outside." They exit to sea air and walk counter-clockwise on the hardwood promenade. There are few late-night strollers, all out of earshot. Malcolm takes Cynthia's hand. "Earth to Cynthia. What else did you learn about me?"

She stretches her neck, a nervous habit she's trying to break. "You said you're worth over two billion. My sources say it's more like one. Why overstate your wealth?"

Laughter catches in his throat.

"What's so funny?" she says.

"Not funny, actually. I've gone to a lot of trouble laying smokescreens so that bidders underestimate me. The extra billion is shielded in various shell holdings under ownership that can't be traced."

Cynthia considers challenging his explanation—some of her old friends have access to ultra-sophisticated technology, and she is sure that they uncovered all Malcolm's assets. Instead, she says, "My contacts must have misinformed me."

"Are these contacts from the prior life you avoid talking about?"

"Nice try," Cynthia says. "We agreed—nothing about my past."

"You brought up it up."

"Let's get back to business. Tell me how the countess and Julia got their money—and how you know them. Everything."

They stroll for a few yards before Malcolm speaks.

"You've heard the expression old money. Well, the countess is *ancient* money. Her family has been rich for so many generations that they've evolved with sticky fingers."

Cynthia hides her smile. "How about Julia?"

"I told you: she married money. Several times. Between funerals, she goes after *my* fortune."

Cynthia arches an eyebrow. "How did you first get to *know* Julia?"

"Nothing biblical. Strictly business—a fundraiser for the

Prado, years ago."

"And the countess?"

"No one can pretend to know Countess LaCroix. She's the coldest fish in the Arctic Ocean. But she has tremendous influence, so people humor her. Do you think a woman with Julia's *joie de vivre* would socialize with her otherwise?"

"Dumping Latin on me again, huh?"

Malcolm laughs out loud. "You're funny—for a stoic body guard."

Cynthia gazes out across the ocean. They walk more slowly now. She asks, "How did *your* family get rich?"

"My grandfather smuggled liquor during prohibition, along with old Joe Kennedy. But Malcolm Golden, the First, kept a low profile, knowing you can sucker more people when they don't know who you are. Grandpa was into money, not power."

"But aren't they the same thing?"

Malcolm doesn't respond, so she asks, "And your father?"

"A penny-pincher. The toughest businessman I've ever known."

"Did *he* get you interested in art?"

"Heavens no. It was my mother. She was the artistic one."

"Are they still alive?"

"Both deceased. What about yours?"

Cynthia shrugs. "The same."

"I'm sorry. What happened?"

She shakes her head. "That qualifies as part of my past. Off limits. Don't ask, because I won't tell if you do."

"We have a whole week. I'll get something out of you before we disembark."

Cynthia, leery of encouraging his charm, doesn't reply.

Amidships, Malcolm stops and leans his palms on the railing. "I bet your past is full of vivid stories."

"Why won't you let up?"

"You're an intriguing woman. I appreciate intrigue. I'd like to know your story."

She gazes at the stars.

"I *want* to know." He touches her shoulder.

Cynthia draws back. "You and your search for *intrigue*. I was raped when I was seventeen because my stepfather found me *intriguing.* It took me ten years to get over that, so excuse me if I don't genuflect. Don't ask me again, *okay?*"

"Okay.... I'm sorry."

"Apology accepted." Cynthia starts walking; Malcolm follows. She stares skyward. "Do you know anything about astronomy?"

"Ursa Major," he says, pointing, "and Ursa Minor. And there, Ursula Andress."

She tap-punches his arm. "Who's she?"

They retrace their steps on the promenade, the breeze now in their faces. He takes her hand. She walks for two steps, her pulse spiking, before she pulls her fingers away. She whispers, "Too much play-acting is a mistake. Let's just enjoy the night."

Malcolm and Cynthia go inside and climb eight flights to check out the Magic Carpet Drive-In Movie, an open-air theatre with double-chaise loungers—each shaped like a flying carpet. The latest Pixar animated feature is playing.

They recline. Stewards bring popcorn, soda, and blankets. A movie, stars, clean air, sea breeze—Cynthia thinks, pretty darn nice for February.

Their first night in adjoining cabins. Cynthia and Malcolm enter, as always, into hers, L105, the nearest to the stairs. Miguel has turned down the beds, placed chocolates on the pillows. He has also left tomorrow's newsletter, promotions for the ship's spa, and a reminder to set the clocks ahead one hour as the ship sails southeast into the Atlantic Time Zone. The light is low—just one soft reading lamp.

Tension tightens her neck; silence encourages her imagination. Cynthia couldn't stop the tingle if she wanted. Nothing will happen, but something *could*—that's all her nerves require. She spends a minute half-heartedly checking his room for bugs and bombs, listening to him tell a joke about breakfast cereal.

He offers to keep the connecting door open. "Good night," she says, closing it.

Cynthia tiptoes out into the hall. At Malcolm's door, she Scotch-tapes a fresh two-inch strip across the exterior seam.

Back in her cabin, Cynthia slips into comfort sleepwear—

gym shorts and a frayed cut-off T-shirt—then goes through her nightly yoga ritual. By the end of Shavasna, her body is soothed, but her mind doesn't unwind until she hears Malcolm snoring through her pearl-stud ear-speakers. She turns the volume down, removes the left pearl, and rolls onto her side.

At 3:30 a.m., Cynthia's watch alarm beeps—time for an audio check. She turns up the volume on the right ear-speaker.... No snoring. No breathing. Nothing. She puts on the second earring.... Still nothing. She adjusts her eyes to the darkness before easing open the adjoining door.

Malcolm's bed is empty, the sheets cold.

She hurries through her room, grabs the cardkey, then darts into the hall. The tape on his door is broken. "Shit!" She kicks the door, jamming her toes on the frame. "Shit, shit, shit." The ship is too big for a search; she will have to wait.

Malcolm sneaks into his room shortly after 4:15. Cynthia sits curled on his loveseat, listening to noises in the dressing alcove. When he flips on a light, she says, "Have a nice rendezvous?"

Mr. Smooth flinches.

She sniffs, smells perfume. "You're not gay, are you?"

"I never said that I—"

"You're such a moron. What piece of ass could possibly be worth your life? Was it the Dominican party doll?"

"What makes you think—"

"Cut the crap." The k-sound catches in her throat, as it does whenever she's angry. "Who did you meet?"

"That's none of your business."

"The hell it isn't! You're paying me to protect you, so where you put your dipstick is *very much* my business. Like I said, you're a moron."

He grins.

"This isn't funny."

"But it is."

"How is you sneaking off unprotected supposed to be *funny*?"

"Have you ever seen Butch Cassidy and the Sundance Kid?"

She squints. "Huh?"

"Well, there's a line that's *à-propos* to this situation." He gives her a knowing nod. "But you'll have to figure it out yourself. I'm going to sleep. You can stay or go." Malcolm slips out of his shirt and pants—unconcerned that she sees his golden briefs.

She tries not to notice, but everything is far too noticeable.

He climbs into bed. "Remember, you work for me. And please, turn off the light."

"We'll talk about this tomorrow," Cynthia says. She leaves the light shining and slams the door. Her big toe throbs.

In bed, she searches her memory bank for memorable Butch Cassidy lines:

"For once, I wish you'd get here on time."

"I'm better when I move."

"Who are those guys?"

While listening to Malcolm breathe evenly, Cynthia ponders: who is *this* guy? He's smart, charming, rich, and her best student, but those characteristics don't explain the riddle. One of Cynthia's former colleagues investigated Malcolm Golden— controversial but clean. He has been consulted regarding art heists—as an expert. Rumors flutter about fishy auctions, but no specific allegations ever took root. Malcolm lends exhibit pieces on *his* terms and plays no favorites with museums, which means he has no allies. Within the intense competition for limited masterpieces, if one isn't an ally, then one is an adversary. Malcolm appears to relish the role of lone eagle. If Cynthia had to describe Malcolm Golden in two words, they would be: charming rogue.

The first time he mentioned the cruise job, she had laughed, a reaction that piqued her interest because she rarely laughed. But she isn't laughing tonight, and there's no one to blame but herself. Malcolm charms everyone, so Cynthia's beguilement means nothing, which is as it should be. She is his *bodyguard*, she reminds herself, *not* his date.

The alarm wakes her at 6:00 a.m. Cynthia listens....

Malcolm snores on. She thwacks the snooze button and closes her eyes.

Three rapid *thumps* awaken Cynthia. Her watch reads 6:15.

Malcolm's voice growls through her ear speakers. "I'm coming."

Someone is at Malcolm's door.

She bounces from bed, opens the connecting door, and bolts through his room in time to be behind his shoulder before he opens the door to the corridor. She notes that he took the time to put on a bathrobe. They exchange glances. Hers says: "You should have called me." His says: "Oops."

Malcolm opens the door.

The caller is a beanpole officer in dress whites. "Ensign Billingsley, security," he says in a stodgy British accent. "Sorry to bother you so early, Mr. Golden, but there has been an incident at the art vault."

Day 2 — Sunday

At Sea

7

Wardrobe

Cynthia, muscles tensing, steps in front of Malcolm, who asks, "What kind of incident?"

"Nothing to worry about," Ensign Billingsley replies.

Cynthia looks at the man's huge hands. One holds a manila folder; the other flexes near his belt. There is no visible weapon—he's probably who he says he is. With the rush of fear disappearing, she's aware of being underdressed in gym shorts and a cut-off T. There are several glances, one directed at her bare abdomen. "I'll throw something on. You can come on in."

Under the circumstances, Cynthia can't leave Malcolm alone with anyone. Backing into Malcolm's dressing alcove, she sees his hanging windbreaker. As the men walk past her toward Malcolm's bedroom, she grabs Malcolm's wrist long enough so that Billingsley goes first. With her eyes locked on the officer's hands, she slips into Malcolm's jacket and zips it up, after which she walks in ahead of her client.

"Have a seat, Ensign," Malcolm says, gesturing at the chair.

"No, thank you. I'll stand."

Malcolm stops his downward motion toward the mattress, then straightens up.

Cynthia stands between the men.

"So what happened?" Malcolm says.

Billingsley opens his folder. "The lock of the art vault's door was tampered with early this morning."

"Tampered with?"

"We don't believe it was penetrated, but Sophia Caporetto thought that you, as President of the Picasso Society, should be notified at once."

"Tampered with?" Malcolm's pitch rises, his face colors.

"We have photographs."

"What about the security camera?"

"It seems to have malfunctioned, an electrical problem. We're having it repaired—"

"I want to see the vault!"

Billingsley shakes his head. "We're dusting for fingerprints, doing other tests, treating the area as a crime scene—at least for now." He removes photos from the folder. Cynthia focuses on his hands, ready to intervene in the event of any sudden motion, but Billingsley merely lays out seven photographs on the bed. The shots are close-ups of the safe door and combination dial.

Cynthia recognizes the door and lock—a stainless steel Brown S&G 6730. The dial and surrounding area are scuffed, as if scraped by a chisel. Not the work of a professional.

Billingsley bends over and taps one picture. "The 05:35 security round detected the marks."

"What about the Picasso?"

"It's fine."

"How can you be sure?"

"The door wasn't opened. The sensor log would have a record if it was. And afterward, Sophia and I went in and verified that the Picasso's protective case had not been tampered with in any way. All the signed tapes are in place."

"So what do you want me to do?" Malcolm says.

"We just thought you should know. Now you do."

Malcolm stews with furrowed brow.

"Thank you, Ensign," Malcolm says. "You can go now."

The officer gathers up the photos and leaves.

Malcolm paces in the bedroom. "A *crime scene*? I'm just supposed to *sit around and do nothing*? I'm the President of the god-damned society!"

Cynthia tunes out his venting while she thinks. A pro would

have drilled out the locking mechanism or used amplifiers on the tumblers. Very strange.

He has stopped talking and is frowning at her. "I said: what do you think, Cynthia?"

"Whatever it was, I don't think this was a serious attempt to steal the painting."

Malcolm's eyes widen. "Then what was it? That's supposed to be a secure area."

She shakes her head. "I don't know. But we might as well get ready for breakfast. Neither of us is going back to sleep now."

"*Then* what?"

"I suggest you don't react," she says. "See if anyone else does. In the meantime, let's do what you said we should do this morning—catch some rays."

From her balcony, Cynthia watches the sun climb from the horizon into a warm, cloudless sky of breathtaking blue. According to the newsletter, the ship is cruising southeast at 18 knots. If they can forget about the safe-tampering, the peaceful Sunday morning promises to be a good sunbathing day.

After breakfast, Cynthia squeezes into a black one-piece swimsuit featuring horizontal back-straps—$125 on her wardrobe account. Very chic, but she's wary of modeling for Malcolm—it will be the first time he sees her neck uncovered. Six nickel-sized pink scars are spaced every two inches around her throat— souvenirs from her days as a patriotic assassin. The scars are why she wears chokers and turtlenecks, none of which will complement a bathing suit. She tries on a turquoise scarf, but it looks silly.

Malcolm frowns when she walks into his cabin. "You'll get even darker than that, won't you?" he asks.

Cynthia peeks at her naturally tan shoulder. "Uh-huh. After a half-hour broiling with Brazilian tanning oil, you might not recognize me."

"That's what I'm afraid of. Let me see the dress you're wearing tonight."

She wonders what leap has taken him to ask about wardrobe choices several outfits into the future. After a long squint, she pulls out two hangers and holds one in front of each shoulder.

"Either or."

"And the backs?" She flips them over. He examines the dresses then laughs. "A word of caution: don't wear that swimsuit today."

"Why not?"

"Look at the pattern of the cross straps. Now look at the dress necklines, front *and* back."

He's right. The back of each dress is too low—horizontal tanning lines will look ridiculous with either dress. She muses: did her mother or father pass on her idiot gene?

"I guarantee we'll see women tonight who don't coordinate swimsuit and gown. Lucky for you, I have another present." He disappears into his room, then returns with a small purple Empire Lines plastic bag, which he hands over. "Here."

Cynthia pulls out a skimpy orange bikini. She turns dark pink. "You want me to wear this... this *thong*? I'm thirty-five, not eighteen."

"You'll look fabulous," he says without a hint of sarcasm.

"No way. Thanks, but I'll change into my *own* bikini." She stuffs the orange suit back in the bag. "Here."

Malcolm puts the bag in her lower bedside table drawer. "It'll be here if you change your mind."

Cynthia hoped to delay showing the circled "80" on her abdomen, but revealing the brand is a lesser evil than zebra stripes... and certainly better than wearing a thong in public.

When Malcolm sees her in a powder-blue bikini, he says nothing about the circled two-inch-high "8" and "0" seared onto her abdomen, just as he said nothing about the neck scars. Before leaving the room, Cynthia slips on an oversized University of Texas Hook 'em Horns T-shirt.

Two minutes later, they are searching for optimum sun-bathing conditions—two adjacent chaises with protection from a brisk headwind, plus close proximity to a bar—Malcolm's preference. The Lido and Sun Decks are busy with other people looking to do the same. Cynthia chooses not to say something flip about morning casino attendance. As the two of them walk among occupied chaises, several passengers stare at her scarred throat. Cynthia gets a kick out of the way people pretend *not* to look at such ordered scars, which resemble ruby studs on an invisible choker.

The *Persian Prince* has four swimming pools. The adults-only Spa Pool near the bow on the Spa Deck is little more than an oversized bath tub. The Veranda Pool has adequate wind protection and the most striking setting—hanging off the stern—but, with the ship sailing southeast, the sun-bathing patio is shaded. The Atrium Pool features a giant video screen—grating sound from all-day movies is too loud for reading. That leaves the Persian Gulf Pool—according to Malcolm the largest pool on any cruise ship. The pool is shaped like the Persian Gulf, with facing patios oriented as Arabia and Persia. For a bodyguard, the whole area is a security nightmare because there are so many people and so much open space. But despite her statements of concern, she still gauges the risk acceptable, and this pool has the best variety of sun and shade.

Malcolm leaves books and towels on a set of Lido Deck chaises under the Sun Deck overhang.

"The signs say we shouldn't reserve chairs," Cynthia says.

"Look around." He gestures at a row of chaises. Many have towels or books, but no people. "Nobody else follows the rules. I'm paying for us to enjoy ourselves, so I'm saving seats."

For tanning, Cynthia and Malcolm select the Sun Deck, overlooking the pool in one direction and the ocean in the other—two chaises, with blue-tinted Plexiglass at their backs. Malcolm says, "Let's go for a swim before we grease up."

They drop a second set of towels, then walk down a flight of metal stairs to the pool level. Malcolm jumps into the water immediately. Cynthia removes her T-shirt and sits on the edge of the pool, legs dangling in the water, watching Malcolm porpoise around the shallow end. He moves with confidence, despite his baggy bathing trunks, a comical pair of knee-length, fish-patterned boxers. For a moment—just an instant, really—she pictures him in his gold briefs.

Malcolm gets out and heads up the steps for their chaises. He rolls one hand, encouraging her to go in. After he's bought the painting, she will be on full alert, so now's the time. The pool is too small for *real* laps, but Cynthia likes to swim so much that she vows to make the best of it. She slips in, ducks her head, and pushes off on the first freestyle mini-lap between Iraq and Oman.

8

Malcolm Golden

Malcolm ensconces himself on a chaise, sipping iced tea while watching Cynthia swim effortless laps down below. She strokes, flips, and drives off the end walls in a continuous, gliding figure-8—artistry in motion. After each turn, she takes her breaths to his side, dutifully checking up on her client.

He could watch her swim all day, but on her 23rd lap, she aborts in mid-pool when a gang of kids splashes into the water. Her expression is more miffed than angry. It's clear that the children aren't going anywhere when two cruise staff members string up a volleyball net.

After Cynthia ascends the ladder, her slick hair glistens, but it's the subsequent walk up the stairs that captivates Malcolm's artistic senses. She surges with the balance of a diver on a springboard, each step like one that precedes a slow-motion catapult to the sky. He has appreciated her walk before, but there is something passionately alive about Cynthia James dripping water.

Some experts, Malcolm included, believe that great art is defined by contrast and ambiguity. Cynthia qualifies on both counts. The contrast between her masculine and feminine traits is most vivid in a bikini. And ambiguity? She is mystery personified—prison record, murky past, simmering sexuality. Such living art will surely keep the cruise interesting until Thursday's auction.

Malcolm understands the power of human beauty—the way

line, texture, and proportion are enhanced by vitality. And by motion. Cynthia swings a towel behind her neck as she glides toward him. Part dancer, part athlete, she is a masterpiece, effortlessly bewitching. Resisting her will be more difficult than Malcolm expected, but his obsession for the Picasso is even more powerful than charms of the flesh.

Malcolm lowers his eyes to page 33 of *The Cider House Rules*. Don't get ahead of yourself, he thinks. He will adhere to his plan, which includes a professional relationship with his bodyguard. After all, she has a crucial role to play in getting him and the Picasso safely off the ship.

Malcolm hears gentle splatters next to his chaise but doesn't look above her ankles. "Nice swim?" he asks.

"The water's a little warm, but yeah, it was good."

Seconds ago, she was swimming like a torpedo, yet from two feet away, Malcolm hears no evidence of exertion, no heavy breathing. He's tired from just watching. "You can swim more if you like."

"No," she says. "They're organizing a volleyball game."

"Oh?" He glances toward the pool. "I hadn't noticed."

He knows that she saw him looking before, so she knows he has seen the volleyball net. He waits for her to call him on his silly lie.

"Besides," she says, "I don't want to take my eyes off you for too long." In a whisper, she adds, "The job, you know."

Malcolm is sure that she's looking at him, and he has a primal urge to flirt back, but he flips a page, his head remaining down. "Suit yourself." He uses the word "suit" on purpose. His mind always processes on multiple levels. Cynthia is bright but not bright enough to match wits with him. She has no idea that he just gave her a clever compliment, just as she has no idea that he learned something about how far he can push her.

When Malcolm searched for the perfect bodyguard, he hadn't expected to find one so… so what? Not beautiful, per se. Her face is flawed. The eyes, too far apart, are haunted; the nose, too prominent. So she's not beautiful—until she moves. He settles on the concept of athletic sensuality. No matter, the result is a distraction.

Again, he contemplates physical beauty. Just understanding

its components, understanding how the brain perceives these components, isn't enough. The beholder must surrender a piece of his soul before enjoying the ultimate reward. Malcolm cannot afford to surrender any part of himself to Cynthia James. He needs to remain focused, and he needs her vigilant. He can't remind himself of that too often.

Malcolm watches her extract a brown bottle from her tote bag.

"May I get your back?" he says. He imagines how deep her mocha skin will tan after a week broiling under the Caribbean sun. Imagination is okay, so he allows it. His fingers tingle as he anticipates spreading oil on her shoulders and back. He will be Michelangelo, sculpting a life-size Incan goddess, the feminine equivalent of the David. He can already feel his hands slide underneath her halter—

"I'm okay," Cynthia says. She sits down and slathers her own chest, shoulders and neck.

Malcolm looks down at his book and the fingers that hold it. A wave of depression engulfs him. Why, with all his expertise, does he lack the talent to create even a mediocre work of art? Why is he cursed merely to analyze the genius of others? That personal deficiency is why he must possess great art like the Picasso. And Cynthia James will help him.

9

Rays

Cynthia adjusts her chaise, raising the back to reading position. Preoccupied with tanning lines—thanks to Malcolm—she unties the halter behind her neck. Her bikini's outer corners flop down, revealing a tad more of her modest bust than she prefers, but nothing compared to what several nearby women are flaunting. Then she props her book on raised thighs, thus partly shielding the abdominal brand. Her eyes pan the deck from behind mirrored sunglasses. In the unlikely event of trouble, it will come quickly. Hands and feet will be the ready weapons, and she's skilled using them. She endured three years in prison without being raped.

Thirty minutes later, after she flattens the chaise to lie on her stomach, Malcolm again says, "Let me get your back."

Cynthia shivers. "Don't bother. I can get—"

"It's okay," he whispers, caressing her shoulder blades, easing her down onto her stomach. "Remember, we're supposed to be an item." He deftly unclasps the back of her bikini.

"What are you doing?"

"So you'll get an even tan. Relax."

Cynthia says nothing while he applies the oil.

"Your shoulders are already darker," he says. Malcolm has the touch of an artist—she was afraid that he would.

Cynthia remembers the last time she sunbathed with her top unfastened. She was seventeen, in the backyard. Her stepfather insisted on rubbing lotion over her back.

Malcolm gets up to stretch his legs.

"Stay close by," she says.

"Or what? You'll follow me into the men's room?"

His joke snaps her alert. Cynthia refastens her back strap so she can sit up and watch him.

Malcolm strolls around the deck, gazing first at the ocean, then at the one reclining sun goddess amidst a sea of fleshy middle-aged mortals. He stops to flirt, out of Cynthia's earshot. The striking blonde, who looks to be in her early twenties, holds a book, not to be read, but to frame breasts that are one breath from overflowing a canary-yellow bikini. The girl poses in oiled majesty, somewhere between art and pornography. Above the double-feature is a surfer-girl face, not that Malcolm appears to notice. *Absolutely not gay.*

When he returns to his chaise, Cynthia says, "Meet anyone interesting?"

"Everyone is interesting if you ask the right questions."

"What questions did you ask Ms. Hooters?"

He laughs. "Her first name—it's Francesca. Seems like a nice girl. Fine Arts major at Rutgers, on the cruise to be part of history."

"No last name?"

"You're psychic. It's Hooters."

Cynthia doesn't laugh.

"Actually," he says, "it's Goode."

Cynthia frowns.

"Goode with an E."

She shakes her head.

"Jealous?" he teases.

Cynthia bristles.

Malcolm reaches over and taps her wrist. "Notice her bathing suit?"

Cynthia glances at Francesca. "It's flattering, but obvious."

"No. Look at the cut of her halter. I'll bet you a bottle of wine that tonight she'll be sporting shoulder straps out of sync with tanning lines."

It's a harmless wager—he'll pay for the wine, either way—so Cynthia says, "Okay." Wanting to change the subject, she asks, "What do you like best about the cruise?"

"Our art lesson. How about you?"

She delays answering while a waiter replaces her empty glass with a full iced tea, then glides away.

"The service," she says. "Having so many people wait on me. It's decadent, but for a week, a very pleasant decadence."

"What do you *dislike*?" Malcolm asks with a mischievous grin.

Cynthia inhales a lungful of ocean air, pans the indigo vista, listens to the hum of tourists. Something is missing—something important. It's freedom. She doesn't like being trapped on a ship, no matter how large. But she murmurs, "Nothing."

Silence gives her time to align events of the last 24 hours. "You bought that thong at the all-night boutique when you snuck out, right?"

After a pause, he says, "Yes."

"Strange time to be shopping."

"I wanted to surprise you. Then, when you were so angry, well, it was amusing to watch you fuss and fume."

"It wasn't funny then, and it isn't funny now."

"You're right," he says, sounding contrite. "I'm sorry."

"And what about the perfume I smelled?"

His eyebrow rises ever so slightly. He taps his index finger to her nose. "Your olfactory sense has quite the imagination."

10

Auction

Cynthia wants to arrive early for the afternoon art auction so that she and Malcolm can secure chairs with their backs to a wall. Alexander's Lounge is a tiered cabaret-theatre that seats several hundred. Malcolm humors her precautions, and they sit on the far left, their backs duly protected and everyone else in view.

With a few minutes to kill, Malcolm talks Cynthia through Cruise Art 101. "Empire Lines offers auctions every voyage, but this week is special because of the Picasso, although today is only an appetizer—the usual limited-edition prints that you can buy on any cruise."

"Why prints instead of originals?"

"Registered prints are one way commercial artists promote themselves." He points to a framed killer whale on the near side of the stage. "That's a limited edition Wyland. He produced two hundred numbered copies. Much better quality than museum posters. Amateur collectors get their kicks buying a Wyland. They go home and boast to their friends. Now the friends have to have a Wyland, too. Next thing you know, Wyland's spitting out prints and minting money."

Cynthia's eyes twinkle. "Who's Wyland?"

He laughs at her feigned ignorance. "It's all about exposure. In a Chelsea gallery, a handful of people see a piece. On this ship, a few thousand stroll through the gallery every week, and hundreds sit in on the auctions. That's exposure you can't buy."

"Is the bidding like on sit-coms—pick your nose and you

inadvertently bid a thousand dollars?"

"Not unless you alert the auctioneer that your signal is a nose-pick."

"Alert the auctioneer?"

"Yes. I meet with Sophia before every auction to get our signals straight—like a pitcher and catcher. I may not want the competition to know when I'm bidding. On some pieces, you won't see any hands, but the bids keep rising, via pre-arranged signs. That's when you know the serious collectors are in the hunt."

"So what's your secret signal today?"

"See if you can figure it out. Oh, there's Sophia, the auctioneer." Malcolm points toward the cabaret stage where a slender, olive-skinned woman—mid thirties—paces on stiletto heels. At a table, she taps a flurry of keystrokes on a laptop. Sophia's purple dress qualifies as a uniform by virtue of its corporate color, but it fits like a cocktail dress, with a hemline showcasing skinny thighs. Exaggerated eye makeup enhances Sophia's lean, hungry look.

"Who's the guy to her left?" Cynthia says, looking at an exceedingly handsome blond in a purple blazer and white slacks.

"Brent Burns, her assistant. His specialty is charming rich women into buying over-rated rubbish they don't need." Malcolm leans close and whispers, "Sophia says that he's very good at his job."

Cynthia notices one of the costumed International Escorts by the stage, this one Asian, posing with two middle-aged men for a ship's photographer. Cynthia points. "It looks like Empire gives Sophia help softening up the men, huh?"

"Affirmative. Ziyi has a Masters in art history."

Cynthia notices that Malcolm knows the first name of every escort.

From the moment that an unseen voice introduces Sophia Caporetto, Sophia's every step and gesture are choreographed. In a lyric Italian accent, she explains the mechanics of the auction: once, twice, sold. And how, on most pieces, anyone can match the winning bid and buy a duplicate print. She repeats what Malcolm said about exposure, which explains why artists accept lower prices from cruise lines than boutique galleries. Artists aren't the only self-promoters. Sophia mentions her book: *Art Collection Made Easy*.... but doesn't reveal what Malcolm told Cynthia—Empire takes a healthy cut from each sale.

There are a few questions from pudgy men with European accents before Sophia announces the first piece, a Nechita print, the bidding to start at $700.

"Nechita was a child prodigy," Malcolm says. "They used to call her The Petite Picasso."

The print is striking, but $700? Cynthia sets her mind to "get it." She glances at the standing-room-only crowd of would-be bidders. No Countess LaCroix, no Julia Sotelo, but Cynthia sees the buxom blonde from the Sun Deck. Cynthia wonders if Ms. Goode's presence, only ten feet over, is a result of Malcolm's flirting.

"Do you see Julia or the countess?" Cynthia asks him.

"They won't be here. Neither will John Poindexter. The major players only care about the important originals, which won't be auctioned until Thursday. A Dali, a Chagall, and the Picasso, of course."

From the stage, Sophia says, "Before we begin, "I almost forgot." She waves to the wings. "Guys, bring out the Picasso."

Cynthia guesses that nothing here is *forgotten*—everything is part of the show.

"There." Malcolm points center-stage where two uniformed guards carry an easel—upon which rests a 2' x 3' bluish composition of harsh facial features on a gray background—to center stage. The painting is less imposing than Cynthia expected.

The audience applauds.

"It's called, 'Winter Prince,'" Malcolm says. "An example of analytical cubism."

Cynthia doesn't ask what analytical cubism is. She will observe, absorb, just as Malcolm has taught her. She assesses the Picasso, which looks too small to be worth so much money. The prince is neither glamorous nor masculine—it could be a winter *princess*. The subject has multiple superimposed faces, so it's difficult to count noses. The net expression is dark, more troubled than sad. Something glistens on the subject's head. A crown? Snow? Experts must be hedging their bets, hence the name,

"Winter Prince." Cynthia tilts her head to connect with the most dominating set of features. Does she see greatness? Or does she see evil hiding behind four eyes, danger too shady for a vacation? From this angle, the painting looks like something her brother drew when he was ten, using the same paper twice. "I know I'm showing my ignorance," she says, "but it's hard to believe that it's worth eighty-five million dollars."

Malcolm laughs—Cynthia isn't sure if it is *with* her or *at* her.

When Sophia opens the auction for the Nechita, Cynthia is disappointed—no yodeling of unintelligible words. Sophia speaks English in a lilting, Italian accent, her rhythm a mixture of lecture, patter, and promotion.

The Nechita goes for $850.

"Only eight-fifty," Cynthia says in her pretentious voice.

"Not Nechita's best," Malcolm deadpans.

After three pieces, Cynthia knows the routine. She whispers in Malcolm's ear. "If it's just ho-hum prints, why are we here?"

"You'll see."

"Next up," Sophia says, "dolphins by Wyland."

Cynthia leans close to Malcolm's ear. "Tell me about Thursday's auction."

"In addition to the Winter Prince, there will be two other important pieces on the card: a Chagall, painted shortly after he arrived in Paris, and an ultra-surrealistic Dali that lampoons Franco."

The bidding on Wyland's dolphins is up to $600. Malcolm pays no attention, continuing to whisper to Cynthia. "There will be off-site bidders to contend with."

"Off-site bidders?"

"Two kinds. Proxy bidders submit several interval bids and a maximum for certain pieces. Crew members execute the proxies by speaking into microphones hooked to the auctioneer's earpiece. There'll be six or seven major proxy bidders. More serious off-site bidders will hook in by satellite phone. The Uffizi will have a trustee, plus the d'Orsay, the Guggenheim, the Met, and the Musée Picasso. They follow the audio feed from the auctioneer's mike and place bids through operators who'll relay the bids to Sophia. The phone call is expensive, but cheaper than a one-week cruise."

"Sounds complicated."

"That's what makes it exciting."

Sophia drops the gavel. "Sold, for eight hundred. Is there anyone else who would like the Wyland at eight hundred?"

Cynthia looks for hands. Malcolm touches her wrist. "Don't turn your head. I told Sophia that would be your signal."

"You're teasing. Seriously, how does a bidder get an edge with all the sharks lurking? Cozy up to the auctioneer? Convince her to look at you last? Or maybe to ignore the competition at just the right moment?"

He shrugs.

"Perhaps you were doing some convincing last night?"

"Sophia's the fairest auctioneer in the Empire fleet."

"You didn't answer my question."

Malcolm smiles. "This isn't the proper time or place."

Cynthia could counter with a witty comeback but lets his platitude stand.

Sophia strides across the stage in short, clipped steps, always impatient to get from Point A to Point B, never reveling in the journey. Sophia is at the top of Cynthia's short list of people Malcolm might have met the night before. Cynthia assumes the rendezvous was either about sex or the Picasso—Sophia qualifies on both criteria. So does Julia Sotelo. And, perhaps, the countess is a closet tigress in the sack.

The long list includes John Poindexter plus serious bidders unknown. Cynthia will refine the lists—she is obligated to do something for her $1,000-a-day besides eating, working on her tan, and studying over-priced art.

"Oh," Malcolm adds. "I just bought a copy of those Wyland dolphins for a friend."

"Who's the friend?" she whispers.

"Someone who has a place on St. Thomas."

"What was your signal?"

He touches her wrist. Again. His hand is warm.

Cynthia watches a porter carry her fountain woman to an easel, center-stage. Sophia announces the artist's name, Sevastini, and recites background, but Cynthia isn't listening. "How should I bid?" she whispers.

"Don't," he says. "Remember, it's a print. They have five on board. You can get one for the same amount as the buyer, so you don't want to push up the price. The only way you'll bid is if nobody opens at the minimum. If they don't, you'll raise your hand after she says, 'two.'"

"Shouldn't I have a secret sign," she says. "Being your date, and all?"

"Just raise your hand. Do you have in mind how high you'll go?"

Cynthia pictures the lone painting in her condo. "Five hundred." That would make it her most expensive piece of art— by about $450. Her heart-rate accelerates. She smiles, admitting to herself: this is fun.

"Do I have three hundred?" Sophia asks the audience.

Cynthia holds her breath until a man in back raises his hand, bidding the minimum, $300. She squeezes her hands together when another man bids $400. At $450, she grabs Malcolm's wrist and holds her breath again.

"One. Two. Sold for four-fifty."

"Now what?" Cynthia whispers.

"Wait."

Sophia says, "Is there anyone else who would like the Sevastini for four-fifty?"

"Now, raise your hand."

Cynthia shoots her left arm into the air. She's a collector.

11

Vault

After getting some fresh air on the Promenade Deck, Malcolm takes Cynthia to the Art Department on Deck 5—to see the vault. Malcolm puffs up the word "vault" as if there will be thick steel walls and a gleaming, multi-wheeled door, like Fort Knox in *Goldfinger*. But, of course, she has seen the ordinary door in photos. The vault room turns out to be a 12' by 15' climate-controlled storeroom entered through the Brown safe door on a side wall of the auctioneer's office. Very *un*glamorous. On the way into the office, Cynthia sees only one security camera—in the hall.

The office is crowded: Countess LaCroix, Julia Sotelo, a rumpled man (whom Malcolm points out as John Poindexter), Malcolm, Cynthia, Sophia Caporetto, and the exceedingly handsome assistant auctioneer, Brent Burns. In the corner stands Billingsley, the tall security officer, in his crisp white uniform. Cynthia feels like a party-crasher. She backs up and stumbles over a narrow, oblong box, one of a row of packages leaning against the desk. She checks the address label—*her* framed print, already boxed for shipping.

Sophia turns toward a hard-plastic case, which sits off the floor on two chairs. One end is open so that Cynthia can see the edge of a gilded picture frame. "Time for verification," Sophia says.

While Burns holds the case, Sophia slides the framed masterpiece out of its squeaking, protective foam. They set the painting on an easel. The face in the picture frowns with multiple mouths. No matter which way Cynthia studies the various eyes, all are sad, maybe haunted.

Cynthia notices a similarity among the experts: they all have active eyes, although in different ways. John Poindexter scans the room with laser precision. The countess's eyes are furtive, darting, never lingering. Julia doesn't seem to notice objects but makes eye contact with every person in the room. From a distance, Cynthia thinks her eyes scream, "Don't ignore me!" Malcolm's eyes are the most intriguing. Cynthia concludes that it's his gentle eyes that make people suspect he's gay.

Cynthia finds herself squeezed next to the hunky Brent Burns. "Hey there," he says in a deep voice that belongs in a pick-up bar. She expected a British accent, but he is American. She doesn't want to stare at his nametag, so asks, "Where are you from?"

"L.A."

"Don't tell me you're a surfer."

Burns nods with a grin, looking like a young Brad Pitt. Up close, she notices his dimpled chin is ever so slightly off-center. Some innate instinct—possibly natural selection—compels her to offer a smile.

Sophia claps her hands. "It's unusual for a non-certified guest to see the lockdown procedure," she says, looking at Cynthia. "But Malcolm insists that you observe, and any friend of Malcolm is a friend of ours."—There is no sincerity in her voice.—"Okay, we're ready for verification." She hands a jeweler's loupe to Julia, who bends down and squints at the signature corner of the canvas.

"Genuine," Julia says as if the fate of the world hangs on her pronouncement.

Countess LaCroix repeats the process. She is able to make a half-squat appear graceful. "Genu-*wine*," she purrs.

"Genuine," agrees Malcolm after a more thorough perusal.

Poindexter merely nods after his inspection, briefer than the previous three.

Sophia takes the eyepiece, bends, and squints. "Verified. The genuine Picasso."

During this ritual, Cynthia sidles behind the desk to get a

closer look at the tampered lock. Her impression is confirmed: whoever made the scratches wasn't trying to open the safe, or else was a total incompetent.

Burns holds one end of the case while Sophia slides the painting, frame, and packing back into its plastic shell. She snaps closed a padlock and spins the combination dial. "Once again," Sophia says, "the prince is locked in his cell."

Next, Sophia extracts a ten-inch strip of tape from a Pitney Bowes date-time stamp machine, wraps the tape across both edges of the locked end, and flattens it tight with her palm. One-by-one, Malcolm, Julia, Countess LaCroix, John Poindexter, and Sophia initial the tape across an edge, each using a different pen. Last, Ensign Billingsley, who hasn't said a word, steps forward and initials the tape.

Two porters heft the multi-million-dollar painting into the vault, where they lean it against boxes that, Malcolm whispers, contain the Dali and the Chagall. Malcolm almost genuflects. The countess looks faint. Cynthia thinks the tedious procedure is anti-climactic, like the changing of the guard at Buckingham Palace.

Sophia swings the vault door closed and spins the locking wheel. She logs the time: 16:43. All four verifiers initial the security log. "That's it, everyone," Sophia says. "See you Thursday, when the prince will get a new owner."

Out in the art gallery, Cynthia waits for the others to walk away before asking Malcolm, "So what was that all about?"

"Special security. There are four certified elite-level Picasso experts on board, as recognized by the International Picasso Society: Julia, the countess, Poindexter, and me. Worldwide, there are only nine, which gives you an idea how important this auction is. Every time the Picasso is logged into the safe, three of us, one of the art staff, plus a security officer, must verify the painting's authenticity."

"So you're really hot stuff, huh?" It feels natural to tease him, yet somehow inappropriate, so she turns serious. "A few observations about the so-called *special security*," she says. "There's only one surveillance camera outside the office—none inside and none in the vault. I peeked. The walls aren't reinforced. That particular model Brown safe door has no time restrictions, and it's kid-safe, meaning it can be unlocked from the inside by a lever. A pro could splice in a dumb video feed to the camera in a few seconds, cut a small hole through the wall, snake in a retractable arm, and flip open the door. All in less than three minutes. And I could crack that safe with a stethoscope."

"No! Not *the vault?*" He smiles.

"That's no vault. That's a medium grade safe door on a storage room with a thermostat and dehumidifier."

"The painting really can't be *stolen*. We're on a *ship*. At sea."

"Granted," she says, "but a pro could get it out of that room, roll it up, and hide it anywhere. It's insured, I guess."

"For eighty million," he says as casually as she might say a hundred bucks.

"Then the ship has an eighty-million-dollar painting with dollar-store security." Cynthia pulls him to a stop. "But you knew that. No high-falutin' President of the Inter-galatical Association of Picasso Ass-Kissers would mistake that storeroom for first-rate security. The walls are probably sub-standard—no steel— because extra weight is a no-no on a ship. Jeez, anyone with a saw could cut through the sheetrock—"

"It's a ship. Requirements aren't the same as if we were on land." His face breaks into a grin.

"I'm insulted," Cynthia says, trying, unsuccessfully, to look insulted. "If you really thought I was top-notch security, you wouldn't have laid that *vault* crap on me."

"You're my bodyguard. How was I supposed to know you're a safe-cracker, too? By the way, how *do* you know so much about safes?"

She shrugs. "Maybe I had to steal a few things."

"Is that why you went to prison?"

"No. End of subject. Now, Mr. Hot-Shot Art Expert, is there time to run off some of this cruise-fat before dinner?"

Every time Cynthia returns to the stateroom, there are more promotional flyers in the mail rack beside the door. This afternoon, the ten International Escorts are featured in costume, complete with color photos. They are billed like super models, first names only: Liat, Talia, Elsa, Charisse, Ziyi, Inga... All are beautiful; their races vary from Scandinavian ivory to African ebony, their figures ranging from emaciated to voluptuous. Cynthia locates Miranda's picture—her smile sweeter than the others'—and reads a thumbnail bio. Home: La Romana, Dominican Republic; shopping specialty: jewelry; spa specialty: Swedish massage; dance specialty: Latin.

Cynthia pushes the paper in front of Malcolm's eyes. "Do the other cruise lines have anything like these escorts?"

"No. They're part of niche marketing—another way to lure international high-rollers."

"High-rolling *men,*" she huffs.

"Men spend the big bucks." He removes a water bottle from the mini-bar then sits down on her loveseat. "Take jewelry. Women wear most of the big-ticket items, but it's the *men* who pay the bill, whether for wives... or mistresses."

"Okay. About that jewelry," she says, sitting on the bed. "It says Miranda's shopping specialty is jewelry. What does that mean?"

"It means that with Miranda's TLC, a man is more likely to buy expensive Persian jewelry in the onboard boutique."

"I thought the *islands* have the bargains. Why would someone overpay for bling on the ship?"

Malcolm purses his lips as if about to chose words carefully. "First, the boutique's Persian designs aren't available anywhere else—unique, coveted by aficionados, made by Persian craftsmen exclusively for Empire Lines."

After a pause, Cynthia prompts, "And?"

"And in exchange for large purchases, passengers get onboard credits... for perks."

"What kind of perks?"

"Chips in the casino, exclusive behind-the-scenes tours, dinner with the captain, spa splurges—those sorts of things."

"Do *you* get perks for what you spend?"

He smiles. "As a matter of fact, I do."

While changing to go exercise, Cynthia does a double-take at the mirror. Her skin has darkened already—from mocha to antique brass, no shoulder lines. The lavender dress will look smashing. Her scar tissue doesn't tan the way healthy skin does, so her neck studs and "80" belly brand are now lighter than her skin, which makes her feel like a film negative—exposed. She massages moisturizer into all the baked surfaces, a process she will have to repeat throughout the week. She stretches on bicycle shorts and a sports bra—both black—and adds a sweatband around her neck.

On their way up one flight of stairs to the running track, she catches Malcolm glancing at her midriff, but again, he doesn't comment on the brand. He does wave to John Poindexter on the far side of the Sun Deck. Two people wave back: Poindexter and a woman, whose head is obscured by a post. After a few more steps, Cynthia makes out the profile of the woman. It is the auctioneer, Sophia Caporetto.

12

Sophia Caporetto

Sophia's crewmates mistake her impatience for agitation, calling her hyper. They don't know that her mother died of ovarian cancer at 35. If Sophia's journey is to be brief, at least it will be lucrative. That's why she cuts off her disappointing conversation with Poindexter and hustles to the elevator, which she wills to *go faster* on its way down to the art gallery.

She likes money and people—in that order—although she has little use for Malcolm's girlfriends. They are always taller than she—a petty concern, but real, nonetheless. This week's eye candy probably likes Malcolm for the same reasons they all do— he's richer than Croesus and much more fun. Judging from the navel-screwed-to-the-spine abdomen, this one is a fitness fanatic, reason enough to dislike her. And that metallic tan!—asking for skin cancer.

What was her name? Cynthia Something. Not that it matters. Next time, the girl will have hair down to here or legs up to there. One thing for which Sophia gives Malcolm credit: there is little pattern to his flings.

Sophia has no time for flings. She's too busy going places. Men are only useful if they give her a boost. Like Malcolm, who used his influence as President of the Picasso Society to lobby for her as auctioneer, a fantastic opportunity. So few elevators go all the way to the top; deciding to ride this one took five nano-seconds. The express is always best when there may be no tomorrow.

Cynthia is different from Malcolm's usual dates in one respect: she doesn't grovel. A typical gold-digger fawns over her sugar daddy as if he were a comedian. But Cynthia's wary eyes defuse amusement like a cold rain at the Magic Kingdom.

Could Cynthia be a problem? Unlikely, but with the Picasso, Sophia worries about everyone. For instance, will Cynthia allow Malcolm to sneak away tonight? Sophia almost hopes that she won't. Malcolm can be so damn charming, and right now, she doesn't need his charm. What she needs is another Valium.

But first things first. Brent Burns hasn't helped her on a Sunday inventory in over two months, but Sophia leaves nothing to chance. She knows Burns's moronic tastes and noticed where his eyes lingered during the afternoon auction, so she invited Francesca Goode, eager art student, to the auctioneer's afternoon tea.

Sophia hears a perky, "Yoo hoo." Francesca is prompt, an admirable trait to someone as impatient as Sophia, who ushers her guest into the office. The girl is all flashing teeth and run-on sentences, but Sophia can speed talk with the best of them. They exchange mindless chit-chat about the ship.

After a minute, Sophia segues into gritty girl-talk, which lasts longer. The two women trash ex-boyfriends as if they had dated the same losers, which in a metaphorical way, they have. Francesca repeats a complaint about men being insensitive. Sophia thinks: keep it moving, honey.

Art-talk. The saving grace. Sophia can talk nonstop about art, and Francesca is a willing sponge. Mixing romance with art, Sophia volunteers, as if only half-joking, that the best make-out spot on the ship is in the vault. Getting Burns to sneak a girl into the vault later in the week isn't necessary, but it will be a nice touch when the shit hits the fan.

Sophia knows that Burns is perpetually late for everything, but she fidgets anyway. The good news is that Francesca turns out to be more than a bimbo. If only she didn't have those bulging melons. Still, the conversation is as tolerable as wasted time can be.

Burns strolls in. Finally. A smile wider than the Caribbean lights his face when he lays eyes on Francesca. Sophia figures:

they'll be an item within five minutes. It takes only ten seconds for him to offer Francesca more wine. He hovers over her while pouring, barely aware that Sophia is in the room.

Sophia taps her foot, waiting for wine and cheese to be nibbled, hormones to percolate. She peeks at her watch. Two more minutes should do it. She tops off the wineglasses and listens to Burns brag about the Picasso as if his role as assistant auctioneer has actual importance. Enough frivolity. Time to move things along.

"It's a lovely evening," Sophia says. "Brent, why don't you show Francesca the pieces displayed up in the Hanging Gardens? Take the champagne with you. Tell her about our preferred collectors' promotion." With a conspiratorial wink, she adds, "Francesca, don't forget what I told you about the vault."

Burns is a willing dupe, guiding Francesca out the door. He's such a lazy slug, except when it comes to pursuing young lovelies. The last thing she overhears is Burns asking, "So, what did she tell you about the vault?"

The blonde is perfect bait. Sophia figures the odds are two-to-one that Burns and Francesca will end up making out in the vault—along about Wednesday.

The waiting is almost over—less than a week until the payoff. Take it easy, Sophia reminds herself. She inhales several deep breaths in a futile effort to lower her heart-rate. The Valium is in her purse, but she doesn't swallow one. At least not yet.

Emile, the day watchman, ducks his head into the office right on schedule. Sophia gives him an innocent smile, watches him move on, then counts to ten before locking her office door. She spins the vault's silver dial... 25... 13...6...Tumblers catch; the door opens. From a drawer in her desk, she removes a canvas satchel. With the inventory clipboard and satchel in hand, she walks inside, then swings the vault door closed.

13

Formality

Cynthia bought two expense-account cocktail dresses for the formal nights. Tonight's is silky lavender, with a scooped back and a tasteful slit up one side. Facing the mirror, Cynthia is impressed. Normally, she doesn't obsess about appearances, but there's something about the Caribbean, the ship... the company? She turns sideways and rotates her hips so she can see the low-cut back—no tanning lines. The dress flatters her figure, and a lavender choker adds a touch of elegance. Matching eye shadow hints at intrigue. She feels special....

Until she sees Malcolm in a classic tuxedo with shimmering lapels. It brings out the best in him—expressive eyes, a distinguished touch of gray at the temples.

Their dinner companions are John Poindexter and his wife, Gladys. Pointdexter is bald, with a dumpy build that makes his aging tux look rumpled. His full-figured wife wears a stylish black dress, drinks too much, and keeps adjusting Malcolm's silverware. Neither Malcolm nor Poindexter seem to mind. Cynthia certainly doesn't mind the absence of art in the dialogue. Poindexter is conversant on a variety of topics: the secret of good *coq au vin*, how to imitate the song of an Indigo Bunting, and what makes Google the best search engine.

After dinner, Malcolm takes Cynthia lounge-hopping in search of a decent dance band. "I'm not a very good dancer," Cynthia says at the entrance to the Arabian Nights Lounge. "Never learned the ballroom steps."

"Don't worry," he says. "I'll make you look like Ginger Rogers." She figures that if anyone can make good on such a boast, it's Malcolm.

He hears what he likes at their third stop—Alexander's Lounge, site of the afternoon art auction. "This is the place," he says. "They'll be playing our song any minute." The temporary thrust stage that was used for the auction has been retracted underneath the permanent stage, leaving a half-moon, parquet dance floor. Poindexter and Gladys wave Malcolm and Cynthia over to a front-row cocktail table. A purple-coated waiter appears; Malcolm orders wine; Cynthia, a Diet Coke. There are fifteen or twenty couples either dancing or thinking about it. The serious ballroom crowd knows the schedule.

When the band begins the next number, Malcolm coaxes Cynthia onto the hardwood. Assuming the dancing position, Malcolm whispers, "Slow, slow, quick-quick," into her ear, twice, in sync with the beat. Before she can think about which foot to move first, they are gliding. He says it's a Foxtrot, then sings softly, "Some-*where*...beyond the *sea*...." He has a mellow voice and moves like an Arthur Murray instructor, drawing her into steps she doesn't know, beguiling her feet into compliance. It's her most enjoyable ballroom dance—ever. At the end, they *pat-pat* polite applause.

The beat picks up—*In the Mood*. Malcolm twirls her through an energetic swing. By the last syncopated bar, Cynthia is into the spins and loving the motion.

Poindexter and Gladys double-cut for *I Left My Heart in San Francisco*, too slow to do much more than sway. Poindexter holds Cynthia respectfully away from his paunch. After they settle into an acceptable rhythm, he looks into her face and asks, "How long have you been seeing Malcolm?"

"Oh... a few months."

"Serious?"

Cynthia glances over at Malcolm, who is enveloped by Gladys.

"You think I'm nosy," Poindexter says.

"Not at all," she lies.

Poindexter squeezes her hand. "He's a snake-charmer."

Cynthia exhales, saying, "Tell me something I *don't* know."

Ten feet away, Gladys clutches Malcolm to her bosom.

"When things are too good to be true," Poindexter says, "they usually are."

"I thought you'd be talking about the weather. Instead, you're grilling me about my love life."

"You seem like a nice kid."

She blushes. At 35, she enjoys being called a kid.

Poindexter steers them through traffic. "Malcolm has a lot of baggage, that's all."

"What sort of baggage?"

"Obsessions. Like for the Picasso. He won't get it, and the failure will devastate him. You don't know what he's like when he loses."

"So tell me."

"Well, there was a fund-raising auction for a hospital. Malcolm wanted a particular Degas. I'm not even sure why it was so important. Anyway, the auctioneer quick-closed for another bidder, a man we'll call Jackson. Malcolm went ballistic. He bought the business of Jackson's primary customer then cancelled Jackson's contract, running him into bankruptcy. And he hired a private investigator to catch the auctioneer with a woman—then told the wife."

Poindexter allows the story to settle. "As I said, he's a sore loser."

"He's pretty confident he'll win this time."

"He's the consummate actor, but he knows the handwriting's on the wall."

"You think the auction is rigged against him?" she asks.

"No."

"Then you don't think he can afford the Picasso."

"That's right."

Cynthia thinks about Malcolm's possible accounting games. "We'll see…. But why tell *me* all this?"

The song ends. While clapping, Poindexter says, "He's not what he appears. It's only fair that you know."

"Thanks for the warning," she says as they part. "I think."

Back in Malcolm's arms during *You Belong to Me*, she is a loyal spy. "He doesn't think you can afford the Picasso."

Malcolm tugs her closer. "That's good."

At the touch of Malcolm's chest, all the heat absorbed while sunbathing releases into her bloodstream—too much energy. Keep talking, she tells herself. "Do you want to know what else he said?"

He nods against her flushed forehead.

"That you're obsessed and a poor loser—and a bad boyfriend risk."

"Do you care?"

The question surprises her. A pivot, Malcolm's subtle pull, their chests kiss again. Her heart flutters. Trouble. It's only day two.

"I was right; they played our song," he says, before crooning, "*You belong... to... me.*"

When the band takes a break, Cynthia and Malcolm walk forward to the Empire Theater for Anton the Illusionist's 10:30 show. There is a line at the ladies room. Cynthia frets during the seven and one-half minutes that she isn't in position to protect her client.

On their way down the theatre's left-center aisle, Malcolm taps Cynthia's shoulder and points to the right. "You owe me a bottle of wine."

There sits the stunning blonde, Francesca Goode, in a strapless black dress that reveals—in sunburn-pink—the cut of her bathing suit. Cynthia thinks: there, but for the grace of Malcolm Golden, go I.

The Poindexters, having saved two seats, wave Cynthia and Malcolm down front. It appears to be more than coincidence that they keep running into the Poindexters.

14

John Poindexter

John doesn't need tailor-made clothes or a mistress to be happy. He learned at a young age that the most valuable gems lie below the surface. Gladys, faults and all, is his life partner. Malcolm's date is merely a passing acquaintance, someone in whom John will find the best because that's what he looks for in everyone. Take their dance. Cynthia, young and fit, made him feel twenty years younger. What's the harm in that?

John can tell by her imitation pearl ear studs that Cynthia isn't rich, and by her vocabulary that she doesn't have an Ivy League education. Yet here she is, swimming in waters infested with wealthy art sharks. She doesn't know whether to use a fork or spoon on her Tiramisu, but she savors food. She doesn't know a Foxtrot from a rumba, but she enjoys melding movement with music.

Cynthia's social naivety can't disguise her physical confidence. Malcolm is notorious for spitting out overmatched women, but John suspects that Cynthia will survive Malcolm Golden—possibly even come out of the experience stronger. John certainly prefers her company to that of pushy women like Sophia.

He watches Cynthia and Malcolm approach the fifth row— John has been on enough cruises to know that the fifth row is the best vantage point. Cynthia sidesteps between the seatbacks in front of her and the line of knees behind. She's trim enough to slip through with little contact. She sports a deep tan and athletic figure. Very nice slit up the thigh. Lavender loveliness. Okay, he does notice what's on the surface, but for him it's the same as admiring a Manet. Yes, think about sunsets, he tells himself when he stands to let her taut backside brush past his sucked-in stomach.

"Excuse me," she says, then, "Thank you," as she settles into the adjacent seat. The seating odds have fallen John's way—he didn't want to get stuck next to Malcolm.

"Are you having a good time on the cruise?" he asks, a clichéd opener that he wishes could be taken back.

She smiles—or is it more of a smirk? "Yes, especially when we keep bumping into you and Gladys."

She can lay it on thick…or is she really a sweet girl? No, she isn't sweet. Kind perhaps, but not sweet. He glances at her copper shoulder—muscular. He sees an image of her as a jungle cat. Definitely not sweet. She chats with Malcolm, to her right— something about her owing him a bottle of wine.

Gladys, on John's left, says, "Dear, do you want a drink?"— her code for: *I* want a drink.

"No," John says, "there isn't time before the show." One of the reasons he likes attending the theatre shows is because the row seating isn't conducive to ordering cocktails. Delaying the inevitable is a small victory. After the show, Gladys will drag him to the Tehran Salon for nightcaps. If John can hold her to two, that will be another victory. His life is a non-stop series of such skirmishes, the fate of an alcoholic's spouse.

Gladys waves to a cocktail waitress who is looking the other way. More good fortune.

Cynthia turns toward him and whispers, "I appreciate what you said to me earlier. I really do." Her tone is sincere. She lets her words settle before asking, "Have you seen this magician's act before?"

"Oh, yes. Anton's the best, although he prefers to be called an illusionist rather than a magician."

John loses himself in the performance. Anton is a master. He ties up his lovely assistant, Carlotta, and lays her in a gilded box; he slices the box in half and then in quarters; he makes her vanish; and each time, she reappears, lovelier than ever. Anton even adds an illusion created especially for this cruise. He places a large painting by Pino—of a reclining woman—into a glass box, spins the box, and *voila*, the painting disappears.

At the end of the show, after the empty box spins for the last time, Anton opens it with a flourish to reveal not only Carlotta inside, but the missing Pino.

John is enthralled. He prefers Anton to the production stage shows, even though the plucky kids sing and dance their hearts out in sequined costumes, rush to change into new sequined costumes, then lay even more heart on the line. Those shows would be better without the charade of having the dancers wear fake headset microphones while lip-synching to pre-recorded background vocal tracks. John detests anything fake. Why then does he like sleight of hand?

15

Intrigue

Filing out of the theatre amidst the buzzing crowd, Cynthia stays next to Malcolm's shoulder. He is animated in his praise of Anton's genius at making his assistant disappear. Cynthia is more impressed with Carlotta, who contorted herself inside tiny sliding boxes while shedding ropes, changing clothes, and invisibly moving from one point to another. The act shouldn't be "Anton the Illusionist," she thinks, but "Carlotta the Contortionist." Anton is merely the misdirector of attention.

Outside the theatre's exit, they come upon Anton hawking DVDs with Carlotta by his side. At close range, the costumes are less dazzling than they appeared under spotlights. Anton's tux looks like permanent-press aluminum. Carlotta's sequined teddy has the consistency of tinsel and reveals a figure maintainable only—Cynthia knows from experience—with brutal exercise. Close up, they appear older than their stage personas; Anton is pushing fifty, Carlotta looks about forty. Anton's waxed moustache could be painted black, and Cynthia detects hair plugs. Carlotta's poofy platinum do is straight from a tube, and her heavily-made-up eyes, sparkling on stage, now appear ghoulish.

Malcolm pumps Anton's hand and says, "Great show. I loved the Lady and Vanishing Painting Illusion."

"Tank you; eez noting," Anton says in his stage accent. "Come back later een zee veek, ven I vill double zee dazzle."

"Anton is a collector, himself," Malcolm volunteers.

"Oh, boy," Cynthia mutters. Malcolm catches her eye-roll.

"Yez," Anton says. "Dat eez vy I love to vork zee big auction cruise. Friends like Malcolm are great zource of informazion."

With the men occupied, Cynthia shakes Carlotta's hand. "There's no way he could do what you do—whatever it is."

Carlotta flashes perfect teeth and nods, but doesn't reply. Cynthia wonders if she speaks English.

The two men start talking about art, but Cynthia pulls Malcolm away to make room for people who might actually buy the DVD.

Back in their cabins at midnight, Cynthia grills Malcolm while she makes a show of inspecting his room. "Now that I've met John Poindexter, tell me all about him—like you did for the ladies. How did he get his money? Why does he collect? How does he know you? How well does he know Sophia?"

Malcolm glances at his watch, yawning. "You're a slave-driver."

"Just tell me about Poindexter."

Malcolm slumps onto his loveseat. "John wasn't born to money—not like the countess—although he did inherit some from his father. He's really more a facilitator for MOMA's rich trustees. His personal collection is quite modest, but he works hard for his museum—a sincere art lover."

Cynthia, having finished her inspection, sits on Malcolm's bed and crosses her legs. He notices, losing his train of thought. Although her pose wasn't planned, Cynthia's ego is pleased. "Go on," she says.

"I first met him years ago at a fundraising dinner. We're acquaintances, not friends. He wants my money for the museum, so he tolerates me."

"But he doesn't like you?"

"John doesn't approve of my lifestyle. He's a one woman man."

"So he never cheats?"

"No. Not with women. And not with art. He's proud of his values."

"What do you mean?"

"The art world is very passionate. Look at me. I'm focusing all my energy on the Winter Prince, despite the presence of beautiful women." He gazes at Cynthia's face, making her feel, for an instant, like a masterpiece. Then he says, "That's an incredible focus on art."

She blushes.

Malcolm continues. "John never gets caught up in the pursuit of beauty. At the end of the day, he can block out work until the next morning. That's why he stays with Gladys. If I ever married, I'd be divorced as soon as my wife realized that I loved a hundred paintings more than I loved her.... At least until now."

Cynthia's chest tightens; her throat locks. In search of a diversion, she fires a pillow at him, the bedtime chocolate sliding onto the floor. "You need to get some sleep," she says. "Good night."

In the safety of her cabin, she realizes that Malcolm didn't tell her how well Poindexter knows Sophia Caporetto. Cynthia slips into the hall to tape the doors before returning to don her gym shorts and sleeping T.

After yoga, she flops face-down on the bed to lose herself in a Grisham thriller.

She has been reading for thirty minutes when her ear studs pick up Malcolm making a muffled phone call. Cynthia turns up the volume, holds her breath.

"Room service?" he whispers. "This is Mr. Golden in Lido-103. I'd like a bottle of chilled Dom Perignon sent to Sophia Caporetto's cabin—crew quarters.... Yes, right away."

Tense, Cynthia lies still, the pearl speakers' volume on high. She waits.

After thirty minutes, Cynthia hears noises: sliding drawers, tinkling coat hangers, running water, a latch click. She bursts out her door in time to catch Malcolm, wearing a white silk shirt and black pants, sauntering down the hall.

"Hold it!" she calls to his back.

Malcolm stops and pivots. When he approaches, it's with a swagger, not the slouch of a kid caught red-handed. Cynthia grits her teeth. She sees the glint in his eyes a second before smelling cologne.

"Am I busted?" he says.

"Damn straight. You're *still* a moron." She grabs his arm and leads him back inside her stateroom. "You're going to Sophia's cabin, aren't you? I heard you call room service."

"How? I was whispering."

"You're a loud whisperer." She lets go of his arm and pushes her door to make sure it's locked. "We have to talk." She shoves him through the dressing alcove and sits him on her loveseat. "Sneaking out is *unacceptable*. Did you forget why you hired me? What did we agree about your movements? Always together, right? What the hell's the matter with you?"

He raises his chin, looking supremely Brahmin. "Are you finished?"

She puts her hands on her hips. "For now."

"Good. Have a seat. I'll explain." He pats the cushion next to him.

"I'll stand." She bores her eyes into his. "Well?"

"I have a tradition with Sophia. Every year on the first formal night, we—"

"So she's a *tradition*." Cynthia's face flushes redder. She is aware of irrational jealousy. "Don't you think the auctioneer might make good bait for your enemies? You're a moron."

Malcolm laughs, extending his legs, almost tripping her.

She steps back. "It's not funny."

"But it is. Remember in Butch Cassidy, when Newman and Redford are going straight as payroll guards, trying to guess where the ambush will take place on the way to the bank? Strother Martin spits and says, 'Morons. I've got morons on my team.'" Malcolm beams. "He knows the bandits won't rob them until *after they have the money*. The notes warn me not to bid on the Picasso. That can't happen until Thursday, so there's nothing to worry about until then." He winks. "So who's the moron?"

"I knew that." Cynthia bites her lip, seething. Rather than ripping out his throat, she rips her hands through her hair. "But why didn't you remind me?"

"It was too much fun watching you do your bodyguard thing." He stands. "Now, I'm late for a very important date."

She touches his shoulder. "You're paying me to—"

"Stop." His voice turns solemn. "I'm acutely aware of

exactly why and how much I'm paying you, Cynthia. Come with me, if you like. Check out Sophia's room for bugs or whatever—explosives—if you want. You can sit in while we talk, and that's all it is. Talk. I'm going, with or without you. She's a champagne sponge; I want to get a taste of my Dom Perignon before it's all gone."

"Okay. But call her while I put on some clothes. Tell her I'm coming, too, so she won't greet us in her birthday suit."

Cynthia ducks into the changing alcove where she yanks on sweatpants, slips her arms into a short-sleeved blouse, and, just before leaving, snatches a pink choker. Walking into his room, she fastens on the choker. Malcolm grins, apparently still enjoying her tantrum.

"Sophia's phone is busy," he says. "We'll just go down. This isn't a birthday-suit-kind-of-meeting. Trust me."

Trust, she thinks, is something that Malcolm will have to re-earn.

He reminds her to bring her cruise card. "Don't want to lock yourself out."

On the way to the stairs, Malcolm asks, "How'd you get so good at this—the bodyguard stuff?"

She doesn't answer.

A dozen flights down, they wend through a maze of narrow, uncarpeted hallways. She didn't slip on shoes, so her bare feet absorb the chill. Cynthia feels like a lab rat. They pass three signs that read: "Crew Only Beyond This Point." Malcolm knows his way around. After all the walking, Cynthia has calmed down, but she isn't sorry that she blew up—she hopes it will instill some fear, or at least a little respect.

At Sophia's door, he knocks.... Silence.

"Maybe she's already passed out," Malcolm says with a laugh. "Maybe..." He reaches for the door handle, which turns.

"I thought all the cabin doors locked automatically," Cynthia says.

"Crew doors still have to be locked with a key."

Cynthia is impressed that he knows so many details about the ship, but troubled that he knows *this* detail. She grabs his arm. "I'll go first." She pushes open the door. "Sophia?" she calls. "It's Malcolm and Cynthia."

She hears muffled beeping, a phone left off the hook.

Inside, a bedside lamp illuminates a tiny windowless cabin mirrored on facing walls to make the room appear larger. The twin bed is made, but no chocolate graces the pillow, no purple comforter adorns the beige blanket and white linens. The carpeting could have been bought at Walmart. An open bottle of champagne chills in an ice bucket, which takes up most all the surface space atop a small bureau.

A champagne glass lies on the carpet an inch from a wastebasket. The beeping phone receiver hangs out of sight. Cynthia sees curled fingers at floor level, peeking out from behind the bed.

"Oh, shit!" Cynthia pulls the bed away from the wall.

Sophia, dressed in a sheer short-robe and pink nightie, sprawls on the carpet in the narrow gap between the bed and far wall. The tragic pose in minimal clothing exaggerates her skeletal limbs. The phone dangles over her ankles. Shiny nail polish matches the negligee. Her grotesque mouth is open, lips garish blue. Hollow eyes stare to infinity.

Cynthia kneels and checks for a non-existent pulse. "She's dead. Looks like poison.... Maybe meant for you."

"What? No. I don't think... don't think..." Malcolm, mouth ajar, shakes his head.

Cynthia stands, wobbles as blood rushes from her head, then shakes his shoulder. "Don't touch anything," she says. "Go outside and call security." She nudges him toward the door. "I saw an emergency phone in the hall—to the right."

Malcolm, his hands extended like a blind man, stumbles out the door.

Crimes of her past flicker through Cynthia's mind: a series of corpses that energized her when death was her doing. But not this time. The cushy art cruise has turned as dark as Sophia's lips.

Malcolm returns. "Someone's on the way."

They gape at the corpse, unable not to.

Less than a minute later, three *thuds* shake the door. "Security!" A man's voice, breathing hard, British accent. "Open up!"

"It's unlocked," Malcolm says.

An officer ducks slightly while passing under the lintel. It's

Ensign Billingsley again. With his cap, he has less than an inch to spare through the door. His trim white uniform makes him appear even taller. He takes in the scene with deep-seated eyes.

"She's dead," Cynthia says.

They all stare at Sophia, who, indeed, looks very dead.

"Don't touch anything," Billingsley says. "We'll wait for Lieutenant Fist."

"I pulled out the bed," Cynthia says. "That's all I touched—except her neck, to feel for a pulse."

The ensign bends down, feels Sophia's neck for himself. He shakes his head and stands. During a wait that stretches from one slow minute to another, Cynthia catches Billingsley glancing at her bare abdomen. She buttons her shirt, thinking: creepy how he arrived so quickly.

16

Officers

After a five-minute wait, Ensign Billingsley is outranked by three somber officers—each of normal height—all in starched white uniforms. They pull the bed toward the room's door, then lean over Sophia's corpse as one. The officers speak English in three different accents: Italian, Dutch, and British.

"Yes, she's dead," the Italian with a stethoscope tells the Dutchman with the most ribbons on his chest. Cynthia infers that they are the ship's doctor and captain.

"I can see that," the captain says. "Do something about the eyes."

The doctor reaches down and closes them.

The captain turns to the stockiest of the three. "Lt. Fist, we need to keep a lid on this. Don't want to set off a panic. I'll call Sophia's family before we tell the crew—then only the officers, at least for now."

"Right-oh," Fist says. "Ensign, clear the adjacent cabin for interviews."

Billingsley slides the bed enough for the door to open. Then he departs.

The captain rises from his crouch. "So, Mr. Golden, you found the body?" From his tone, Cynthia concludes that he knows Malcolm.

"Ms. James and I, yes."

The other officers stand up, too.

Fist says, "Captain, I suggest we move next door. That

cabin's free…. Keep the crime scene tidy."

"In a minute." The captain scrutinizes Cynthia as if just now noticing that she's in the room. He glances down at the dead woman. Back at Cynthia. "What were you two doing here?"

"I arranged a meeting with Sophia, as I do every year," Malcolm says, his voice shaky. "I called room service and ordered champagne sent down, but I was delayed. Looks like she started drinking without me."

The captain eyes the bottle, then Sophia's distorted face. "Doctor, can you run any tests for poison?"

"Not on board. All we can do is save the champagne for the investigators."

"From the visible symptoms, what do you think?"

"It certainly looks like poison of some kind, but I'd rather not guess as to type."

"We'll check the cork for a syringe hole," Lt. Fist says.

The captain turns to Lt. Fist. "And find out who delivered the champagne. Review the security tapes. Check the phone logs to verify Mr. Golden's statement."

"Yes, sir. But again, I suggest we move next door."

"Yes, yes. We'll do just that in a minute. Carry on."

Fist (first name Sebastian, according to his nametag) clicks on a walkie-talkie as he moves toward the door. "Billingsley, I want you to…" Fist's British accent trails into the hallway.

"Show me your cruise cards," the captain commands Cynthia and Malcolm. She is thankful Malcolm reminded her to bring it.

The captain stares at the IDs, then takes another look at each member of what must look like a love triangle gone tragically wrong—longest at the one on the floor. Cynthia fears that the red-faced Dutchman suspects *her*.

"Mr. Golden," the captain says, "Ms. James is your traveling companion, yet you have separate staterooms and you were sending champagne to my auctioneer?"

"Um… yes."

"Ms. James, do you have a problem with this?"

"Yes, of course. I caught him sneaking out. He insisted on coming here when Sophia's line was busy. I thought I'd better come, too."

"It's not what it looks like," Malcolm says.

The captain slaps a fist into his palm. "A member of *my* crew lies *dead* on the floor! This is *exactly* what it looks like."

"I was just going to talk," Malcolm says. "About the auction—go over my signals. We do it every cruise—"

"Don't insult my intelligence, Mr. Golden. Look at her... clothes."

Fist steps back into the cabin. "Are you coming?"

The captain nods at Fist. "You're right. Treat this as a crime scene, Lieutenant. No one goes in or out without my approval. Photograph every detail. Call the U.S. authorities in Miami, and have investigators meet us in St. Thomas."

"Perhaps, sir, you should consider changing course for San Juan. It's closer."

The captain purses his lips before saying, "No. We'll hold to our present course for St. Thomas. Only a few hours difference. Now get me that room service steward."

Fist nods with British efficiency. "Ensign Billingsley is tracking him down, sir, even as we speak."

The captain appears rattled for a moment before snapping, "Right. Everybody next door."

Cynthia, Malcolm, Lt. Fisk, the doctor, and the captain step into the hall then into the adjacent cabin, which looks the same as Sophia's room, except for no dead body. There, they stand in silence for a few awkward moments.

"Whose cabin is this?" the captain asks Fist.

"Stephanie Roberts. Assistant Purser. She has the night shift at the Passengers' Services desk."

The captain taps his foot, appearing to ponder his next move.

"Captain," Fist says, "would you like me to get cracking?"

"Yes, I think that best. What will you—"

Billingsley, the tall ensign, pushes open the door. "I have the steward, Paul Radzna. Should I bring him in?"

"Just a minute," Fist says. He turns to Malcolm and Cynthia. "I'll have to ask you two to wait in the hall for a few minutes."

As everyone maneuvers in the cramped room, Cynthia slips off one pearl ear stud and switches it from receiver to transmitter. She bumps Malcolm, losing her balance, and sits on the bed. In the act of getting up, she leaves the stud under a pillow.

She sees Paul Radzna as they pass just inside the door. He's a lanky blond, not more than 22, who looks like he wants to be anywhere in the world but jammed inside a large closet with three irate officers.

The door closes. Billingsley ushers Malcolm and Cynthia twenty feet down the hall. She moves a few yards away from Malcolm and listens to the interrogation through her remaining speaker.

"At ease," Fist says in the interrogation room. "Earlier, did you bring champagne to Miss Caporetto's cabin next door?"

"Yes, sir," Radzna says.

"What time was that?"

"Just before one a.m." The steward's English is good, his accent mild; Radzna sounds Polish.

"Can you be more precise?"

"Ah... I'd say five minutes before one, sir. I could check ticket to be sure."

"Do you remember who placed the order?"

"Yes, sir. A Mr. Golden, Lido-103."

"Who answered your knock next door?" Fist asks.

"Ms. Caporetto, sir."

"Was she alone?"

"Uh, yeah."

"How was she dressed?"

Silence.

"What was she wearing?"

"A skimpy robe and nightgown, sir. Pink."

"So you set up the champagne in an ice bucket?"

"No, sir."

"What?" Fist says. "Why not?"

"There was a bottle already *in* a bucket. She had full glass. Singing. Almost kiss me. She said her bottle was already delivered by another stewardess. It was right there in ice bucket on her desk. She give me two dollars and say, 'Get lost.'"

Fist's voice rises. "Did she say who delivered the first bottle?"

"She said it was a stewardess, sir. A *she*."

"How long was that before you arrived?"

"I didn't ask."

"Anything else?"

"No, sir. I do as she say—get lost. Return the double order."

"Anything else?" Fist asks.

"No, sir."

"All right," the captain says. "Dismissed."

The door opens; Radzna and Fist come out. Fist calls down the hall to Malcolm and Cynthia, "You two can come back in."

As Cynthia enters, the captain points a finger at Fist's round face. "Verify his story. Now what *else* are you going to do?"

"Perhaps, Captain, we shouldn't discuss that in front of passengers." Fisk nods sideways at Malcolm and Cynthia.

"Yes, of course."

There is a moment of silence.

"Are you through with us then?" Malcolm asks.

"Oh," Cynthia says. "There's my earring on the bed." She snatches it from underneath the pillow. "I must have dropped it when I stumbled."

The captain's icy gaze holds on Cynthia.

17

Captain Dirk De Vries

Dirk abhors trouble on his ship, and Cynthia James is trouble with a capital T. He frowns at her attire: bare feet, lavender sweatpants, white shirt, and pink choker. Dirk can read people, one reason he is the youngest captain in the Empire fleet, and he reads her eyes. They're dark, the eyes of jealousy; perhaps the eyes of vengeance. He has no objection to attractive women—is rather in favor of them—but Ms. James has predatory body language. Death has followed her onto his ship and threatens his triumph.

His brilliant triumph!

True, Dirk had nothing to do with Empire Lines actually coming into possession of a valuable painting, but he was the one who made this gala cruise happen. The company executives scoffed when Sophia presented her idea to auction Picasso's Winter Prince on a winter cruise. Those poltroons wouldn't recognize a publicity bonanza if it bit them in the arse. They wanted to play it safe—farm out the auction to Sotheby's and pocket a quick profit. The brass didn't want to strain a "sideline" like the art department, didn't want to bother with increased security.

But Dirk schmoozed the board of directors, partnered with the Picasso Society to guarantee authenticity, and finally prevailed, getting the auction on his ship, of course. The publicity was phenomenal—everyone who is anyone in the art world is onboard. Dirk has a week of dinners and parties scheduled with the richest art collectors in the world. But a murder could spoil everything, especially if it remains unsolved.

Thank God, *Persian Prince* has the best security man in the fleet. Fist will control the crisis, solve the crime, and allow Dirk to do what captains do best: rub shoulders with the rich and famous. They don't call him Captain to the Stars for nothing.

Sophia will have to be honored tastefully, of course— perhaps a memorial service in place of the next regular auction. Then the special auction must take place on Thursday as scheduled. The world is watching.

Dirk gives Golden's girlfriend a condescending glare. He doesn't care if Golden *is* an art mucky-muck. Something isn't right with her and Malcolm. Separate staterooms? Malcolm's champagne rendezvous with Sophia? Cynthia tagging along? Why? She appears too cool, as if accustomed to finding dead bodies. Yes, he will have Fist keep a close eye on Ms. James.

Dirk wants to escape the scene—free Fist to, as Fist put it, get cracking. Still, Dirk is the captain, which means the ultimate responsibility is his and his alone.

"May I ask a question before I leave it to you?" Dirk says to Fist.

"By all means, sir."

Dirk looks straight at the woman. "Ms. James, you don't appear dressed for a social call."

"I already explained that I caught Malcolm sneaking out and just threw on—"

"So you were already in bed when Mr. Golden 'sneaked out'?"

"Yes."

"You heard him get up?"

"Yes. He, ah, bumped something in the dark."

Dirk wants to tell Golden, man-to-man, that he should be more discreet next time, but such a flip remark would be inappropriate. He has made a mistake by lingering, trying to be an investigator. "Carry on," he says to Fist before departing.

The walk to the bridge is a long one. On more than one occasion, Dirk's legs buckle. A vice clamps on his forehead. He stops and leans against a bulkhead to ward off dizziness. The situation seems worse than when he was barking orders. Now alone, the implications erode his ego. He knows of no other cruise ship captain who has lost a crew member to murder. That's a black enough mark, but to have it happen this week, of all weeks, while the world is watching!

After a few measured breaths, he steadies. Yes, it's bad, but leadership will carry the day—it always does. Dirk knows what he must do: 1.) Honor Sophia with a tasteful memorial service. 2.) Cooperate with the land-based authorities upon arrival in St. Thomas. 3.) Make sure all the ship's activities continue undisturbed. And 4.) Announce, without equivocation, that the auction will take place on Thursday, as scheduled.

Buck up and push ahead, despite the tragedy. The auction will write the biggest headlines. Take it one day at a time. Don't blow this, Dirk. Don't blow this.

Stronger, he juts his chin and strides for the bridge. Two steps later, his bravado collapses. How will he endure the phone call to Sophia's family?

18

Pressure

With the captain gone, Cynthia watches Lt. Fist assume command. His voice strengthens; he even seems taller. Turning to Malcolm, Fist says, "Tell me exactly what you two saw and did from the moment you opened Sophia's door. Everything you touched. What you smelled. I want to know how often you *breathed*. Did you touch the phone?"

"No," Malcolm says. "It was off the hook. After she moved the bed and saw… Well, Cynthia reminded me not to disturb any evidence."

Fist measures Cynthia with accusatory eyes. "I think everyone would be best served if we separate you two for further questioning. Just a formality, really, to get better perspective."

Right, Cynthia thinks, warier than ever. She considers leaving the ear piece again, but Fisk doesn't take his eyes off her, so she resigns herself to relying on Malcolm's veracity.

For twenty minutes, Cynthia stands alone in the under-lit corridor not far from the cabin where Lt. Fist questions Malcolm. Looking down, she sees her swollen, purple toe, but there's little pain—too much else is going on in her mind. Antsy, she paces until Billingsley appears from around a corner.

"Sorry to keep you waiting," Billingsley says, "but I had to review the security videos. Nothing there—we don't have cameras in every crew quarters hall, just on the staircase landings—but you'll be interested to know that we found two dishwashers who saw the back of a woman steward approaching

Ms. Caporetto's room with an ice bucket. It wasn't your boyfriend in drag. The suspect is too short. A person can make themselves taller, but not shorter. Now you, on the other hand..." Billingsley doesn't have to complete his thought—he thinks she's a suspect and he doesn't care if she knows it.

He flips open a notepad. "Ms. James, I'm going to have to conduct your interview here. We're quite pressed for space, what with a full ship and the murder and all—all—all." His voice echoes in the metal hallway.

She leans against the corridor bulkhead, one bare foot flat against the wall. She hasn't smoked since her second year in prison, but now, she craves a cigarette.

He asks precise questions: exactly where was she earlier? when was she was separated from Malcolm? and for how long? He jots her answers in his notebook. One thing doesn't make sense: if she is the primary suspect, why is Fist questioning Malcolm instead of her?

Twenty minutes later, Cynthia and Malcolm meet back in her stateroom. They exchange summaries of their individual interrogations. Cynthia learns nothing new from Malcolm's account. Not wanting to reveal her bugging system, she doesn't tell him what she overheard of the interview with the Polish wine steward.

"Thank God that's over," Malcolm sighs. "I'm exhausted."

"No rest for morons. Get out the warning letters. Both of them."

Malcolm slouches. "You're not serious. It's three in the morning."

"Get them!"

He returns with the envelopes and sits next to Cynthia on her loveseat. She reaches for the first note. "It's time to tell Lt. Fist about these."

"No." He pulls it away from her hand. "We can't do that."

"Come on, Malcolm. We *have* to. The security staff may be able to—"

"No! If they suspect Sophia's death is tied to the Picasso, they'll cancel the auction. That's unacceptable."

"But—"

"But nothing! I'm on this ship for *one reason*: to get the painting. You're here to get me off safely after I have it, *not* to compromise the acquisition."

She stares at his fiery eyes. It's as if he drank Dr. Jekyll's potion.

"I'm pulling rank on this, Cynthia. We keep the notes to ourselves."

Cynthia takes two deep breaths before saying, "Okay."

They silently re-read the first letter while sitting on Cynthia's loveseat.

Mr. Golden, Do not bid on the Picasso. If you do, dire consequences will befall you.

The letter was printed by a laser printer. Cynthia inspects Malcolm's name and address on the envelope, also computer printed. Not much to trace.

"Manhattan postmark," she says, thinking out loud. "Do any of the Picasso Society elites live in New York?"

"John Poindexter."

"But I bet the others visit museums and auction houses... or know people who do." Cynthia chooses her next words carefully. "What happens to your estate when you die?"

"*When*?" Malcolm says, "Not if?"

"Everybody dies, Malcolm. Knowing about your will may shed some light on the situation."

"Oh. I thought you were tiring of my company." His joke falls flat. Still, he forces a tired grin. "My estate will be complicated; much of it goes to various art foundations, but one segment is very straightforward, in a trust—set up by my grandfather—for the Museum of Modern Art. Thus, about thirty million will bypass probate and go straight to MOMA."

"John Poindexter's museum." Cynthia taps her good foot. "How much time does Empire Lines give a bidder to pay for auctioned art?"

"Normal purchases are charged to your shipboard account, due upon debarkation, but the Picasso will be sold on special terms: ninety days."

"If you died, how long before the museum might gain access to the trust money?"

"Much faster than probate. Maybe a month—" He nods. "I

see where you're going. MOMA could pay for a good part of the painting with the bequest. But why the warning note? And why kill Sophia?"

"And why not bump you off sooner?" Cynthia says. "So the money would be there for sure."

"It gives Poindexter motive," he says. "I'm embarrassed I didn't think of it before."

Cynthia studies his eyes. She sees some murky emotion, but it isn't embarrassment. She taps the second envelope, then opens it and reads the second note. "It would be helpful if we could test printers belonging to the elites and major bidders."

"Right," he yawns. "No judge would issue warrants."

"What's the protocol for a murder on the high seas? Who has jurisdiction?"

Malcolm barely shakes his head.

"Never mind," she says, glancing at her notebook. "We need some way to narrow the field. The A-list is the likely bidders on board: Poindexter, Sotelo, and LaCroix. Plus anyone close to the Picasso. The auction staff. How many people work for—" She hears snoring.

In repose, Malcolm appears harmless. Cynthia wakes him just enough to lead him to his bed. Once on his back, he quickly falls asleep again. For a moment, she considers undressing him. Instead, she lays the comforter over him, returns to her room, flips off the light, pulls off her sweatpants and blouse, then slips into bed. Sleep is hours away.

Over and over, she tries to fit Sophia's murder with Malcolm's death threats, three pieces of a sinister puzzle. Every way she twists the facts in her head, the events end up linked, even if she isn't sure how. Malcolm is warned not to bid, then the person who will handle the bidding is killed. Clearly, someone is going to great lengths to obtain the Picasso. Cynthia guesses that it must be someone who has no hope in an auction. She starts at the top of the list. Again.

Countess LaCroix...

Day 3 — Monday

At Sea

19

Morning After

Cynthia makes sure that Malcolm is still asleep before she slips out of her stateroom at 06:15 and tapes an exterior edge of each cabin door. She wants to sample early rumors and, more importantly, be seen *without* Malcolm. She finds Miguel at the bow end of the hall, cleaning the stateroom of early-risers.

"Anything new this morning?" she asks. Miguel tries to smile, but his eyes betray sadness. "What?" she says.

"Lady auctioneer killed last night. They say murder."

Cynthia guesses that the Polish steward put two-and-two together, then told everyone he knows. If rumors have leaked to the crew by 06:20, the passengers will be buzzing at breakfast.

Cynthia hustles down the stairs to the Internet Café on Deck 6. From there, she sends an e-mail to Bruce Swenson, friend and surveillance magician.

Bruce,

Greetings from Persian Prince. The ship's art auctioneer, Sophia Caporetto, was murdered last night. Poison in her champagne. My client, Malcolm Golden, may have been the target, but he's okay. Get everything you can, level four, on

Caporetto, plus art collectors Julia Sotelo, Countess Yvonne LaCroix, and John Poindexter. Finances, affairs, associations with museums, history with Malcolm Golden, etc. Respond ASAP.

Weather's great. Food, too. Working on a tan. Won't get much reading done because watching Malcolm is now a full-time job.

—*Cyn*

While online, Cynthia does a few minutes of basic research on the Louvre, the Prado, and MOMA.

After jogging back up to the Palace Buffet, Cynthia helps herself to iced tea before walking through each seating section, hoping to see the Poindexters. She spies them and swings past their table, close enough to be noticed, but far enough away to ignore them.

She is positive John Poindexter sees her, but he doesn't say anything—not "Hey, Cynthia, where's Malcolm?" or "Care to join us?" or even "Good morning." If he *is* involved, he doesn't tip his hand. In any event, Cynthia has planted "no Malcolm" seeds on the assumption that he was the killer's intended victim. She hurries back to the staterooms where she verifies the unbroken door tapes. Then she sits on her balcony and gazes at the endless sea, waiting for Malcolm's alarm.

At breakfast, every table hums about the auctioneer. There is a posted bulletin announcing the tragic death—with no reference to murder—and cancellation of the day's art auction, replaced by a memorial service.

Cynthia and Malcolm change for sunbathing, then walk down their hall to the outdoor section of the Lido deck.

"I need to know more about the other major bidders," Cynthia says. "A lot more." She tugs his elbow, leading him to a round table with a view of the ocean, bluer than the day before. She sits. "But first, we need to talk about security."

Cynthia suggests tighter measures. While they argue over how much time to spend on the open decks, an officer with a Jamaican accent summons them down to Passenger Services on Deck 6. There, the officer leaves them in two chairs across a tiny desk from an empty seat. This is the future cruises sales booth, but it is the head of security, Lt. Sebastian Fist, who enters carrying a hard-shelled briefcase.

Fist grimaces as if there are pebbles in his shoes. Before he speaks, his walkie-talkie crackles. "Yes, Captain.... No.... Yes... Yes, *sir*." Fist signs off. "Blasted turf wars—jurisdiction hell. You two better hope no bloody evidence points your way, because if it does, you'll rot in the brig before the U.S., Netherlands, Bahamas, Virgin Islands, Empire Cruises, Interpol, and the FBI decide who gets first crack at you."

Cynthia and Malcolm exchange wary glances.

Fist clicks open the case and pulls out two giant Q-tips. "I need mouth swabs from both of you. And fingerprints. For the investigators on St. Thomas."

They open their mouths so Fist can take saliva samples. Then they stand up so they can reach the ink pad. The Jamaican officer moves in from the door and helps Fist take fingerprints the messy, old-fashioned way.

Fist bags the DNA samples and fingerprint cards, then offers hand-wipes and paper towels. "Have a seat," he says. They comply. Fist shuts the case and places it on the floor. "There's an important question I forgot to ask last night. How the blazes did you two get into Sophia's cabin if she was already dead?"

"The door was unlocked," Malcolm says.

"Strange," Fist says. "Not like her. Had you ever been inside her cabin before?"

Malcolm peeks at Cynthia before saying, "Yes. On three previous cruises."

"You arranged for the champagne. Did she leave the door unlocked for *you*?"

"Discretion was important to Sophia. She didn't want knocking to attract attention. If people got the wrong idea, she might lose her job."

"Well, it seems she *has* lost her job...along with her *life*. Just pray your DNA or fingerprints don't show up where they shouldn't." While he says this, Fist is looking at Cynthia.

20

Suspects

By 11:00 a.m., Cynthia and Malcolm are oiled up, trying to bake out depression on the highest, most forward section of the Spa Deck. It isn't working for Cynthia, whose shoulder and neck muscles won't relax.

"Do *you* think the poison was meant for you?" she says.

Malcolm removes his sunglasses. "All the insiders know I'm here for the Picasso. If I'm dead, the painting's up for grabs."

"Suppose the murderer knew you were sleeping with the auctioneer."

Malcolm stares at Cynthia's reflective lenses. "I never said that I was."

"So were you?"

"We had a professional relationship. That's all."

She reads his eyes, can't tell if he's lying.

"The murder still eliminates a potential ally," Cynthia says. "The person who can ignore a bid as the gavel comes down." She takes a moment to think. "Who stands to gain with her out of the picture?"

"I don't know."

"Who'll conduct the auction now?"

"Brent Burns, I expect. Her assistant."

"What do you know about him?"

"Not much except the superficial. As I said, he's there to charm the ladies. Three or four years with the company. He's a face man—doesn't say much, at least to me. Smiles a lot. Perfect teeth."

"Do you think he favors any particular bidder?"

Malcolm shuts his paperback. "You're way off base. All the Empire auctioneers are impartial."

Cynthia aims her reflective lenses at his nose. "I thought you said you didn't know much about him."

Malcolm looks away.

"Do you think he suspected you were seeing Sophia—professionally or otherwise?"

"We were discreet."

"Ordering champagne from room service is *discreet*?"

"All right. It's possible. He can't be as dumb as he looks." Malcolm gets up to stretch his legs.

"Remember, stay where I can see you."

"Yes, mother."

Malcolm circles the deck, chatting with several passengers. Periodically, he smiles in Cynthia's direction.

Two men catch Cynthia's eye, one a bouncer type—built like a trash can, shaved head, bicep-to-bicep snake tattoos—who bumps Malcolm when he could have avoided it. The other is the same slim man whom she noticed three times on the first day. He looks too much like a tourist to be for real. His wardrobe is straight from the ship's Persian Bazaar: *Persian Prince* T-shirt, *Persian Prince* baseball cap, as if his luggage was lost. Aside from his clothes, the man is nondescript, shorter than average but not short, slimmer than average but not skinny.

The slim man goes from noteworthy to suspicious when he follows Malcolm onto the jogging track and leans on the rail next to where Malcolm faces the ocean. Cynthia watches them across thirty feet of deck, through a Plexiglas wind barrier. The men talk for two minutes before Malcolm comes back to his chaise.

He and Cynthia chat for a while about countries each of them has vsited. He asks her questions about Spain; she asks him about China. Cynthia breathes the fresh air, takes in the endless blue. The effect is dulling; her eyelids are heavy. Lack of sleep is catching up to her....

Malcolm shakes her shoulder. "Time to turn so you don't get burned."

Cynthia snorts awake. *Some bodyguard!* She rolls onto her

back, sits, raises her chaise, and flips open a book. Before she has read a page, the brassy voice of Julia Sotelo cuts through the background noise.

"Malcolm, thanks for saving me a chair." Julia sheds a flowery shirt and sits down on the chaise next to Malcolm. Her figure, pleasing enough in formal attire, is eye-catching in a bikini for a different reason: rolls of fleshy overflow. Cynthia would be embarrassed to wear such an inappropriate suit, yet Julia oozes confidence—as well as bosom—as if she has the body of Miss World.

"What are you reading?" Julia asks, touching Malcolm's hand.

"A John Irving novel," he says.

Julia laughs. "Does it say who murdered Sophia?"

Cynthia faces her own book but slides both eyeballs sideways.

Julia fawns over Malcolm as if she's in heat. Cynthia knows how easy it is to flatter men off balance—she once did it for a living. She studies Julia Sotelo, woman of excess. Julia touches Malcolm more than is proper. She laughs loudly so that everyone within earshot turns her way.

"You must be *devastated* about Sophia," Julia says.

"It's a shock," Malcolm mutters.

"Everyone knows you two were having an affair…. Well, you *were*."

Malcolm snaps his book shut. "A gentleman doesn't tolerate such—"

"A gentleman?" Julia coughs. "You forget—I know better."

"Julia, I don't think Cynthia appreciates—"

"Be a dear…" Julia, still sitting, hands Malcolm a tube of sunscreen and rotates her shoulder blades toward him. "Do my back."

He complies. Cynthia studies his hands, suspecting that he has rubbed Julia's back before.

"Don't stop there," Julia says. "Lower."

He puts down the tube and wipes his hands on a towel. "As I started to say, I don't think Cynthia appreciates your flirting with me."

"I don't hear *her* complaining. Maybe she wants to learn

more about her boyfriend's fidelity."

There are several seconds of awkward silence. Cynthia closes her book and smiles gamely. "I'm in favor of education. What should I know?"

"That Malcolm slept with Sophia... and half the women at Sotheby's."

Cynthia raises an eyebrow. "Only half? And only the women?"

Julia laughs. "Most women would feel threat—"

"I'm not most women. And whoever he slept with in the past is only a prelude to who he'll be sleeping with tonight." Cynthia reaches over and squeezes Malcolm's hand. "And Julia... that won't be you."

Cynthia enjoys her little performance and expects Julia to leave in a huff, but the flamboyant Spaniard laughs louder. "You have a catty edge—I like that. I think we'll get along famously. So about the murder, who do you think did it?"

The next ten minutes are all Julia—spouting conspiracy theories, most pointing to John Poindexter. "...and I hear that John treated Sophia's assistant to dinner. Coincidence? I think not."

Malcolm shakes his head. "You're way off base about John. He wouldn't do anything like that."

Julia smirks. "Maybe you don't know him as well as I do."

"Probably not." Malcolm stands. "I'm getting iced tea. I'll bring back three."

Cynthia wants to remind Malcolm not to roam, but he can't see eye signals through her sunglasses. Rather than blow her cover, Cynthia lets him go. After all, the iced tea station is nearby.

Once Malcolm is out of earshot, Julia says, "He never stays with the same girl very long, but if anyone can change his nomadic ways, I'll bet it's you."

"I'll take that as a compliment." Cynthia waits two seconds, an acceptable pause for a smooth change of subject. "Did I read somewhere that you're a distant relative of Picasso?"

Julia laughs. "Not really. My first husband was Pablo's third cousin twice removed. Or was my second husband a first cousin, thrice removed? However tenuous the connection, the Society

Board wanted a relation with ties to a major Spanish museum. Now they can't get rid of me."

"Malcolm also says that you know your stuff."

Julia lowers her chin. "What stuff would that be?"

"You know, about art."

Julia pouts. "I was so hoping he was referring to a different sort of talent."

Cynthia colors.

"Oh, I forgot. You Americans are such prudes.... I'm joking. If you stick around, I'll grow on you. You'll see." Julia peeks at her watch. "Look at the time. I have an appointment at the spa." She stands, gathers her belongings, and walks away, her butt cheeks rolling like a pair of Slinkies.

Cynthia opens her book but looks at Malcolm, who appears to be flirting with a pretty Asian server at the iced tea bar. Cynthia ponders the main suspects: Julia, John Poindexter, and the countess. And the swarthy little man. Cynthia thinks about the murder, the warning notes, the tampered safe lock, the confined space of the ship, and motives. *Damn, I'm a character in an Agatha Christie mystery:* Murder in the Caribbean.

What to make of Julia Sotelo? An actress? Yes. A flirt? Definitely. Happier than Cynthia? Absolutely. Cynthia envies any woman who isn't a slave to her body. While Cynthia religiously does stomach crunches, fighting a futile battle against aging, Julia lets her voluptuous body hang out, full of life. Yes, Julia's thirst for life is fierce. But could such a thirst have led to murder?

Malcolm returns with three iced teas. "Where's Julia?"

"I'll drink hers," Cynthia says. "I'm thirsty as a camel."

Across the deck, Cynthia notices John Poindexter looking at her as if she were under surveillance. The next time she glances up from her book, Poindexter is gone.

After a much-needed move to shaded loungers on a sparsely populated corner of the Lido Deck, Cynthia reads a few pages, but her mind wanders to a nagging question. She decides on an ambush. "Malcolm," she says, leaning over to whisper. "Why did you *really* hire me?"

He clears his throat. "As I've said, I wanted someone non-threatening, and I'd heard about what you did for the senator—"

"No. I mean why not a licensed pro? You must have looked into the corporate services, like Guards To Go. They hire out women."

Malcolm grins. "It's complicated."

"I *hate* it when men tell me: *it's complicated.*" She removes her sunglasses. "Try me."

"Shhh," he says. "Not out here. I'll tell you later."

"Why not just tell me now?"

To Cynthia, his evasive expression looks like that of a liar in search of bullshit. Lucky for him, a ponderous woman in a flowing red muumuu chooses that moment to wander by.

"Is this one taken?" she asks, pointing to the chaise next to Malcolm's.

He winks at Cynthia, as if to say: I win. To the woman, he says, "No. Please take it."

Cynthia wants to dislike him for looking far too pleased with himself, but it's at such moments that his charm is most engaging.

Madame Muumuu says she is from Algeria, but Cynthia thinks Brooklyn is more likely. She's quite the talker, proving that there *is* justice in the world, after all. She jabbers at Malcolm in her artificial French accent about everything on the ship, including the murder. Cynthia hides behind her shades, book, and purse-lipped smile, while the obese woman wears at Malcolm's patience.

"I need to stretch my legs," he finally says.

"Don't go yet," says Madame Muumuu. She presses a fleshy palm on his knee. "I figured out who did it, who killed the woman auctioneer."

Malcolm frees his limb. "I don't really—"

"Oh, but I have to tell somebody, and you're such a nice man. Hear me out. It has to be the auction assistant. These things always turn out to done by the people closest to the victim. Like in the book I'm reading."

Cynthia subtly turns to see the woman's book, a Miss Marple mystery, which brings a smile to Cynthia's lips. Malcolm tries to catch her eye, but Cynthia feigns inattention behind reflective shades.

"There's no spouse," the woman prattles, "so the next closest person is the assistant. He stands to get her job—unless he's caught, of course. It's just like those Patrick O'Brien books where the third mate bumps off the second mate to move up the ladder." The woman goes on without a breath. Malcolm stoically absorbs her verbal assault.

When Cynthia thinks that he has paid enough for his arrogance, she clears her throat. "Raoul, dear, would you please get me some more iced tea?" Cynthia sits up straight and says to the woman, "I hope you won't mind. I've broken my toe and..." She points to her left big toe—black-and-blue.

Malcolm doesn't have to be asked twice—even though Cynthia still has a full glass. He bounces to his feet. "Right away, Gwenevere."

"Make sure you don't *spill* any," Cynthia says to his back.

Now it's just Cynthia and Madame Muumuu, who asks whether Cynthia bought her bikini in the onboard gift shop. "Maybe I should get one, too," the woman says. Cynthia thinks the woman is joking but doesn't laugh—the thought of Madame Muumuu in such a suit is painful. The woman keeps talking, but Cynthia ignores the stream of words and looks at her own book.

Malcolm returns with three iced teas triangled in his hands.

"Did you forget my fruit?" Cynthia says, sounding bitchy.

"Oh, I'm sorry, darling. I didn't hear. I'll get—" Malcolm spins, bumps Madame Muumuu's knee, spilling all three glasses onto her massive thighs.

There follows a flurry of gasps, apologies, muumuu wringing, and calls for a towel. Cynthia covers her mouth to muffle laughter. The end result is a damp, empty chaise.

After Malcolm sits down, Cynthia whispers, "Well done, Raoul."

"Broken toe?" he says. "Nice touch, Gwenevere."

Cynthia gazes at the ocean and smiles. Yes, Malcolm Golden is a charming rogue.

Later, they move back into the sun and reclaim lounge chairs saved by their towels. The day is perfectly gorgeous, and Cynthia has to remind herself that she is working and that Sophia is dead. Malcolm endures the sun for only a few minutes before he gets antsy for another walk.

"Not too far, Raoul honey." The joke has worn thin, so she blinks Raoul out of existence. She watches Malcolm banter with strangers on the far side of the Spa Pool. She studies the body language of the people—men and women, passengers and crew—all caught in his spell. Malcolm thrives, totally in his element. He waves, letting Cynthia know that he hasn't wandered out of sight. She pans her eyes from port to starboard, paying attention to anyone moving toward Malcolm. As her neck twists left, two figures startle her from close range.

"What are those?" asks a chubby eight-year-old boy in dripping, oversized bathing trunks. He holds two ping-pong balls in one hand and points the index finger of the other at Cynthia's neck. "My sister says tattoos, but I think they're birthmarks. She's six." At his side, a pixie wearing a doll-sized pink bikini nods, thumb jammed in her mouth.

Cynthia is speechless, as if the kids are aliens—which, in a sense, they are. These are the first children onboard with whom Cynthia has spoken. She finds it refreshing that the kids look and sound totally American.

"So what are they?" the boy says. "Which of us is right?"

"They're scars."

"No way."

"Way." Cynthia smiles. "I got a belt with little spikes caught around my neck, real tight, like a noose. The spikes punched holes in my skin that got infected."

"How'd you do that?"

"I was careless. But I was lucky and got loose before… well, it was a close call."

"Is that why your voice is scratchy?"

Cynthia smiles. "Uh-huh."

"So are scars more like tattoos or birthmarks?"

"Why?"

"Which one of us is righter?"

Cynthia smiles at the silent girl and shakes her head. "Neither. Things aren't always a simple question of right and wrong."

The boy shrugs. "Well, okay. Thanks, lady." He pulls his sister's hand.

"Wait," Cynthia says. "What are your names?"

"I'm Jake. This is Nora. She's shy."

Cynthia flutters five fingers toward the girl. "Hi. My name's Cynthia."

The girl smiles briefly then yanks her hand away from Jake's and points at Cynthia's belly.

"She wants to know about the numbers on your tummy."

Cynthia reflexively tightens her abs. "What does it look like?"

Jake twists his head and wriggles his nose as if smelling rancid food. "Looks like a brand. I've seen 'em in old westerns my dad watches on AMC. Looks like you're a cow, property of the Circle-Eighty Ranch." Jake nods, pleased with himself.

Cynthia, never having been called a cow, laughs. "You're right. That's exactly what it is. Bet you haven't seen one on a person before."

"That's for sure. So who owns the Circle-Eighty?"

"Nobody owns me anymore. I'm a maverick."

"What's a maverick?"

"A calf that gets separated from the herd—travels her own trail."

"So you're lost?"

"More like escaped. I don't want to go back to the Circle-Eighty Ranch. I like it right here. How about you? Are you kids having fun on the cruise?"

Nora nods. Jake fumbles one of the ping-pong balls but snatches it out of the air after one bounce. "It's okay, but it's no Disney World. Come on, Nora. Let's go swimming *now*, 'cause Dad's gonna take us rock climbing after lunch. Bye, lady."

Nora slides her thumb out and whispers, "Bye." The little girl waves as Jake drags her sternward.

Cynthia holds a smile long after the children disappear.

21

Exchange

After lunch, Cynthia and Malcolm settle back onto their lounge chairs in the shade. There, they listen to a steel drum band play pop American songs with a calypso beat. The slim man from the running track appears again, wearing a Hawaiian shirt, baggy shorts, and baseball cap. He loiters on the far side of the pool, glancing Malcolm's way. Cynthia pretends to focus on John Grisham.

"I'm going to the bathroom," Malcolm says. "Okay?" Cynthia nods. He picks up his paperback which has an envelope for a bookmark—an envelope she hadn't noticed earlier—and ambles toward the far end of the Persian Gulf Pool.

Cynthia can see the alley entrance to the men's room. She watches the slim man disappear. Malcolm follows. Cynthia checks her watch. Twenty-two seconds later, Malcolm exits. A minute after that, the man walks out. Cynthia notes a few oddities: the man has an envelope stuffed in his right rear pocket that wasn't there when he entered; Malcolm wasn't inside long enough to urinate and wash his hands; and his fat bookmark is gone.

Malcolm resettles on his lounger.

"Anything I should know about?" she asks.

"No, but everything came out in the end."

Cynthia doesn't even smile; she can't let the slim man slide any longer. "You gave something to the guy in a baseball cap while you were in the bathroom. The same guy you talked to earlier up on the track."

He laughs, higher pitched than usual. "What are you talking about?"

She slaps her book. "Cut the crap. You carried an envelope into the men's room in your book. *He* left with the envelope in his hip pocket."

Malcolm studies her, as if forming a new opinion. "Okay. He's Cliff Gorman, a fellow-collector, an ally. I asked him to keep tabs on Julia Sotelo's movements. Just now, he gave me a report, and I gave him a new list of things to watch for."

"Can I see his report?"

"It was verbal."

Cynthia chooses not to point out that 22 seconds isn't much time for an oral report—or that a public bathroom is an odd locale. All she says is, "Then what did he tell you?"

"That Julia ate lunch with John Poindexter."

"Is that significant?"

Malcolm adjusts the back of his chair. "Maybe. When major players from rival museums meet, I'm interested."

"Do you think the Prado and MOMA are in cahoots?"

"That's what I want Cliff to find out."

"Tell me about Cliff… Gorman, is it?"

"Yes. He's a small-time collector who likes to rub elbows with major-leaguers. He does favors for me, especially if I make it seem like espionage."

"Is he any good—at getting information?"

"Sometimes."

Cynthia sips iced tea before asking, "What was on the list?"

Malcolm returns a blank stare.

"The new list of things you want him to find out?"

"Right. Just the routines of other players, the countess, and John. What time they get up, where they eat and with whom."

Cynthia taps her book—something about Gorman is off. "How much does Cliff know about me?" she says.

"He knows you're not a real date, if that's what you mean."

"Why the secrecy then? From me."

"You're a surveillance pro, Cyn. Maybe I was afraid you'd think I'm a clumsy amateur."

"You *are* a clumsy amateur, so I suggest you clear your

stunts with me next time." Cynthia returns to her book, thinking that Cliff Gorman looks nothing like an art collector. The next time she glances up, John Poindexter waves to her from across the pool.

"Lets' get out of here," she says.

"Why? Where?"

"Anyplace," she says. "Let's see if Roly-Poly Poindexter is shadowing *you*."

"What?"

"He's popped up again. Over there. By the hot tub."

Malcolm looks up, sees Poindexter. "Big deal—he's around the pool. So are a few hundred other people."

"Still," she says. "Humor me. Let's go. I'm the boss about security, right?" What she wants is to take the initiative.

Malcolm sighs. "Right."

"Let's swing by the rooms and get some long pants on."

"Huh?" he says.

"To protect your knees."

Malcolm and Cynthia stand fifteen feet apart at the base of the rock-climbing wall, each armored with a helmet, knee pads, elbow pads, and clipped into a harness around their haunches and thighs. A safety rope goes from the front waist of each harness, up to a pulley at the top of the wall, and down to a bulky spotter, who stands on the ground behind the climber. Malcolm cranes his neck to stare up the 40-foot face. "I can't believe I let you talk me into this."

Cynthia walks over to him and tugs his harness rope against the hitch—solid. "Ten times safer than jogging by the railing. You're good to go."

"I'm only doing this because you whined," he says.

"If I whined, it was only because you were *moping*. And after you buy the painting on Thursday, we won't be doing stuff like this in the open, so we better try it now."

"Did we ditch Poindexter?" he says, forcing a smile.

"He's nowhere in sight," she says without looking. "Now get moving. Remember the rule of three."

Cynthia sidesteps to her starting point, from where she watches Malcolm secure two hand holds and start up the rocks, which aren't rocks at all, but a molded composite, with strategically placed nubs that act as hand and foot holds. There are four pulley systems for four climbing routes, left to right: kids, beginner, intermediate, and advanced. She is on the far right. On the far left is Jake, the boy from the pool, already half-way up the easiest route, with his father calling instructions from below. The pot-bellied father appears too heavy to get up the wall himself, but he's full of advice. "Above your right shoulder, son…. Good…. Now move your left foot up…. Grip with your knee."

Malcolm moves his left foot, finds a step. Then his right. Once he has ascended fifteen feet and is making steady progress, Cynthia starts up. She has never rock-climbed on a molded wall, but in her twenties, she did some real climbing. She acclimates quickly, as with anything athletic. Her hands and thighs are strong, which makes the going quick. She hears Malcolm huffing from the left, so she veers that way to be closer. In thirty seconds, she is twenty-five feet up, even with Malcolm. She stops and calls over, "How ya doing?"

"Okay," he says, although he is struggling for his next handhold. "Glad you told me to wear long pants." He reaches awkwardly with his right arm, first too far left, then to the right, twisting his arm around the slack rope—a no-no. The spotter below tightens the safety line, pinning Malcolm's arm to the wall. His next step should be with his right foot, but the taut rope restricts his balance. He's frozen and in danger, if he releases the handhold, of being spun like an unwinding rubberband. His spotter further tightens the safety rope, increasing Malcolm's predicament.

"Damn!" Malcolm shouts. "My arm's caught! I can't move!" His right foot looks about to lose its toe hold.

"Stay cool," Cynthia calls. She scrambles horizontally across several nubs and is next to Malcolm before a lifeguard can get hooked up to the free harness between Jake and Malcolm. Cynthia presses her left knee under Malcolm's buttocks; her heel has enough traction to support his weight. "I've got you. You okay?"

Malcolm nods.

"Wait," Cynthia calls down to the cavalry. "I've got him."

She checks Malcolm's eyes—no panic. "Loosen his line a tad," she shouts down. When there are a few inches of slack, she tells Malcolm, "Let go with your right hand. Good. Now get your arm out of the rope. Good. Grab the same hold. Good."

Malcolm inhales a deep breath.

"Do you want to go down?"

"Hell no," he mutters.

"Okay," she says.

The harnessed lifeguard—an athletic blonde in shiny purple Lycra—appears off Malcolm's left shoulder.

"Voud you like me to help you descend?" the lifeguard asks in a German accent.

"No," he grunts.

"He's okay," Cynthia says. "Let him finish."

"You are sure?" the lifeguard asks.

"Yeah," Malcolm says. "I'm sure. Just give me some space, okay?"

The lifeguard pushes off and rappels down.

Malcolm takes several seconds to regroup, then resumes the climb. Cynthia matches his pace, staying a few feet away, despite her own spotter's attempts to guide her back to the far right.

The going is slow, but they finally reach the top, side-by-side. Malcolm rings a victory bell at the apex. He is huffing but smiling.

"Way to go," Cynthia says. "Great job!"

Malcolm beams. His spotter calls up, "Ready to rappel down?"

"Huh?" Malcolm says.

"Like in the instruction video," Cynthia tells him. "Hold the rope with both hands and push off with your legs—just a little. The spotter will slide your rope. You'll half-bounce/half-glide down. Enjoy the ride."

She watches over her left shoulder as Malcolm bounces down the wall in four ten-foot leaps—not smooth, but without serious bumps. Once he is on the ground, she calls below, "I'm ready."

Cynthia swoops down in two 20-foot drops. It's like flying. As soon as she touches the deck, she wants to do it again, but of course, she won't—Malcolm is exhausted, and she has to stay with her client.

They unhitch. "Good job," she says, patting his back. "I'm proud of you."

"I'm proud of *you*," he says. "I think I have the best damn bodyguard of all time."

Cynthia shrugs. "We should get—"

"Hey, maverick lady!" It's Jake's high-pitched voice.

Cynthia turns to see the boy with his sister and their father.

"That was a pretty cool rescue," Jake says.

Cynthia colors.

"No way any cowboy'll ever own *you*."

"I hope you're right about that," Cynthia says.

Nora slides her thumb out of her mouth. "You're Spiderwoman."

"No she's not," Jake says.

"Is too!" Nora tugs her father's hand, and they step toward Cynthia. "Can I..." the girl murmurs. "Can I have your autograph?"

Her father holds out a pencil along with a deck plan. "Please?" he says, before adding in a whisper, "She really thinks you're Spiderwoman. So if you could... you know."

Cynthia hesitates.

"Go ahead, Spidie," Malcolm says, "sign."

So Cynthia takes the pencil and signs *CJ Spiderwoman*. "Here you go."

"Thank you," the father says.

"Gee, thanks!" Nora gushes, clutching the talisman. "You're the best!"

"That she is," Malcolm says. "That she is."

22

Memorial

Sophia's memorial service takes place at 3:00 p.m. in Alexander's Lounge, standing room only, more crew than passengers. The heavyweight bidders attend, dressed as somberly as vacation wardrobes allow. Cliff Gorman sits behind them. Cynthia watches Cliff crane his neck, apparently to hear what Julia is saying.

For her part, Cynthia wears a mix-and-match combination—gray pants and a blue top—that she had planned for one of the non-formal dinners. Malcolm, in a perfectly cut sport coat, looks more suave than a man should for a memorial service. Something about expensive clothing brings a sparkle to his eyes.

Instead of flowers, the stage is adorned with Sophia's favorite prints from the art gallery—including a copy of Cynthia's fountain woman. The ship's timid chaplain steps to the podium. Cynthia half expects him to auction off salvation. She is eager to hear what crew members will say about the deceased.

The eulogies have a common theme: Sophia was the most dedicated and energetic crew member on the *Persian Prince*. The Aussie Cruise Director brings a tear to 'most every eye with a story of how Sophia saved a retired couple $17,000 when she discovered a billing error on their art purchases. Ever the cynic, Cynthia wonders how large the invoice must have been for the couple to overlook seventeen grand. Captain DeVries calls Sophia prophetic in her marketing vision for this cruise before stating that Sophia would have wanted the special auction to go on without her. Cynthia muses that death has a way of canonizing the deceased.

Brent Burns doesn't appear broken up as he sits next to Francesca Goode. Had there been a problem between him and his boss? Cynthia wonders where the crew has stored Sophia's body. Certainly there's no morgue. Her best guess: inside one of the jumbo kitchen refrigerators.

Following the benediction, crew members wander away in tears. Cynthia believes that Sophia would still be alive if Picasso's Winter Prince wasn't on board. She notes that Cliff Gorman follows the Poindexters toward the ship's bow.

After the service, Cynthia and Malcolm have multiple choices for entertainment. They walk aft to the Magic Carpet Club— decorated with 101 hanging carpets—in time to catch the St. Thomas shopping seminar. Malcolm quips that this allows the passengers to segue from worshipping God to worshipping Mammon.

Cynthia and Malcolm slip into the last row while the onboard "shopping expert," a slinky redhead wearing extravagant jewelry, extols the virtues of Empire-approved jewelry stores on St. Thomas. Cynthia listens to the expert's Irish brogue for a few minutes before leaning close to Malcolm. "Am I missing something, or is this seminar just a way to direct women with too much money to specific stores? Maybe for a kick-back?"

"My-my, you're cynical. These people *want* to be told where to shop." Malcolm winks. "It's good business to give customers what they want."

"It will be very hot tomorrow," the shopping guru reminds the audience, "so drink plenty of water."

"I'll bet Empire sells water at the gangway," Cynthia says. "And for more than the natives sell it on the streets."

The program ends; everyone heads toward the exits.

"So," Malcolm says, "do you want to go jewelry shopping tomorrow?"

"No, thanks." Cynthia touches one of her studs. "I'll stick with my genuine fake pearls."

Malcolm wants a drink at the Tehran Salon. She tells him that it's a little early for cocktails, but he's paying the bills. They sit at the bar, where he orders beer for himself and cranberry juice for Cynthia. They spin around on their stools to observe people walking through the atrium. Cynthia can't stop herself from saying, "This is a bad idea."

She's right, but for an unexpected reason. A staggering, overweight woman spills an ice-cold strawberry margarita onto Cynthia's lap, in the process tipping the cranberry juice onto her pants, too. The woman slurs apologies. Malcolm jumps up, angrier than Cynthia, who holds his arm. "It's just clothes," she says. "I have to change for running anyway."

Cynthia and Malcolm are the only early-evening joggers on the track. They run side-by-side. "Did Sophia have any enemies among the crew?" she asks.

"She never said anything."

"Do *you* have any enemies among the crew?"

"No," Malcolm says. "And why focus on the crew? Don't you think the killer is one of the bidders?"

They sprint past a lone walker before Cynthia says, "The murder looks like an inside job. The ship's doctor suspects poison, and Fist verified that you called room service, so a crew member has to be involved. How else would the killer know when Sophia was expecting champagne?"

Malcolm clicks his tongue. "Maybe it was a coincidence. The killer might have delivered the poison without knowledge of my call. That explains the second bottle."

She shakes her head. "When something looks like more than coincidence, it usually is."

They jog in silence for half a lap before Malcolm limps to a stop. "Damn! Cramp coming on." He raises his foot and kneads his instep with a preemptive massage. "I got it in time. It's fine." He puts weight on it. "I should keep going before it stiffens up. Come on." He gimps ahead.

Cynthia catches up within a few strides. "Burns looks like a ladies' man," she says. "Was he sleeping with Sophia?"

Malcolm chuckles. "Oh, no. He prefers well-endowed blondes. The crew is full of young eastern Europeans. They work nine-month tours. Burns is literally a kid in a candy store."

"That could get awkward, him juggling girls, all trapped on

the same ship."

"Sophia said he's a tease."

"What do you mean?" Cynthia says.

"A rare duck for a man. Sophia said that three pretty crew members complained that Burns wouldn't go to bed with them."

"But he acts like such a Don Juan."

Malcolm shrugs. "It's what she told me. I didn't say that it makes sense."

"How long has Burns been Sophia's assistant?"

"About a year."

"You said he was a three-year employee. What did he do before that?"

"Wine steward, I think."

Cynthia grabs Malcolm's elbow and stops. "What! *You didn't think that was worth mentioning?* Where do you think the room service attendants get champagne?"

"But he wasn't—"

"*Think.* If he's dating crew members, he could easily enlist a groupie in his conspiracy. We should make sure that Fist checks him out."

"But first, can't we relax?" he says.

"This isn't a vacation any more."

"My foot's tightening up. Let's go shower and get ready for dinner."

As they reach the stairs, Cynthia sees Cliff Gorman one flight down on the Sun Deck. Gorman spreads the fingers on his right hand, as if flexing arthritic joints. Malcolm hesitates.

"Jeez," Cynthia mutters. "He's supposed to be your friend, right? Cut the spy crap and let's talk with him."

While Cynthia and Malcolm walk down a flight, Gorman glances around, looking for an escape.

"Cliff," Malcolm says. "Cynthia wants to meet you."

Gorman beams.

She extends her hand. He shakes it, his eyes dropping to her abdomen. She forces a smile—men are so predictable.

"Since we're all on the same team," Cynthia whispers, looking around—there is no one nearby—"we should be working together. Malcolm tells me that you know I'm a bodyguard, not a date, and he says you're acting as his eyes and ears."

Gorman nods.

After an awkward pause, Malcolm asks, "What did they do this afternoon besides go to the service?"

"The Poindexters stayed in their cabin—napping is my guess. The countess still hasn't done anything without Julia, outside of that meeting with Sophia Saturday night—"

"What meeting?" Cynthia says.

Gorman catches Malcolm's subtle nod before answering. "The countess met briefly with Sophia Caporetto on the Sun Deck Saturday night. Right after her dinner with you guys."

Cynthia turns to Malcolm. "You knew about this?"

"Just found out this morning. That was my first contact with Cliff. You've kept me on a short leash."

Cynthia keeps her manner friendlier than she feels. "Don't you think I should have been told about covert meetings between the deceased and a major bidder?"

"I wanted Cliff to get more information."

"More information? She's dead, remember?"

"Don't get huffy."

Cynthia is fully huffed. She starts counting to ten, making it to five. "Okay. At least you're telling me now." She turns to Gorman. "What about Julia?"

"She's a gadfly. When she's not with the countess, she's yakking with half the passengers. Hell, she asked *me* for my cabin number."

"We're getting off track," Cynthia says. "What about Poindexter?"

"He hasn't met with any players since lunch… that I'm aware of."

Cynthia frowns. "You're forgetting the service. They all sat together."

"But they wouldn't talk about anything important in public," Malcolm says.

Cynthia shakes her head in disgust. "A lot of secret information is exchanged in public places… like *restrooms*."

When Gorman adds nothing but a shrug, Cynthia says, "Back to Julia Sotelo. Did she meet with anyone this afternoon?"

"Like I said," Gorman says, "just flirting with men, which is good because I can hang around naturally. But she'd rather be flirting with Malcolm. She's pissed that you have him all to yourself—she doesn't know you're only a *virtual* ball and chain."

Cynthia ignores the joke and asks, "What did the countess do this afternoon?"

"She stayed in her room while Julia went sunbathing... in a bikini she had no business wearing, if you catch my drift. Now *you* would look good in—"

Cynthia, fuming, steps close, her glare in Gorman's face. "What's your problem? If you're not leering at my abs, you're making sexist comments."

Malcolm moves between them. "He doesn't mean anything—"

"I'm talking to *him*." She nails her eyes to Gorman's. "What's your problem?"

Cliff leans to within an inch of her nose. "Look at you. You go running in stretch underwear. You're not really *with* Malcolm, so I figure, maybe I have a shot. I compliment you, and what do I get? Hostility! Stop being so self-righteous."

Gorman stomps off, leaving Cynthia more convinced than ever that he's no art collector.

"I think he's sweet on you," Malcolm whispers.

"And *you?* You let a guy talk to your date like that?"

Malcolm laughs. "I'm your date when it suits, but not—"

"Shit. We have an unsolved *murder* and you guys are... you're just so... Oh, shit! You know *exactly* what you are."

He watches her simmer before saying, "Calming down yet?"

"I have a right to be angry."

"Perhaps, but you're wound tighter than a golf ball. Remember what I said about needing to relax?"

She knows he's right. Since the murder, every little thing gets under her skin. Cynthia says, "Okay. Let's go back to the cabins."

She can't wait for the week to be over.

23

Picasso

Twenty minutes later, Cynthia and Malcolm, freshly showered, relax on his balcony, gazing at the endless sea. Actually, only Malcolm sits and relaxes; Cynthia stands, leaning her palms on the rail, her fingers twitching. It strikes her how easily one could fall overboard. Or be pushed, especially at night. The perfect murder would have been to toss Sophia over the side, disposing of the evidence, but that was impossible from the auctioneer's interior room. Cynthia decides that Malcolm should avoid railings. Then she laughs at herself—*she's* the one leaning; *she's* the one in jeopardy.

"I heard you call Fist while I was getting dressed," Malcolm says.

"He wasn't in," she replies without turning away from the sea.

"You need to chill out, Cyn."

"Funny, coming from a guy obsessed with a painting."

"I'm not the one too jittery to sit down."

"Wait until Thursday," she says over her shoulder. "*You'll* be the basket case."

"With good cause; it's not just any painting."

"Why is it so important?"

"It's a *Picasso*." He says it in a way that makes Cynthia feel naive.

She turns, braces her rear on the rail. "So what makes Picasso so great?"

Malcolm grins. "You still want to climb Everest before the foothills, don't you?"

"No. But I want *you* to tell me what it's like to climb Everest."

"All right." Malcolm takes a breath. "Picasso is more than an artist. He's a philosopher. His paintings deconstruct the emotions of man, reconstructing them with a spiritual tension. The result combines conception with perception." He stares at her as if he's uttered a profound truth.

"Sounds like more B.S. I still don't get it."

"Would you *like* to get it?"

She nods. "But start with the short version."

"All right. I just happen to have a book with me—lots of pictures." He goes inside and returns with an 8 x 10 book about Picasso—by Malcolm Golden—which he flips open. "First, the blue period, triggered by his best friend's suicide—Carles Casagemas..."

Cynthia sits next to him. Using examples in the book, Malcolm explains Picasso's blue period, rose period, and the origins of cubism, which used "a sculptural sense of space."

Whoosh. Right over her head.

"...Which brings us to *Winter Prince.*" He pulls a loose 5 x 7 print from inside the back cover. "The object of my quest."

Cynthia studies the shapes and colors—gloomy features, icy hues. The distorted man (or woman) wears a weathered crown and peasant rags. The closer Cynthia looks, the more an invisible weight compresses her own chest, as if she were facing whatever troubled Picasso's blue phantom.

"Why do you want this particular Picasso so badly?"

"Answering that would be like unburdening my soul."

"Try me."

"All right. To start, this painting may be a missing link."

Cynthia shrugs.

"What did I tell you about Picasso's three early phases?"

"Blue, rose, cubism," she recites like the ABCs.

"So in which period does *Winter Prince* belong?"

Cynthia scrutinizes the print. "Multiple geometric features. Cubism. *Analytical* cubism." She is proud of remembering the qualifier.

"Yes, but what about the colors and subject matter?"

"Depressing blues. The man—if it's a man—looks beaten, like his whole family died. So it's the blue period. Or maybe a transition piece, from blue to cubism."

"But remember, the rose period came between the blue period and cubism."

"So is it blue or cubism?"

Malcolm smiles. "That's why it's so fascinating. The blue period was over by 1904, but Picasso and Braque didn't start dabbling in cubism until late 1906. At least that's what art historians believe. But maybe the seeds of cubism were planted before we think, or maybe Picasso reverted to melancholy blue. We're not positive when he painted it. But we'll figure it out."

Cynthia thinks before asking, "I get the missing link idea, but what does it have to do with your soul?"

"Everyone's behavior is a series of causes and effects—links. Sometimes they're easier to see in others than in oneself. This painting helps me bridge inner gaps, understand an inconsistency in my psyche. That's what great art can do."

"But why do you have to *own* it? I mean, you could see it in a museum and even have your own Giclée print, right?"

He shakes his head. "In a print, you can't see the brushwork, the texture."

"It's nice, I guess, but..."

"There's no other painting in the world like this—the way it sings to me." His face glistens like a stained glass window. "I'll be complete when I own it. Not before."

Cynthia shakes her head. "You really get off on this stuff, don't you?"

"I suppose."

"Okay, I think I get why you want it so badly, but why is it worth so much? I mean—eighty-five million for one painting?"

Malcolm closes the book. "First, the obvious: it's a Picasso. That makes it worth ten million in the dark. Second, it's a *good* Picasso. That bumps the value to around fifty million, plus. The fact that this one is brand new to the art world is worth another fifteen. But the real boost is that this is a high-profile auction, and so many wealthy people want it. That works against me—I figure that the show-off premium will be about twenty million, maybe more." He places the book on a plastic cocktail table. "I have to have this painting."

Cynthia opens the book, flips pages, looking for a painting she noticed during the lesson. She finds it—a double-nosed woman with yellow skin, sitting in a chair. The right hand has two sets of fingers, one blossoming out of the other like flower petals. "Tell me about this one."

"That's a Portrait of Dora Maar."

"Who's she?"

"Picasso's lover from 1936 to 1945. One of many. A great photographer and his muse for a number of paintings."

"Why'd he paint her hand like that?"

"She self-mutilated her fingers playing the Knife Game—where a person spreads one hand on a table and jabs a knife between the fingers."

Cynthia winces.

"You asked. Dark passion often goes hand-in-hand with great art. Some call it the price of genius." Malcolm's intense gaze makes her feel empty.

Cynthia considers her own mutilations. Indirectly, they were self-inflicted. What would it feel like to be Malcolm's inspiration? She shakes off the fantasy, closes the book, picks up the print of the Winter Prince. "May I keep this?"

He nods.

She stands. "Thanks for the lesson. We should call Lt. Fist again.... Er, is that what you're wearing tonight?"

Malcolm looks down at his moderately dressy shirt and pants. "What's wrong with this?"

"Nothing. But if you switch to a tux, I'll have to change."

Malcolm laughs while scanning Cynthia's sleeveless yellow jumpsuit, from turtleneck to flared pant legs. "You're fine. More than fine."

Lt. Fist proves elusive. He's out of his office, and the security man on duty says that Fist is "busy." After futilely traipsing over half the ship, Cynthia and Malcolm stop at the Internet Café, an interior room with twenty terminals crammed into space for ten. She sits at a screen back-to-back with his terminal, so she can watch behind him but he can't see her e-mails. There's one from

Bruce Swenson with information on Countess LaCroix.

From there, Malcolm and Cynthia ascend to the Tehran Salon where they ease onto their usual bar stools, all cleaned up from the earlier spill. Malcolm orders wine; Cynthia, Diet Coke. When Malcolm excuses himself to chat with a Spanish collector, Cynthia engages the barmaid, a pretty young Romanian named Ceresela.

"I used to tend bar on a riverboat," Cynthia says. "Six weeks on, two off."

Ceresela sighs. "I have nine-month contract. Three more months before I go home."

Cynthia remembers how antsy she got after five weeks on the rivers. Nine months at sea is way beyond her limit.

"Pay much better than at home," Ceresela volunteers. "Good opportunity."

Cynthia glances at Ceresela's ring finger. "You're married?"

"Yes. Things work out best this way—for future." Ceresela nods in Malcolm's direction. "How about you?"

"He's just a boyfriend," Cynthia says. "I'm not sure what I want to happen." After a pause, she says, "Maybe you can help me. What can you tell me about Brent Burns? The assistant auctioneer."

Ceresela wipes the bar.

"Does he have any girlfriends among the crew?"

"I should not gossip."

"He's cute," Cynthia says, "but I heard he's a tease. Does he have any special favorites among his old bar colleagues?"

The barmaid colors. "I should not say."

Cynthia slides a $20 bill across the bar. "A name?"

For a moment, Ceresela looks at the money. Then she slips the bill into her apron. "A bartender named Olga had a thing for him—the jealous type, works the late shift in the Casbah Café. She might give you something."

24

Fencing

"Ready for serious cocktails?" Malcolm asks from his bar stool.

Cynthia, dreading the evening's party, clinks her glass of Diet Coke to his wine. "This doesn't count?"

"The countess is expecting us."

As much as Cynthia wants to investigate the suspects, she dislikes their snobbishness more, and cocktails in the countess's suite will be tedious. She offers a non-committal sigh.

"That sounds like a whine. I dawdled here for *you*—so we'll have less time with the stuffy art crowd upstairs. Now come along."

They agreed: no whining. She follows two steps behind as they take the stairs up to Deck 14, where they walk toward the stern.

Cynthia touches his hand before he knocks. "Let's not stay too long, okay?"

"I *have* to at least put in a token showing."

"One of the people inside may be plotting to kill you."

"Only one?" He *raps* three times. "Anyway, they won't try anything with so many people around…. But just in case, you'll be watching my back, right?"

An Indonesian bartender, whom Cynthia recognizes from Alexander's Lounge, opens the double-doors of the Presidential Suite to reveal unbridled affluence. Cynthia feels under-dressed in her expense-account jumpsuit. The décor is beyond lavish, with a sitting room large enough for a Viennese waltz. One server mans a portable bar in the corner, another offers *hors d'oeuvres*—the current tray is caviar. Cynthia passes.

Oversized sliders open to a long balcony cantilevered over the stern. The patio furniture is wicker, not plastic. There are fifteen guests chatting on the balcony, ten more in the sitting room—the space could handle twice that. Cynthia would like to see the bedroom, but the door is closed.

Countess LaCroix greets Cynthia with a cool nod and Malcolm with a kiss that misses his cheek by six inches.

"You're late," the countess says to Malcolm. "And you could have worn a coat and tie." Without deigning to look at Cynthia, the countess glides toward a conversation group that appears posed, awaiting her return. Malcolm heads for the bar. Cynthia feels like the outsider in a Woody Allen comedy.

Julia Sotelo, draped on Captain De Vries's elbow, dominates the outdoor conversation, holding the attention of several men whom Cynthia doesn't recognize.

In the sitting room, the countess intimidates Brent Burns and three interchangeable couples with gray hair and blue blood. Cynthia is surprised to see Anton the Illusionist—alongside Carlotta—chatting with John and Gladys Poindexter. Malcolm hands Cynthia a Diet Coke.

"This is her own art," he says, gesturing at the walls. "All originals. The countess travels in style."

Once he mentions it, Cynthia notices that the pieces far outshine the tranquil Arabian Nights reproductions in her cabin. She examines a gaudily-framed oil painting of a pastel pond. "Monet, right?"

Malcolm smiles. "You're learning. Why don't you study these paintings for a few minutes? Then tell me what you think." He slides away.

Cynthia analyzes the largest painting, keeping one eye on Malcolm's reflection in a wall mirror. She watches him gravitate to Julia's side.

A moment later, Cynthia does a double-take; the countess's austere reflection appears in the mirror's frame—very close. "What do you think of my Monet?"

"It's beautiful—rich texture and..." Cynthia wants to add technical jargon but comes up empty.

"It's one that Malcolm wasn't able to steal." The disdain in the countess's voice is thinly veiled.

"If you really dislike him so much, why invite us to your party?"

"I didn't invite *you*. Only him, because I had to. He chose to bring you along."

"I'm surprised you're talking with me."

"Don't flatter yourself. I'm simply making sure you don't vandalize my painting."

It takes Cynthia a moment to recognize the dry wit. "I'm surprised that you have a sense of humor."

The countess purses her narrow lips until they disappear entirely. Then she says, "I wasn't joking."

Cynthia, chilled, rubs her upper arms and turns to the left. "That's a Picasso, isn't it? I'll bet the blue period's your favorite."

"Why do you say that?"

"You're unhappy, like Picasso was."

"My life is very—" The countess flinches when Cynthia abruptly raises a hand—to adjust her turtleneck.

"I don't laugh much myself," Cynthia says, "and I know all about the blues. I understand you better than you think."

"You don't know the first thing about me."

"Oh no? Let's see…." Cynthia speaks with her eyes focused on the sad Picasso. "You married for position and title. You travel often, but never with your husband. Despite having the run of a floating palace, you only leave your suite for meals and art functions."

"Recounting common knowledge doesn't mean that you know me."

Cynthia plays her e-mail ace. "When you were eighteen, you poisoned your brother."

"Where did you—" The countess stifles her outburst. "That was one of the cooks, an accident, and Jean Claude recovered."

"Only to fall off a cliff and break his leg two years later… when you were the only witness. Just how did he lose his balance?"

"It was raining. We were trying to rescue his dog. And I don't have to dignify—" The countess places a fluttering hand over her heart. "Mademoiselle James, remind me to specifically exclude you from the guest list next time. You are a gold-digging tramp."

"And you're a pompous snob."

Both women stare at the blue Picasso.

Malcolm approaches. "Am I interrupting?"

"We were discussing my painting," the countess says. "Cynthia thinks the poor wretch reminds her of me. I don't see a resemblance."

Malcolm picks up on the temperature. "Cynthia, perhaps we should be going."

The countess nods. "Perhaps you should not have come at all."

Malcolm takes Cynthia's hand. On the way to the door, they encounter Anton the Illusionist. "If I might have a vord about zee Picazo auction," he implores Malcolm.

Cynthia digs her nails into Malcolm's palm. He flinches. "Some other time, Anton," he says. "I promise. But right now, my date reminds me that we're late for dinner."

In the hall, Malcolm asks, "What was that all about with the countess?"

"We were talking about her past."

"Oh...?"

"Her brother had a few unusual accidents."

"How did you find out?"

"It's not important."

Malcolm stops on the landing. "I'm the one paying you. If I think it's—"

"No! You're paying me to *protect you to the best of my ability*. That's what I'm doing. I told you all you need to know. Now let's go to dinner. I don't eat caviar, so I'm starved."

25

Brew-ha-ha

After a delicious dinner, Cynthia and Malcolm track down Lt. Fist in the Casbah Casino. With a background of *ba-bling, ba-bling*—the soundtrack of electronic greed—Cynthia, her voice scratchy with impatience, lays out her suspicions against Brent Burns: that he stands to gain promotion by Sophia's death, that he has knowledge of room-service procedures, and that he has girlfriends among the wine stewardesses.

Fist responds in a patronizing tone, "Are you a licensed detective, Miss James?"

"No."

"Then I suggest you leave the investigation to professionals."

"I didn't mean to sound presumptuous. I just want to remind you why Burns—"

"For your information, we looked into Burns right away. Seems he was up in the disco all night. Ten patrons swore he was there until the wee hours. The passenger he was groping confirms he never left her side. Not even to go to the loo."

"So did you check out room service stewardesses who were working that night?"

Fisk frowns. "There weren't any."

Cynthia tries to ignore the maddening *ba-bling, ba-bling.* "Did you get a better description of the *mystery* stewardess?"

"Actually, yes. The witnesses worked with a police sketch artist in Miami via ship-to-shore and faxes. Very slow going, but we have something to work with."

"May we see the sketch?"

Fist scowls.

"Look, Lt. Fist," Cynthia says. "Mr. Golden received a—"

"*I'll* explain," Malcolm says, giving Cynthia a *stay cool* glare. "As a possible intended victim, I have a right to know who may still be out to get me."

"I suppose…" Fist removes a folded sheet of paper from his pocket. "Here."

Cynthia blinks to be sure. The sketch resembles both herself and Countess LaCroix.

"I know what you're thinking," Fist says, snatching back the sketch. "Yvonne LaCroix says she was in her room alone, but she has no one to corroborate her story. Just as nobody can verify that you didn't leave your cabin. Now if you'll excuse me, I have work to do." Fist marches out of the casino.

"I don't know if she's capable of murder," Malcolm says.

"If murder requires ice-water in one's veins, then she's quite capable."

The conversation has nowhere to go. Malcolm clears his throat. "As long as we're here…" He leads Cynthia toward a craps table.

The *ba-blings* sound like an electronic xylophone inside her head—annoying, but escape will have to wait. "Have you ever played?" Cynthia asks.

"I wrote a college paper on craps odds for a probability and statistics course."

"So you know what you're doing?"

"In theory."

Malcolm buys $500 worth of chips and positions himself opposite the two croupiers. Hands are everywhere—placing bets, pushing and pulling chips with rakes, rolling dice, clutching the sideboards, flaunting diamond rings. Cynthia takes in the chaos. For a few minutes, Malcolm merely watches.

"Aren't you going to bet?" she finally says.

"When the time's right. Depending on the situation, you can have the odds in your favor… if you know what you're doing. But you need to make a lot of bets."

After the snake-tattooed man from the Sun Deck rolls for the fourth time, Malcolm lays down six $20 bets. "As long as he doesn't roll a seven or craps, I win."

Cynthia is impressed.

Tattoo guy rolls a seven.

"Oooo." Malcolm grimaces. "That's why you need a lot of money to make money."

An hour later, he's still playing—up and down—now down about $200 and controlling the dice. He hands them to Cynthia and lays five $20 chips on the pass line. "Roll a seven," he tells her. She tosses the dice.

Seven.

He lets it ride. She rolls again. A six. Then an eight. Malcolm covers the two points with $50 each. Cynthia rolls an eight, then a six. Malcolm collects each time.

"All right," Malcolm says. "This is how it's supposed to work. Just keep 'em coming."

Cynthia blows on the dice and rolls... snake eyes. The croupiers rake in all of Malcolm's chips.

Cynthia pokes his ribs. "I should have asked what grade you got on that paper."

"Enough of this." Malcolm flips each croupier a $20 chip. "Let's blow some change on slots poker. Just for fun."

"Too noisy in here. Headache. I'll stand over there." She points toward the arched entrance fifteen feet away. "I'll be able to watch your back." What she thinks is: he's not the slots type.

Malcolm sits at a poker machine next to Gladys Poindexter. Cynthia observes from the casino entrance, where the *ba-blinging* is less annoying. Gladys has a gambling rhythm—every time she presses Deal, she follows with a sip of her drink.

"What's he been playing?" John Poindexter asks from behind.

Cynthia turns, flustered at the way Poindexter keeps popping up. "Craps."

"I'll bet he lost."

"A little."

"He's much better at face-to-face gambling, like poker... and auctions."

She shrugs and turns toward Malcolm.

Poindexter moves close so they can whisper. "I hope you're not angry about what I said last night. I should probably tell you the whole story—the reason Malcolm doesn't have enough money for the Picasso."

Cynthia keeps her eyes on Malcolm. "I'm listening."

"Trustees from the Louvre and Prado have joined forces on this one."

"Why would they do that?"

"The people running those places hate Malcolm enough to do anything to keep the Picasso out of his hands."

"You should tell Malcolm, not me."

"He already knows."

"Why isn't MOMA aligned with them, too?" she says. "Is it because your museum will get thirty million from his estate? Or maybe that's a reason to wish him dead."

Poindexter produces an acidic smile. "You know more than you let on."

"I'm learning. And you didn't answer my question."

"Pragmatic politics. A museum can't throw money away on vendettas. I don't have the personal wealth that the countess and Julia have."

"Why tell *me*?"

He shrugs. "Let's just say that I like you and keep it at that."

Cynthia ponders a witty reply but decides on an indirect approach. "Do those other museum people really hate him?"

Bling-bling-bling! Gladys hits a jackpot. She throws her arms around Malcolm. Cynthia glances at Poindexter, who says, "I know what you're thinking, but she doesn't mean anything by it. My wife's a very friendly person. I accepted who she is long ago…. As to your question, Malcolm is a very *un*friendly person when competing for art. Nobody plays harder. Some say he plays dirty. If you double-cross people, they take offense."

"So what did he do to piss off the Louvre and Prado?"

Poindexter makes sure nobody is close enough to hear. "He's burned them on contracts, promising extended loans of pieces. In exchange, the museums' trustees didn't bid against him. Then he whipped out extremely fine print. In short, the museums didn't get what they bargained for. The countess and Julia were involved in some of those negotiations. You can understand how they might be angry."

"Interesting. Has Malcolm done anything to piss *you* off?"

Poindexter hesitates. "Not yet."

Cynthia makes eye contact. "You're just saying that because I'm Malcolm's girlfriend."

Poindexter studies her face. "I got the impression you thought he walked on water."

She gazes at Malcolm while saying. "Jesus pissed off a lot of people."

Poindexter laughs.

Cynthia and Poindexter pass time talking about the perfect Caribbean weather until Malcolm and Gladys tire of slots. The Poindexters say goodnight and head toward the elevators.

Malcolm glances at his watch. "How about a turn around the Sun Deck?"

Cynthia says, "Anything to get out of this noise factory."

They trot up the stairs, keeping to their pledge—take every opportunity to burn calories.

Out on the open Sun Deck, the salty breeze is a pleasant change from the air-conditioned interior. There are two young couples taking in the moonlight, one kissing, the other about to. Cynthia whispers, "Seems to be the make-out deck. Want to go someplace else?"

"No," he says. "It's nice up here under the stars. We can act out our parts." Malcolm places one hand low on her hip—or is it high on her buttocks?

Maybe it's the stars, but Cynthia, unsure of his intentions, waits two seconds before pulling his hand up to her waist. "Not really a good idea, Malcolm."

A third voice from behind. "There you are." It's the little pest, Cliff Gorman, whom they last saw before dinner. This time, Cliff reeks of beer.

"Helluva night for romance," Cliff slurs.

"And drinking, it appears," Malcolm replies.

"I've been taking shots for the team. That Julia drinks like a fish. Can't keep up with her."

"Did alcohol loosen her tongue?"

"She says she's gonna bring a box of Kleenex for you when she buys the Picasso."

"Did she talk to anyone else?"

Gorman shakes his head. "Too busy with me."

Malcolm chuckles. "You could do worse."

Gorman eyes Cynthia's torso and says, "Could do a lot better."

She rolls her eyes.

"You're a quiet one," Gorman says to her.

"Not much to say."

"Like you didn't say anything just now when Malcolm put his hand on your ass."

"Easy, Cliff." Malcolm lays a palm on Gorman's shoulder.

Gorman shakes it off, staggering, almost falling. Cynthia catches him.

Gorman steadies himself by grabbing her buttocks. "Thanks, babe."

"You're drunk!" She nudges him away. "Don't make me hurt you."

He clutches hard with both hands. "Promise? I like it rough."

26

Pool Party

Malcolm lunges at Gorman, is grazed by a wild punch, and slips down. Cynthia takes out Gorman with one knee to the crotch followed by another to the jaw. Just reacting. Over before she knows it.

Cynthia's knee burns. She helps Malcolm to his feet and tells four gaping bystanders. "Just a misunderstanding. Everything's over; nothing to see here."

The witnesses linger until Cynthia stamps her foot. Scurrying away, one of the two men mutters to his girlfriend, "Trust me. I'll never lay a hand on *that* woman."

Gorman, on his knees, tries to get up. "Sorry—don't know what got into me."

"Budweiser," Malcolm says. "Or maybe Bud-stupider."

Cynthia and Malcolm deposit Gorman on a chaise, but he wobbles to his feet. "I'm okay. I just want to go back to my cabin and lick my wounds."

"We should take him down to the medical office," Cynthia says.

"He's fine."

"Look, I'm fine." Gorman shakes his jaw. "I think I needed that. You two run along. Do whatever fake dates do."

"We should at least walk you to your cabin," she says.

Gorman holds up a hand. "Don't touch me! I'm going on my own." He shuffles toward the elevators, hunched over, a man with private pains. Malcolm holds Cynthia to keep her from following. "Let him go. You've done enough for one night."

"Do you think those couples will report it?"

He shrugs. "I hope not; don't want people to know my date finished my fight."

Cynthia puts a hand to her forehead. The balmy breeze, the fight, adrenaline—she's over-heating. "I need some water."

He feels her forehead. "*El fuego.*"

"Just what Picasso would say."

He laughs. "I know of extra-special, refreshing water." Malcolm takes her hand and leads her down the outdoor stairs to the Persian Gulf Pool. The night lighting is dim. One hundred empty chaises are precisely aligned for next morning's sunbathers. Nobody else is in sight.

Cynthia steps onto the Arabia-shaped patio and approaches the pool, illuminated by under-water spots. The refracted light looks like yellow ribbons flowing in a breeze.

"How about a swim?" he asks.

"The sign says the pool's closed."

Malcolm chuckles. "You and signs."

"And we don't have our suits."

"You'd really like to cool off, wouldn't you?"

"Yes, but—"

He snatches her purse and shoves.

The pool swallows Cynthia; the jumpsuit shrinkwraps her body. The cooling release is palpable, the moment absurd. "You're gonna get it," she warns. He merely grins down from Arabia—very roguish. She reaches under water, takes off her pumps, fires one at him, then the other. He deflects both with his hands.

She splashes him. "Come on in and fight like a man."

He sets her purse on the nearest chaise. "Sorry. I'm afraid of the creature from the Black Lagoon. My shoes alone cost a small fortune."

She ducks under, swims to the wall, and comes up quickly, swiping at his foot, but he dances away from her grasp.

"*Brock-brock!*" she squawks. "Chicken!"

"But a *dry* chicken."

She sloshes out of the water and chases him, splattering across Arabia. Malcolm laughs, back-pedaling toward Iraq until he trips over a chaise. He doesn't resist when she hoists him onto her shoulder and lugs him to the edge. He manages to kick off his expensive shoes a second before she dumps him into the pool, momentum carrying her in alongside.

They splash, frolicking like children. The spontaneity dissipates Cynthia's tension. She imagines them running to their rooms in sopping clothes, leaving a trail of puddles—

His splash ends her fantasy, sending water down her throat. She coughs.

"Sorry." He glides close and brushes her shoulder.

"I'm okay." She pushes free and swims to the other end of the pool, slowed by waterlogged clothes.

He follows, walking on the bottom. "Cynthia, may I ask you a personal question?"

Here it comes, she thinks. Day three, earlier than expected, but the murder has added danger to the mix. The scuffle with Gorman has drawn them closer. He's about to ask permission to kiss her. Stop it, she reprimands herself. Let him surprise you. So she says, "Depends on what it is."

"Well then— Uh oh…" Malcolm turns toward approaching footsteps. Cynthia sees white legs and an extremely long shadow.

"What the blazes are you doing in there?" Ensign Billingsley says from poolside. "Can't you two *read*? The pool's *closed*!" From Cynthia's perspective, looking up with water lapping at her chin, Billingsley looks like the Washington Monument.

"Come in and get us," Malcolm taunts.

Cynthia laughs, wishing she could be so spontaneous.

Billingsley kneels by the pool, extending an arm. "Just give me your hand, Ms. James."

Her first impression is to let him help, but then she remembers the way he ogled her abs the night of the murder. When Cynthia comes out, this lush will see a contestant in a wet jumpsuit contest.

Cynthia enjoys a mischievous rush—somehow Malcolm's attitude blots out common sense. Billingsley is so tall that, even kneeling, his center of gravity is high enough to be toppled. *Why the heck not?* In quick, coordinated moves, she reaches up, braces both feet against the side wall, grabs the officer's wrist, and yanks him into the pool.

Billingsley flails for his floating hat while she and Malcolm splash out of the water. She snatches her purse, Malcolm grabs his shoes, and they hurry toward the stern. Cynthia would be embarrassed if she weren't laughing so hard.

Malcolm and Cynthia's dash aft is blocked by two approaching deck hands at the door to the elevator concourse, so Cynthia angles up the outdoor stairs to the Sun Deck, Malcolm close behind, both of them leaving a trail of water. Cynthia is energized by the chase. Adrenalin kicks in, which enhances her awareness. "Follow me," she calls over her shoulder.

It's a game of hide and seek with no chance of escape—after all, they're trapped on a ship—but she wants to see how long she can remain free. When they reach the Sun Deck, the question is: how to separate themselves from the pursuers long enough to get lost in the maze of decks, stairs, halls, and landings? Cynthia darts up the next flight to the Spa Deck. From there, she sprints inside to the staircase. Malcolm is falling behind. At the head of the stairs, she turns and sees him accelerate toward her, his sopping socks leaving moist footprints a few seconds ahead of three men in uniform. The whole episode is bizarre. She drops down the steps six at a bound.

Three flights down, she is still laughing. Since the pursuers are behind them and the stairwell is unguarded, a half-baked plan takes shape: shake off most of the water while descending to Deck 8, then hide in a laundry room.

From a half-flight above, Cynthia hears a thump and a groan. She stops and goes back. Malcolm has fallen, crashing into the wall on a mid-deck landing. The idea of the *man* falling is funny, once she sees that he is unhurt. She is laughing when two guards grab her elbows. She could dispose of them... but wisely doesn't try.

It is no longer funny. Cynthia and Malcolm stand side-by-side, dripping water on the chief of security's gray carpet. Lt. Fist is lobster red. The two officers who nabbed the pranksters loom by the door. A fourth officer, the sheepish Billingsley, stands to one side shivering in his damp uniform, holding Cynthia's yellow pumps.

"Miss James," Fist says. "I could lock you in the brig for

assaulting an officer."

Cynthia says nothing, although she doubts that a cruise ship even has a brig. But surely it has rooms with locks.

Malcolm steps forward. "I was the instigator. I pushed her in. It was a reaction to a long, draining day—a release from the grief, sir. We promise it won't happen again."

Cynthia nods contritely.

"Is that blood on your pants?" Fist says, pointing toward Cynthia's knee.

She looks down. "Um…"

"Several passengers reported a fight on the Sun Deck. There was a woman involved—in a *yellow jumpsuit*."

"Just a minor misunderstanding," Malcolm volunteers.

"Must have been quite a row. We heard there was a kick-boxing knockout. Who was the fight with?"

"Just a friend of mine named Gorman," Malcolm says. "No harm, no foul—a playful little nothing. But we feel terrible about Ensign Billingsley. I'll pay for any damage to his uniform and equipment. And to make further amends, I'd like to treat both you and him to dinner at the Emperors' Room Wednesday night."

The fire ebbs from Fist's eyes. "The Emperors' Room, you say?"

Cynthia forces down the corners of her mouth—Malcolm could charm a charging elephant.

"Agreed," Fist says. "Against my better judgment, but anything to move on." His mood darkens. "About the murder. You're material witnesses. Your interview time for tomorrow is two p.m., here in my office with the shore authorities, FBI, Interpol. As I told you, jurisdiction issues are dicey. We'll be hashing that out all morning with the lawyers."

"So we can go ashore, right?" Malcolm asks.

"Yes. But all the boat-charter companies will have your pictures with orders not to rent to you. Make sure you're back on board by fourteen-hundred. You don't want me to have to track you down."

27

Lt. Sebastian Fist

Sebastian is paid to be suspicious. He's certain that Cynthia James is not whom she appears to be. No specific allegations come to mind just yet, but apprehension itches deep in his bones. What gold-digger, shocked by a corpse, shows the foresight to worry about fingerprints? And who volunteers theories about alternate suspects unless she's involved? And what slim woman is strong enough to dunk a trained security officer? Ensign Billingsley said he had no idea how she did it—he swore he had been cautious, weight back from the edge.

Sebastian distrusts Miss James. There will be no more breaks for her after this ridiculous incident. He takes a breath and manufactures anger. The trivial escapade doesn't warrant his time, but since the culprits have been brought before him, he must play his part.

"I suppose I won't throw you in the brig," he says.

"Thank you, sir," Miss James replies. "It won't happen again."

"It bloody well better not."

Malcolm takes her hand. "Are we excused, Lieutenant?"

"You can go. The lady stays. I have some questions for her about our pesky unsolved murder."

"Surely this can wait until she dries off," Malcolm says.

Sebastian shakes his head. "Billingsley, find a towel and dry clothes for Miss James. Goodnight, Mr. Golden."

Five minutes later, Miss James, wearing a purple Empire

Lines sweat-suit three sizes too large, sits stoically still on what Sebastian knows is an exceedingly uncomfortable chair.

Sebastian doesn't sit. Rather, he puts one shoe on a second chair and leans over her damp hair. Intimidation probably won't work, but he'll give it a go. "What are you doing on this cruise? You're no trophy date. You ask too many questions. You flip my best man into the pool. Who are you?"

"Cynthia James, Mr. Golden's girlfriend." She sounds cool.

Sebastian isn't surprised, but he has a Plan-B. "All right. Play dumb. Just listen. Right now, you match our mystery stewardess's description, so you're the most suspicious character involved."

"But I'm not involved."

Sebastian stomps his foot to the floor. "I said, listen! I can throw you to the FBI when they come on board in St. Thomas. When I tell them you're the only suspect, they'll tear into you like piranhas. If you have any record, any kind at all, they'll be relentless. I'm giving you an opportunity here." He eases up on his glare. He wants her to relax. "Talk to me."

After a long pause, she says, "Okay…. I'm not technically Mr. Golden's date."

"What does that mean?"

"I'm his bodyguard."

Sebastian rubs his chin, relieved to finally be getting somewhere. "Go on," he coaxes.

"Malcolm received a warning—a death threat—to *not* buy the Picasso. He hired me to protect him."

Sebastian wants to blare: You imbecile! But he remains professional, saying, "Did it occur to you to alert Empire to this threat?"

"Mr. Golden wanted to keep it quiet; he thought that was the best way to maximize his chances of purchasing the Picasso."

"What about Sophia Caporetto's chances?"

The James woman lowers her eyes.

"And after the murder?" he presses. "Didn't you think it was important then?"

"Yes. But I did what my client wanted—I kept quiet. The painting is very important to him; it's why I'm here."

Sebastian thinks she's lying, at least by omission. Maybe

that's why he asks, "How much is he paying you?" Immediately, he regrets the question, but what's said is said.

She doesn't flinch, just looks through him and says, "I need to… I mean, I'd like to get back to my client."

"Dismissed," Sebastian says. He hands her a plastic bag— her clothes and shoes. Watching her go, he has a disturbing thought: that if there is trouble, he should like Cynthia James on his side.

28

Third Night

Cynthia's shower is hot enough to peel nail polish. Still chilled after five minutes in the tiny stall, she feels no responsibility to save a drop of hot water for the other 3,499 passengers. More steam—she increases the temperature. The water's pulse on her skin brings to mind the fountain woman. Cynthia wants to lose herself in the association. She turns up the pressure, going past fountain to waterfall. She rubs her ears to magnify the roar, to escape the craziness. Somewhere, she hears a faint voice. "Sin! Sin!" *Ignore the man behind the curtain.* She rubs her ears harder. Almost warm now, she faces the nozzle, eyes closed, her skin pricked by the pulsing—

"Cyn! Cyn! Are you alright?"

Shit! What's Malcolm doing in my bathroom? A dream? She turns the faucet off and looks over her shoulder. No dream. He stands behind her, holding the shower curtain aside with one hand. She turns her face away, keeping her back toward him. A fresh chill starts in the neck, plummets to her toes. She stares at the tile wall six inches in front of her face.

"Sorry," Malcolm says. "You were in so long, I was worried. I knocked. I called. You didn't answer. I was afraid something was wrong."

She hugs her forearms; her heart punches the inside of her chest. "Get me a towel, please."

One wraps around her shoulders. She clutches it, wonders why she isn't demanding that he leave.

"If you're okay… I'll be going. Sorry."

She nods to the shampoo shelf. In two seconds, he's gone.

With adjoining rooms, an awkward moment was bound to happen. "Don't blow this out of proportion," she mutters to herself. "Be professional."

She dries, dresses for bed, then knocks.

"I'm decent, Malcolm," she says through the door. "You can come in."

He sits on her mattress, so she takes the loveseat. She wears her sleeping shorts and T-shirt. Malcolm sports a purple Empire Lines bathrobe over whatever he does or doesn't have on underneath.

She offers an icebreaker. "Should we talk about you seeing your bodyguard's naked body?"

"I already apologized. What more can I do?"

She shakes her head. "Nothing, I guess."

"What did Fist ask after I left?"

She's relieved to talk about something other than the shower scene. "He asked again about why I wasn't flustered by the murder. I told him that I—I just have good self-control. And he wasn't happy that you held back the death threat."

"You told him?"

"Yes."

"Anything else?"

"Yes," she says. "I also told him that I'm your bodyguard."

Malcolm says nothing, appears to be thinking.

Cynthia asks him to get the warning notes.

Waiting, she lets out a sigh, realizing how tired she is. She lays her head on the armrest and closes her eyes—for just a few seconds. She listens to running water in his bathroom, hears a fountain.

"Tired?" Malcolm says.

"Just a little," she murmurs without opening her eyes. The notes are forgotten. "Talk to me about something other than murder… or art."

She hears the rustle of him sitting on the bed. "Like what?" he says.

"What was it like growing up as a rich kid?"

"That's what you're thinking?"

She breathes slowly, says, "Tell me a story from your childhood."

"All right. Let's see..." Malcolm settles on her bed. "I was eight or ten, I think. Kids in the park used to taunt me by saying, 'You think your shit don't stink?' So I snuck into my parents' room and drank some perfume. I threw up, and my shit still stank."

She laughs. "Yeah, right. Tell me something that's true."

"One time, my parents made me..."

An hour later, she wakes, still on the loveseat, floating in an easy torpor. Her eyes remain closed. "Still there?"

"Yes," he says.

"Have you been watching me sleep?"

"Yes."

After three slow breaths, her lip curls. "Why?"

"For centuries, artists have expressed the line of a woman lying on her side. Your hips are slim enough so the angle isn't too steep, yet shapely enough so the slope is compelling."

Such compliments, coming from a world-renowned art expert, go straight to her addled head. "Go on."

"The soft light bathes your face. When you're awake, your eyes are dynamic and dark, always wary. Asleep, that undercurrent is removed; the curved lids reflect perfect peace."

She smiles and listens to his voice. Soothing.

"Your face relaxes, revealing a different person—softer. I'm seeing something that no one but your lover ever sees. That makes the beauty all the sweeter."

She knows bullshit when she hears it, but *this* B.S. is what she wants to hear. "I'm not beautiful," she says, hoping he will contradict her.

"You've been looking in the mirror," he says. "Your expectations filter what's really there. I'm talking about what the world sees with no filter."

She opens her eyes. "I'll bet you say that to all the girls."

"You're not just any girl."

Cynthia doesn't know how to replay, so she says, "I'm tired."

"Then let me help you."

She closes her eyes. "You can't get me into the sack that easy."

He pulls down her covers. "Get into bed and go to sleep. I'm not trying to seduce you."

"No? I feel rejected."

Malcolm laughs. "See? I'm going to my room." He walks to the connecting door, then stops. "Go to bed."

Opening her eyes to slits, Cynthia stands, staggers one long step, and rolls into bed. She opens her eyes for a second. A sensual connection—subject to admirer. She wonders, *if I hold the sheet up, will he accept the invitation?* Deep in her gut, she craves it all.

But wanting isn't enough. She pulls the sheet to her chin, closes her eyes.

The door *clicks* shut.

Day 4 — Tuesday
St. Thomas

29

Land Ho!

At 4:00 a.m., Cynthia's watch alarm wakes her. Malcolm snores peacefully. It's too late to catch Olga, the jealous cocktail waitress in the Casbah Café. Cynthia steps into sweatpants and sneakers, pulls on a shirt, flicks her hair, and walks into the hall. She tapes fresh exterior strips to both doors before heading down to the 24/7 Internet Café. There is another e-mail from Bruce Swenson. According to Bruce, there's no evidence that the Louvre and Prado have joined forces.

Cynthia is back up to the rooms on Deck 15 by 04:40. Both tapes are in place. She goes through a series of yoga exercises before lying in bed. After thirty minutes of wondering whether Julia and the countess are double-crossing each other, she drifts to sleep.

Cynthia's watch alarm beeps again at 6:00 a.m. She activates the pearl speakers and hears Malcolm's monotonous snore. Relieved that he's still in his room, she inhales slow, even breaths but can't get back to sleep. Cliff Gorman is on her mind, and the more she thinks about Gorman, the less she believes that he is who he says he is—or more accurately, who Malcolm says he is. After all, *she* isn't who Malcolm tells people she is.

Gorman has popped up too often, as if he's tailing Malcolm instead of the suspects. If Gorman isn't an art collector, who is he? And why does Malcolm mislead her about him? Maybe Gorman is really a second bodyguard. If so, not telling Cynthia is believable because human nature causes people to relax when they have a safety net. But she has problems with that theory—paid protection should never get drunk on the job.

Perhaps Malcolm is telling a half-truth—maybe Gorman just works for him on the side. That would account for Gorman's covert behavior but doesn't explain why Malcolm would lie to Cynthia about it. Nor does it make sense for Gorman to make a pass at his friend's date. Then she remembers that she isn't a date.

Shit. Think about art.

She clicks on a light and pulls her 5 x 7 Winter Prince out of the nightstand drawer. The painting has multiple faces, multiple personalities. Her mind selects an eye, ear, nose, and mouth, piecing them together like a jigsaw puzzle. She shuffles features, covers some, turns the face forty-five degrees. With imagination, she can see Malcolm.

Picasso depicted a troubled person when he painted the Winter Prince. Troubled, as in obsessed? Someone like Malcolm, whose personality is intertwined with obsession?

Cynthia's stomach growls. Despite consuming mountains of food for three days, she hungers for breakfast.

From her Deck 15 balcony, she watches while the *Persian Prince* docks at St. Thomas. Ant-sized men secure the ship with ropes that look like strings. Waiting near the pier, along with a line of matchbox taxis, is a squat ambulance and three tiny police cars. The first people off the gangplank are porters carrying a body bag on a stretcher.

Cynthia is no longer hungry.

An hour later, her body's need for energy compels Cynthia to face food. The breakfast buffet loses a bit of luster each day—with slight variations, the fare is the same. Good and plentiful, but the same. The fruit isn't living up to Malcolm's luscious prediction. Cynthia is even bored with the golden pineapple. He notices her playing with her oatmeal. "Tomorrow," he says, "we'll eat breakfast in the dining room—get something cooked to order. You'll like it."

She takes solace from his confidence.

On their way down to the art gallery, Cynthia and Malcolm encounter Cliff Gorman on the Deck 9 landing. Again. He appears to be expecting them. "I need to talk with Cynthia in private," Gorman says.

Malcolm sidles to the far end of the landing, a strange retreat after last night's encounter.

Cynthia says, "Were you waiting for us?"

"Look," Gorman whispers. "I'm sorry if I upset you. The fact is that you're a good looking woman, and I like you. I'm not as sophisticated as Malcolm, but I like you for real. That's why I look—and compliment. I'm sorry I was drunk, and sorry if you weren't flattered."

"Apology accepted."

"Good. So we're friends, right?" He extends his right hand. For an instant, his eyes stray below her neck.

She forces a smile and shakes. "Let's just say that we're not enemies and call it a truce." That's enough to get rid of him.

Three flights down, Malcolm says, "What was that about?"

"Tell your friend to stop hitting on me."

Malcolm and Cynthia are waiting outside the art gallery office on Deck 5 when it opens at 8:00 a.m. They wear Hawaiian shirts over swimsuits, ready for a day of island recreation. Brent Burns, normally all dimpled grins, is somber. The men mutter generic banalities:

"I'm so sorry."

"Still can't believe it."

"What a tragedy," Cynthia adds as if she's another heartless guy.

Nobody wants to sound downright pitiful. A triangle of silence makes Cynthia listen for what isn't there.

Finally, Burns asks, "So what are you doing here at this hour?"

"I'm here to pick up my Wyland," Malcolm says. "It's a gift for a friend on St. Thomas. Sophia packed it up and filled out the necessary—" Malcolm's voice cracks. He wipes his eye, although Cynthia sees no moisture.

Burns's frown eases.

"I do this every year," Malcolm says. "Check my file."

Burns paws through a drawer. "Here it is." He scans the paperwork. "Everything looks to be in order, but…"

"But what?"

"For this cruise," Burns says, "nothing leaves the art gallery without a physical inspection. Special security orders from your Picasso Society."

"I forgot," Malcolm says. He turns to Cynthia. "We'll have to wait while they inspect it."

Cynthia is surprised—Malcolm is not the forgetful type.

"Maybe it's overkill," Malcolm says to Cynthia, "but my idea, so I can't really complain."

Burns calls Security, and they wait five minutes for an officer, who turns out to be the ever present Billingsley.

Only then does Burns slice the shipping tape and open the cardboard box. He slides out the frame, then pulls off a blanket of bubble-wrap. Turning the frame backside up, he lays it on his desk. Then he slits open the brown back-paper. There is thick cardboard backing, the Wyland print, and two layers of matting. Nothing else.

"All in order," Burns says.

"Right-oh," Billingsley adds.

Malcolm realigns the matting and re-secures the picture. Burns mutters, "You and your security rules."

"Where do I sign?" Billingsley says.

While Malcolm re-tapes the shipping box, Burns gathers some papers for Billingsley, who scribbles his name. Then Burns staples two more pages for Malcolm. "Sign here."

Malcolm complies. Cynthia, reading over his shoulder, notes the recipient's name: Marcie Green. She also notes Malcolm's hurried taping job, with two brown strips over one end of the box forming a misaligned X.

Burns stamps the paperwork. "You'll have to check this through customs. But you know that. Security will direct you at the gangway."

Cynthia volunteers to take one end of the box, but Malcolm

declines. She wonders: who is Marcie Green? Colleague? Friend? Lover? Cynthia doesn't ask for fear of sparking her own jealousy. She has been on the ship too long—the voyage has played havoc with her rationality, much like scuba diving thirty feet down. It occurs to her that after this week, she will need decompression.

Cynthia's first steps on land are pure rejuvenation—stability is therapeutic. For a moment, she stops and smiles at the green hills surrounding the harbor.

There is a customs trailer near the pier. Inside are two jet-black male officers in powder blue uniforms. Both speak with British accents. One sits in a chair by the exit door. The other stands behind a counter, looks at the package, glances at Malcolm's paperwork, stamps several documents, then waves him through. The process takes less than a minute.

During a twenty-yard walk from the trailer to the street, five taxi drivers solicit them for private tours. Malcolm, both arms clutching the package, avoids eye contact while pushing past, which is unlike him. She and Malcolm prepare to cross the street. A tiny pickup truck from the right almost barrels into Cynthia. Malcolm, with one hand, pulls her back to the curb. He almost drops the painting. The truck whooshes past.

"Watch it! St. Thomas is a U.S. territory, but they drive on the left."

"Now you tell me."

They cross and duck into a dilapidated stucco building that looks like an auto repair garage. The whole place could use an overhaul. The sign says "Rico's Tourist Services." Rico looks as if he wants to hug Malcolm like a long-lost brother, but the package is in the way. Malcolm asks about renting a Ford compact—previously reserved. This strikes Cynthia as odd because taxis are everywhere. Malcolm explains that cab drivers rip off the tourists, and he wants a car for the whole day. Cynthia convinces him to rent a different car—a Toyota—in case anyone with nefarious intentions may have known about the Ford. Rico hands over the keys. A minute later, they are inside their Toyota Camry—a black furnace without air-conditioning. They roll down the windows. "Step on it," she jokes.

During the drive, he rattles off the history of St. Thomas, but

Cynthia is too taken by the scenery to pay attention. The island, teeming with lush vegetation, is a visual delight. She is happy to be off the ship. After spending three years in prison, any confinement itches. St. Thomas might be a small island, but it's huge compared to the *Persian Prince*, which looks like a toy when it comes in view from high on the curving road.

Driving up a mountain (which, from the ship, appears to rise straight out of the harbor, but in reality turns out to be gently sloped), she realizes what was missing on the ship. Trees. St. Thomas's trees aren't the oaks and maples of home. These trees look stunted, with delicate bark, some sporting pointed leaves and orange berries, others flaunting shiny foliage and smooth trunks. Each home has a flower bed—so pristine and colorful that Cynthia wonders whether every resident has a green thumb. When the car stops to let a truck pass, she sticks her head out the window to savor the sweet scents of island flora. Malcolm names half the plants and trees, guessing at their ages. He would make a good contestant on *Jeopardy*. Two-thirds up the mountain, at a hairpin turn, they see a silk cotton tree that he says is unusual this high on the mountain.

Three lots further up the hill, they stop in front of a white bungalow—potted plants on the front steps—with a postcard vista of the harbor. There are faint shadows on the stucco where a house number used to be. Two-forty-something.

On the small porch, Malcolm sets down the package and knocks. When there is no answer, he finds a key underneath a flower pot, unlocks the front door, then ushers Cynthia in. The cottage is cozy, decorated with artistic flair. He sets the package inside a coat closet. An envelope addressed to him sits on the foyer table. He tears it open and says, "The note is dated two days ago. 'Dear Malcolm, I decided to go to New York for a few days. Sorry I missed you. Say 'Hi' to your babe of the week. — Marcie.'"

Malcolm reddens.

"Babe of the week?" Cynthia teases. "I thought I was your Eliza Doolittle."

He's too angry to laugh. "After this, she doesn't get the Wyland. And we're raiding her fridge." He stomps into the kitchen and returns with two Cokes.

"Take it easy," she says.

"You're right, you're right. It's just that I brought it all this way…"

"What will you do with it now?" she says. "Lug it back on board?"

"Why not send it to your business partner? You said you want to give her a gift from the cruise. And you said she likes dolphins."

"She'll think it's too expen—"

"Better than a postcard, right? We'll consider it part of your entertainment allowance. So far, you've been a cheap date." He goes to the closet and retrieves the package.

Again, Cynthia notes the ugly taping job, saying, "X marks the spot, huh?"

"Just my luck to have an anal bodyguard," he jokes. "We'll hit the Post Office on our way to the snorkeling beach."

Malcolm locks up on the way out, slips the key into his pocket. "I hope the bitch can't get in," he mutters.

Soon, they're heading down the mountain, back toward the town of Charlotte Amalie. Malcolm drives too fast and seems to enjoy Cynthia's anxiety each time they come within inches of sliding off the mountain."

Back in town, Malcolm parks across the street from the Post Office, a stucco colonial building. They get out, and Malcolm opens the hatch. "He hands Cynthia a wad of money. "You know the address. Have them slap on a new label. Insure it for a thousand. I need to buy sunglasses. I must have left mine at Marcie's."

Cynthia raises an eyebrow. "No. We'll stay together."

"What," he teases, "tough bodyguard can't handle mailing a package by herself?"

She laughs. For an instant, his eyes flash. She enjoys a surge of warmth up her spine but tries not to let it show.

After Cynthia advises Malcolm on his sunglasses purchase, they return to the car. Malcolm takes the long way to the far side of the island, driving Cynthia through paradise, avoiding shanty towns. She thinks it's the most beautiful drive ever. At the beach, he points. "That's our snorkeling tour over there. Get in line while I park."

Cynthia glowers. "Did you sign up for this tour in advance?"

"Sure. No need to get testy."

Cynthia grabs his elbow. "You keep forgetting: don't do anything predictable. How easy would it be for the killer to see what tour you're scheduled for and make a phone call? If you really were the target Sunday night, the killer may try again. Don't make it easy for him... or her."

"Sorry. We'll take a different tour."

"Better yet, we'll go by ourselves. That way we won't be looking over our shoulders at every stranger."

"Okay. Anything to calm you down."

They drive to a different beach, rent masks and fins, then wade in and set out on their own. With no idea where the good reefs are, they aimlessly swim in circles. The water is brilliant, but they see few fish and no coral. Cynthia gets more irritated by the minute—at Malcolm and herself. The outing is a budding disaster.

Then Malcolm splashes her breathing tube. "Shark attack!" He dives and grabs her ankle. A few counter-moves later, they are frolicking like teens at a pool party—like last night. The water washes her senses clean... She sheds her flippers and swims, free from the confines of tiny shipboard pools. The day is glorious.

Malcolm and Cynthia drive back to town and park in a sun-baked lot filled with taxi drivers hawking guided tours. They walk Main Street, crammed with jewelry stores and full of shoppers from the cruise ships. Cynthia sweats from heat reflecting off macadam. Malcolm pulls her under a brick arch, into Hibiscus Alley, a narrow passageway lined with shops and conveying a sense of seclusion. They duck into a cave of a bar called Calico Jack's. The ceiling is battered timbers; the walls are antique brick. Instantly, her sweat evaporates. She smiles—if she could be anywhere in the world, she would be right here. Sitting under the slow-twirling fan blades straight from the set of *Casablanca*, they order two iced teas, which turn into four iced teas and two grilled tuna sandwiches. They relive the snorkeling, then critique their favorite books. He completes one of her sentences. Each new topic brings more smiles.

After lunch, they hit the streets. As a tourist town, Charlotte Amalie is somewhere between quaint and phony, with charming pass-throughs like Hibiscus Alley tipping the balance toward quaint. But there are far too many dubious characters, any of whom could be an assassin. She urges Malcolm to stay off the street, but he wants to shop, and he's the boss. Every third door is a jewelry store. They enter one. He says, "What kind of diamond would you like?"

Cynthia smiles politely, waving the backs of ten bare fingers. "I don't wear jewelry."

"You wear chokers. Maybe you'd like an emerald-studded one."

"You don't get it. I don't want you to buy me expensive presents."

"Why not?"

He really doesn't get it. Cynthia shrugs and retreats to the sidewalk where they stroll toward the parking lot, keeping on the shady side of the street.

"Let's go over there," Malcolm says, pointing to a crowded tent bazaar. "I'll buy you some cheap island jewelry."

She grabs his elbow. "I don't want you to buy me *any* jewelry. Okay?"

Malcolm, sulking, looks at Cynthia as if she were an angry lover. "I'm sorry," he says. "It's just that you would be beautiful with…" His voice trails off. "Can't we at least look?"

She squeezes his cheeks with one hand, pointing his face toward the bazaar. "See all those people jammed together. If someone wants to kill you, they'd pay money to get you into chaos like that."

She gets a queasy feeling, checks her watch. "Shit. We're late. Fist'll be pissed. She leads him towards the car, but something makes her stop.

From the waterfront street, Cynthia looks across the harbor, so blue that it isn't any shade she has ever seen, but some novel palette that results when nature filters everything that doesn't belong. Somewhere beyond azure, the sky and water mate, male and female of perfect blues, shades that Wyland himself couldn't capture.

30

Island Grill

Malcolm and Cynthia are laughing about his lost sunglasses when they encounter a tall white specter at the base of the gangway. Billingsley's grumpy expression erases their reverie. "You're thirty minutes late."

"We're sorry," Cynthia says. "We lost track of time."

Billingsley doesn't look forgiving. "Lt. Fist and the authorities are waiting," he says. When Cynthia and Malcolm don't snap to, Billingsley adds, "In his office, about the murder."

"Can't we change first?" Malcolm says.

"Interpol, the FBI, and the local police all request that you two come along *now*."

Malcolm mumbles, "Well, I suppose."

They follow Billingsley down two flights, then through a warren's den of hallways. Cynthia buttons up her Hawaiian shirt. At Fist's office, Billingsley knocks. A voice barks, "Come in."

"One interview at a time," Billingsley says. "Ladies first." He opens the door. Cynthia hands her tote bag to Malcolm, then walks into Fist's crowded office.

"Break a leg," Malcolm says as the door closes.

Inside, there are five men seated on folding chairs, their hips touching. Each one stares at Cynthia.

Fist stands up from behind his desk. The others don't, due to tight quarters. "Sit here, Miss James," he says, indicating his rolling chair. She squeezes around the desk and sits. Fist strides to the door, then makes the introductions—too many names, ranks, and titles for Cynthia to remember them all. It's truly an international gathering: one FBI agent from Miami named Duvall; a Crime Scene Investigator, also from Miami, whose toupee appears to be pasted on; a black St. Thomas detective whom Fist calls Jumper; a skinny man from Interpol; and a Dutch man whose role Cynthia misses in the flurry of titles.

The FBI agent stands and adjusts his suspenders. "We've reviewed your statement to the ship's security," he says with a southern drawl. "And I have a few questions. I'll try to be brief and cover new ground." Cynthia doesn't believe him on either claim. Duvall stands directly in front of her. "Are you ready? Would you like a glass of water?"

Cynthia looks up at her interrogator. "No, thank you."

Duvall smiles with false benevolence. "Ms. James, what the heck are you doing on this ship?"

His folksy bluntness is meant to intimidate her, but she has faced off with tougher adversaries. She answers in measured tones. "I'm on the cruise as the paid bodyguard of Mr. Malcolm Golden, who received a death threat concerning his intent to buy the Picasso painting. I would expect that Lt. Fist has told you this."

"As matter of fact, he has, Ms. James, but... well, what interests me is that you've got one heck of an interesting FBI file."

She resists the urge to reply.

"An interesting criminal record, too."

She waits for a question.

"That, by itself, makes you a person of particular interest, if not a prime suspect. And you seem to match the description of the likely murderess."

Still no question. She takes a calming breath.

"Now, you told Lt. Fist that you and Mr. Golden have separate cabins so you could have easily slipped away and delivered the poison, right?"

"That's clever phraseology, Mr. Duvall."

"What do you mean? I just asked a simple question."

"But the way you phrased it was meant to trick me."

Duvall looks genuinely shocked, for which Cynthia would nominate him for an Academy Award. "Miss James, I'm perplexed as to why you would think that I'm trying to trick you. Please enlighten us all." He waves a hand toward the other men.

"If you insist. It's true that I told Lt. Fist that Mr. Golden and I have separate rooms, but you phrased your question to make it sound like I also told Lt. Fist that I could have easily slipped away. You and/or Lt. Fist may *think* that I could have easily slipped away, but I never said it, so the answer to your question is no."

Duvall leans close and squints so that only Cynthia can see a flash of hatred. Then he pulls back, adjusts his suspenders, and paints on his aw-shucks grin. "I'm sorry. I didn't know we were in advanced English class. I'll rephrase. You could have slipped away from your room without Mr. Golden knowing it, correct?"

"Yes, I could have, but I didn't."

"You could have, but you didn't. All right. Let me ask you this, Miss James...." Duvall stretches out the moment. "Ever poisoned anyone before the other night?"

"You wouldn't have asked that question," she says coolly, "if you hadn't seen my confidential file. And since you've seen the file, you know that it's classified. I'm surprised that you would embarrass the United States in front of these international law enforcement officials by using a cheap stunt intended to pin this murder on me."

Duvall is momentarily shaken, for which Cynthia suppresses the smug smile she wants to lay on him. He hems and haws for a moment.

"I'll answer," Cynthia says, "if you allow me to tell these gentlemen the circumstances."

Cynthia can see the anger on Duvall's reddening face. He works his gums while gathering composure. "I think we get the picture, Miss James. Perhaps we'll move on."

Duvall proceeds to question Cynthia for twenty minutes, but neither his repetitive questions nor her equally repetitive answers shed any light on who killed Sophia Caporetto or why.

When Duvall runs out of questions, he asks if anyone else requires information from the witness. The other men look at the worn, gray carpet. Fist dismisses her.

Billingsley is waiting outside the door. He leads her to a nearby crew cabin not unlike Sophia's. "Wait here. I'll be right outside," he says, tapping the walkie-talkie on his hip, "in case they need you back."

Cynthia wants to return to her own stateroom. This one is small, like a prison cell. There's a twin bed, one chair, no TV, and nothing to read. She sits in the chair and notices her reflection in a mirror. Her eyes look worried; perspiration dots her brow; there is more, unseen beneath her armpits. She holds up her fingers, trying to look like Picasso's mistress with the mangled hand.

31

Picasso Society

As soon as Malcolm is released from his interrogation, Cynthia and he hustle up twelve flights of stairs, then quickly shower for a cocktail party hosted by the International Picasso Society in the Tehran Salon. Malcolm takes longer to blow-dry his hair than she does. He urges her to wear the skimpy black cocktail dress, which he has hung in her open closet, but she opts for a black pantsuit with turtleneck, classy enough to fit in with whatever the upper crust wears.

She and Malcolm arrive fashionably late. One man, posted in the corner, is obviously not a guest—dark suit, ear piece, thin cord disappearing beneath the collar. From a bodyguard's point of view, Cynthia hates this sort of function—people milling about everywhere, no control over access from the atrium. Worse, the small-talk will be dreary.

As long as she has to be there, Cynthia makes the most of it. Keeping Malcolm in sight, she sidles over to Countess LaCroix, who is standing alone near the top of one of the atrium's curving staircases. The countess cringes at Cynthia's approach, but she neither says nor does anything overtly rude.

"Having fun?" Cynthia asks in a goading tone.

"You don't want to be here anymore than I do," the countess says, the first statement of hers with which Cynthia agrees.

"*Touché*," Cynthia says.

"Your French needs work."

There is an awkward break in the conversation. Cynthia

looks over at Malcolm. "Just two more days, and—"

"You're a vulgar woman. Whatever does Malcolm see in you?" She casts a judgmental glance at Cynthia's pants. "Well, he *is* a man, I suppose."

"Man enough to bid on his own, without trustees from other museums."

The aristocratic throat tightens. "Whatever do you mean?"

"I know a bit about conditional auction alliances. You and the Louvre and the Prado—"

"The Louvre is a magnificent institution, my dear, but they have no influence over my purse strings."

"But they do over your collection. Both you and the Louvre want the Picasso. They'll make it worthwhile for you to bid high, but how high will you go?"

The countess exhales, champagne on her breath. "Malcolm doesn't have the resources to outbid me." She leans close to Cynthia's ear and whispers, "Or—how would Julia say it?—the *cajones.*" Before Cynthia replies, the countess spies an escape. "Oh, Captain DeVries…"

With the countess gone, Cynthia wedges between Malcolm and Julia Sotelo, who is radiant in kelly green. Cynthia smiles and says, "The vain in Spain dress mainly in the gree-ain."

Malcolm squeezes her hand. "Still my fair lady, huh?"

"You make a good Henry Higgins."

"Marvelous," coos Julia. "You're growing on me, Cynthia."

"So," Cynthia says, "how much money is the countess contributing to your bid?"

Julia glances at Malcolm. "Have you been asking your squeeze to throw smoke bombs?"

Malcolm shrugs.

"I'm serious," Cynthia says. "You all know everyone else's numbers. Why not admit it?"

"You *are* naïve," Julia says.

"Perhaps." Cynthia snatches a champagne flute from a passing tray—not to drink, but as a prop. "All this money chasing one little painting, all these buyers willing to pay the market value, *plus*. The amount of the plus is the depth of one's pockets. Or the number of pockets one dips into."

Julia gives Malcolm an insider's squint. "Sharing wild

theories in the bedroom, are we? Be a dear and get me another drink."

He looks at Cynthia, who gives him a sideways nod.

Once Malcolm is out of earshot, Julia leans so close that her lips brush Cynthia's pearl stud. "He's loco, you know—will stop at nothing to get his hands on a masterpiece."

"Isn't that a little harsh—"

"He's a dangerous egotist, hoarding a private collection that should be in museums for all to appreciate. I think he was behind the Gardner heist."

"The Gardner heist?"

"The Isabella Gardner Museum in Boston, where thirteen priceless treasures were stolen."

"What treas—"

"Vermeer's 'The Concert,' for one."

"Malcolm?" Cynthia asks. "He may be passionate, but—"

"Selfish and obsessive are more like it, honey."

"You call him selfish, but look how attentive he is, getting your drink."

Julia smirks. "If he seems gentle, it's only acting. And remember, I said obsessive, too."

"He's not obsessive," Cynthia says. A real girlfriend couldn't have been more defensive.

"With a capital O, dearie. He's outbid me for Rembrandts and a Degas, but this time, his grandfather's money won't be enough. He won't get the Picasso. We won't let him."

"We? You and the countess?"

Julia pivots with perfect timing and takes a wineglass from Malcolm's hand. "Oh, thank you, Malcolm. I was just telling your squeeze that you're a loco snake who will stop at nothing to deprive the public of inspiring art. Have a nice evening." Julia swivels toward the captain.

"What was that about, Cyn?"

"She tried to turn me against you. I think she's jealous."

"Of you or the Picasso?"

"Both, I'd say. I need some air. Walk with me on the promenade."

Once they can talk freely outside, she stops by the railing. The ship is pulling away from the dock. The harbor's turquoise blues dance toward golden green in the late afternoon light.

"So what did Julia say?" he asks.

"That you have a personal hoard of priceless art."

"That's ridiculous. If you check the records, every piece I've bought has been circulated to museums."

"She was referring to pieces that can't be shown." Cynthia raises an eyebrow. "Possibly stolen?"

Malcolm laughs. "Her little game. She tells all my dates that I'm crazy, to scare them off. She wants my money for herself."

Cynthia gazes out at an elegant yacht, so photogenic that it should be moored permanently. Her question slips out. "Tell me the truth—have you slept with Julia?" She holds her breath.

"No," Malcolm says. "Did she say I had?"

Cynthia exhales. "No, but it would explain why she said those things to me."

"It isn't true."

Cynthia turns to study his eyes. "What isn't true? That you slept with her or stole those paintings in Boston?"

"Cynthia, we've had a good time together today. Don't let Julia spoil it."

32

Julia Sotelo

Julia envies Cynthia James, who is young, lithe, and sleeping with Malcolm. That last one hurts. Julia tries to disappear inside an inane conversation with the captain, but she can't help but recall when she was thinner. Never as slender as Cynthia, mind you, whose tapered torso is sinfully indecent.

It has been years since Julia seduced Malcolm—while she was in mourning over husband number one. Then, she was Malcolm's co-conspirator. They traveled the continent, meeting for trysts in Capri and Monte Carlo while plotting to conquer the art world. Malcolm was so amusing. With him, she was the most beautiful woman on earth. Now, she is middle-aged and plump, clinging to a shaky alliance with a passé aristocrat. Life with Malcolm was so much more vital.

Self-conscious, Julia tugs at her hem, too short for a 52-year-old woman with chunky thighs, but she can't help herself. As for her cleavage, Julia owns nary a garment that doesn't flaunt it. Ten years ago, she could still be called voluptuous, but time has taken its toll. These days, she avoids mirrors—they reflect an excess of flesh at every curve. Next year, it will be worse. When did she stop working out? After the second funeral? Or after Malcolm abandoned her in Barcelona?

If only she had been lucky in marriage. *Señors* Constantine and Sotelo had both been rich, both loved her passionately, and both tolerated her affairs. Too bad Constantine had been cursed with a love of speed and Sotelo with a weak heart. How many women suffer the dual misfortunes of watching one husband explode in a fireball at Le Mans and screwing the other to death in a Jacuzzi?

Self-pity might ruin her day, but the captain nods at her assets. His salute is the slightest dip of his chin, but enough to flatter her. Thank God for men in uniform. Thank God for captains who know how to make passengers feel special!

Julia holds his elbow and smiles with the radiance that only a desperate woman can muster. They chat, but he isn't engaged. His eyes dance toward younger women with shiny hair. Julia laughs at the captain's bad joke—anything to buy precious seconds of attention. But she's losing him. He responds to her point about the genius of Picasso by mumbling, "Whatever you say, Ms. Sotelo."

Ms. Sotelo! Last cruise, she had been Julia. Next cruise, she will be ma'am.

The captain, with another almost imperceptible nod in her direction, excuses himself to join a nearby conversation of art groupies, where he nods vigorously at the chest of a twenty-something blonde. Julia sees the countess approaching.

"What did the American concubine say?" the countess asks.

"So now you're interested in her opinions?"

"She's with him, so she's the enemy. One should always know what one's enemies are thinking."

"Thinking and saying aren't the same thing, Milady." Julia curtsies.

The countess turns to stone.

Julia, herself again, laughs. "You would be surprised at what she said—had the Prado-Louvre partnership right on."

"*Louvre*-Prado. Remember that."

"Fuck off, Yvonne." Julia enjoys a rush from telling the cadaver what she thinks. "If Cynthia suspects we've teamed up, she got it from Malcolm."

"What can he do?"

"He could throw in with MOMA."

The countess blanches. "He wouldn't!"

"Would you bet the Picasso on wishful thinking? Or on Poindexter's loyalty?"

"Perhaps I should make inquiries." The countess slithers off, doubtless to conspire with Gladys Poindexter.

Julia sets down her champagne flute and orders a ginger ale from a passing waiter. He's handsome, so she swings her hip toward his, but the waiter pivots around her as if she were a piece of furniture.

Aha! Julia spies a man who has been furtively admiring her all cruise—that little friend of Malcolm's. What's his name? No matter; he's breathing. She swivels over to where he stands looking out the window. From there, she, too, stares through the glass at Cynthia and Malcolm, who lean side-by-side on the railing, gazing at the harbor. Julia focuses on Cynthia. Why? Julia reminds herself to ignore the taut derriere and tapered torso. Cynthia James is a distraction. Everything is about getting the Picasso to the public. Does it really matter if the Louvre gets the painting seven months and the Prado only five? Five is so much better than nothing. As is the little man.

Julia rubs her arm against his shoulder. He turns and smiles into her bosom. She remembers his name: Cliff. For some silly reason, the name seems appropriate.

33

Smart Casual

For nine months, a lifetime ago, Cynthia worked as a bartender on the *Louisiana Lady*, where intimate river life had a pleasant rhythm that soothed her damaged psyche. She misses that life—the fog, the oxbows, the subtle motion that was only sensed when it disappeared as you stepped ashore. One reason she wanted to take this ocean cruise was to compare modern excess to historic charm. To her surprise, excess is holding its own.

The imperial facilities are new, the food tasty and plentiful, the entertainment varied and first-rate. The passing scenery is monotony incarnate—flat, flat sea—but there is a peaceful escape within endless blue.

Socially, there are too many passengers for Cynthia's taste, and interaction with the crew is stiffly formal. On the riverboat, the crew was American. On the *Persian Prince*, most of the non-officers are Asian or Eastern European—exceedingly polite and hard-working, but incapable of American banter.

The biggest plus is the weather. In mid-February, it's a sunny 75 degrees, with 1,000 crew members at your service. Sipping cold drinks is deliciously decadent. Feeling lazy, she suggests to Malcolm that they skip their daily run so they can relax until dinner.

He has no objection.

At the cabins, Malcolm says, "Why don't you get some rest? I have work to do." He closes the connecting door. Cynthia feels a stab of disappointment. She lies on her bed and listens through her ear-speakers to his pen scratch whatever it is he's writing.

Cynthia wins the fashion negotiation, convincing Malcolm that they should dress down to smart casual. She selects spring colors—loose white pants, a lightweight pink pullover, and a maroon scarf. Malcolm wears a powder blue shirt and gray slacks. On the way to the cocktail lounge, they debate the pros and cons of having drinks with strangers. Cynthia wants to sit with other couples, so she won't get sucked back into the romantic atmosphere of St. Thomas. Malcolm wants a cocktail table for two. They compromise by joining a single rotund Dutchman, who turns out to be another art collector.

Later, outside the dining room, Cynthia touches Malcolm's elbow. "I don't want tedious small-talk with any more art snobs tonight." There. It's out. Cynthia feels honest, a weight lifted from her shoulders. "Let's eat by ourselves—try the buffet at the Palace Café. You said yourself that tonight's sit-down menu didn't excite you."

"Look," Malcolm says. "There's John and Gladys. We can eat with them. John isn't snobbish like the countess. Or me." He smiles.

"Jeez, Malcolm," she whispers. "We spent time with them at the afternoon reception. Just for tonight. Say I'm seasick." She wants to forget Julia's calculated lies and talk about anything but art.

Cynthia stays out of the offers and counter-offers between Poindexter and Malcolm, just as a seasick date would. She tries her best to look green. Poindexter is persistent, but Malcolm defends her illness, insisting that Cynthia must go back to her stateroom to rest. Eventually, the Poindexters demure. Malcolm takes Cynthia's hand as they watch the older couple disappear into the dining room. Then Malcolm leads her aft through the art gallery. They are suppressing childish giggles, as if they have ditched annoying kids. At the aft staircase, they break out laughing.

"I'll race you up." Malcolm darts onto the steps. She sets off after him.

She is a tomboy, mindless of her clothes, taking stairs two at a time, dodging his elbows. Each large stairwell has two staircases, side by side, so Cynthia splits off to the right-hand stairs to be unencumbered. She is younger and in better shape than Malcolm, but her pumps even the odds. On the Deck 9 landing, she swerves through a unisex pack of teenagers. She stumbles while avoiding the kids, stoops just long enough to snatch off her shoes, then races on in stocking feet, straining to catch Malcolm. Her thighs burn as she gains ground. Only a few steps behind. She passes him halfway up the last flight.

On the Lido Deck, Cynthia bends at the waist, breathing heavily. Happiness radiates from her body. Malcolm is panting and smiling, his cheeks red, his forehead moist. He enjoyed the race, too. Another surprise.

The buffet is terrific. Or maybe Cynthia is jazzed by the race, or perhaps food just tastes better when savored with an attractive man. "So," she says. "Now that we're alone, no more stalling. What did they ask you in your interrogation?"

"They went after both of us," he says. "Asked if I overheard you make any phone calls, why I sent the champagne to Sophia, whether you were in your cabin before you caught me in the hall."

"What did you tell them?"

"The truth," he says. "The same things I told Fist that night."

"Did they ask about why you hired me?"

"Yes," he says. "I just told the truth about that, too."

Cynthia chews a tasty bite of lamb, swallows. "Did they ask anything that made you think they're looking at other suspects?"

"The mysterious stewardess, of course. But I couldn't help them."

"What about the Polish steward?"

He shakes his head. "They don't suspect him. Or the room-service dispatcher."

She sighs. "No questions about any of the other bidders?"

"No," he says.

"What about—"

"Relax," he says. "I told you everything they asked, everything I answered. Give it a rest, okay?"

Cynthia sits down at their table with thirds. "This lamb is to die for."

"So you're really enjoying yourself?" Malcolm asks.

Cynthia glances around—nobody within earshot. "That's a strange question. There's been a murder. I'm a prime suspect. You may be the next target, yet you ask me if I'm enjoying myself."

He twirls a fork. "It's just that you were laughing on St. Thomas. And you laughed again after our little race. It suits you. And I had fun today. I guess I hoped that you did, too." A mischievous grin spreads across his face. "Diz iz de Caribbean, wo-mon. No worries, be happy."

She fights off a smile. "You're a regular Jekyll and Hyde. Obsessed about a painting one minute and joking the next."

"We're entitled to have some fun until Thursday."

"And if you happen to get yourself killed in the process?"

"That won't happen." His eyes twinkle—such a silly word, but they really do. "My bodyguard won't allow it."

A shiver tiptoes up her spine. Cynthia thinks about her lips, exposed, vulnerable. She takes the final bite of lamb. The smell of mint jelly stimulates her nostrils an instant before her taste buds respond to the flavor. Sophia may be dead, but Cynthia is incredibly alive.

An elderly couple, the man in a wheelchair, chooses the table next to theirs. Malcolm rises to hold the woman's chair.

"That was sweet," Cynthia whispers after he sits down.

"Dessert?" Malcolm says.

Cynthia grins. "Oh, yeah, mon."

After splitting a raspberry tart and a slice of pecan pie, they linger over cappuccinos. The elderly couple must be hard of hearing because they talk loud enough to be heard back in St. Thomas. Cynthia figures that they don't know who Malcolm is because they talk about the murder, conjecturing on who did it. Malcolm pretends that he doesn't hear. Cynthia is stuffed, glad to have worn her loosest pants.

With no warning, Malcolm asks, "Where do you want to be in three years?"

"For real," she whispers, "or for the benefit of the couple at the next table."

"Let's find someplace more private."

34

Illusions

Malcolm takes Cynthia to the Tehran Salon, adjacent to the atrium, where they select a loveseat by a window, isolated from the other tables. Malcolm sits on Cynthia's left, close enough for her to smell spearmint on his breath, close enough to feel his warmth. A Filipino cocktail waitress appears in purple waistcoat, a picture of efficiency. Malcolm orders drinks.

"So," he says, "do you want to still be teaching self-defense in three years?"

"Probably not."

"Then what? What are your hopes and dreams?"

Cynthia knows it isn't smart to verbalize her dreams—she doesn't know Malcolm well enough. "Let's just enjoy the night," she says. "The dreams will come." The unspoken truth: she is tired of acting one part, yet afraid to live another.

Their fingers are touching, but she doesn't know who reached first. "Do you want to go somewhere else?" he asks.

A deep breath. Goose-bumps prickle her forearms. "No. We better stay here."

Malcolm's complexities intrigue her. He can be shallow, as when buying her a bikini in the hope that she will model it. Or he can be deep as the ocean, as when explaining the genius of Picasso. He can be as intense as any man she has ever met, yet his eyes caress her as if she were a butterfly. He is older than she, but younger at heart. He allows her to control their movements, yet he manipulates her—in ways that she doesn't mind. He trusts his life to her, and she dares to wonder what reciprocation might feel like.

But just when she is primed for meaningful dialog, Malcolm starts pontificating about art, museums, and auctions. Talking about art pleases him, so she lets him go on, nodding during the appropriate pauses.

They listen to the piano crooner, a Latino hunk named Luciano. Malcolm relaxes with a margarita. Cynthia keeps alert with a Diet Coke. The current object of her attention is the jewelry boutique, on the far side of the atrium, where Cynthia observes Miranda—the Dominican escort, in all her island regalia—assisting the Dutchman with whom they earlier shared cocktails. Miranda models diamond necklaces, brushes the customer's arm, flirts up a hurricane. The man's pink face reddens, but he doesn't buy anything. Miranda gestures toward the rear of the shop and leads him through a swinging saloon-style door. Cynthia thinks, perhaps to a storeroom.

She and Malcolm finish their drinks. Malcolm orders another round. The crooner completes his set with "My Way." Miranda and the Dutchman have still not returned to the store. Malcolm talks about the differences between artistic beauty and natural beauty; Cynthia, distracted by Miranda's absence, merely nods.

The crooner returns for his next set. He has been on break for 25 minutes.

Miranda and the customer finally slip back into the boutique after being gone 55 minutes. The man leaves the shop, weaving like a sailor. Miranda waves to him and watches until the man is out of her sight, then she checks her watch before leaving the store. Miranda walks toward the amidships elevator bank.

Cynthia's face breaks into a bemused smile. She leans her lips close to Malcolm's ear and whispers, "This ship's a floating brothel, isn't it?"

Malcolm spits a mouthful of margarita onto the cocktail table.

The piano man keeps playing, but several patrons gawk at the disruption. An efficient cocktail waitress appears with a towel. Malcolm says, "Let's go for a stroll." He and Cynthia pick up their drinks and exit the lounge with twenty eyes upon them.

Once outside on the breezy promenade, Cynthia blurts,

"Those so-called escorts are really prostitutes, right?"

"Well," he says, "it's not really a secret."

"Not a secret?" Cynthia's eyes widen; her face flushes. "Prostitution on a cruise ship?"

"It's completely legal."

"Legal? You're kidding, right?"

Malcolm shushes her as a young couple giggles past. "This way." He pulls her the other direction. "All forms of massage service are permissible in international waters, just like gambling. All perfectly legal. The ship is registered in Amsterdam, so on the open seas, Dutch law takes precedent over—"

"I don't believe it—not exactly featured on the website."

"Not on the *U.S.* website. But on the international site, massage services are prominently marketed."

Cynthia shakes her head.

He touches her wrist. "Your prudish Protestant upbringing is showing."

Cynthia raises her jaw. "I'm not a prude."

"Your reaction certainly shades that way."

They walk for a few paces. "So how do they stay in business? Most Americans must be offended when they find out."

"You see how international the passenger list is. Empire's bread and butter are Europeans. Do you think the French or Danes mind?"

"Maybe not, but…"

"Look," he says. "Empire wants the high roller business. They offer single-passenger cabins without premiums. They have a lock on the sex crowd. It's a lucrative trade."

They stroll for almost a minute. Malcolm nudges her hip. "Say something, Cyn."

"Now that the cat-house is out of the bag, what do you do with *your* credits? Your perks."

"Fair enough." He stops, faces the rail, and gazes into the black night. "I sometimes spend time with Miranda."

Cynthia flinches, rubs her upper arms. She hoped he would say gambling, jewelry, anything but sex.

"Why?"

"Miranda's the best lover I've ever been with. Phenomenal, actually."

"What makes her so great? Excess silicone?"

"You shouldn't be jealous."

Cynthia tries to read his eyes, but his expression is a blank. "Just tell me," she says.

Malcolm rubs his chin as if enjoying himself. "They *are* magnificent. And deliciously real, but that's not what brings me back. She's amazingly sensual—soft, inside and out. And patient. Exquisite muscle control. Unselfish."

"Oh, *please*."

"You're the one who asked."

She looks at the moon, relaxes. "You're right."

He rubs her shoulders. "You thought something might happen between us, didn't you?"

"No," she says too quickly.

"You're an attractive woman…"

She shakes her head, aware that he didn't say intriguing this time.

"…but we have a professional relationship."

"A professional relationship apparently doesn't stop you from sleeping with Miranda."

He exhales, then take another breath. "It's not like that," he says.

Cynthia waits for an explanation.

"She's a good kid," he says. "I'm helping her."

Cynthia rolls her eyes. "Helping, huh? Like teaching her bedroom tricks?"

"No," he says. "Arranging to get her a green card."

Cynthia nods for him to go on.

"Enticing rich tourists is no life—long term. She knows that. She can get a new start in America."

"Continuing in the oldest profession?"

"She has other skills. She's a trained dance instructor and masseuse."

"Oh. I *forgot*. And jewelry consultant."

Malcolm shrugs. "Like I said before, you're a prudish Protestant."

Cynthia's jealousy is spent—her self-righteousness, too.

"When you take some time to think about it," he says "you'll see that there isn't anything bad going on here."

She almost reminds him that Sophia Caporetto is dead.

Back in the Tehran Salon, Cynthia sees Anton the Illusionist and Carlotta sitting at the bar. Without costumes, they look like any other passengers. Carlotta's platinum hair is pulled into a ponytail. If not for Anton's waxed mustache, Cynthia wouldn't have recognized them. Carlotta wears wedding and engagement rings, both absent during the performance. The two of them make no effort to talk with each other, merely staring at their strawberry daiquiris between sips.

Malcolm leads Cynthia over, saying, "Anton. It's great to see you again. I have a few minutes."

Anton slides off his stool; the men shake hands.

"This is Cynthia," Malcolm says. "I should have introduced you the other night. Anton and Carlotta Perrault."

Carlotta swivels to face them but doesn't get up. Everyone exchanges nods and hellos.

Anton says, "I wanted to ask you what you think the Dali is worth." His accent has the night off.

Malcolm slaps the magician's back. "Only if you'll teach me an illusion."

The men disappear into a blended world of magic-art, sidling toward a framed Nechita displayed in the atrium. Cynthia shakes her head, and Carlotta smiles insincerely, her eyes looking withered from years of performing under ponderous mascara.

With the men out of earshot, Cynthia says, "I want to tell you again that I think you're the star of the show. Whatever the trick is, you have to be unbelievably supple and quick to make the switches."

"Tell that to Anton." There is a depressed slur to Carlotta's words. The accent is American; Cynthia thinks: North Jersey, to be precise.

"What do you mean?" Cynthia asks.

"I'm the Amazing Anton's third lovely assistant. And third wife. You do the math."

Cynthia can think of nothing to say.

"He told me today—today!—that he's bringing the understudy on for the last night of the cruise. Phoebe. Only twenty-five. I know what *that* means. Ten years ago, *I* was the understudy."

Cynthia thinks of an optimistic spin. "That must be for the two ladies vanishing trick he alluded to outside the theatre."

"On stage, two, but at night, he only makes one disappear. Care to bet on which bed he'll be sleeping in?"

"I'm sorry."

"I shouldn't complain," Carlotta says. "It's been a good run for a high school drop-out from Hoboken, and it's not like I didn't know this day was coming." She takes a drink. "He's the best." She shakes her head. "Illusionist, that is. The best illusionists go on and on, but lovely assistants get replaced."

Cynthia glances toward Malcolm, hoping to be saved from way too much information, but the men are thirty feet away. So she says, "The act is good enough for A.C. or Vegas. Why do you work the cruise ships?"

"He's lazy," Carlotta slurs. "The money's okay, only three shows a week. And he likes to travel, see the world." She sips her daiquiri. "I wanted kids. Shit."

"What makes Anton the best?" Cynthia asks, hoping to lighten the gloom.

"Do you want me to have to shoot you?"

Cynthia smiles. "You don't have to be specific."

"He's a master of the box—any box. And I can say this: he knows that every illusion can be enhanced to make it look like something new."

"Is there anything he can't make disappear?" Cynthia asks.

Carlotta looks at her reflection in the mirror behind the bar, shakes her head. "Nothing."

35

Anton Perrault

Anton hurries toward the bar where his wife is talking with Malcolm's girlfriend. Anton shouldn't have left Carlotta—in a vindictive, inebriated state—alone with another woman. Carlotta has a way of unburdening herself. He hears her say, "Nothing."

"Nothing what, my dear?" Anton asks, forcing a smile.

Carlotta scowls. "I was just telling Cynthia that there's nothing you can't make disappear, most especially yours truly."

"Don't you think you've had enough to drink, my love? We should be going to our cabin."

"My love?" Carlotta says.

From Malcolm's fidgeting, he clearly wants nothing to do with anyone's marriage woes, but Cynthia isn't taking the hint. She says to Carlotta, "Are you sure you're ready to leave?"

"No. I'm just getting started." Carlotta's speech is slurred.

Anton has to get her out of there. He pokes his elbow into Malcolm's arm and adds a sideways nod that means: get your nosy girlfriend away from my wife.

Malcolm complies, tugging his date's elbow.

Carlotta says, "No. Don't go." She reaches an unsteady hand, regrettably the hand holding her daiquiri, which sloshes onto Cynthia's white pants. This accident turns out to be a good thing because it hastens their departure. Malcolm and Cynthia are escaping while Carlotta mumbles her third apology.

"Well," Anton says to Carlotta, "you drove them away."

"Bartender," she says, "another daiquiri over here."

"I don't think so," Anton says, shaking his head at the bartender. He caresses his wife's shoulders, but she doesn't relax the way she used to. That makes him think of Phoebe, who melts to his touch, who makes him feel magical.

The new illusion will make him rich, rich enough to afford art masterpieces of his own. He needs Phoebe for the trick, which will soon be known as "The Anton." No one has done it. No one has even conceived that such a feat could be attempted.

It's not Carlotta's fault that she must be left behind. It's the nature of the business—*what have you wowed me with lately?* Phoebe is more alluring, far more acrobatic, and thirty pounds lighter. Thirty pounds that will make all the difference when "The Anton" is unveiled Thursday night.

Poor Carlotta.

Poor Carlotta needs Anton's help getting into the elevator, into the cabin, even into bed. Drinking is her latest attention-getting device. Did it commence before or after he began working with Phoebe? He can't remember. Looking down at his once-lovely wife, Anton finds it hard to believe that there was ever a time when he wanted her.

Phoebe will join the cruise tomorrow on St. Maartens. That gives Anton a day and a half to assuage Carlotta, convince her that putting on a happy face for the last show is in her best interest. In the end, Carlotta will be a professional and perform her part in the show because, with her future in limbo, she needs the money.

Anton turns off the light and lies down as far away from Carlotta as the double bed permits. His anticipation allows him to ignore the depression that is suffocating his wife. He can't help but feel giddy at the effect Thursday's illusion will have, not just in the world of magic, but in the world of art.

36

Fourth Night

Lying in bed after yoga, Cynthia does a lot of thinking. About the day on St. Thomas. About why she is drawn to Malcolm, and why it's wrong. About artistic muses. About the murder. About the upcoming auction.

Malcolm is a bundle of surprises—sexy in a dangerous way. Funny. Not to mention filthy rich. Cynthia aches to feel his warmth pressed to her skin. But is that enough? Hardening nipples suggest otherwise.

Stop it! Do your damn job. Protect your client. That means: solve the murder because it's no coincidence that the victim was the auctioneer. Did Malcolm go to Sophia the first night? Probably. What if they *were* having an affair? If so, why did Malcolm lie about it?

Cynthia has to learn more about Sophia's relationships with Brent Burns, Julia Sotelo, the countess, and John Poindexter. And possibly, secret bidders unknown. Cynthia needs Malcolm's help, and she will have to cut through his charming defenses to get it.

Malcolm snores in her ear speakers. Her watch alarm beeps. 01:45. Time to hustle to the Casbah Café before closing. She checks on Malcolm, then sneaks into the hall and pushes tight the tape on both doors.

The Casbah Café is winding down at 1:55. Three drunk gamblers—all men—nurse their last round. Two costumed belly-dancers wipe empty tables. Behind the bar stands a pretty bartender, whose shirt, bowtie, and purple vest can't disguise a full figure.

Cynthia sits on a stool and offers a smile, which is returned by the round-faced girl, who can't be more than 23. Her long hair is twirled into an elaborate bun, the excess falling in a ponytail. The nametag reads: Olga. "We're closing," she says with a mild Russian accent.

"I don't want a drink," Cynthia says, sliding forward a $20 bill. "Just information."

"What about?" Olga says, glancing at the money.

"Brent Burns."

Olga's lips part. She peers at Cynthia with calculating green eyes. "What kind of information?"

"Girlfriends among the crew."

Olga's eyes widen; she licks her lip—the look of greed. She puts one hand on the bar, slides it toward her apron. The money is gone.

"Meet me out on the starboard promenade," Olga says before nodding toward the nearest door. "Five minutes."

"Okay."

Ten minutes later, Olga steps outdoors with a pocketbook slung on her shoulder, bowtie loosened, vest unbuttoned, and a cigarette dangling from her lips. She lights up before nodding to Cynthia. Forced air whirs out through a nearby vent.

"So," Olga says, exhaling smoke.

Cynthia fights the urge to bum a cigarette. "Is Brent Burns seeing any girls from the bartending staff?"

"What's it worth to you?"

"Depends on what you have to give."

"It's been a long day," Olga says.

"Tell me something for the twenty. About Brent Burns...?"

Olga puffs, thinks, exhales. "He's a shit-head. He dumped me when he got promoted to the Art Department." She squints at Cynthia. "You can do better."

"I hear he's a tease."

Olga laughs. "He's saving himself for marriage. Can you believe that shit?" She takes in a deep draw. "What's this really about?"

"If Burns needed a favor—a big favor—is there a barmaid,

cocktail waitress, or wine stewardess who would do *anything* for him?"

"Like what do you mean by anything?"

"Something illegal."

Olga shrugs. "Maybe." She stares at the $20 bill in Cynthia's hand.

"Somebody about my height," Cynthia adds. "Slim."

"There's a bartender like that who thinks Burns is a god." Olga nods at the money.

Cynthia hands it over. "What's her name?"

"Svetlana. She rotates shifts at the pool bars."

"What makes you single her out?"

"Svetlana would do anything to sleep with Dimple-Dumb."

At 05:00, Cynthia hears Malcolm rustling about in his room. She rises. Rather than waiting for him to sneak out, she taps on the door. "Malcolm? Are you okay?"

There follows ten seconds of more rustling followed by a click, then five seconds of absolute silence before the door opens. He is wearing a gray T-shirt and gym shorts—both unwrinkled. She guesses that he pulled them on over golden briefs.

"What?" he whispers.

She extends one arm and leans on the doorframe, a challenging pose. "You're the one who was up."

"Oh, yeah." He's trying to act half-asleep but is unconvincing.

She sees his briefcase on the desk, closed, with the corners of a few pages protruding.

"I couldn't sleep," Malcolm says. "Um, maybe we can talk for a while." He pushes past her arm and sits, perched forward on her loveseat, chin on his fist. Cynthia sits on her bed Indian style. They whisper across five feet of space that seems much narrower.

"What do you want to talk about?" Cynthia says.

"I don't know." His voice is thin, like a ghost's. "What do *you* want to talk about?"

Cynthia ponders in silence. What was he doing at the desk? She decides that this isn't the time to press.

"You never answered my question," Cynthia says. "Why you wanted *me* for your bodyguard."

"Oh, yes. I gave it a lot of thought."

"Did you? Are you ready to share those thoughts?"

"Wait here." He rises and steps into his room.

Cynthia doesn't get up to confirm that he is going to his briefcase. In ten seconds, he returns holding a folded piece of paper. "I was just finishing up," he says, sitting on the love seat. "I promised you an explanation, didn't I? Here it is—in writing." He unfolds the paper and reads. "Tonight's Top Ten List is from Malcolm Golden of Upper Montclair, New Jersey."

Cynthia is already smiling.

"The top ten reasons why Malcolm Golden selected Cynthia James as his bodyguard are:"

Cynthia's smile widens.

"Number ten," he reads. "She gives you what you pay for.

"Number nine: She's on time and serious about her work.

"Number eight: She can handle drunks.

"Number seven: None of the art snobs like her.

"Number six: Her skin is tailor-made for Caribbean sun."

Cynthia muffles her escalating laughter with both hands.

"Number five: She's easy on the eyes."

Cynthia blushes.

"Number four: Her hands are registered as lethal weapons.

"Number three: Her feet are registered as dancing weapons."

Cynthia snorts into her palm.

"Number two: She distracts everyone, including the bad guys.

"And the number one reason why Malcolm Golden wants Cynthia James as his bodyguard... She took out two would-be assassins while protecting a U.S. Senator."

Cynthia, dumbstruck, stops laughing. The fact that she killed two men was never reported. The information available for public consumption is that Cynthia thwarted an attempt on Senator Patel's life by pushing him away from a stream of bullets. According to all accounts—and the press—a police officer shot the attackers as he was slain by the assailants' fire. Such misinformation was fortunate because Cynthia had been carrying a weapon, in violation of her parole.

Cynthia unfolds her legs, stands, walks to the sliders. "I didn't kill anybody protecting Patel. You can check all the reports." Her heart isn't in the lie; deep down, her ego wants Malcolm to know what she did.

He holds eye contact, either teasing or measuring—she isn't sure which. "Okay," he says. "I guess I misinterpreted something I heard."

"From whom?"

"Doesn't matter," he says, "especially if it's not true."

Suddenly, she is feverish. She slides open the balcony slider. A breeze flutters unruly strands across her eyes.

He stands, steps close.

The hairs on her neck stiffen. Cynthia expects a kiss.

Malcolm shifts his weight and smiles. "Well, thanks for talking. Goodnight again, Cyn. Or should I say, good morning." Then he slips into his cabin and closes the door. His top-ten list remains on her comforter.

Cynthia lies in bed, rolling the left pearl ear stud between forefinger and thumb, listening to Malcolm snore. She replays his Top Ten List over and over, like counting sheep, but is unable to accelerate the exceedingly slow passage of time. She tries to scoff at number five, easy on the eyes, but a smile softens her jaw. His top ten reasons were for entertainment and should be forgotten, yet she can't forget them.

Day 5 — Wednesday

St. Maartens

37

Magic

Cynthia knocks on Malcolm's door at 7:30. "Rise and shine," she says. "We have work to do."

He groans.

"I'll bring you a muffin and coffee. Don't go anywhere until I get back."

He groans louder.

At 8:00, they eat in her stateroom, both dressed for their shore outing—she in a white T-shirt over a black bikini; he with a Hawaiian shirt over burgundy swim trunks. Although it's a beautiful morning, Cynthia has the sliders closed. She says, "I need to know where you sneaked off to the first night."

"I told you. To buy the bathing suit. You would look so—"

"Flattery won't get me out of your face today. You're hiding things—things I need to know. You were gone too long to just buy a swimsuit. Who did you go see? Sophia, right?"

After a short stall, Malcolm sighs. "Yes. She was meeting everyone on the A-list. Cliff witnessed her meeting with the countess. I'm sure Julia and John were in the mix somewhere."

"Why would the auctioneer meet bidders?"

"Sophia is... *was* very ambitious, always looking for an edge, a stepping stone. This auction was her shot at the big time.

My guess is that the museums sent their agents to feel her out—
see if there was anything they could do for her career."

"You said she was honest."

"That doesn't mean she wouldn't accept favors. That night,
she told me she was getting a thousand dollars from one of the
other bidders just to hear what they had to say."

"What did *you* pay her?"

"Nothing. Didn't have to."

"Because you two were involved?"

"No. Because I can outbid the competition."

Cynthia is dubious but doesn't say it. "Who has the second
most money?"

"The countess." Malcolm resettles himself on the loveseat.
"Like I said, totally devoted to the Louvre."

"Why would she take the cruise? Why not send an agent or
call in bids?"

"The Picasso Society named her to authenticate. And she'd
rather be alone in her cabin than anyplace with her husband."

"Does she have affairs?"

Malcolm laughs. "You're kidding, right?"

"She may not have personality, but money can be a hell of an
aphrodisiac."

"I'd be very surprised. She has such an elevated opinion of
herself that nobody is worthy. It wouldn't surprise me if she's
never had sex and adopted her only child. She married strictly for
status—his title was better than hers."

"I almost feel sorry for her," Cynthia says. "By the way, why
does the countess hate you?"

"I've outbid her on several occasions. There was one Degas
she particularly fancied. I bought it just to watch steam emanate
from that cool façade."

"Does she hate you enough to kill you?"

"Perhaps."

"What about Julia? Does she hate you, too?"

"Ah, Julia is interesting, an example of vitality and wealth
coming together in an Olympic ego." Malcolm scratches his chin
as if contemplating something important. "The truth is: we *did*
have an affair."

Cynthia isn't surprised. She considers rubbing the previous

lies into his smug face... but decides that honesty is better late than never. After a short pause, she asks, "When?"

"Ten years ago. After her first husband died. After number two checked out, Julia has auditioned me for the part, but recently, she cooled."

Cynthia gives him a "go on" nod.

"She wanted to marry me. I *didn't* want to marry her. I refuse to be the latest husband, because I don't love her. And her husbands end up dying prematurely."

"Former boyfriends, too?"

He shakes his head. "I don't think that's likely."

"But possible, if a fiery flame thought you stood between her and the Picasso, right?"

"Anything is possible, but, as I said, that would be highly improbable. She's genuinely fond of me."

"Would John Poindexter be more likely to want to kill you?"

Malcolm crosses his legs. "You know about my will, but except for... well..."

"Except for what?"

"Nothing. John is a model citizen. Great for the art world."

"*Except for what?*"

Malcolm stands and paces the room. "John's father died in murky circumstances—one of those incidents where a child with power-of-attorney tells the doctors to pull the plug. There are some who say that John was eager for his inheritance, modest as it was. But I don't believe that."

Cynthia smirks. "Yet you tell me anyway."

"Hey," he says, annoyed, "you're nagging me for dirt. I'm just giving you what I know. If you don't—"

"You're right," she says. "How old was John when this happened?"

"It was eight or ten years ago; so he was about fifty."

Cynthia stands, too. "Sounds like all three have skeletons in their closets, and each has a motive to want you dead. Sophia is already disposed of. Why aren't you more worried?"

"I *am* worried." His eyes turn steely gray. "But I refuse to run scared. I want that painting so badly I can taste it!" He sits down on the love seat and glares at a muffin, which he then flips into the trash. "Speaking of taste, what about a decent breakfast?"

"In a minute. First... about Julia. At the cocktail party, she said, '*We* won't let him get the Picasso.' Who's the rest of her 'we?' The countess?"

"Unlikely. Those two have never cooperated on anything except ruining reputations. Their museums would never join forces—far too competitive."

"Poindexter told me that they *are* together. Just to beat you."

"Don't believe it."

"He says you already know it's true."

"He's lying. Those ladies are no team."

"Then why are they hanging out together?"

"The countess has to show the flag with someone."

Cynthia touches Malcolm's wrist. "Suppose Julia didn't mean 'we won't let him get the Picasso' by *outbidding* you, but by *eliminating* you?"

Malcolm is silent.

"Who could *that* 'we' be?"

"Julia is playing with your head. She knows you'd tell me. Honestly, I don't see Julia being a 'we' with anyone. Her ego is far too big."

Where the ship docks at Phillipsburg—on the Dutch side of St. Maartens—disembarking passengers are routed through a plaza of tourist shops. Once out of the secure cruise ship zone, Cynthia and Malcolm negotiate a gauntlet of pushy taxi drivers, each begging for business. After a hundred yards, Malcolm lets the two of them get snared by a driver whose rate to Pelican Key is 30% cheaper than the ones close to the checkpoint.

After Malcolm and Cynthia rent snorkeling equipment, they seek good water on their own. The colorful fish are brilliant, the coral inspiring, but for Cynthia, dead-tired after another restless night, the experience is as flat as the ocean's surface. They swim back to shore after 35 minutes, each pretending to have seen enough. There are twenty cab drivers bidding for their return business. Malcolm selects one he recognizes, a bear named Luis, who drives them back to town.

Philipsburg is grittier than Charlotte Amalie. The people are poorer, their pitches more desperate. In Wathey Square, a young native woman in skin-tight blue jeans is so persistent hawking tours of a time-share that Cynthia wants to visit just so the girl will get a $10 bonus. Ten dollars! Malcolm is paying thousands for the cruise and willing to bid $85 million on a single painting. When Malcolm isn't looking, Cynthia slips the girl a twenty.

The relentless sun blazes hotter than yesterday, but the natives are impervious to the heat. Most women wear blue jeans—not shorts, but full length denim. Just looking at them makes Cynthia's thighs sweat. She walks the blistering streets in a daze. It's so hot that she removes the T-shirt from over her halter, soaks it in a fountain, and wraps it around her neck. Cooled, she encourages Malcolm to do the same with his Hawaiian shirt, but he insists on wearing it. She pays little attention to the clothing in the windows and bypasses every jewelry store. The shopping highlight is a sign reading: "Water $2.00; Heineken $1.99." Malcolm buys a beer for himself and a water for her—ice cold. She chugs it, bringing on instant brain freeze.

The infernal heat! She starts up conversations that worked on St. Thomas, but every topic peters out. Malcolm suggests a nude beach tour of the French side, trying to make it sound like a joke. Cynthia declines with rolling eyes. Neither smiles. The temperature has made Cynthia forget how.

At noon, they give up on recapturing yesterday's magic and agree to return to the ship for lunch. Malcolm makes a pit stop in a public restroom off a courtyard surrounded by four gift shops selling identical trinkets. Cynthia waits outside, watching the time-share girl work tourists fresh off the ship.

"Let's go around," Cynthia says when they approach a cramped flea market. Every vendor has a tent for shade, the tents defining a maze of pedestrian alleys.

"Let's look," Malcolm says. "We'll just breeze through."

She grabs his elbow. "No."

He shakes her off. "I have to pick up a gift for my nephew. This is the last chance to get something authentic. Give the bodyguard act a rest, will you? If the killer wanted me dead, he or she would have got me by now, right?"

Cynthia can't deny that. Despite her presence, he has been an easy target.

"That's what I thought," he says. "Now don't ruin the day."

Too late, she thinks.

"Just let me pick out a belt buckle for my nephew, okay?"

Against Cynthia's better judgment, she nods.

They squeeze through the shoulder-to-shoulder bazaar. She would like a pack of note-cards by a local artist but doesn't want to get distracted. Malcolm stops at a table lined with scores of belt buckles. "How much is that one?" he asks, pointing to a pewter horse-head.

The vendor is a charcoal black woman, wearing blue jeans and six colorful scarves. She looks like a voodoo fortune-teller. "Fifteen dollar," she hisses.

"Six."

"Ten."

"Seven."

The woman nods. "Seven... fifty."

"No. Seven." He makes a level slice with his hand. The woman shrugs okay. Malcolm has clearly bargained before. After letting Cynthia fondle the workmanship, he slips the buckle into his breast pocket.

After a brief stop browsing at another table, they push through a crowded aisle amid the tents. An instant after Cynthia's eyes dart right—toward a rack of flowery sarongs—Malcolm lurches into her left shoulder.

He groans, clutching his chest as if punched. He crumples to one knee, gasping.

Cynthia snaps her head to the left as she holds Malcolm's head against her hip. She swivels her neck, eyes searching for anyone retreating.

"What happened?" she says.

"Gun," Malcolm gasps. "Silencer."

So much to do in a few seconds. She reaches for his chest, she sniffs for gunpowder but smells only grilled fish. She looks for a flashing reflection.

Two seconds... No flashes. Her hand feels around his chest—no blood. She listens for a clicking gun action, running feet. There is nothing but people milling about, none of them running.

"You're hit?" she asks.

Three seconds. No gun barrel. No thin woman who looks

like the countess—just a crowd, with each tourist like a hundred others.

"Yea—" Malcolm is breathless.

Four seconds. She forces her hand under his shirt—definitely no blood. She looks up again. Somewhere, a single perpetrator escapes.

Five seconds—the attacker is lost forever. A wave of helplessness washes over Cynthia. "Shit," she mutters. "Shit, shit, shit."

She looks down at Malcolm. His right hand clutches her leg to keep himself from toppling. His fingernails bite into the skin above her knee. As he slumps, his hair slides down the moist skin of her thigh. She bends low. "Exactly where are you hit?"

"Chest," he coughs.

"Let me see." Still no blood. She kneels next to him. The multitude passes by as if there weren't two tourists on their knees in the middle of the market.

There is a tear in the pocket of his shirt—a bullet hole—surrounded by discernible powder burns. Point-blank range. She rips open his shirt. His chest is red as if hit by a hammer, but there's no puncture, no blood.

He coughs.

Her fingers feel something hard. She removes the belt buckle from his breast pocket. "Oh my God, Malcolm! Look!"

The dented horse-head is fused to a squashed bullet. They share stares of disbelief. Malcolm pulls her to his chest and whispers, "I'm so lucky," into her hair. The crowd quiets in waves of concentric circles. People recede, leaving Cynthia and Malcolm as a one-ring circus.

An old fish vendor, black as ebony, wearing an orange sarong over jeans, limps forward. "Can I help?" she says in a thick island accent.

Cynthia breaks the embrace. "No," she says. "We're okay." She stands, doesn't notice that her knees are scraped. She helps Malcolm rise and shuffle to a nearby bench. Her T-shirt is gone, but she doesn't care.

The woman follows them, pulling a cart, muttering, "Help, help." Cynthia buys three water bottles from the woman, gives her a $10 bill, says, "Keep the change."

The woman hands Cynthia a wad of paper napkins from her cart and points to their scraped knees. Then the woman backs away, smiling. Two gold teeth flash. "Help is good," she says.

Malcolm guzzles water.

"Sure you're okay?" she says.

He nods, gulps down more. Rivulets dribble off his chin.

Cynthia uses water and paper towels to wipe his chest and clean his knees, which, like hers, are purple. "We should report this," she says, moving on to her own scrapes.

He swipes the back of his hand across his mouth. "No."

"It's attempted murder!"

"But I'm okay. If we get involved, we'll get mired in red tape and miss the ship. Then I'd miss the auction."

"Is the damn painting more important than your life?" She sees in his smoldering eyes that it is. "Suppose," she says, "we don't tell the local authorities, but we tell Lt. Fist."

"No."

"You'll have to stop me then," she says, "because I'm telling him. You won't have to pay me. I'll quit. Whatever, I'm telling."

"Well..." Malcolm shakes his head. "As long as I don't have to get off the ship. I'm not filing a complaint. I'm fine. Just a little pain—as if I got hit by a baseball." He grimaces.

Cynthia's chest aches just looking at his darkening bruise. "We'll tell Fist right away," she says. "He needs to know. There's a damn good chance this is related to Sophia's murder."

"Let's just get on board before we decide anything."

"Okay," she says.

They step to the sidewalk. Five taxi drivers hawk their services. Without negotiating, Malcolm and Cynthia climb into the nearest cab.

38

Distractions

Cynthia tugs Malcolm's sleeve to get him to take the final steps into the security office. Lt. Fist sees their bathing suits and frowns. "Looking for a skinny-dipping permit?"

"This is serious," Cynthia says. "Somebody tried to kill him on St. Maartens." She unwraps the mangled buckle from a paper towel. "This was in his breast pocket. It saved his life."

Fist examines the buckle and flattened bullet. "Looks like a twenty-two. Anything more would have punched through. Still, you should have quite a bruise."

Malcolm opens his shirt. The welt is purple. Soon it will be black and blue.

"Where and when did this happen?"

Malcolm relates the time and describes the market of tents.

"Did you see who shot you?"

"No. All I saw was a barrel, silencer, and black-gloved hand receding into the crowd. It felt like I'd been slugged in the chest. My knees buckled. I went down. Then all I saw were legs."

"Did you report it to the island police?"

"No."

"Why not?"

"As a foreigner, I didn't want to get mired in red tape. If I missed the ship…"

Fist faces Cynthia, makes no effort to disguise his contempt. "And what did the *bodyguard* see?"

"My head was turned the other way. By the time I verified

that Malcolm was okay, the shooter was gone."

Fist switches back to Malcolm. "So what do you want me to do?"

"Catch Sophia's killer. We think today's shooting is related."

"Perhaps. Did you see a mysterious woman?"

"No."

Fist glares at Cynthia, says to Malcolm, "Not much we can do on land. And the shooter could have been anyone."

"But at least you have evidence," Malcolm says. "Keep the buckle and shirt. If a gun turns up, you can have it matched when we get to Florida."

Fist frowns at the buckle in his palm. "This bullet is so squashed that ballistics couldn't match it to *any* gun."

For a moment, there is silence. Then Fist says, "I have to advise the captain to cancel the auction."

"Don't do that," Malcolm says. "The auction has to go off on schedule. Too much is riding on this."

"I'll give him my advice, but knowing the captain, I expect your sacred auction will proceed against my will." Fist shifts his weight—body language for: *this meeting is over*. "I'll get on this as best I can. You let me know if you remember anything else."

"There is one thing," Cynthia says. "I have a lead. You might want to question a bartender named Svetlana. She's slim, like the mystery wine stewardess, and she would do anything for Brent Burns."

Both Malcolm and Fist raise their eyebrows. Fist says, "Where did you get this?"

"From one of Burn's jilted flames."

"Svetlana? You sure? The pool bartender?"

"Yes. That's what my source said. Svetlana."

Fist shakes his head.

"What?" she says.

"There's only one Svetlana on board. She's five-ten, a moose. I'm afraid you've been had, Ms. James."

Had to the tune of $40.

Fist excuses them with warnings to be careful. After they leave, Malcolm says, "Where did this Svetlana idea come from?"

"Drop it. I made a mistake. At least I'm trying."

After stopping in their stateroom to clean up and get Malcolm a new shirt, he and Cynthia eat a late lunch in the Zagros Dining Room. Neither talks much. She can make out the bruise through his white shirt. If she weren't so thankful he was safe, she would tear into him. He disregarded her advice—again—by entering the crowded flea market. But she's angrier at herself for not insisting.

"So," Cynthia says, "are you going to listen to me in the future about precautions?"

He nods his head. "Yes. Does that mean we circle the wagons, never leave the rooms?"

"No. We just use common sense. We don't have to worry about guns on board." After an awkward silence, she shakes her head. "You know, I felt like a failure out there. If you want to let me go..."

"I'm not going to fire you." He covers her hand with his.

The warmth is reassuring.

Although shipboard activities go on as scheduled, the *Persian Prince* is a different place for Cynthia, glitz replaced by tension, fun by distrust. They sunbathe on the Penthouse Deck to be higher than every threat, but there is no leisure. Every ten seconds, she stands, or sits, or stretches, her nervousness contagious. Malcolm twitches, becoming just as antsy. The bruise on his chest is a constant reminder of her incompetence. It takes Cynthia an hour to read five pages of Grisham.

"Let's go for a jog on the track," Malcolm says. "I need to stretch, and I could use something to take my mind off the throbbing in my chest."

Although anxious to exercise as well, she says, "No. Circling the track makes you vulnerable next to the railing. Indoor machines are safer."

The health center, located at the bow of the Sun Deck, is busy. There are nine treadmills, side-by-side, facing the island through blue-tinted Plexiglas. The second and third machines from the left are free. Malcolm and Cynthia jog without speaking. She hates the quagmire of running in place. Equally unpleasant is having CNN glare from overhead monitors. A middle-aged man, laboring to her left, drips perspiration like rain.

A swath of moving color catches Cynthia's eye. It's

Miranda, in costume, all flowers, bosom, and gems; totally out of place amid the stench of sweat. Miranda strikes up a conversation with the huffing man to Cynthia's left. He stops the treadmill and wipes his glasses.

Cynthia strains to listen. It's hard to hear over the noise of the machines, but the man obviously knows Miranda, who compliments his physique, going so far as to squeeze his sweaty bicep. Miranda mentions free massage therapy if the man purchases a deluxe beauty package for his wife. The man says he'll think about it. Cynthia pictures the perverse "beauty"—the man's wife being pampered with hot towels, cucumbers, and cream, while the husband beds Miranda.

The man turns on his machine and goes back to jogging, a smile on his flushed face.

From behind, Cynthia senses more than hears Miranda talking to someone else. Cynthia glances over her right shoulder. It's Malcolm, smiling, flirting.

There are several reasons why Cynthia considers interrupting the *tete-a-tete*, but in the end, she keeps running in place, watching their reflections in the TV screen. Still, Cynthia glances over her shoulder every few seconds. Malcolm catches her, and waves. Cynthia dislikes herself for being jealous.

When Miranda leaves the gym, Malcolm returns to his treadmill. Cynthia waits, hoping he will explain, but after he jogs in silence for a minute, she says, "What was that about?"

"Personal. Nothing to do with the Picasso. Trust me."

"Everything you do has to do with the Picasso, so I *don't* trust you.'"

"I have to stop," he says, turning off his machine. "My foot's tightening up."

They wipe down their treadmills, towel off, and drink from water bottles. Cynthia suspects that Malcolm used a non-existent cramp to divert the conversation, but she lets it go. Deep down, she's better off not knowing what he plans with Miranda.

Back in her cabin, Cynthia hesitates before stepping onto her balcony for the breeze. Malcolm, instead of heading for his shower, joins her. It is just the two of them, side-by-side. No art collectors, no Miranda. That thought gives her pause. For all the danger, all of Malcolm's misdirection, all the chaos, she is relieved to be alone with him, perspiration and all.

Malcolm has charmed her—almost out of her pants. It isn't the money. Or is that just wishful thinking? The money is why she came, isn't it? She thinks about $10,000 while standing next to him, feeling the wind cool her skin. She watches him fidget. He isn't faking his nerves. Raised veins in his forehead—which weren't visible yesterday—are real, as is a tic in his eye.

Malcolm clears his throat. "You know," he deadpans, "we should have taken that nude beach tour."

There it is: the last thing she expected. The surprise! One sentence lessens her sense of failure. She laughs. Out loud. Selfishly, she craves his energy, wants to press herself against his sweaty body as much as she has ever wanted to hold anyone. Making love would bleed the tension, stroke her ego... and be a huge mistake. He knows it, too, which is why he doesn't make a move. But he's thinking about it. She can tell.

Once he retires to his room, Cynthia exercises. Sit-ups, push-ups, crunches, over and over until breathing hard. Anything to distract her from what is taboo. Then a shower to wash away everything she sweated out. What a disastrous trip! Sophia's dead, Malcolm's been shot, and Cynthia has fallen for her client.

She lets the water run until her fingertips shrivel like prunes.

Time to dress for dinner with Fist and Billingsley—payback for the pool stunt. Apprehension gnaws at Cynthia's gut. Played straight, the evening will be tedious. If Fist isn't grilling them about the shooting on St. Maartens, the questions will be about Sophia or the pool prank. She won't be able to look at Billingsley without remembering how water dripped off his pointed chin.

Cynthia brought the perfect white outfit to contrast with her bronzed skin—a sleeveless turtleneck with matching pants that display a narrow band of midriff. Seeing herself in the mirror, she feels wicked. Perhaps she can distract the officers, keep their attentions away from the case. It's worth a try. Out comes the portable iron for a touch up. Cynthia can't resist adding purple eye-shadow to match the ship's décor. With her professional ego shaken, this is the tightrope she chooses to walk.

"What time is the dinner reservation?" she asks after walking through the adjoining door.

"Seven-thirt—" He gives her a twice-over.

"Enough time for cocktails. Give me the cabin numbers of the three other elites."

"What are you up to?" he asks.

"You'll see."

Cynthia takes the numbers and dials Julia. "Hello, Julia. This is Cynthia James. I'd like you to meet me in the Tehran Salon for cocktails at seven."

"I'm sorry," Julia says, "but the countess and I have a previous commitment."

"This won't take long. I have an important message from Malcolm, as president of the society, for all the elites. Malcolm is too ill to attend himself, so he has asked me to deliver his message."

"Malcolm is sick?" Julia gasps, now interested. "What's wrong?"

"I'll tell you all together. At seven. This is very important."

"Well, I don't know about the countess."

"You'll convince her," Cynthia says. "You're very persuasive."

"I'll see what I can do."

"Excellent," Cynthia says. "See you at seven."

She hangs up.

"What's this important announcement?" Malcolm says.

Cynthia checks her watch. "You have one hour to think of something good."

"What are you up to?"

"We'll wait for them together. When they each arrive, we'll see how your good health surprises them."

"I see now," he says. "If one of them ordered the hit, he or she may not know I returned without serious injury."

"Right. While I call Poindexter, use the other phone to call the restaurant and order a bottle of wine for the officers—in case we're late."

Cynthia and Malcolm perch on stools at the bar in the Tehran Salon, her favorite of the many lounges—the décor is straight from a Persian museum. "Remember," Cynthia says. "Watch their eyes when they see you. The ladies will probably arrive together, so you take the countess."

"Rather clever," he says.

She doesn't feel clever, just nervous. They sip Chardonnay and wait. Her glass is half-empty. It's the first time on the cruise she has consumed more than a few drops. She sets her glass on the bar.

John and Gladys Poindexter arrive promptly at 7:00. John's reaction at seeing Malcolm appears normal enough. "Glad you're feeling better, sport. What's so important?"

"Wait until the others arrive," Malcolm says, playing his part.

Gladys spurs the conversation, gushing about a St. Maartens emerald the size of a marble weighing down her right hand. Cynthia swivels on her stool so she can listen to the Poindexters while watching for the others.

Julia and the countess exit the elevator together, fashionably late. Julia wears peacock blue. The countess makes forest green appear gray.

Contrary to the stated plan, Cynthia doesn't focus on Julia's eyes—they will flash with Spanish fire, no matter what. Instead, she watches the countess—same old mannequin, except for a judgmental glance at Cynthia's midriff.

Everyone wants to know Malcolm's news, so Cynthia says, "Go on, Malcolm, tell them."

"Well," he says, "you are all invited to my New Jersey home on Memorial Day weekend for an elites-only unveiling of Picasso's Winter Prince."

"That's *it*?" Julia says.

"Always the dreamer," the countess says down her nose.

"You must be on drugs from your illness," Poindexter jests.

Julia laughs. "Ah, the joke's on us for tonight. But come tomorrow afternoon…"

"What was wrong with you, anyway?" Poindexter asks.

"Indigestion," Malcolm replies. "Probably from bad water on the islands."

Cynthia listens to the elites discuss the dangers of drinking the water in various locales around the world. She watches each of them, looking for tell-tale signs. She sees nothing.

Eventually, conversation fizzles. At 7:25, Julia and the countess excuse themselves for dinner, but the Poindexters are in no hurry. They engage Malcolm in a spirited discussion about rumors of the Louvre-Prado alliance.

Malcolm wraps an arm around Poindexter's shoulder, his wagging finger in Poindexter's face. "If what you say is true, John, then there would be rumblings in the art world...."

Cynthia sees the Dominican escort bouncing through the atrium. She breaks away from Malcolm and the Poindexters.

"*Hola*, Miranda!" Cynthia calls.

Miranda stops. "*Si.*"

"Got a minute?"

Miranda looks behind her, hesitates, then nods.

"Malcolm tells me that you're his favorite *escort*," Cynthia says, making the last word sound seamy.

Miranda manages a fragile smile. "Girlfriends and wives get wrong ideas."

"Then help me get the right idea," Cynthia says. "Can I buy you a drink?"

Miranda glances at her watch. "No liquor, but okay." They walk to the quiet end of the bar. Miranda sits on a stool. "Coke Light," she says to the Filipino bartender.

The bartender asks, "How's the diet coming?"

"Just two kilos over," Miranda says. "Getting there." She shrugs at Cynthia. "Wish I had your abs. I like real Coke, but..."

Cynthia glances at the girl's belly roll, exaggerated by sitting. No appropriate response comes to mind, so Cynthia returns Miranda's shrug. The bartender places a napkin on the bar in front of Miranda.

Cynthia shows her cruise card before glancing toward Malcolm—who is still working the Poindexters.

"So," Miranda says, her fingernails tapping on the bar.

"I was wondering how Empire Lines hired you."

Miranda smiles but doesn't reply. The bartender brings the Diet Coke, and Cynthia signs for it. They watch the bartender retreat.

"I know what you do," Cynthia says. "I know you service passengers, including Malcolm." After an uncomfortable pause and a monitoring glance toward her client, Cynthia asks, "How did Empire Lines find you?"

Miranda smiles slyly. "What, you looking for a new job?"

Cynthia laughs. Against instinct, she likes Miranda, who sports perkiness Cynthia will never regain.

Miranda takes a gulp. "I was costume girl—at a resort. For photo-ops. A man from the ship see me there and say he might hire me as tourist escort."

"Did you know what he meant?"

Miranda smiles. "My English not so good then." She drinks more cola. "But I *comprende* lots of dollars, so I go for tour, and *wow*. Ship is a palace." Miranda knocks back more Diet Coke.

Cynthia looks over Miranda's shoulder at her own employer. "Malcolm says that you want to move to the United States?"

"Sure. Why else would I sleep with men who are..." Miranda makes a see-saw "not-so-hot" motion with her hand. She glances at her watch then finishes the soda. "Thanks for the drink, but I have appointments." Miranda teeters her hand again and smiles.

They laugh together. Miranda's affability is contagious. Cynthia leans close and whispers, "Malcolm says that you're *very* good."

Miranda blushes as she slides off the stool. "I bet you good at same thing."

"Why do you say that?" Cynthia asks.

"Malcolm's other girlfriends not spend so much time with him. But he sticks close to you all day. So, you must be good all night."

It would be Cynthia's turn to blush if she had anything to blush about. "See you around," Cynthia says. She watches Miranda swivel away, then rejoins Malcolm. The Poindexters depart for the dining room.

After the older couple leaves, Malcolm says, "So what did you think of their reactions?"

"If Poindexter paid to have you shot," Cynthia says, "he's a great actor. Julia is so animated, it's impossible to say. What about the countess?"

"She flinched," Malcolm says. "Not a lot, but a definite flinch." He pauses. "Why did you want to watch Julia's reaction? Do you think she's the one?"

"Picasso was Spanish," Cynthia says. "Julia is Spanish. The Prado is Spanish. If anyone has the passion to commit a crime for this painting, it would be a Spaniard."

Cynthia keeps her own observation about the countess's reaction to herself.

Cynthia and Malcolm are fifteen minutes late to the Empire Room. The bottle of wine that Malcolm sent is half-empty, so the audience is softened up. Both officers rise from their seats. Good genes and thousands of crunches have made her abdomen worth noticing, and right now, Cynthia wants to be a distraction. Her walk toward the table is a practiced mix of elegance and athleticism, enhanced by designer pants. Locking her smile in place, she clenches her abs, showcasing the band between white garments. Yes, both officers glance. After smiles and salutations, she sits. With the table blocking their view of her midriff, she relaxes her muscles. After all, she's not a kid any more.

Billingsley sits down and extends his Ichabod Crane neck.

39

Ensign Winston Billingsley

Miss James disgusts Winston. Not just because she might be a murderess, and not because she dunked him in the pool, but because she is a typical American trollop, flaunting her body as if morality no longer matters. Yes, he noticed her entrance, but only because it's difficult not to look when a temptress struts her stuff.

Miss James may think she is God's gift to men, but Winston will not be beguiled. As shapely as she may be, it is still a 35-ish shape. Winston's wife at home in Liverpool has a 25-year-old shape—plus the discretion to cover it for everyone but him.

He is British to the core—stiff upper lip, and all—so he will resist Miss James's provocative charms, which are nothing compared to those of the costumed whores who masquerade as escorts. If those seductresses can't tempt him, the James woman certainly won't. The hard part will be suppressing his distaste. Fist never wants anyone on his staff to make a scene with passengers, even arrogant Americans. Winston always does what the boss says; he only came to dinner because Fist ordered him.

Winston disliked the James woman from the moment he saw her in that harem costume the night of Sophia's murder. After the pool incident, dislike grew to loathing. Such thoughts upset Winston. He brings his wineglass to his lips for a steadying sip. Empty. He reaches for the ice bucket. The stand is positioned so that as he leans for the bottle, he sees her abdomen around the edge of the table. She notices before he averts his eyes. The hussy probably thinks that he's interested.

"Ms. James, would you like wine?" he asks with forced civility. "It's very dry."

"Yes. Thank you." Her smile strikes him as predatory. "But just a half glass, please."

Winston smiles back—only because his commanding officer is watching. He pours her half a glass and Mr. Golden a full one before topping off Fist's and his own.

Mr. Golden offers a toast—some banal apology for being late—as if rude behavior can be excused by expensive wine. They all clink. Ms. James uses her water glass, which Winston takes as an intentional reminder of how she yanked him into the *water*. His color rises. Lt. Fist, to his left, is likely thinking about the same incident. Winston drains half his glass. Ms. James offers a second toast of her own. "To forgiveness." She is looking at Winston as she speaks.

Such unsuitable attention is disconcerting. Winston empties his glass—faster than he intends. He shouldn't have drunk any while waiting for the tardy Americans. That's another reason to abhor the slinky siren—her delayed arrival implies that *her* time is more valuable than his. Winston reaches toward the ice bucket. He can't help but peek. Blast, she catches him, again. A few idle glances made against his better judgment, and she thinks he's a cad.

Winston holds up the empty bottle.

Golden orders another.

Cynthia smiles Winston's way. She is definitely flirting—and not with her date. The ship's roster lists them in separate cabins, and Lt. Fist has told the security staff about the bodyguard-client relationship. Sweat beads on Winston's forehead. Don't fall for her act, he tells himself. Smile, be polite, don't let her under your skin.

The new bottle of wine arrives. She asks for a refill. Good breeding obliges him to comply. While he reaches for the bottle, she crosses her legs. His eyes flinch. She surely thinks that he's on the prowl.

Relax, have more wine. Treat her like just another woman. Ha! Cynthia James is not "just another woman" and never will be. She discovered Sophia's corpse—quite a coincidence. The dunking was a catastrophe. And she is a paid bodyguard. Winston wonders, only half in jest, whether Golden pays her extra for shagging.

Something is odd about her. Is it the flirting? Perhaps she is playing him for a sap. Winston juggles several hateful scenarios, but a sliver of midriff distracts him. He senses the heat radiating from her smoldering skin. More wine is needed. He reaches for it without looking, fumbles the bottle, saves it, finds himself staring straight at—

He looks up at the carved ceiling, angry to be so flustered. If an attractive woman wants to flirt, who is he to complain? If she is guilty of murder, he will catch her. After all, he is a trained security officer. He will use her wiles against her—let her distract herself.

Eat your steak, man, and figure out what the James woman had to do with Sophia's death. Remember that she has no alibi.

Cynthia has just said something to him.

"Sorry?" he says in his deepest voice.

She smiles, an invitation. "I said: it looks like Lt. Fisk could use some more wine."

Keep your hand steady, old boy, and go with the flow. Don't let Fist see that you're tipsy. There, poured without spilling a drop.

40

The Emperors' Room

"Is the crew excited to have such an important auction on the ship?" Cynthia asks Billingsley.

"I suppose," he replies, "but we always do our duty."

He's acting aloof, trying to ignore her, but she has seen enough such clumsy attempts to suspect that he likes what he sees. She uses tricks from her former life—a smile, a breath—to keep him hooked. It's like old times, play-acting to distract men. She has no purpose in mind beyond making Malcolm a teensy bit jealous. Her first alcohol of the week has made flirting fun.

For the most part, the men engage in pleasant conversation. Once, Billingsley gently presses for information about Cynthia's whereabouts prior to Sophia's murder. Cynthia excuses herself for the ladies' room. When she returns, Billingsley's focus is back where she wants it. Both officers stand as she re-enters, for the improved viewing angle, she thinks, rather than out of good manners.

As for conversation, she tosses out art terms (that Malcolm has used) without understanding half of what she says. She manages to insert "contrast" and "ambiguity" into the same sentence. The officers know even less than she, and they devour her performance. If the murder were to come up again in conversation, Billingsley might say, "Sophia who?"

The tensest moment has nothing to do with pool pranks or murder.

"I'm sorry, sir," the Romanian waiter says to Malcolm. "We

are out of Beef Wellington."

Malcolm furrows his brow. His lower lip quivers. "Why didn't you tell me that *when I ordered?*"

"I'm sorry, sir. I just found out. It's quite late and the last piece—"

"Don't give me excuses!" Blood vessels pulse at Malcolm's temples. "What am I supposed to eat now? The menu?"

Comically, the waiter presents a menu, which Malcolm swats aside. "I don't want to delay the others' food. It's late enough as it is."

Cynthia touches his hand. "We'll split my filet. I'm already full." She turns to the waiter, who nods, impatient to retreat.

Under the table, Cynthia squeezes Malcolm's thigh, just above the knee. The poor man has been shot, so his loss of temper is excusable.

"Thank you," he whispers so only she can hear. "I'm sorry."

The incident surprises her—twice. The tirade over Beef Wellington is a bad surprise, but she diffused it. The whispered apology is a good one.

Picking up her water glass, she toasts again, "To the crew. Tell me again about the computerized ballast tanks that keep my stomach from rolling."

Fist explains, but Cynthia's mind wanders. Malcolm, facing one of the biggest days of his life tomorrow, is fragile. Even if there is to be no romance, she will do whatever she can to help him gather his composure.

Malcolm's voice brings her back to the present—he compliments her outfit. He clinks her wineglass. She sips. Cynthia has made a mistake by drinking—very unprofessional. The first four nights, she consumed no more than a half glass per dinner. Tonight, she is on her second half-glass. Actually, she realizes, counting the half-glass at the Tehran Salon, it is her *third*.

She puts down the glass, pushes it toward Malcolm, telling him, "You can finish mine."

The final bites of dessert disappear. The coffee cups are empty. Almost time to go. Cynthia feels polished, proud of herself, with only the parting conversation to carry off. They push back their chairs and stand.

"I hear the singers and dancers are up at the Hanging Gardens tonight," Malcolm says.

"Where's the Hanging Gardens?" she asks, detecting a slurette in her speech.

"Will you be going?" Billingsley asks. He sways like a lofty tower in a stiff breeze.

"We're not sure," Malcolm says.

Cynthia, concentrating on enunciation, asks, "Is it anything special?"

"They put on quite a show," Billingsley says. "Code name: Dirty Dancing."

She likes the sound of that, but doesn't want to appear eager. "What do you think, Malcolm?"

He smiles. "Not our cup of tea, Cyn."

In her relaxed state, she thinks it appropriate that Malcolm call her Cyn.

During goodnights outside the restaurant, the officers each shake her hand, then take their leave.

Malcolm removes a folded cruise schedule from his coat. "It says there's karaoke in the back lounge. Could be worth a few laughs." He's calm, himself again.

After a 150-yard walk, they slip into the last row of cocktail tables and watch the current singer on several huge monitors. It's Francesca Goode. Although she sings a plucky "Man, I Feel Like a Woman," Shania Twain's rank in pop music is safe. "That was unfortunate," Malcolm says. Without consulting Cynthia, he orders two margaritas from a roving cocktail waitress.

"I'll have water," Cynthia tells the waitress.

"*And* two margaritas," Malcolm adds. "I order you to have a drink with me, Cyn. We should unwind tonight. It's okay to laugh at American Idol wannabes."

"Ten bucks says you can't do any better."

"You're on," he says. "Watch me." Before she can laugh, he's striding toward the MC's booth. Her eyes pop. She would have bet serious money that Malcolm was *not* a karaoke man.

She considers following him—to stay close on the job—but she can see him fine from her seat. He *does* look fine, moving with assurance. It's a treat to admire him without hiding it.

Minimal wine has gone to her head. She shouldn't have any more alcohol. Absolutely.

The water and two margaritas arrive. Malcolm isn't there—the only person to argue with is herself. Drinking margaritas would encourage the naughty ideas percolating in her head—and between her legs. So she sips the water.

Ten minutes and two forgettable Karaoke performances later, Malcolm Golden takes the mike. "Some-*where*... beyond the *sea*..." Malcolm sounds more like Bobby Darin than Bobby Darin. Cynthia isn't the only woman hooting encouragement all the way to the last line: "And never again, I'll go *sail*-ing."

When he arrives back at their table, she throws her arms around him, a hug worthy of a girlfriend. "You were fabulous."

He holds her lower back, where his hands warm her skin.

The waitress appears for Malcolm's cruise card, which he fumbles onto the floor by Cynthia's feet. She bends down and picks it up. The waitress copies his number and glides away.

"Have your drink," he says holding the full margarita up to her.

"No thanks." Cynthia sips more water. The next performer can't carry a tune.

Five minutes later, Cynthia feels more buzzed than when she left the restaurant. The last half-glass of wine must be kicking in. She downs the rest of her water, but is still thirsty. "I need some more water," she mumbles, feeling dizzy.

"Here," Malcolm says, handing her a glass.

It doesn't smell like water, but she drinks. Margarita. *How did I get drunk so fast?* Strangely, it doesn't seem to matter. "Your singing was great," she slurs, willing her head to stop spinning.

They each celebrate the night by downing half a margarita. The alcohol mellows her brain, but the ship keeps right on sailing. Mystical kisses bathe the inside of her skull—she's past drunk now, on the way to downright blitzed.

She laughs at something he says—nothing in particular. The party is just getting started. Her reflexes may be dulled, but her street-smarts remain keen enough. Be unpredictable, keep moving, go places they never frequent, and nothing bad will happen. "Wheretonext?" she says. "Thenight'syoung."

"What about the dirty dancing? Let's check it out."

Hearing him say the words makes her feel sexy; she rationalizes away the last vestige of common sense. An assassin won't suspect them at the late-night disco, so it will be okay to entertain her fantasy. She offers him a flirty smile and sways to her feet. Malcolm takes her hand and tugs her toward the door.

Exiting the lounge, Cynthia almost bumps into Francesca Goode, who, tonight, shows no tanning lines. Her escort is the dimpled auctioneer, Brent Burns.

41

Brent Burns

Brent has the perfect job. He gets paid to sell art to unfulfilled women who flock around him as if he were a movie star. Every new cruise supplies a steady stream of admirers to supplement the best-endowed females in the crew. He flashes his radiant smile and takes his pick. Relationships with passengers—the less meaningful, the better—last no longer than seven days and never progress past harmless petting. He pushes women away before they discover he has no interest in commitment. Best to keep things on the surface, one pretty façade to another.

Brent is a breast man, so he focuses on the bodaciously buxom—like the lovely Francesca, currently on his arm. Burns's credo: spend a week getting to second base, and make every feel count. He has no delusion of respect for the woman behind the breasts. Someday he may outgrow his sophomoric fetish, but until then, let the good times roll.

Brent and Francesca amble past Cynthia James, who scares the piss out of him. He feels her distrusting eyes x-ray his core. Under different circumstances, he might have made a pass at her, but she got Fist onto his case, and she doesn't have as much up front as Francesca.

He glances down Francesca's dress—a dose of inspiration. Five days of anticipation are about to conclude with a victory. He licks his lips. "Still want to see the vault?" he whispers, knowing she craves a private tour. One more drink, and she'll be ripe.

Brent deserves a little quality time with Francesca's breasts.

Since Sophia's untimely demise, work has been a bitch with a capital B. He's sorry she was murdered and all, but he had no idea how much work Sophia did behind the scenes. There's been non-stop Picasso hoopla, auction preparation, interviews with the press, plus being hounded by the bidders. Dinner with Julia Sotelo was fun, but Countess LaCroix is one of the few women alive who makes his blood run cold.

The worst has been Lt. Fist, interrogating Brent as if he bumped off Sophia for her position. Only a demented type-A workaholic would want that stupid job. The hassle isn't worth all those questions about room service stewardesses whom Brent might have seduced. Aside from Francesca, the week has been a living hell. Brent can't wait until *Persian Prince* gets a new head auctioneer, so he can go back to doing what he does best, what he has missed out on this week... but what he's finally getting to now.

Brent stops and squeezes Francesca's hand. The auctioneer's office is right around the corner. "Wait. I need to block the camera. You're not really allowed in after hours." He pulls over a chair then stands on it. "Ready?" She nods. He covers the lens with an art brochure. "Go. Quick."

Francesca scurries around the corner and into the office as nimbly as stiletto heels allow. He lowers the brochure after three seconds—a blackout that will merely look like a blip of bad pixels. Walking normally, he steps into the camera's field of vision then out of sight. It's not an ingenious trick, but nobody ever reviews the tapes.

She presses shoulder to shoulder. "This is so exciting, Brent. I can't wait."

Neither can Brent. His eyes are on the zipper running up the back of her white dress. He rubs his fingertips together and spins the combination dial. The metaphor is inspiring.

42

Margaritaville

It's ten or so minutes after a number Cynthia can't read on her fuzzy watch when she and Malcolm exit the elevator at the Hanging Gardens of Babylon, a discothèque aft on Deck 18. The club is a greenhouse, with artificial flowers suspended from the ceiling in Persian carpet patterns. She is disappointed to hear a DJ instead of live music—such a waste with so many talented musicians on board.

Billingsley wasn't kidding about dirty dancing. Tonight's gimmick is that the ship's singers and dancers, dressed in slinky show costumes, invite passengers to bump and grind. To provide inspiration, seven large TVs display scenes from the movie *Dirty Dancing* while the sound track blares. There are prize raffles to lend respectability to the pairings, but pseudo-sex is the real draw. The crowd is raucous, the dancing steamy. More hands are on buttocks than not. Cynthia scans the patrons, seeing mostly young adults whom she hasn't noticed over the course of five days. Malcolm is the oldest person present. She may be second—a sobering thought, which she needs in her current state.

The walk hasn't revived Cynthia, who is vaguely aware of being drunk, but she's not sure how it happened. Three half-glasses of wine hit her like thirty. The margarita hardly mattered—she was already gone. She pulls Malcolm close enough to be heard over the thudding baseline. "Since they're selling sex, how come the escorts aren't here?" Her sluggish tongue feels twice its normal size.

"Night is their big-money time," he says. "This"—he waves at the dancers—"is chicken feed. Empire runs it for fun."

Several hands beckon them onto the dance floor. "What's the deal?" she shouts at the nearest singer, a young, muscle-bound Tony Bennett.

The music's volume makes it difficult to hear. From the singer's hand signals and moving lips, Cynthia guesses that $20 buys a drink, raffle ticket, and a dirty dance with one of the entertainers. She nods at Malcolm, who orders two more margaritas and charges them on his room card.

"Sure this is a good idea?" she shouts into Malcolm's ear.

"What can it hurt? Stop working. Have a good time, and see what happens."

See what happens. Cynthia knows nothing good can come from her guard being down, even as she sips her next margarita. But she rationalizes: since being sober hasn't prevented one murder or a second attempt, what the heck?

Maurice Williams's "Stay" plays over the sound system. Kitty, a feline dancer in half a costume, pairs off with Malcolm. The muscular singer—appropriately, his name is Raul—grinds with Cynthia. The dancing is more hand-to-haunches than feet-to-floor. Based on her form-fitting pants, Cynthia is asking for it, so she goes with the flow. The alcohol helps. After she gets used to Raul's palms sliding where they don't belong, the pelvic pumping is therapeutic, not sleazy. Well, maybe a little sleazy. She pretends that Raul is a terrorist whom she has been assigned to eliminate.

The song ends. Raul excuses himself to entice other passengers. She looks for Malcolm, but he's hooked up with another dancer, this one a willowy blonde. Cynthia is surprised to see Ensign Billingsley talking with one of the male bartenders. Cynthia wants to make Malcolm jealous, so she sneaks behind the towering ensign. Billingsley turns when she taps his shoulder.

"MayIhavethisdance?" She presses herself into his chest.

"I don't think so," he says, stepping back, wide-eyed.

"Why not, Winnie?" the bartender says in an Aussie accent. "You're off duty, mate, and the sheila obviously fancies you."

The bar blocks Billingsley's retreat. Cynthia pivots so that her back is tight to his front, a position from which she can see

Malcolm dance with his surfer girl. Cynthia takes Billingsley's huge hands and presses them to her abdomen. "I'veseenyou looking," she slurs. "Nowyoucantouch."

Billingsley shakes off her grip. "You're drunk, Ms. James. I suggest that we both forget about this indecent... whatever it is." He stomps out of the lounge.

Useless flat foot, she thinks, although the word "thinks" is over-stating her current mental capabilities. She sees what looks like her margarita on a cocktail table, staggers over, and downs it, spilling some on her white pumps. No pain, no inhibitions. The current song from the *Dirty Dancing* soundtrack is "In the Still of the Night." She cuts in on Malcolm and Barbie Doll so that client and bodyguard can finally get dirty.

Malcolm does a decent Patrick Swayze impersonation for two minutes of simulated sex. Together, they undulate like the untamed sea. She thinks: all is right in this screwed up world.

Tequila drowns her last qualms; all sense of responsibility evaporates in the pulsing beat. Any woman who says that alcohol is a depressant has never been inebriated while Malcolm Golden pressed close. He slows the tempo of their affection—his lips kissing her ear without quite touching. She smiles, thinking: *he's doing this with me, not Miranda.*

"You knew about this smut dancing," she mumbles. "You just wanted an excuse to feel my ass."

"Did I need an excuse?"

She thinks, no, but lets her hands say it—squeezing his back. It has taken Malcolm, the Caribbean, and alcohol five days to seduce her.

Their stroll toward the cabins is roundabout foreplay—down a corridor, into an elevator, out onto an unfamiliar landing. "We should get you some air," he says before leading her outside. Too tired to speak, Cynthia clutches a railing with both hands. She thinks it may be the Sun Deck, or maybe the Sport Deck—one of those S-decks. The breeze evaporates perspiration on her tingling midriff. She's feverish, motions for another margarita. Malcolm says, "Sure." A bartender at an out-of-the-way lounge pours them what tastes like two waters a tick before closing. Cynthia slurps hers like a castaway. She excuses herself for a much-needed trip to the ladies' room and the best pee of her life.

Amidships on whatever-the-hell-deck it is, they pause to star-gaze. When he doesn't kiss her, anticipation builds. Swollen breasts press against her bra. Deep breathing does what she hopes his fingers soon will... and his lips. Her high is exhilarating. Every delay makes the impending first kiss that much more necessary.

Cynthia weaves down the hall on Malcolm's arm. Her shoulder bumps the wall, and he steadies her. The ship must have hit rough seas. She can't get her ID card out of her tiny purse, so Malcolm opens her door.

Inside her stateroom, she takes a deep breath, leans into his chest. The tension, shared experiences, pleasurable diversions, all culminate in this moment, this connection. Sure it's wrong, but she doesn't care. Call it Tequila Therapy.

He rubs her bare waist, his fingers gentle as evening mist. She flinches, giggles, closes her eyes, parts her lips.

"Goodnight," he whispers. His lips peck her forehead.

"Nomoreteasing," she murmurs.

"No tease. It's time to say goodnight."

"Not yet." She flutters lashes over her fogged eyes; then, when he doesn't react, she goes up on tiptoes.

He pulls away. "Not like this."

Her legs wobble. She wishes she could go back in time and decline those last few margaritas. She blinks. Again. And again. *Malcolm can't be rejecting me, can he?*

"If we're to be lovers," he says, "don't you want to be sure? And sober?"

Her head nods as her body presses forward.

He eases her away. "I agreed to your deal—no fooling around."

She remembers how he made fun of her old-fashioned expression. Now, she wishes she never said it. "Thatwasthen." Does she sound as desperate as she feels?

"And we should both be sober."

"I thought you wanted—"

"Not like this," he says. "Not without both of us being in control. You deserve that much. *We* deserve that much."

Anything is allowable to get what she wants. In one motion,

she pulls her top over her head. He's wavering; she can tell by the way he stares at her bra. But he shakes his head and says, "What are you doing?"

Here, the alcohol fails her, blocks all synapses.

He shakes his head again. Sadly. "We can't do this."

"Why not? Because you're my client?"

"No. Because you're better than this. Say goodnight, Cyn."

That's it? Cynthia's head spins like she's in a dryer. The door between rooms has indeed closed, and Malcolm is on the other side. For a moment, she stands, tottering. Then she staggers to the closet for her sleepwear, but she has trouble staying upright. More heavy seas? Lie down, she tells herself—hold on until the storm calms. She flops on the mattress. Prone atop the spinning bed, she starts to wriggle out of her pants but is fast asleep before either leg is freed.

43

Fifth Night

Lying on a beach, Cynthia listens to Malcolm breathe, over and over, so slowly that at times she fears he has stopped. The exhalations, loud and distorted, vibrate her eardrums, as if his breath were on her skin. He's a client, ten years older, yet she can't stop... Stop what? The emotions or the sensations? She hears waves break in the distance. Might he change his mind and come to her?

She holds her breath...

When he approaches, she isn't surprised.

He brings tanning oil. A whole jug, smeared thick on her backside, from the nape of her neck to the hollows in the bottoms of both feet. His arms are pythons, slithering over her shoulders and thighs, twisting underneath. Erotic, primal, evil. She passes the point of no return, lost in the arousing pulse. She can't remember how he persuaded her to wear an orange thong to the nude beach. The untied top lies on the towel beneath her, and his teeth pull loose the second of two bows that hold... formerly held the bottom. He knows exactly where to spread the oil, and how—with his lips and tongue. Then her responsive twitching wakes her.

For a moment, she is aware of firm nipples and a heart thumping in her chest. Then reality. She is pathetically alone. Disappointment drains her self-esteem. She checks the bedside clock—5:02 a.m. No beach, no thong, no oil, no Malcolm. Just her sweaty skin and pounding head. She squeezes her temples, as if she can push out the pain, but no such luck.

Cynthia shakes out of her clothes, tugs on her sleep T-shirt and shorts, cracks the door. For the longest moment, she stares. He's asleep, maybe dreaming. Cynthia shuts the door and crawls back into bed. Her gut twists—nothing has changed. Except that her head needs thirty aspirins. Did she really beg?

A tidal wave rolls up her stomach. Cynthia races surging vomit to the toilet bowl. The vomit wins.

She would pay the whole $10,000 to go back twelve hours in time. Instead, her brain rolls inside her revolving skull like a giant roulette marble. Round and round, rolling slower and slower until it bumps and jumps. Just when her bouncing brain is about to settle, the rolling starts all over again.

Where the hell is the fucking aspirin? And the damn Pepto-Bismol? Every muscle aches. The bowling ball inside her brain explodes into gravel. She will never touch tequila again.

Day 6 — Thursday

At Sea

44

Game Day

Cynthia isn't sure how best to apologize, or if an apology is even in order. Sure, she got drunk, which let lust out of the bag. But even in the fog of her hangover, she knows that Malcolm has been finessing her all week, and the margaritas and dirty dancing that wilted her resolve were his ideas, weren't they? The knot inside her chest tightens. How presumptuous $10,000 made her.

She swallows three more Tylenols, presses fingertips to her throbbing temples. Time to face the music. Knock very lightly. *Tap-tap-tap.*

"Come in." His voice booms like exploding dynamite.

She grimaces.

Malcolm offers an assured smile. "Last night never happened, okay, Cyn? It was a release from the shooting. Old news. Today, we pick ourselves up. I have a masterpiece to buy."

"You should fire me."

"Nonsense. I'm going to buy the Winter Prince, and you're going to see that I get home safely."

A screw tightens her forehead above the left eye. "Can we really forget about last night?"

"Forget about *what*?" He smiles. "Maybe we need a do-over.

I meant what I said. You weren't yourself. I chose to give you the respect you would have demanded if you hadn't been drunk."

She squeezes out a smile that hurts the roots of her hair. "I promise: no more alcohol."

"Me, too. How about breakfast? We could order Eggs Benedict in the dining room."

The thought makes her nauseous. Her quivering body craves a Bloody Mary, but she settles for two cups of coffee.

During the morning sunbathing hour, Cynthia and Malcolm recline in the shade. Still, she requires sunglasses plus a visor, and squints to minimize the ache caused by reflected light. If she were to stop breathing, that might help. Every gentle rock of the ship feels like a roller coaster. She couldn't possibly be the bodyguard to a billionaire, waiting for the afternoon auction of a priceless Picasso.

She needs distractions. Talking hurts more than listening, so she whispers, "Tell me again why this event is on a cruise ship, instead of at a big New York auction house?"

"Because—"

"Shhh. Softer."

"Sorry," he whispers. "Because Empire Lines owns the painting. It's a fascinating story. Didn't I already tell you?"—She barely moves her chin side-to-side—"Do you want the long or short version?"

"Give me the baby bear version," she says.

"Okay. Empire's a huge operation. With warehouses for their warehouses—"

Cynthia winces. "Don't make me laugh."

"Sorry. About five years ago, an Empire buyer, who was about to be fired, bought four crates of sports memorabilia at an auction in Bayonne, New Jersey. The sports memorabilia market is shady at best—lots of unauthorized garbage, forged signatures, five thousand copies of a one-hundred-run limited edition. Hero-worshipers are easy marks."

Cynthia nods too emphatically, sloshing muddy brains in her skull.

"So, knowing the buyer's track record, Empire thought it was worthless junk. Two years went by. The fired buyer died of liver disease. Then the auctioneer died. Sophia Caporetto was assigned to clean out a warehouse in Ft. Lauderdale, which is where the memorabilia sat collecting dust. She found the Picasso in a secret compartment of a distinctive crate. By all logic, it had to be a forgery, but her nose told her otherwise. She brought in experts from the Picasso Society, including me. We confirmed that it was, indeed, painted by Pablo Picasso.

"When I saw the Winter Prince, I knew I had to have it." Malcolm has a far-away look in his eyes. "But ownership papers, if there ever had been any, were long gone. The painting wasn't known, wasn't stolen, wasn't anything but a Picasso appearing out of thin air. So what does Empire do?"

Cynthia offers a tiny shrug.

"They publicize a world-wide search for the owner. It was in the papers. Didn't you read about it?"

She shakes her head—barely.

"Hundreds of fortune-seekers came out of the woodwork, many with fake inventories that 'proved' ownership. Most were eliminated out-of-hand, but a few of the cleverest advanced to an arbitration council, where all claims were eventually denied. Nobody could identify the box, the kind that even a blind owner would have remembered because of ornate carvings.

"Meanwhile, some of Picasso's family and several museums, including the Prado, claimed the painting. There was a two-year legal battle, after which the cruise line's possession was ruled to be ten-tenths of the law—by an international tribunal."

Cynthia slides to the edge of her chaise.

"So the case went all the way to the International Arbitration Committee, which ruled in favor of Empire a year ago. At that point, Empire had to decide what to do. Their legal fees were already deep into seven figures, so the CEO wanted to go through Sotheby's and wash his hands of the whole mess. But Sophia was savvier than that. She saw the marketing potential—she coined the name Winter Prince. She showed how the company would save over ten million dollars in taxes by selling in international waters. Unfortunately, the executives didn't listen to a lowly woman auctioneer. Enter Captain Dirk De Vries. He envisioned mountains of free publicity for the company and for *his* ship. He had the clout to get the matter a fair hearing, and he won the executives over. After the company agreed—that auctioning the Picasso was a smart move—using the *Persian Prince* was a no-brainer. It's their largest ship. This cruise sold out two days after the auction was announced."

Cynthia wonders how Malcolm booked two rooms when she hadn't agreed to come until a few weeks ago. Then she realizes that he would have gotten somebody else.

"The Picasso Society, after guaranteeing authenticity, made security requests: a locked vault, overlapping verification procedures, inspection of all art leaving the ship—my ideas, incidentally. Empire made the modifications and tripled ticket prices for the cruise. That's an extra ten million in fares. They'll clear another sixty million on the Picasso—maybe more. Plus, the publicity has increased sales on all their winter cruises. Pretty nice return on a forgotten crate of autographed photos."

Cynthia almost smiles. Her hangover has been tamed by Malcolm's voice.

After the story, Malcolm can't sit still. If he isn't in the men's room, he's stretching his legs, which means taking a walk through the ship, which means that Cynthia goes with him. More miles of Persian carpets. Each walk starts in a different direction but invariably leads them to the Empire Theatre on Deck 7 where Malcolm observes the event set-up.

Normal auctions take place in Alexander's Lounge, but today's is anything but normal. Empire Lines is auctioning off several 20th century masterpieces, including the Winter Prince, the most valuable available painting in the world. Seating is by reservation only, 750 seats for 3,500 passengers. Tickets, priced at $100, are being scalped for $500.

Cynthia jests, "The auction should be treated like other extravaganzas in the theater, with an early and late show. That way, twice as many passengers could fork over a hundred bucks."

Malcolm doesn't laugh.

While he obsesses about the Picasso, Cynthia worries about protecting him after he buys it. She will restrict his shipboard movement, of course; they will eat in the cabins. Unbeknownst to Malcolm, she has requested that Fist provide a hallway guard outside their rooms. Fist hasn't said yes, but he hasn't said no.

At 10:50 a.m., Malcolm and Cynthia leave the chaises and swing past their rooms to change for the sign-out procedure. She dresses in her least sexy outfit: a burgundy blouse with black pants, neither with any cling. She knots a black scarf around her neck. Malcolm appears in beige slacks and a white golf shirt. They hurry downstairs where they meet Burns and the other Picasso Society elites in the auctioneer's office. Poindexter and Julia have on shorts, but the countess wears a dress. With Ensign Billingsley and two porters present, the room is stuffy. Nervousness is contagious—after curt hellos, there is no conversation.

Brent Burns opens the safe. The porters carry the Picasso's case out into the office and set it on a rolling cart, which to Cynthia looks like what she used to buy sheetrock at Home Depot. Burns stands by with a clipboard. One by one, the Picasso Society elites verify that the initialed date-time stamp tapes are undisturbed from Sunday.

After the Dali and the Chagall are added to the trolley, the porters roll it into the hall, followed by the elites, who walk reverently toward the elevators, reminding Cynthia of a funeral procession. John Poindexter says, "We can't all fit in the elevator with the paintings. I'll take it from here with Burns."

"I should come, too," Malcolm says. "After all, I'm the Preside—"

Julia puts a hand on his shoulder. "It's John's job as Treasurer."

Cynthia tugs Malcolm away from Julia. "Let it go. You want an early lunch, right?"

"I suppose," Malcolm sighs.

Cynthia and Malcolm watch the elevator door close on Burns, Billingsley, Poindexter, and two porters cramped with the cart supporting three cases. Malcolm looks like a parent sending his child off to camp.

45

The Main Event

Malcolm wants to eat early so his food will be completely digested before the 2:30 p.m. auction. Cynthia agrees, although food still nauseates her. And every bite not eaten will help—in five days, she has gained three pounds.

They eat in the Darius Dining Room, where Malcolm shovels down his lunch and snaps at the waiters. The two of them don't talk. Cynthia picks at a Cobb salad. His tapping toe frays her nerves. At 12:15, she says, "Why don't we take our bodies down to the theater? You're already there in spirit."

They hustle back to the cabins to shower and change—he into a tuxedo befitting the President of the International Picasso Society, she into something suitable for the date of one so important—her black-knit pantsuit with turtleneck.

When Malcolm and Cynthia arrive at the Empire Theater, there is a line at the security checkpoint—two scanners plus more wands than a Harry Potter convention. Malcolm asks for and receives an official bidding paddle—number 101. Still, they reach their first-row seats an hour early. Picasso's Winter Prince, uncased, flanked by guards, sits on an easel, center stage, in front of plush purple curtains. In the giant theatre, the painting looks pathetically small. A female string quartet plays Mozart from the far right of the stage. An empty podium stands to the left. Behind it are several tables, draped with purple fabric and boasting a bank of telephones.

High on the side walls, flanking the curtain, hang two giant

TV screens displaying slides of Picasso's paintings. Of course, Malcolm can't sit still. He paces the front left aisle, back and forth like a psychotic zoo animal. At 2:15, he squeezes Cynthia's hand. "They need me on stage for pre-auction ceremonies. I'll stay in sight."

Cynthia sits in her seat on the far left of the first row—near the stairs to the stage. Her eyes dart around the theater, purple and glitzy, not a pillar in sight—one of many engineering marvels inside a gigantic marvel. Two rows behind her, in the center, Anton the Illusionist sits between Carlotta and a blonde pixie whom Cynthia assumes to be the understudy, Phoebe. Every seat is filled. People jam into standing room at the back. She spies tall Ensign Billingsley at the rear portside entrance.

The pre-auction hoopla is refined—string quartet in pink gowns, soft spotlights, nobody does the wave. Cynthia watches Malcolm on stage in a photo op with his fellow Picasso Society dignitaries—Countess LaCroix and Julia Sotelo. Each wears a red and yellow Society ribbon, which in the case of the countess, spices up her drab gray suit. From what Cynthia knows of Picasso, gray is all wrong.

The ship's photographer, a human walrus named Ferd, cajoles John Poindexter to join the others next to the Picasso.

"Get a shot with Julia scrutinizing the painting like Sherlock Holmes," Poindexter suggests. He volunteers a magnifying glass from his coat pocket. Ferd composes the shot. Julia leans close, peering at the painting. "Ready?" Ferd says. "More to the side."

Julia ignores the photographer and bends awkwardly to get a closer look at the lower right corner of the painting. She wobbles and drops the magnifying glass, its metal rim bouncing on hardwood.

"Malcolm," Julia murmurs, her voice a mere echo. "Take a look at the signature."

Malcolm kneels, picks up the magnifying glass, and focuses on the signature, with Julia peering over his shoulder. "What do you think?" she asks.

"The A is all wrong," Malcolm says, his voice rising in pitch. "If this is somebody's idea of a joke, it isn't funny!"

The countess wheezes.

Spectators react to the body language on stage. A wave of

silence rolls over the first few rows, spreading rearward. The musicians abandon Mozart in mid-measure.

"Burns," Malcolm growls at the auctioneer. "We have a problem."

"What do you mean?"

"This painting is a forgery!" Malcolm's announcement is heard back in standing room—the hanging microphones work perfectly. Silence becomes contagious. Cynthia hears Brent Burns's shoes clip across the stage.

"That can't be!" Burns yanks the glass from Malcolm, then squints at the painting. "Fuck. I'll have to call Fist." Sweat beads on his forehead. He fumbles with his walkie-talkie.

Every passenger in the theater cranes forward, Cynthia included.

The countess, pale as death, clenches both fists. "What does this mean?" she wails to no one in particular.

"It's a fake!" Malcolm calls. "The signature's all wrong."

The bombshell is out. A buzz like a billion cicadas infests the theater. Cynthia, her hangover erased by a far worse feeling, bounds up the far left stairs.

"Was the signature painted over?" the countess asks, desperation squeaking in her thin voice.

"No," Malcolm says. "It has other discrepancies. There on the side." He gestures. "Not his brushwork at all."

"Impossible," the countess huffs. "I verified it myself."

"We all did," Piondexter says. "But that was four days ago. Now, it's as phony as an eighty million dollar bill."

"John," Malcolm says to Poindexter. "You. You were with the painting. What happened?"

"I… I re-verified the seals were unbroken, then I checked the phone banks and backstage wiring. Burns and the porters set it up on the easel. I never dreamed…"

Malcolm spins toward the auctioneer and spits, "Burns?"

"I didn't look at it that closely. Why would I? Honest. How would I tell? I'm just an assistant." His voice evaporates. "It looks the same. Doesn't it?"

The countess twitches her nose; even the white drains from her face. "This is a nightmare," she whimpers. "A nightmare… My Picasso…" She slumps into Poindexter's arms.

Malcolm shakes his head as if staring at a ghost. "First Sophia, now this." He drops to his knees. His face contorts like crumpled paper.

Lt. Fist's voice barks from behind the curtain on Cynthia's side of the stage. "Have Maynard's squad seal all entrances and the backstage area. Get a man at every door. Have them search every bag or package bigger than a Walkman.... Strap sidearms on the kitchen staff if you have to. Then we search backstage with a fine-tooth comb. We have to find that painting. Out."

Fist pushes through the curtains and strides toward Burns. "The auction is cancelled," Fist states. "Make an announcement. Have the people leave via the rear exits—only when their row is called. My men will search everyone on their way out. Everyone but those on stage and all stagehands. *They stay.*"

Burns taps the microphone. *Thud-thud-thud.* "L-ladies and g-gentlemen," he stutters, "due to unforeseen events, today's art auction has been temporarily postponed. Please wait until your row has been—"

Few in the back hear the rest of his announcement over the rumbling drone. The uproar turns into a hostile interrogation by those with the loudest voices.

"What's going on?"

"What about the Picasso?"

"Who's in charge?"

"Was it stolen?"

"What about a refund?"

Burns cringes behind his hands, unable to repeat the announcement.

Security officers, supplemented by deck hands, escort passengers toward the rear, where everyone is searched.

While the evacuation proceeds, Fist lines up the major players on stage like they are misbehaving third-graders: The countess, Julia Sotelo, John Poindexter, Malcolm, Burns, the art auction staff, the theater crew, the porters, plus high-profile spouses, dates, and groupies like Gladys Poindexter, Cynthia, and Francesca Goode. Cynthia holds Malcolm's hand, but a security officer separates them, moving Cynthia to the far right of the stage.

Fist, his face now pink, glares at the experts. "Are you

absolutely positive this is a forgery?"

Malcolm and the countess are too shaken to speak.

"Yes," Julia croaks.

"And not even a very good forgery, at that," Poindexter adds. His is the only voice with strength. "This is definitely *not* the painting that was locked away on Sunday."

Fist stares at Burns. "Any chance the real one's in the vault?"

"Unlikely, but a porter is checking now."

"*My* men will look. Behind every frame. Check every package in there."

"Don't get your hopes up," Poindexter says. "If someone took the Picasso out of its case, they didn't do it to play hide and seek."

"Then tell me how someone could have done this."

"An inside job," Poindexter says, glancing at Burns, who gulps.

Fist asks, "Why do you say that, Mr. Poindexter?"

"The lockdown procedure guarantees that one auctioneer and three experts verify the painting when it's put away. The *real* painting was locked up Sunday afternoon. Between then and now, only the crew had access. Today, the painting was transported by the crew, so an Empire crew member has to be involved."

"Is that right, Burns?" Fist asks.

Burns's knees buckle.

"Get him out of here before he faints," Fist says. "Hold him in the dressing room." Fist issues a barrage of crisp orders to several security officers. One escorts Burns backstage. Another hurries up the aisle. A third calls the captain. Ensign Billingsley hustles to the video surveillance room.

Fist faces his prime suspects. "Find a seat in the first few rows. Leave at least two empty seats between each of you. And no talking. Raise your hand if you need the loo. We'll bring in dinner if we have to. We may be here a while."

Cynthia guides Malcolm off the stage as if he were blind. He tries to speak, but manages only faint gurgling sounds.

Waiting out a series of backstage interrogations, Cynthia sits two seats away from Malcolm in the first row. With arms extended, their fingers touch. He can't seem to focus his eyes. She pats his hand... cold.

Cynthia remembers the framed Wyland, now on its way to her Boonton Township address. Is Malcolm feigning grief? Did he somehow steal the Picasso and smuggle it out in the package? No, she, Billingsley, and Burns witnessed the inspection—backing, print, matting, and frame. No hidden masterpiece.

But still.... Malcolm is *obsessed* with the Picasso. Suppose Poindexter is right—that Malcolm *can't* afford it. She wonders: was there another way that he could have stolen the painting? The only time he escaped her surveillance long enough to repackage a painting was Saturday—the first night—but three other experts verified the Picasso the next afternoon.

The theft and Sophia's murder are surely related. Sophia was either involved and then eliminated by a co-conspirator, or else was removed to facilitate the robbery. As spineless as he appears, Burns is a suspect in either scenario.

Cynthia glances around to assess behavior.

Julia's hand-fan is all that keeps the countess from re-fainting. Cynthia hypothesizes that the two women could have done it together—the countess being the mystery champagne murderer.

Cynthia scans the auction staff: five phone-bank operators and two porters who transported the paintings to the theatre. Did any one of them have access to the vault? Or were any of them alone with the Picasso during today's set-up? If so, the painting could be anywhere on the ship. If the Picasso was stolen *after* Wednesday afternoon—after the ship departed St. Maartens— then the painting must be onboard. Where would Cynthia hide the painting if *she* had stolen it? She thinks: someplace so obvious that it won't be searched.

She flips open her pocket notebook. By the time Burns is led out from his backstage interrogation and up the aisle toward the rear exit, Cynthia has devised an outline of scenarios.

I.) theft inside the vault, or II.) theft outside the vault. Under "inside," she lists: I.A.) walls penetrated, I.B.) safe cracked, and I.C.) door opened in normal operation. Item "I.B." is plausible, given the limited security. The vault could have been opened in preparation for the Monday auction, which was cancelled after Sophia's murder, or for other art deposits or withdrawals. The security camera outside the auctioneers' office *might* show someone going in. Remembering her comment about tampering with the system, she underlines the word <u>might</u>.

Item "I.B." (safe cracked) is related to "I.C." (door opened normally) in that the video surveillance system would have to be bypassed. She circles "I.B." and "I.C." together and writes, "Through the door." Item "I.A." (wall penetration) is more intriguing. Cynthia would have to see the blueprints to be sure, but she speculates that some passenger cabins or crew quarters may be underneath the vault. Above is the Darius Dining Room, which would be unlikely for entry—too open. Of the four sides to the vault, two are implausible, hallway and restrooms. The other two, the auctioneer's office and space unknown to Cynthia, are worth investigating. On her "inside theft" time line, Cynthia brackets 4:00 p.m. Sunday and 11:00 a.m. today, then jots "How to circumvent the date-time tapes on the transport case?"

That leads her to number II.) theft *outside* the vault. Here, she has two items: II.A.) theft on Sunday. II.B.) theft today. "Theft on Sunday" was physically possible but required a conspiracy of all four verifiers or—here she doodles several ink swiggles—someone had to fool the verifiers (or some segment of the verifiers fooled the others). Cynthia wishes she knew exactly what the experts looked for when they examined the painting. After thinking about the problem of the locked box, she adds II.C.) Anton the Illusionist? His magical accessories are here in the theatre. She underlines the word <u>Illusionist</u>."

To Cynthia, an exterior "theft today" is more likely than on Sunday. The painting and its container were carried out of the vault then transported to the Empire Theatre. There, someone removed the painting from the crate and set the Picasso on a display easel. Brent Burns, Ensign Billingsley, and John Poindexter were supervising, but all said they were busy and didn't watch the painting every second. How many people handled the painting? Was it ever left with only one attendant? Or only two? Was Anton near the crate at any time? How long would it take to remove the painting from its frame? That leads to another question. Is the gilded frame on the stage the same as the one that was in the vault on Sunday? It looks similar, but Cynthia can't be sure. And what about the Dali and the Chagall?

A security officer clomps on stage and summons "Malcolm Golden." Malcolm gazes sadly at Cynthia before following the officer up onto the stage and behind the curtain.

Whether the theft was executed on Sunday or today or sometime in between, there is a more important question. While Malcolm is backstage on the hot seat, Cynthia outlines scenarios of: *where is the painting now?*

At the top of a new sheet, Cynthia lists tow columns: 1.) off the ship, and 2.) on the ship. Below number 1.), she writes: "mailed to Boonton; impossible? Then where else?" Under number 2, she lists: a.) in theatre, somewhere backstage, b.) along route from vault to theater, c.) still in the vault, d.) with the thief's baggage, and e.) other.

She studies the list before circling "2.c" and "2.d" together and writing, "rolled or flat?" How tightly can the Picasso canvas be rolled? Certainly to fit inside a golf bag. What about a fishing rod case? Flat, it will fit behind another picture. What else would hide it? A hundred items—from suitcases to shipboard appliances—flash through her head. Suddenly, the ship is a gigantic haystack. She writes possible locations: storage rooms, food pantries, refrigerators, laundry rooms, library bookshelves, etc. This is a waste of time, but she has to keep busy.

Cynthia turns toward someone strutting down the aisle. It's Captain De Vries, his pink complexion betraying a simmering rage. He stomps onto the stage and barks, "Where's Lt. Fist?"

"Backstage, sir," a porter says, "conducting interviews in the—"

The captain has already pushed through the curtain.

46

Backstage

Ninety minutes later—after all the Picasso elites have been interviewed—a dour security officer escorts Cynthia into a narrow backstage dressing room. There, Fist paces like a tiger. Two chairs have been pulled away from an eight-foot-long vanity to face each other. Above the vanity, mirrors double the rows of colored tins, sticks, and vials. She smells greasepaint and thinks of community theater.

The door clicks shut.

Fist's skin is red, as if he applied some of the nearby rouge to his round face. "So we meet again, Miss James."

"I had nothing to do with this." It's the truth, so why does it feel like acting?

"We'll see," he says. "Have a seat."

Cynthia sits, suspecting that he wants to keep her off balance. A tad nervous, she stretches her neck.

"You may be able to eliminate suspects," he says, still standing. "Let's talk about the murder Sunday night. Was Mr. Golden ever out of your sight between six p.m. and the time when you two discovered Miss Caporetto's body?"

Cynthia thinks before she speaks. "Yes. While I was in the bathroom, showering, but not long enough for him to get down to her cabin and back. I was in and out. Three minutes, tops."

Fist taps a pencil on his clipboard. "You and Mr. Golden have separate rooms, not a suite. You admitted you're his bodyguard, not his girlfriend. So you were using different bathrooms, correct?"—she nods—"So you weren't really with him, were you? While you were dressing and later, while you were in separate bedrooms."

Cynthia doesn't reply.

"Remember..." he says, pausing for effect, "...you told me you *caught* him sneaking out."

"I have his room bugged. I heard him through my ear studs. He was in his room. Here." She unpins one pearl stud, pops it open, and hands it to Fist.

He rolls the device in his palm then cocks his head and holds it to his ear, as if listening to a tiny conch shell.

"I only took them off when I was actually *in* the shower."

"Does Mr. Golden also have *your* room bugged?"

"No."

"Interesting." Fist returns the pearl. "While you can verify that he was in his room, he *can't* verify that you were in yours."

Cynthia sits straight, chin up. "We've been over that."

"These look like they can be switched from microphone to receiver."

"Yes."

Fist nods his head slowly. "I recall you dropping one of these in the adjacent cabin the night of the murder. That wasn't an accident, was it?"

Cynthia shrugs before crossing her legs.

Fist flips pages on his clipboard. "Cynthia James. Convicted felon. Served three years, four months in the Tennessee Prison for Women for reckless endangerment and obstruction of justice. I had her picture faxed.... What a surprise," he adds with British understatement. "She *is* you."

Cynthia's throat tightens; her pulse quickens.

"Did those crimes involve poison?"

Her head boils, so she stalls. "You seem to have the report."

"Agent Duvall kept your FBI file a secret, so no, I don't have everything, do I? You're a suspect in the murder. I may not have your motive pegged, but you *are* a convicted felon. I have Scotland Yard and Interpol trying to get the FBI to open your file. I wonder what they'll find."

Cynthia clears her throat. "I didn't kill Sophia Caporetto, and I didn't steal the Picasso."

"Did Mr. Golden?"

"No. We've been together the whole cruise."

"And you were together every second on St. Thomas when Mr. Golden took off a Wyland print large enough to conceal the Picasso?"

Cynthia is impressed that Fist has this intelligence so quickly. Obviously, security personnel are working on the case outside of theater interrogations. "Yes. We were together."

"What happened to the Wyland package?"

"It's not there. Ensign Billingsley inspected the package—"

"Just answer my question. What happened to the Wyland?"

"We mailed it to my roommate in New Jersey."

"Why would you take it off the ship to do that?"

"His friend on St. Thomas—the intended recipient, a woman named Marcie Green—wasn't home. Malcolm was annoyed after schlepping the package all the way up to her house. So he gave it to me to mail to my roommate."

Fist doesn't smile but looks almost pleased. "That's what Mr. Golden said."

"So if you knew, why did you...?" But Cynthia knows why—to try to catch one of them in a lie.

"Murder and grand theft," Fist says, leaning back. He flips two pages on his clipboard. "Do you think the crimes are related, Miss James?"

"Yes. Of course."

"Assuming the stolen Picasso is *not* behind the Wyland, if it wasn't you or Mr. Golden, who was it?"

Cynthia hesitates before saying, "An inside job. Like Mr. Poindexter suggested."

"Still pointing fingers at Mr. Burns, are we?"

She shrugs. "You would know better than I who had access to the vault."

"I don't appreciate the attitude, Miss James."

"Sorry. I just think you should take a look at whoever has access to the security surveillance tapes and/or whoever supervised today's transport."

"You mean my assistant, Ensign Billingsley?"

"If he's the one—yes." She forms a word, dissolves it, then speaks. "But there's another possibility. The safe door on the vault can be opened from the inside."

He squints suspiciously at her but says nothing.

"And because of the ship's weight limits, the walls are..." She wants to say "surely..." but substitutes, "probably substandard. You should check the blueprints for access points to the vault's floor, ceiling, and walls."

Fist rubs his chin... then allows pages to flop back onto the clipboard. "As a matter of fact, the walls and ceiling are cement board, the floor, plywood and carpet. We'll check for holes or patches—"

The door bursts open. Billingsley crows, "We found it! Backstage. Among the magician's props!"

"What?" Fist asks. "The Picasso?"

"Yes, sir. Yes. The Winter Prince.... Sorry to barge in."

Fist processes the news for a moment before saying, "Let's go take a look, Ensign." He rises and strides out. At the door, he turns back. "Wait here, Miss James."

Cynthia is not about to miss the show, so when she finds no guard posted at the door, she tiptoes out of the dressing room and follows Fist through a maze of sets, props, and fly-bars. She passes the Picasso's empty container and comes upon Fist and Billingsley in a corner, staring at the Winter Prince, half covered by a blue plastic tarp. She crouches twenty feet away, where she can hear from behind palm-tree scenery.

"Not very well hidden," Billingsley says. "The tarp was just duct taped around it."

"And these are the magician's props, you say?"

"That's what the stage manager told me."

"And *you* found it?"

"Yes, sir."

"Get the art experts back here, pronto. All of them."

With Billingsley gone, the storage area is quiet. The calm lasts less than two minutes, the time it takes Billingsley to round up the players. Approaching clip-clops announce company. Billingsley trails the eager quartet of elites. They stop, en masse, five feet from the painting.

Fist greets them with a grand wave. "Care to inspect your precious painting?" It sounds like he's smiling.

Cynthia peeks around the side of the papier-mâché tropical

island.

"Is this some sort of sick joke?" Malcolm bellows.

"What do you mean—"

"It's a worse forgery that the first one."

Fist's voice catches. "H-how can you tell from over—"

"This isn't even good enough to *qualify* as a forgery."

"It's not even an oil painting," Poindexter adds.

"It's a fuckin' poster," Julia snaps.

The ghost-like countess appears about to faint. Again.

Fist turns to face them; Cynthia can see him turn red. Again. "Are you telling me we have *two* fakes?"

"Apparently so," Poindexter says.

For a moment, nobody knows what to do. The elites stare at Fist, who grunts. "Go back to your seats. I need to talk with the magician."

This is Cynthia's cue to sneak back to the dressing room.

Cynthia is sitting calmly, legs crossed, when Fist returns. "Did they really find the Picasso?" she asks, keeping a straight face.

"No. Another bloody fake!" He sits. Then stands. Then sits again. "I really thought we had it. I mean, how many blasted forgeries can there be?"

Cynthia knows it's best to let him simmer, so she waits while he drums his fingers on the counter. She watches while he reties shoe laces that don't need tying. Finally, he looks at Cynthia as if *she* executed the latest fraud. "And *you*," he blurts. "You!"

"Would you like me to leave?" she asks.

"No." Fist rubs his forehead. "I need to think."

There's a knock on the door. "Sir," Billingsley says. "I have the magician."

"Bring him in," Fist growls.

"Would you like me to leave *now*?" Cynthia asks.

"Stay where you are," Fist commands.

Anton Perrault steps into the narrow room. Without his costume, he looks common, not an illusionist at all.

Fist says, "Have a seat."

Anton sees only folding chairs. He hesitates, then sits in the one farthest from Cynthia. Billingsley remains, standing just inside the door.

"We found a forged Picasso among your props," Fist says. "Is it yours?"

"Ah, yez. In zee commotion, I forgot all about it. Not a forgery, per se—just a copy, a mere print. I zuppoze I should have zaid zome—"

"What the blazes is it doing back there?"

The harshness of Fist's tone sobers the magician. "Oh," he says, leaning forward. "It is there for tonight's grand finale." The accent is gone. "You see, at my shows on Tuesday, I made a painting disappear and then reappear. But tonight, I planned... Ah, well. I cannot say."

"What about tonight?" Fist says.

"As a professional, I cannot reveal the *denouement* before tonight's performance."

"If you don't tell me," Fist snaps, "there won't *be* a performance."

Anton nods. "All right. If you give me your word not to tell a soul..." He glances at Cynthia. "Her, too."

"I'm like a nun," she says.

Billingsley gives her a frown.

"Quit stalling," Fist says to Anton.

The magician twirls the tip of his mustache. "As on Tuesday, I will make a Pino disappear, but tonight, I will make the Pino *and* the *Picasso* appear." He lowers his head, rubs his forehead. "Ah, but after this unfortunate disappearance, that would be in poor taste, no?"

"Very poor taste." Fist writes something in his notebook while saying, "Don't use your fake Picasso tonight. And one more question. Why didn't you use this copy at your show earlier in the week?"

Anton sits straight. "First, there were *two* performances on Tuesday, so the surprise would be lost at the late show. Tonight, I give only the *one* show. And of course, an illusionist saves the greatest trick for last."

Fist shakes his head. "I'm afraid, old boy, that somebody topped you today."

Anton looks indignant. "May I be excused?"

"You'll have to remain in the theatre with the other suspects. I may have more questions."

"What? How dare you!"

"Look," Fist says. "You have particular skills at manipulating objects. We've lost a very valuable object. Now go and take a seat in the theatre."

"Excuse me, Lieutenant," Cynthia says. "Why don't you have Anton look at the painting's transport case? If somebody had a way to remove the painting without breaking the date-time tape, then he could have—"

Anton springs to his feet. "Are you suggesting that *I* stole the painting?"

"Not necessarily," Cynthia said. "But you might help us figure out how the thief, whoever he or she was, could get the Picasso out of its locked case without breaking the seal."

Anton puffs out his chest. "Oh, like a crime consultant."

Cynthia looks at Fist. "Well?"

"Let's take a look," Fist says.

The four of them exit the dressing room—Cynthia first, followed by Fist, Anton, and Billingsley. They wend their way through obstacles until they stop at the empty carrying container. Fist whispers to Cynthia, "Interesting how you knew right where to go."

"Examine the case," Fist says to Anton. "See if it's solid, or maybe has any hidden trick doors."

Cynthia sees humor in the magician being asked by a layman to verify the integrity of a stage box, but she manages to keep a straight face.

Anton slides his hands along the outside edges. When he gets to the end away from the opening, he stops. "Do you have a flashlight, Lieutenant?"

Fist produces a small one from his pocket. Anton shines the light into the case through the open end. "Yes, yes," Anton says. "Rudimentary, but under the circumstances, quite clever."

"What?" Fist says.

"Your thief knows something about illusions."

"Go on."

"Well, it is of no use to me, rather cumbersome, but the far end has a trick latch."

"How does it work?" Fist says.

"Bring my Picasso print over, and I'll show you."

Fist snaps his fingers and points. Billingsley walks to Anton's Picasso print, picks up the frame, and carries it to the case.

"Please slide it in," Anton says.

Fist and Billingsley strip the duct tape and tarp from the framed print; then they slide it horizontally into the container. Anton closes the end door. "Good, a nice fit. First, I'll show you how it normally stays locked. Tip it up so the open end is on the top."

The two officers pivot the case on a corner and rotate it ninety degrees.

"Now put it back," Anton instructs.

Fist and Billingsley lay it down.

"Nothing unusual," Anton says. "But now observe. Normally such a mechanism is accessed from inside, but this one has these. I merely turn four exterior lock handles. See how they look like ornaments?" At the end opposite the door, he flips tiny levers at each corner. "Now, stand it back up," Anton says.

Cynthia had thought the levers were part of the molding.

Again, the officers tip the crate so the door end rises.

"Now lay it all the way flat on the end," Anton says. "Good. Hear the click? In this position, the mass of the frame trips open the latches. Now, turn it back. Slowly."

As Fist and Billingsley tip the container back onto its side, the end on the floor separates from the rest of the container.

"Voila!" Anton exclaims. "Ze meestery eez solved."

"Part of the mystery," Fist says. "Part." He rubs his forehead. "How hard is it for someone to rig this up?"

Anton shrugs. "The hardware is available in any decent magic shop. They would need a high-quality saw to cut the edges of the plastic case."

"How long would it take?"

Anton thinks. "Thirty minutes, perhaps, for precision cutting. But to install the hardware and refit the molding—at least two hours. Perhaps longer."

"Blast it all," Fist says. "We'll need to establish a chain of possession on the case, from manufacture to the ship."

"When it came on board, sir," Billingsley says, "Sophia said the container had been shipped from the Louvre."

"That's a start," Fist says. "Call down and have someone bring Burns back up here with any paperwork he has on the container. And keep him away from Miss Goode."

"Aye-aye," Billingsley says.

Fist excuses Anton, but asks him to wait in the theatre. Then Fist says, "Dust for fingerprints, inside and out."

"Yes, sir." Billingsley reaches for his walkie-talkie.

"And one more thing," Fist says. "Contact Interpol and the FBI to get anything we can on the magician and his assistant."

"Assis*tants*," Cynthia says. "A second one boarded on St. Maartens."

Two minutes later, Billingsley rejoins Cynthia and Fist in the dressing room. Fist shuffles his notes, mumbling, "Where were we? Oh yes, the vault. We'll check for any breaches in walls, ceiling, or floor." He sets down the papers. "Miss James, are you guilty of any felonies I don't know about?"

Cynthia shakes her head. "I think you know everything relevant about me."

"I doubt that." Fist clicks his pen closed. "Funny how you know so much about safes, vaults, and magic boxes."

She shrugs.

Fist checks his witness list. "Ensign," he says to Billingsley. "Bring in Miss Goode before I re-question Burns." He watches the tall officer depart, then says to Cynthia, "I suppose I should thank you for your tip on the box."

"Then I suppose I should say that you're welcome." They exchange nods.

"You're dismissed for now."

"May I get off the ship at Empire Cays tomorrow?"

"As long as you get back on."

47

Francesca Goode

Francesca makes eye contact with Cynthia as they pass, one entering the makeshift interrogation room, the other exiting. Envying the older woman, Francesca feels one-dimensional, outclassed by Cynthia's posture, waist, tan, eyes, walk—even bust, which is better proportioned than Francesca's. Cynthia has her act together, nobody's fool, dating a rich man, but not as a trophy. Francesca will never be "in control" like Cynthia. Instead, Francesca is cursed by her blessing, defined by the conventional-wisdom of Blonde + Boobs = Bimbo. When you get treated like a sex object, one-dimensional attention erodes a shaky ego, which gets its only sustenance from such attention—a vexing Catch-22.

Her solution is a survival list. Francesca's Rules: Never kiss on the first date. Never go to a guy's room. Never let a guy feel you up on the second date. Never get drunk. And never let a guy inside your panties. Ever. No exceptions. If this makes her the biggest tease on campus, it's better than being a tramp, pregnant, or HIV-positive.

Lt. Fist glares at her. "Sit down, Miss Goode"

Her nervous reflex is a deep breath. She feels cheap, but it's a conditioned response to men. The owner of the pub where she waits tables hired her because she's well-endowed. The regulars over-tip her because she's stacked. By either definition, deliberate breathing helps.

Fist clears his throat. "Miss Goode, have you ever been in the art vault of the ship?"

"What?" she asks. Look dumb, she tells herself, you can do it; you're a blonde. Widen the eyes. Stall. Why is he asking? It has to be because of Brent. When he sneaked her in, he told her never ever to tell a soul—deny, deny, deny. Without video, they can't prove anything, and he blocked the lens. He harped that it was so against the rules—he could lose his job—which made making out in the vault all the more exciting.

"I said: have you ever been inside the art vault?"

More stalling required. "Why would you ask that?"

"Just answer the question."

She tries to read Fist's eyes, pale, almost pink. Then she says, "No, I haven't."

"Are you sure?"

"Of course I'm sure. Yes. How could I be confused about that?"

"You took a while to answer."

"I'm nervous. You make me nervous."

"Are you protecting Brent Burns?"

"N-no. Why would I do that? I hardly know him."

"You're afraid he'll be fired if he let you into the vault, aren't you?"

"No. He didn't let me in. I've never been inside."

"You know why I'm asking about the vault, don't you, Miss Goode?" Fist's sneer makes her stomach churn. He knows something. Has she slipped up? Left fingerprints inside the vault?

"About the missing painting?" she mumbles.

Fist nods.

Francesca feels every bit as dumb as he must think she is.

"There's a surveillance video…" he says.

Dumber by the second.

"…that shows Brent Burns going into the vault area last night. The automatic door sensor verifies that the safe was opened. He says it was to check inventory before the auction. The thing is, there were two suspicious blackouts on the tape—short, but breaks that might have covered another person going in before him and coming out after. Now, if you were really with him in the—"

"But I wasn't."

"If you were with him. *If…* you would have seen whether he

did anything unusual in the vault, wouldn't you?"

She tries a deep breath, but nothing happens. Fist is trying to trick her into tattling on Brent. The good news is that she isn't on the tape. Stick with the story; no video, no proof. "I didn't see anything because I wasn't there."

"But you were with him last night, weren't you? Carpet Club bartenders saw you two together, and there's a bar charge for two drinks on his account less than thirty minutes before the camera recorded Burns entering the vault."

"Sure, we were in the bar. Then he walked me to my room." She's proud of the realistic touch. "That's it."

"Strange then. You were seen together again on the Promenade Deck more than an hour later."

"Uh, after the inventory, he called. I wasn't sleepy, so we went for another walk. But I was never in the vault."

Fist ponders. "Well, that's too bad."

"What do you mean?"

"Because if you *had* been in the vault with Burns, you could testify that he didn't steal the painting. But since you weren't there…"

Her heart misses a beat. If she comes clean now, she'll be branded a liar, which will land her in big trouble. Lies. Truth. The truth would cover her lie. She was there, of course, and Brent hadn't tampered with anything except her bra.

"Care to revise your answer, Miss Goode?"

After three tries, she manages to breathe—deeply enough that he notices. "No. I wasn't there."

Fist shakes his head. "That's really too bad. Your boyfriend's in trouble. You could have helped him."

48

Evening

Cynthia has never seen Malcolm so deflated. Normally a stickler for posture, he sprawls over one of his balcony's plastic chairs like a used towel. He suggests skipping dinner to sulk in his cabin. Half a bottle of room-service Chardonnay is already at work depressing his nervous system. Cynthia tells him for a third time about the magician's release on the container, but the information fails to cheer up Malcolm.

"That just tells us how, not who," he sighs. "Or where it is."

"Billingsley said the container came from Paris."

Malcolm's eye twitches. "Via the Louvre—Paris to Ft. Lauderdale—but I have no idea who may have handled it before the Winter Prince was packed."

"Was the case given a date-time stamp tape in Ft. Lauderdale?"

"Yes. I went down two weeks ago along with John. We met two other elites from South America. A dog and pony show for the press. I watched the painting get taped up. I thought it was secure."

"In theory," Cynthia says, "the case could have been tampered with either in Paris or Ft. Lauderdale."

"I suppose," he says. "Or the case could have been doctored a year ago."

Cynthia thinks that's extremely unlikely. Malcolm isn't making sense, and if he keeps drinking, he'll make even less. "At least they have Brent Burns in custody," she says, sounding upbeat. "If he did something shady in the vault last night, like Fist suspects, then the Picasso has to be on the ship. They'll find it."

Malcolm pours another glass. "Even if they find it, the auction won't happen."

"Then you'll wait until it *is* auctioned."

"But what if it's never found?" He takes a sloppy swallow and tromps to the bathroom. Cynthia follows as far as the dressing alcove. He doesn't bother closing the door. From the splatter, it sounds like he has trouble zeroing in on the bowl. The night could get ugly, which she can't allow.

Before Malcolm returns from the toilet, Cynthia empties his glass and stands the bottle upside down in the ice bucket.

"I guess this means you're ready for dinner," he says.

Cynthia rises. "Take a shower. Then get dressed."

"Says who?"

"Says your bodyguard! Stop feeling sorry for yourself. It's just a painting."

"Just a painting!" He licks the rim of his empty wineglass. "What do you know?"

She grabs his elbow. "I know self-pity. Take a shower and get dressed!"

He laughs, a pathetic, beaten cough. "You've been telling me all week: I'm safest in the room."

"If you stay here, you'll drink yourself into a stupor. Now clean up. You have twenty minutes." She yanks his collar and pulls him toward the bathroom. "Get in!"

After her own shower, Cynthia prepares to dress. She wants to look good for the final formal night—Malcolm could use a distraction from the Picasso *and* alcohol. She hopes to replace last night's embarrassing performance with a touch of class. Her champagne dress is simple yet elegant—perfect for the awkward situation. But when she pulls out the dress, her spirits slump. A coat hanger missed the bar and ripped the bodice. "Shit. Careless idiot," she says to herself. The lavender dress is already crumpled in the smelly laundry bag along with the bloody yellow jumpsuit, the twice-worn black turtleneck, and both stained mix-and-match pants. She will have to appear underdressed in.... Then she remembers: there is another option.

Cynthia tries on the little black dress.

Sheer, provocative, and a smooth fit. Silky fabric caresses both figure and ego. The hem is an inch shorter than she likes... okay, two or three, but what will it hurt? Anticipating the expression on his face, she warms. Cynthia wants to give Malcolm a boost, and this dress might do it. She brushes on a grade-A make-up application. Knowing Malcolm is attuned to all senses, she dabs a few drops of Passion behind the ears and on her wrists. Then she fastens the black satin choker.

Her heartbeat accelerates to maximum speed without adrenaline. After a deep breath, she knocks, half-afraid Malcolm will have raided the mini-bar. But he opens the connecting door, eyes moderately clear, breath rehabilitated by Listerine. He has showered; his tux makes him look in control. His expression is close to a smile. After giving her a head-to-toe, it's a full smile.

On the way down the stairs, they encounter Cliff Gorman, waiting for the elevator on Deck 12. Cynthia tenses until she and Malcolm step onto Deck 11.

49

Cliff Gorman

Cliff watches what he is paid to watch—Malcolm's hands—even though he'd rather be checking out Cynthia's bod in that sexy black dress. Over the years, Cliff has learned to read the signals. The number of fingers extended on Malcolm's left hand designates at which of five pre-determined locations they'll meet. Tonight, Malcolm flashes two, the signal for Cliff's stateroom. The number of fingers extended on the right hand indicates time in one of two ways. Normally, each finger is equal to ten minutes, but when Malcolm *raises* that hand, it means hours. The code takes concentration, like Roman numerals, but it works. This time, the right hand clenches into a fist, raised, knuckles scratching Malcolm's chin, which means: five hours.

Cliff straightens the left sleeve; message received. He checks his watch—18:55—and pumps the elevator's down button.

As Cynthia and Malcolm descend the stairs, Cliff turns to admire Cynthia's backside. Very nice. There are some things a man appreciates under any circumstances.

Cliff has been employed by the Golden family for twenty years, starting at sixteen as a delivery boy, working his way to personal assistant. Malcolm is more driven than his late father—pays better, too, which is why Cliff never questions assignments. Cliff's credo: No job is too distasteful if the price is right.

The day after Sophia's demise, Cliff requested a meeting with Malcolm in the Persian Gulf Pool men's room, at which time he received a cash bonus. They met again the next day, more carefully, while Cynthia was in the ladies' room. Malcolm, preoccupied with his bodyguard's impending return, barely acknowledged Cliff's gathered intelligence about the countess's phone calls.

Then the Picasso vanished. Cliff could only imagine Malcolm's distress. Ever since "Winter Prince" was discovered in a warehouse, Malcolm has been obsessed with the painting. Now that it has been stolen, he's obsessed with finding it, almost as crazy as he was after the Gardner Museum heist. Twice today, Malcolm has passed on impractical instructions jotted in code on the back of postcards left behind the paper towel dispenser in the theatre's men's room. Now, Malcolm wants to meet again at midnight.

Cliff has been on the phone for hours, running up a $2,000 ship-to-shore bill talking with surveillance operatives, but he has nothing. No bank account bumps. No rumors buzzing among known fences. No hiccups from collector big-wigs or museum trustees.

In theory, Malcolm might have stolen the painting himself— maybe enlisted the James woman, no stranger to intrigue. If so, Malcolm is going to great ends pretending otherwise. And he wants *more* information. Cliff has exhausted all leads on Julia Sotelo and the countess, so he'll turn his microscope on John Poindexter and MOMA. That makes sense because of Malcolm's will, so why didn't Malcolm ask Cliff to look in that direction first?

Poindexter and his wife are dull as paint, so Cliff has no desire to devote another second to them. However, an order is an order. Malcolm has taught Cliff to operate indirectly, so that's what he'll do. The magician has been chummy with Poindexter, so Cliff decides to pay a call on Anton the Illusionist. Maybe he'll get close to the lovely Carlotta.

Cliff's money is on the magician, anyway. He has the skills to steal a painting while an entire audience is staring at it—that's what he does every night. The rumored "new assistant" makes Cliff even more suspicious of Anton. Is it a coincidence that Anton brought her onboard the day before the painting disappeared?

Going up the elevator, Cliff contemplates what he's heard

about the new girl—tiny and acrobatic. He hasn't seen the case used to transport the painting, but he suspects that it may be big enough for the pixie to squeeze inside. Yes, he must meet Anton and the new assistant.

Cliff smiles. If he can find the Picasso, his bonus will be huge, even larger than for Sunday night's stunt.

50

Sixth Night

"Pose for another picture?" Cynthia says in the crowded Atrium. "I don't think so."

"Please." Malcolm mopes like a lost puppy. Heidi-girl, the Alpine escort, hovers nearby, looking sinfully photogenic.

Malcolm is suffering, so Cynthia says, "Okay. But only in front of the *Titanic* backdrop." She thinks: that's the only appropriate setting for a souvenir photo of this tragic cruise. "And no slinky escort," she says. "Just you and me."

Ferd, the walrus photographer, poses them in front of a hanging backdrop of the doomed staircase, Malcolm sitting, Cynthia standing. She tries to look like her name sounds— sinfully cynical. The ship's photography department is one more way for Empire Lines to get into her wallet. Well, Malcolm's wallet, actually. She doesn't say "cheese."

At Cynthia's suggestion, they have reservations for two in the Darius Dining Room. They order chicken *cordon bleu* and iced teas. Talking about the Picasso is out, so she brings up motorcycles. The tactic works; Malcolm tells anecdotes about a wild weekend biking through Virginia's Blue Ridge Mountains when he met up with six biker chicks in a Front Royal tavern. They either wanted to copulate with him or torture him— Malcolm wasn't sure there would be a difference—but he didn't stick around to find out. He managed to stay one curve ahead of them while winding along the Skyline Drive. Whether his tale is true or not isn't important; he's himself, joking again.

After their laughter dies, Malcolm says, "You're quite a piece of work, Cyn."

"How so?"

"You try to be some sort of he-woman, above the fray, but deep down, you're like everyone else."

"Go on, Dr. Freud."

"You want to be different, so you act aloof, but you're not. You have a vulnerable side that a black leotard and karate kicks can't disguise."

Blood flows to Cynthia's head, but no words.

Malcolm leans forward. "Right now, you have no idea how beautiful you are."

She flushes. "What are you up to?"

He doesn't respond verbally. Instead he caresses her face with his eyes. The rush is so sweet that she doesn't care whether he's a rogue or not. No use hiding from the fact that she *likes* rogues, always has. Her curse—or, at least one of them.

After exiting the dining room, they stop at the lavatories. Inside the ladies' room, Cynthia encounters an unexpected adversary, Countess LaCroix. Both women pretend to straighten their hair while observing the other in the mirror. "I didn't think you ever went *anywhere* without Julia," Cynthia says with a catty edge.

"I'm here," comes Julia's voice from inside a stall.

"Figures," Cynthia mutters.

"Nice dress," the countess says to Cynthia. "But too expensive for you. Did your pimp, Malcolm, buy it for you?"

"Just the kind of crack I'd expect from a haughty bitch."

"I misjudged you," the countess retorts. "You're not merely a whore. You're a *second-class* whore. And by the way, you're not worth it."

"Worth what?"

"Whatever he's paying you." The countess powders her nose. "Just between, as you Americans would say, *us girls*, let me be frank. Malcolm will *never* get the Picasso."

"So *you* stole it?"

The countess scoffs. "Of course not. But it *will* be found, and when it is, it will be auctioned fairly. Malcolm won't get it, and he will be livid."

"What if you're wrong?"

"I guarantee it. And I suggest you let nature take its course, or misfortune may befall *you*, as well."

Cynthia's color rises. "Are you threatening me?"

The countess raises her chin. "There's more to me than meets the eye. Good evening, *Madame* James." The countess starts for the door. "Julia, are you coming?"

Cynthia and Malcolm take in a lively sing-along set with the Latin crooner in the Tehran Salon. Malcolm orders two cappuccinos. Cynthia sips—quite tasty. Malcolm gets into the "bah-bah-bahs" on *Sweet Caroline*. On the third chorus, Cynthia joins in, too. When Malcolm scratches her pantyhose just above the knee, she doesn't push his hand away.

Later, they search through the photo gallery, killing time before Anton the Illusionist's 10:00 p.m. show. Malcolm finds their portrait taken in front of the *Titanic* backdrop. He orders two eight-by-tens and says they make a striking couple, but Cynthia thinks she looks stiff, as she always does in photographs.

The theatre is almost full when Cynthia and Malcolm arrive at 9:45, forcing them to settle for seats near the back.

Anton's show is Vegas-glitzy, full of smoke and flashing lights. Cynthia sees the ballyhooed Phoebe in action for the first time. She's a sprite in green sequins who flies out of one exploding box like Peter Pan. Carlotta is lithe as ever, showing no symptoms of jealousy. During the set-up for one trick, the two women exchange Anton-bashing banter that gets the crowd laughing. The only trick repeated from the first show is when Anton makes Pino's painting of a reclining woman vanish from an easel.

Tonight's grand finale is *Two* Ladies Vanish, preceded by the two women alternately entering and exiting a spinning, mirrored box that, by appearances, is empty all the time. Then in a flash, the box falls flat, and both ladies are gone! As the music builds to a crescendo, holograms of a magician's top hat and wand float above Anton's head while he spins the flattened box on coasters.

A fireworks *BOOM* bounces Cynthia from her seat. The

accompanying puff of smoke dissipates to reveal Phoebe, sitting on Anton's shoulder, waving a wand and Carlotta where the box used to be, wearing a top hat and holding the Pino. Cynthia squints to make sure it isn't the Picasso.

The theatre empties with the buzz of a hit Broadway opening. Anton's magic has revived Malcolm, who insists on dancing. He smiles as he and Cynthia enter the Roman Forum Lounge, his fingers snapping to a Sinatra classic. Cynthia hums along—*the way you look tonight*. She enjoys lingering eye contact. Malcolm is sinfully handsome in his tuxedo. He asks for two waters at the bar, then carries the glasses to a table, where he and Cynthia sit, facing the dance floor.

"You look fabulous in the dress," he whispers. "And thank you for... well... convincing me earlier that I'd had enough. Enough to drink. I'm okay now. Better than okay." He slips a blue pill into his mouth and takes a swallow of water.

She watches him, appreciates his confidence. Malcolm is dynamic, nothing like the brooding drunk she rescued from the stateroom. Ego swells her head—she has pulled him back from the precipice. That's one thing a woman does for her—

Wait! The thought of Malcolm as *her man* is ridiculous. Yet, he did mention that if they were both sober... And the blue pill...

The music lures them onto the floor. Malcolm draws Cynthia toward his chest, as if for a kiss—90% close. The half-inch between them is an introduction to intimacy—the more his chest almost grazes hers, the more perspiration rings her neck under the choker. She thinks of last night's debacle and shakes her head, reveling in the second chance.

Couples crowd the floor; the space between them disappears. Cynthia nestles into Malcolm's torso—a perfect fit. She holds his shoulder, pulls him snug. She isn't drunk, but she *is* dizzy. Her eyes close. The warmth of his breath melts her ear. She loves the onset of arousal, when anticipation fuels libido. This is about to become the best dance of her—

Malcolm eases her away, checks his watch. "It's almost eleven-thirty. We should be getting back."

"So soon," she says, brushing his lapel. She starts to say more, but what? To protest being hurried to bed? She has wanted this from the third night. "Okay," she says.

Cynthia retrieves her purse, and they stroll out of the lounge. Neither speaks until they reach the landing. "Let's pamper ourselves and take the elevator," he says, guiding her toward an empty car.

Inside, the walls close around them, concentrating hormones and heat. Months of abstinence have her primed; a week of anticipation has lit the spark; energy floods her body; her nipples harden. She's light-headed, light-fingered. Totally alive, she moves her hand, grazes his rear.

"Don't," he whispers.

He can't mean it—the fondling of her knee, the dance. She strokes again, swirling her index finger as if spreading icing on his buns.

Malcolm gently guides her hand away. The tease is inflammatory. She imagines them having torrid sex in the elevator; she can drape his jacket over the security camera. Why leave it to the imagination? Cynthia presses the Emergency Stop button. The car jerks to a halt. She flashes bedroom eyes, but he makes no move, so she snuggles close and pulls his pelvis to hers.

He's hard—a bodice-ripping Billy club! In a few seconds, she'll be—

He pushes her away and presses Start.

She jams Emergency Stop.

"What's going on?" Malcolm says.

"That's what *I* want to know. In the lounge, you caress my knee. And now, I stroke your butt and you're hard as a hammer, but you don't want me to touch you?"

"The camera," he says, pointing. He presses Restart. The car lurches up.

She punches Emergency Stop. "There's no *sound* on the damn camera. Talk to me."

"In the room. We have to go." He presses Restart, then jabs "15" three times.

Cynthia, drained, stands in shock as the elevator ascends.

"This wasn't supposed to happen," he says.

"What wasn't?"

"You and me."

"I don't get it," she says. "You've been leading me on all week, and tonight, we're both sober, and..."

"Wait until we get back to the rooms," he says.

The elevator doors open. In silence, she trails him down the hall, watches him open L105, follows him into her cabin.

Malcolm heads straight through the connecting door to his room.

"What the hell's going on?" Cynthia says to his back. "If we turn each other on, why not—"

"You're just the warm up act tonight, Cyn." He pivots to face her. "I'm sorry."

"The warm up act?" She shakes her head. "Well, I'm pretty fuckin' warmed up." Her eyes beg for an explanation. During painful silence, each waits for the other to speak.

Finally, he says, "Miranda's coming tonight. I should have told you sooner."

Cynthia blinks, lost in dense fog. Blinks again.

"She'll be here in five minutes," he adds. "She's very prompt."

"*Here*? For *you*? You're joking, right?"

"No joke."

Cynthia sees him unbuttoning his shirt. Through the open door, she says, "What's going on?"

"You aren't allowed in the sex suites, and you wouldn't let me go there alone, would you?"

Her tongue swells with intended profanities, but all she can manage is, "You're... you're an asshole."

"Yeah, I know.... I have to take a quick shower."

Cynthia closes the door to within an inch of the jamb, then sits on her bed, from where she listens to the spray of water, listens to Malcolm singing "My Way."

The hormonal high evaporates, leaving her core shivering, her ego shattered. "Shit," she mutters. "Shit, shit, shit."

A few minutes later, he steps into her room, having changed so fast that he doubtless excluded underwear. He sports a silk shirt and thin Armani slacks. He's still visibly hard. Cynthia stares at the floor, not wanting to show that she's devastated. Even if he *is* slime, she doesn't want Miranda to have him.

For an extended moment, Cynthia senses his gaze. She feels

old and used.

"Why?" she whispers. "Why a prostitute?"

"No entanglements," he says. "Sex with intimacy messes up both parties. This way, no one gets hurt."

Cynthia is the no one.

"Then why lead me on?" she says.

"I thought *you* were leading *me* on."

Tap-tap-tap on Cynthia's door. She doesn't move, so Malcolm walks through her alcove and opens the door.

"*Hola*," Miranda says.

Cynthia hears the faint smooch of a kiss and wills composure onto her face.

The couple enters with Malcolm's arm around Miranda's bare waist. She wears another jewel-studded halter. Miranda avoids Cynthia's eyes by keeping hers on Malcolm's smug face.

Cynthia can't even fake a smile. "This is a very bad idea," she says.

"You'll be right next door," he says, "so you can protect me."

Miranda's eyes squint into an unspoken question.

"Or maybe," Malcolm adds to Cynthia, "you'd rather come in and watch."

"Fuck you," Cynthia spits.

Malcolm squeezes Miranda's midriff and replies, "No, that's *her* job."

Miranda smiles too sweetly for a whore. Cynthia despises *him* but not the woman. It dawns on Cynthia that the scumbag can't help himself, which lessens her humiliation—he saved her from making a huge mistake.

He clears his throat.

Cynthia realizes that she's blocking the connecting door. She steps back, so the couple can pass into Malcolm's cabin. The door *clicks* shut. Then, for the first time all week, the deadbolt *thunks*.

51

Hell Night

Keep it together, Cynthia tells herself—no matter how repulsive Malcolm makes it. Technically, she's still on the job, earning her $10,000 even as she wants to wring his neck. First, she slips into the hallway, where she adds a second strip of tape at the top of his door. Back in her cabin, she turns off the light, sits on the bed, and—although she doesn't think of herself as a voyeur—turns up the volume of her ear stud speakers. In the dark, she listens.

From the sounds, Malcolm and Miranda undress slowly—probably on the loveseat—kissing often, talking little. Cynthia imagines Malcolm slobbering on Miranda's naked nipples—not quite the scenario Cynthia pictured in the elevator. She puts two and two together—a kick in her ego. What she *thought* was desire for her had actually been Viagra kicking in.

The couple moves to the bed, where they roll on crinkling sheets. Malcolm says, "You're beautiful." Her purr is cut short by a sloppy kiss. Overall, Miranda speaks more than Malcolm—in Spanish, which Cynthia understands. Miranda tells him. "On your back... There." The noises are soft but rhythmical. Cynthia pictures Miranda straddling him, leaning forward. Cynthia feels dry. She grabs a water bottle from the night table and drinks.

They go at it forever. Cynthia's forehead pounds to their excruciatingly slow rhythm. She hangs her head, presses both palms to her temples. Without warning, Miranda's sighs quicken to staccato. She's a squealer. The rush lasts two minutes, punctuated by vulgarities spewed in Spanish.

The lull is brief. The rhythm of flexing springs and rustling sheets resumes. Miranda comes again, this time longer. And louder. Finally, Malcolm grunts into the end game with the bleats of a dying pig.

Listening is a chore. Cynthia's underarms are damp; her head throbs. She goes to the bathroom and wets a washcloth. Even running water doesn't drown the slow, deep breaths of recovery that roll into her ears like waves onto a beach.

After returning to the bed, Cynthia lies on her back, washcloth draped across her forehead. Malcolm coughs. Miranda jabbers about how great Malcolm was, about how *ready* she is for an encore. Cynthia wonders if the girl will ever shut up.

"C'mon," Miranda coos.

"Not yet," Malcolm sighs. "I'm only human."

"Two minutes ago," Miranda purrs, "you were God."

God! Vile fumes percolate up Cynthia's throat.

There is a reprieve of relative quiet—breathing, occasional kisses, bizarre conversation about rent prices in the Bronx. They whisper so softly that Cynthia can barely hear.

"Ziyi fined me hundred dollars," Miranda says.

"Why?"

"Fat. Five kilos over on last weigh-in."

"Nonsense. You're perfect."

Cynthia hears the faint *smack* of a palm on skin.

"Weight clause in contract," Miranda says. "Fine print."

"So you better lay off the tacos." Another *smack*, louder. They giggle. Cynthia actually *wants* to vomit.

Five minutes later, Miranda is insistent, telling him what a stud hombre he is. "I know how you like to do it the second time," Miranda says in Spanish. "Get behind."

Cynthia holds her breath and listens. Rustling and panting. The sounds are hot, but Cynthia shivers. She is still wearing the little black dress, which provides no warmth.

Next door, the bed creaks loud enough for Cynthia to hear it through the wall.

"Fuckin' prick," Miranda moans in Spanish.

"Fuckin' prick," Cynthia whispers in English.

Cynthia figures that the first round of intercourse went on for twenty minutes, more time than any guy ever kept it up for her.

Now, this round lasts longer. Much longer. *Viagra—the wonder drug*. The talking is softer, complemented by purrs, the kind spawned by fingers sliding in slow, swerving arcs. Based on Malcolm's clear voice and Miranda's garbled sighs, Cynthia pictures Miranda on her knees, her face buried in a pillow. Bad porn.

Endless bad porn. Cynthia is past disgusted, but she doesn't shut off the speakers. Why? Because Malcolm is paying her $1,000 a day to listen, and *damn it*, he'll get his money's worth.

His breathing gets louder; finally he grunts, "You're everything."

"Don't believe him," Cynthia whispers.

Miranda comes, her shrieks muffled. Cynthia feels like a Super Bowl loser forced to witness the winners' celebration.

Again, Malcolm sounds like he's dying. Cynthia can hope.

The audio effects fade to heavy breathing. Cynthia pictures them entwined, each pretending that the moment will last forever. For fifteen minutes, they exchange mindless pillow-talk. The sound quality is excellent. Cynthia wishes it weren't.

Their bed squeaks. Miranda is up, making noise, probably getting dressed. "You see my top?" she asks, her voice far away.

"On the loveseat," Malcolm says loud and clear. He's still in bed.

Silence. Then the *pooch* of a kiss. Miranda whispers, "*Gracias.*"

"*Mucho gracias,*" Malcolm mumbles.

"*Buenas noches,*" Miranda says.

"No! Not that way," he says. "The other door."

Cynthia hops to her feet, flips on the light, shakes out her hair, straightens her little black dress. A bolt clacks, but not from the connecting door. "*Buenas noches,*" Miranda says, sounding a mile away.

"Thanks again," Malcolm says.

Cynthia hears the faint click of a closing door. She hurries through her alcove and bursts out the door in time to see the backside of Miranda swiveling down the hall, her hair mussed, the wreath clutched in her right hand. Funny—Cynthia had pictured the floral tiara in place the whole time.

Miranda stops, looks over her shoulder, and runs five fingers through her moist hair. She is less than ten feet away. Cynthia opens her mouth to say, "Wait," but what would she add after that?

It's Miranda who speaks—in a whisper. "It's my job.... Sorry.... *Muy* sorry."

Cynthia forces a pathetic nod that conveys, "I understand."

Miranda nods back, then walks toward the elevator bank. Cynthia watches until the temptress turns left and disappears.

Cynthia takes a deep breath then *rap-rap-raps* on Malcolm's door. After five seconds, he opens it, saying, "Did you forget some—"

"Sorry to disappoint you, Romeo, but fun and games are over."

Malcolm stands mute, wearing nothing but gold briefs, his mouth ajar.

Cynthia pushes past him and walks to the connecting door. "Have to make sure this is unlocked now that *her* stint as bodyguard is officially over." Cynthia steps into her room and slams the connecting door. But instead of undressing for bed, she slips into the hall, tiptoes to Malcolm's door, and replaces the exterior tape torn loose by Miranda's exit.

Back in her cabin, Cynthia shimmies out of the black cocktail dress. She looks at her laundry bag lying on the floor, then balls the dress into the wastebasket. She dons her trusty gym shorts and cut-off T-shirt, then crawls under the covers. She keeps both speakers on.

Malcolm is already snoring. What a pig! Burning mad, Cynthia wants to blame him for everything, from the theft to... yes, even to Sophia's murder. Thinking back, Cynthia wonders whether he tipped off anything he shouldn't have known. She never told him about overhearing Fist's interview with the Polish Room Service steward. So did Malcolm ever *say* anything about the poisoned bottle being delivered by a *woman* before he heard it from somebody else? Cynthia thinks and thinks, but she can't remember who revealed what when. Before accusing him, she has to be sure.

After Cynthia calms down, she realizes that even with the Miranda debacle, she doesn't want Malcolm to be guilty.

Day 7 — Friday
Empire Cays, Bahamas

52

Trapped

To shock herself alert, Cynthia showers under biting cold water. Then she broods while dressing for the beach stop on Empire Cays—shorts and a Hawaiian shirt over her black one-piece bathing suit. Plus a turquoise scarf. Then she waits.

And waits.

Time moves as slowly as it did last night. She silently curses Malcolm, just as she did last night.

Cynthia waits fifteen minutes after his shower turns off, then bangs on the connecting door. Her muscles tense at the sight of him in a sickeningly-sweet peach golf shirt and beige shorts. His skin radiates vitality. She hates him *and* his GQ tan. "How you feeling?" she says. "Like a stud? Like an asshole?"

"I told you that Miranda and I—"

"Miranda, Miranda, Miranda. Why don't you just give her my whole fuckin' fee?" As soon as the words are out, she regrets them, not only for their vulgarity, but because Cynthia has sold herself, too. "I'm sorry," she mutters. "I'm just pissed at you for being a horny jerk last night. You humiliated me!"

"I'm sorry if you feel that way. That wasn't my intent. I was devastated at losing the Picasso. Perhaps I overcompensated, hoping a good time would help me forget."

"Did it?"

"No." He sits on her loveseat. "You know, Cynthia, a man can care deeply about more than one woman. Do you know why I care about you?" He uses his schmoozing voice.

She braces against his gall. "Go on."

"You're a pleasure to be around."

Cynthia paces, waiting for the punch line. "And?"

"You're one tough bodyguard, but you can be soft, too."

He *is* good, she thinks. What a load of crap!

"And one more thing."

Here it comes, she tells herself, some crack about her ass.

"You've been a good friend this week. You deserved better from me. I'm truly sorry for last night." He pats the seat beside him. "Sit down. Let me—"

Cynthia freezes him with a rigid, raised palm. "Last night you were drooling over Miranda's tits. This is bullshit. A few trite lines don't undo the damage." She feels better getting that off her chest.

Breakfast is tedious. Malcolm dotes on her as if they were lovers making up. She responds with the silent treatment. It infuriates her that Malcolm should be so amiable. Cynthia looks out the window, feeling bluer than the Plexiglass-tinted ocean. A skinny Danish man eating bran flakes at the next table pokes his even skinnier wife, points, and whispers. Cynthia recognizes them; they are in cabin L101 next door to Malcolm's room. Cynthia wants to scream: *it wasn't me squealing like a pig!*

The good news: today is the last full day of the cruise with an island stop in the Bahamas. But a wave of bad news breaks over the loud speaker: "Due to high winds, it is unsafe to tender passengers ashore to Empire Cays."

The impact sinks in: There will be no snorkeling over vibrant coral reefs, no swimming in turquoise water, no walks on pristine beaches. She counted on escaping to land, getting nature between herself and him. The ship is suddenly small.

Malcolm shakes his head. "What did I predict? The same thing happened last year."

"Screw your predictions," Cynthia snaps. She blames the cancellation on Malcolm. Everything is his fault.

Lt. Fist interrupts, striding to their table with a frown. "Excuse me, Mr. Golden, Miss James. I need to speak with you both in private."

"What's this about?" Malcolm asks indignantly enough to pass for a Brit.

"It's a delicate matter," Fist says. "I'd rather not talk about it in the open."

The skinny Danes must have complained about the noise. Cynthia rolls her eyes at the thought of being reprimanded for boisterous sex that she didn't have.

"Is this about Miranda?" Malcolm asks.

"Miranda?" Fist says with a tone of surprise not shared by his calculating eyes.

"Miranda," Malcolm repeats. "The Dominican escort."

Fist rubs his chin, thinking. "Let's go sit in the back. For privacy." He leads them into a seating section that is temporarily closed. They walk to the most secluded corner table where the three of them sit.

"What *about* Miranda?" Fist says.

Cynthia thinks Fist is fishing, so she is surprised when Malcolm says, "I had Miranda in my cabin last night for massage therapy, not in one of the designated suites. It was at my insistence, for security reasons. Please don't blame her."

"You'll have to explain yourself, Mr. Golden."

"I had an appointment with her," Malcolm says. "But for obvious reasons, I don't feel safe without my bodyguard present. So I insisted Miranda come to my cabin."

"Excuse me for a moment," Fist says. He flips open a tiny walkie-talkie. After it crackles to life, he says, "Send Ziyi to the starboard stern section of the buffet—with Miranda's log." He pockets the device. "Ziyi's office is in the Spa one deck above us. She'll be right down."

After a short pause, Fist turns to Malcolm. "So she serviced you in your cabin?"

"Yes."

"And exactly how was this safer for you than the suites?"

"Because Cynthia was..." Malcolm seems to be weighing a problem of infinite complexity.

"Cynthia was *what*?" Fisk prods.

"Because Cynthia was there in the room with us."

Cynthia, relieved to be wearing sunglasses, almost gags. Luckily for her, Fist is looking at Malcolm. She swallows, weighing Malcolm's motive for such a whopper. He's a smart man, so there has to be a reason.

Fist's voice cracks. "In the room? While you were shagging the escort?"

"Yes."

Fist huffs. "The escorts are forbidden from any three-way—"

"No-no," Malcolm says. "Ms. James never moved from the loveseat. I just wanted her there in case something happened. Isn't that right, Cynthia?" He gives her a raised eyebrow that Fisk, who has just turned toward Cynthia, doesn't see.

She gulps, wanting time to think. Then she offers a vague nod, hoping it's enough to keep Fist from demanding a definitive yes or no. She sees the Chinese escort at the far end of the dining area. "I think Miranda's supervisor is here." Cynthia says, pointing.

Fisk turns to look. While he does, Cynthia gives Malcolm a "what the hell is going on" squint combined with a full-body shrug. He answers by mouthing, "Trust me." In any event, they wait while Ziyi walks the length of the buffet, buying Cynthia much-needed time.

Ziyi strides past the "Pardon our maintenance" sign and approaches the table. She is dressed in an Oriental silk sarong— intricately patterned in red, yellow, and blue—and carries a manila folder. Her classic beauty outshines Miranda's.

"You have Miranda's file?" Fist asks.

"Yes, sir." Ziyi does not sit, nor does Fist invite her to.

"Well, I don't have all day," Fist says. "Out with it. Tell me what you have on Miranda and Malcolm Golden."

Ziyi glances daggers at Malcolm before opening the folder. "Two hours last night. There's a handwritten note; they met in Mr. Golden's stateroom, at the customer's insistence." Ziyi's accent is British. She must be from Hong Kong, Cynthia guesses, with some western ancestry for height.

"And their history?" Fist prompts.

"Four previous appointments on prior cruises," Ziyi says, looking at the paper. "Always for the three-hour maximum, and, of course, always in the suites."

"And did Mr. Golden have enough credits for three hours last night?"

"Yes, sir. He is Emperors' Club, with ten hours of credit."

"I see," Fist says.

"I'd like to add, sir, that Miranda is my best escort, consistently rated excellent across the board. She has the highest customer retention in the fleet, and..."

"And?" Fist says.

"Well, sir, I wouldn't want you holding the room violation against her. I'll speak to her and make sure that it never happens again."

While Fist ponders, Cynthia suppresses her simmering anger. She is insulted by them speaking as if she isn't there, and offended at the business-like tone about something that shouldn't be anyone's business.

Finally, Fist says, "I'll have to talk with her, get her side of it."

"Very well, sir, but she's with a client right now."

"Then send her down to the tombs as soon as she's free. Dismissed."

Ziyi pivots, gives Fist a sneer that only Cynthia notices, and strides away. Malcolm and Fisk both watch the escort depart.

After a moment, Fist stands. "We should continue this down in security. I'm afraid I'll have to ask you both to come with me."

Cynthia tries to catch Malcolm's eye again, but he doesn't turn toward her.

"Well, all right," Malcolm says with overt disgust. "I guess—since we're not going to Empire Cays."

53

Gut Check

Cynthia trails Malcolm and Fist to the elevators. During the ride to Deck 5, Malcolm mouths behind Fisk's back; it looks something like: "Follow my lead... Miranda will, too."

Cynthia remains puzzled.

From the last stop, they descend two flights of stairs, below the water line, and walk a long, narrow hallway painted in battleship gray. Cynthia has been down here before, but for some reason she's noticing more details today. Their footsteps echo like they're in a culvert. No purple Persian carpets here—this is the bowels of the bowels of the ship. Malcolm is ushered through a doorway by Billingsley.

Fist directs Cynthia into a different windowless room with gray indoor-outdoor carpet. The door closes, leaving Cynthia and Fist facing off in a cramped space that's nothing but four blank walls—gray as fog—two metal chairs, and one square table. Fist sits across from Cynthia and shuffles through a sheaf of papers. He looks like a man searching for scapegoats.

Cynthia asks "Did you find any breaches in the walls, ceiling, or floor of the vault?"

"No," Fist says. "The ship's carpenter verified the surfaces are sound. No cracks or repairs whatsoever."

"Was the safe door tampered with?"

"We found nothing amiss with the locking mechanism or tumblers. Just the superficial scratches from early in the week."

"Who has access to the combination?"

"That's none of your business," Fist says.

"Then I'll assume it had to be at least Sophia and Burns, plus you and your next-in-command."

Fist blinks before stonewalling his expression, but it's enough for Cynthia to conclude that her guess hit close to home.

"And what about the chain of custody on the painting's security container?" Cynthia asks.

"That's not important right now. I asked you down here for a different reason. I'll be asking the questions, if you don't mind."

"You can't be this concerned over an escort skirting the rules."

Fist shifts his weight and leans forward, indicating that the dialog is entering a darker phase. "Miss James, do you have any orange clothing onboard?"

Cynthia squints. "What?"

"Simple enough question. Do you have any orange clothes?"

She shakes he head. "I don't wear orange."

"Not even a bathing suit? According to the Persian Boutique's records, Mr. Golden purchased..." Fist looks down at a computer printout. "...an orange bikini at our gift shop early Sunday morning. Was it for himself?"

"Oh that," she says. "He gave me a bikini, a miniscule thong really, but I told him I wouldn't wear it."

"Where *is* this bathing suit?"

She thinks before answering. A few days ago, she rummaged in the lower night-table drawer, looking for socks. Yes, the purple shopping bag was still where Malcolm had put it.

"In a drawer in my cabin," she says. "By the bed."

"I'll have to search your stateroom."

A damage-control horn blares in her head—she is a submerged submarine, barraged by Fist's exploding depth charges. "What's going on?" she asks.

Fist stares at her shades. "I'd prefer it if you take off the sunglasses, Miss James. I don't want to think you're hiding anything from me."

She hesitates before removing them.

"You look like you could use some sleep," he says.

She knows she looks haggard but forces herself to hold his gaze. "I don't sleep much when guarding a client."

"Do you have a sweat-suit on board?" he asks.

"Yes.... Why?"

Fist leans as far forward as the table allows. "There's been another murder. Security cameras caught the back of a person in a sweat-suit, with hair about your length, on the landing of the victim's deck around the time of the murder."

Her throat closes tight. Tight and dry.

Fist slides a photo across the table. "I think you know this man, correct?"

Cynthia blinks twice to be sure. It's Cliff Gorman. "The victim?" she asks, her throat catching on the k-sound.

"How well did you *really* know him?"

Cynthia resists an urge to loosen her scarf. "Malcolm introduced us on the ship. We chatted a few times here and there."

"What about?"

"About who might get the Picasso."

"And he made a pass at you, did he not?"

Cynthia wants to reply, but she can't think of what to say. The room feels smaller.

"That's what witnesses told me about your *fight* with him."

She nods amid tedious silence. She swallows, then whispers, "Is he dead?"

"You tell me."

"I don't know anything. What happened?"

"I'll ask the questions, Miss James." His pink nostrils flare. "Exactly where were you last night around midnight?"

Her left eye twitches. She assumes that because Fist chose to interrogate her first, *she* is the prime suspect. Be very, very careful, she thinks—*if they hang either of these murders on me, a convicted felon, I'll die in prison.* But there's a glimmer of light—she sees the alibi in Malcolm's madness.

She answers vaguely. "You heard Malcolm say that I was in his room."

"Last time the subject came up, you said you and Mr. Golden slept in *separate* cabins."

She takes a deep breath. Is Malcolm sticking to his lie? Cynthia figures she has no more than three seconds to answer before she comes off as guilty. She thinks quickly about the essence of truth, the effect of a four-inch wall on literal truth, the value of an alibi.

"We were in the same cabin between eleven-thirty and one-thirty," she says

"*With* the escort?"

After a short pause, she says, "Yes. With Miranda. I sat on the loveseat, making sure that he was safe."

"Safe? So you made him wear a condom?" Contempt drips off Fist's words.

"There had already been one attempt on his life," she says. "And there was an element of risk with Miranda because she could have told people where she was going, told people that Malcolm would be distracted, vulnerable." Cynthia is satisfied enough with this rationalization to almost believe it.

"If Miranda was such a risk, why have her come at all?"

"Not my call." Cynthia takes a breath, hoping to keep the hurt from showing. "Malcolm insists on *his* pleasure, his way. I'm only a contractor. I protect him as best as I can, under the circumstances."

"And they didn't mind having you watch?"

"Apparently not."

"What did you see?"

"They had sex."

"Intercourse?"

"What does this have to do with the murder?"

"If you have nothing to hide, just answer the question. Did they have sexual intercourse?"

She pauses, aware of very thin ice. "Going from the sound, I would say probably yes, although I was watching the door, not them." She braces for more specific questions.

"Who was on top?"

"Does that really matter?"

"Yes, I'm afraid it does."

Cynthia thinks before easing into a vague lie. "It was difficult to watch; that's why I shifted position and looked at the door. I didn't really see."

"But you heard?"

"Yes. Quite clearly."

Fist jots a few notes. "How long did they, ah…have sex?"

"Pretty much the whole two hours. With recovery time in between. You should ask the passengers in the neighboring cabin for confirmation. It was pretty loud."

"So Malcolm has a *golden rod*." Fist raises a goading eyebrow.

Cynthia's frown deepens—his pun is in poor taste.

"Sorry. Unfortunate choice of words." He straightens the papers. "Well. Let's go look for your orange bikini."

"Why?"

"Because Mr. Gorman was strangled. We found orange fibers on his throat consistent with the gift shop bathing suits.... Care to amend your story?"

"No. And why me? There are certainly other passengers with orange clothes."

Fist scowls. "None of those other passengers discovered the body of a murder victim. None of those others got into a fight with the newly deceased. And none of those others has a history of strangling men with their bikinis. We don't care who *wore* an orange suit; we only care who *killed* with one."

A history of strangling men with their bikinis! Cynthia's mind races. Only a handful of people know such specifics of her past as a patriotic assassin. Did the FBI hand over her file? Who is framing her? Malcolm? Two days ago, she would have scoffed at the notion. Now, she isn't so sure.

Cynthia realizes that she has to say something. "What the hell are you talking about?" she fires back. Weak on content, but the best she can do in the circumstances.

"Let's just find that bikini," he says. "And your sweat-suit, all right?"

During the walk and elevator ride to her cabin, Cynthia takes slow, deep breaths, gathering her wits. She has no answers, but at least she's thinking.

At her stateroom, she opens the door, goes straight to the bottom drawer of her nightstand, and pulls out the purple and white Empire Lines Boutique gift bag....

Empty. No orange bikini. Not even the receipt. She mutters, "Shit."

Cynthia tears through every drawer, ransacks her changing alcove, opens her suitcase, looks under the bed. No orange bikini, although the pink sweat-suit is folded on an alcove shelf. Fisk crumples the sweats into a plastic evidence bag. If the pinstripes match what is on the security tape, then Malcolm might be framing her. He's the one person with easy access to her clothes. Malcolm could have lifted the sweats when she was showering yesterday—or when she was asleep—and returned them this morning.

"So where *is* this alleged gift?" Fist asks. "The bikini you supposedly put in the drawer?"

"I don't know why it isn't there."

"Think again. Might you have thrown it overboard after using it to strangle Mr. Gorman?"

She glares at Fist.

"Miss James, we're going to—"

A card-key opens the lock. Malcolm barges in. "Thank heaven I found you. They just finished with me." He notices the disheveled room. "What's going on?"

She takes a long look at Malcolm, measuring him, then says, "They think I strangled Cliff Gorman with the orange bikini you gave me. It's gone."

"That's ridiculous," Malcolm says. "Cynthia was in the same room with me last night from eleven-thirty until well after one."

Cynthia's sigh of relief could fill a sail.

Fist clears his throat. "With all due respect, Mr. Golden, you're her employer or boyfriend, or both, so you're not the most unbiased of alibis."

"I'm sure Miranda will verify the facts," Malcolm says

Fist looks unconvinced. "I'll be interviewing the Dominican girl next."

"Good," Malcolm says.

"Miss James," Fist says, "tell me again about the fight with Mr. Gorman. Maybe there's something you forgot to mention."

Cynthia stretches her neck. "Mr. Gorman appeared drunk. He made some sexist remarks, grabbed my butt. Malcolm took offense, came to my aid. The situation escalated. I dropped Gorman with a well-placed knee. No big deal. There were no hard feelings."

"If that's true," Fist says, "then why is he dead, and where is the orange bathing suit?"

"*I* threw it away," Malcolm says.

Fist turns. "You?"

"Cynthia refused to wear it. I thought about returning it, but I hadn't kept the receipt, so I tossed it."

"Where? When?"

"Yesterday. I was upset about the Picasso. When Cynthia took a shower, I chucked the bikini in my waste basket—in the afternoon, I think."

"We have all the rubbish, of course," Fist says. "We'll look for it. We'll also have to thoroughly search both of these staterooms. For the time being, I'll have to ask you two to go elsewhere." Fist frowns. "Just don't disappear." He uses the phone to call housekeeping and ask where yesterday's Lido Deck trash is stowed.

Cynthia waits until he hangs up. "Lieutenant, may I look at the picture of Mr. Gorman?"

Fist hesitates before removing the picture from his manila folder. "Here."

Cynthia studies the facial proportions. "Cover his hair," she says. "See if you think he looks a little like the mystery stewardess."

"But so do *you*, Miss James." Fist stands silent for several seconds before clicking on the walkie-talkie. "Billingsley? Come supervise the search in Mr. Golden's and Miss James's cabins. I need to talk with the escort."

Cynthia avoids Malcolm's gaze. She wonders what Miranda will tell Fist.

54

Miranda

Miranda nibbles her fingernails after Ensign Billingsley pulls her out of the jewelry boutique. He escorts her to Lt. Fist's office down on Deck 3. There, she sits in a chair while Billingsley hovers over her floral wreath. Lt. Fist's glaring pink face is even more upsetting than having his subordinate leer at droplets of sweat forming between her breasts.

Miranda suspects that she's in trouble. She went to Mr. Golden's cabin—even though paragraph 3.4 of the Escort Handbook clearly states that all massage therapy shall be administered only in designated areas—no exceptions.

Lt. Fist scowls while tapping a pen the size of a cigar on the metal desk. He stares at her, unable to hide his known disapproval of the escort program, of insects like her. Miranda hears ticking from a clock on the desk, right next to a picture frame and a pocket tape recorder. She has trouble breathing. Finally, Lt. Fist nods.

Billingsley leans over her shoulder and pushes the Record and Play buttons. Miranda swallows, braces for undeniable accusations. She needs this job.

"Do you know why you're here?" Lt. Fist asks.

Her face flushes. Coherent thoughts are difficult to identify, much less control. She tells herself: say exactly what Mr. Golden told you to—no more, no less—but she wonders if she heard Mr. Golden right. Her English is okay, but he was whispering so that the woman next door wouldn't hear.

"I said," Lt. Fist enunciates, "do you know why you're here?"

Miranda parts her dry lips to whisper, "Yes," but nothing comes out. Her brain is frozen with a fear of being cast back into the barrio.

"Would you like an interpreter?"

A lifeline. Miranda nods.

"Get Garcia in here," Lt. Fist orders Billingsley, who promptly exits, lessening the pressure on Miranda's chest. She squeezes her palms together and inhales several times.

When Billingsley and Pablo Garcia return a few minutes later, Miranda is resigned to repeat exactly what Mr. Golden told her to say. What choice does she have? He promised to arrange for her brother and sisters to emigrate to New York. Without Mr. Golden, her family is doomed to poverty.

Pablo pulls a folding chair next to hers and sits. His presence steadies her. Pablo is stocky, about 35, slightly balding, with a pencil-thin mustache and rimless glasses. His white uniform crinkles from starch. She knows him well enough to say "*Hola, Pablo*" when they pass in the corridors. Now, he assures her, in Spanish, to relax, that he will translate precisely, and that she has nothing to worry about. She nods but thinks: easy for you to say.

"Miranda," Lt. Fist begins again, "were you—against escort policy—in Mr. Malcolm Golden's cabin last night, cabin L103?"

Pablo translates into Spanish.

She squeaks, "*Si.*"

"What time did you arrive?" Lt. Fist says deliberately. "What time did you leave? And what happened while you were there?"

Pablo starts to translate, but Miranda holds up her palm. "I understand these questions. I tell you when I need you, okay?"

Pablo nods.

"Mr. Golden arrange for two hours," Miranda says. "Eleven-thirty to one-thirty. He insist I come to his room. I arrive on time. I leave on time." She waits, not wanting to volunteer anything else.

"Why not three hours? Mr. Golden usually books for the maximum, correct? Ziyi confirmed that he had enough points."

Miranda shrugs. "You have to ask him."

"And what happened in Mr. Golden's cabin while you were

there?"

What to say? Booby-traps loom everywhere, but Mr. Golden holds her family's future in his generous hands. She turns to Pablo and whispers in Spanish, "We kissed, he sucked my breasts, then we spent most of the time having sex. He has great endurance and is a pretty good lay, but maybe you can say it so it sounds better."

Pablo thinks for a moment before slowly saying, "We kissed, then engaged in sexual intercourse."

Miranda nods approval to Pablo.

"For the whole two hours?" Lt. Fist asks.

She forces a weak smile. "Mr. Golden is strong like bull."

Fist appears uncomfortable, as if he doesn't want to ask his next question. "Mr. Golden told us what... positions you two... shared. May I ask you the same question? We need your description to confirm the veracity of his account."

Some of his words are strange. "*¿Qué?*" she says to Pablo.

Pablo moves his lips close to her ear and whispers in Spanish, "Golden gave them details about screwing you. Fist wants to know if it was the truth. Perhaps he's trying to catch you or Golden in a lie. Be careful how you answer."

"Oh." Turning to Lt. Fist, she says, "I don't have to answer dirty questions."

Lt. Fist turns red. "I'm sorry if I was indelicate. Let me rephrase it this way—when you were having sex with Mr. Golden, could you see the door?"

"No," she says. "Not really."

"Why is that?"

"Very busy. And facing wall."

"Could you see the loveseat?"

Miranda thinks. She doesn't like these questions, which make her feel cheap. "No. My back toward small couch."

Lt. Fist's red face grows crimson, but he presses on. "He says he was behind you some of the time. Is this true?"

Miranda explodes in Spanish. "Why do you need to know this shit? So you and that pig"—she points at Billingsley—"can get off hearing about it?"

Lt. Fist holds up a palm. "I'm sorry. Let's calm down, all right?"

Pablo squeezes her wrist.

She takes a few breaths and nods.

"Good," Lt. Fist says. "Now, Miranda. He pauses for dramatic effect. "Were you and Mr. Golden... alone?"

Miranda's heart skips a beat. Out the corner of her eye, she sees Pablo flinch. Although Mr. Golden told her how to reply, she is surprised Lt. Fist bothers to ask this.

When she doesn't answer, Pablo clears his throat and translates. "*¿Eran usted y él solos?*"

She weighs a white lie against the impossibility of getting her family to America without Mr. Golden's help. "Not alone," Miranda says meekly. Her pulse quickens. "Mr. Golden's girlfriend was in room, too."

"Cynthia James?"

"*Si.*" Miranda waits, praying silently that Mr. Golden has said the same thing.

"Where was Miss James while you and Mr. Golden were having sex?"

Miranda inhales a weak breath. "On small couch," she says.

"Behind you?" Lt. Fist asks.

"*Si.*"

"So she could have sneaked out of the room without you seeing, right?"

This question confuses Miranda. Mr. Golden told her to say that Cynthia was in the room, watching from the couch, the implication being that Cynthia was there the whole time, but he didn't specifically tell her to say that.

"Do you understand?" Pablo asks in Spanish.

"*Si.*" She turns back to Lt. Fist. "I would notice if she left."

"While your back was to her?" Lt. Fist says incredulously. "While your face was buried in a pillow? How can you be sure?"

Miranda cringes; she shrugs her shoulders at Pablo, stalling.

Pablo translates but gives her no further guidance. He looks nervous himself.

"Okay," Miranda says. "Maybe she could sneak out, but I didn't see her or hear her go. Why is this important?"

Lt. Fist rubs his chin, scowling. "Because a passenger on the ship was murdered last night, and Miss James and Mr. Golden are both suspects."

Miranda's heart misses two beats; she gulps for air. "Translate, *por favor*."

Pablo explains. She understands perfectly, horribly. The stifling heat sucks her lungs empty.

"You look nervous, Miranda," Lt. Fist says. "Have you been lying to me?"

"No," she gasps. "All true."

"Do you have anything to add?"

In Spanish, she babbles to Pablo, "Tell him that yes, the woman could have slipped out. Once I got over the shock of her being there, watching, I wasn't really paying attention. But Mr. Golden *couldn't* have left. We screwed the whole time. Tell him."

Pablo translates, inserting "had sex" for "screwed."

"Okay," Lt. Fist says. "Thank you. You can go back to work now."

It takes Miranda two tries to stand on jellied legs. Doing her best to look proud, she straightens her shoulders and says, "Lt. Fist, you believe me, yes?"

"We have more investigating to do before I can answer that."

55

Suspicions

On their walk to the open-air cinema, Cynthia keeps her distance from Malcolm's shoulder, as if he has a contagious disease. Moving her legs is cumbersome, like playing a video game with balky controls. They find two chaises and pretend to watch the end of the morning movie, a mindless thriller at the Magic Carpet Drive-in. Noisy explosions and machine-gun fire cover their whispered conversation.

"What did you tell Billingsley?" she asks.

She listens while Malcolm describes his interrogation, most of which harped on the timeline. According to him, he told security that Cynthia had been in the room—as his bodyguard—the whole time while he and Miranda were making love.

When he's done, she asks, "Did you tell them anything about my past?"

"Just that we met when you started teaching me self-defense. That's all I know because you haven't—"

"Fisk knows classified secrets that I never told you."

"What?"

"You heard me." She looks out to sea. "I just hope to hell my house-of-cards alibi holds up."

"It will, Cyn, because you didn't do it. I know that's the truth."

Truth? Cynthia shakes her head. He's acting like last night never happened.

"There *is* one thing," Malcolm offers. "The countess. Maybe *she* knows about your past."

"The countess?" Cynthia says. "Because she resembles Gorman in a wig and Gorman's dead?" Cynthia has a revelation, takes off her sunglasses. "She could have hidden the Picasso behind one of her *own* paintings. Maybe she thinks no one will look for a masterpiece behind *another* masterpiece. But how can she know about my past?"

"Perhaps you and she have a common acquaintance," Malcolm suggests. "Someone else into collecting art."

"Paulson," she murmurs.

"Who?" Malcolm asks.

Cynthia pauses before she speaks again, thinks that Jerry Paulson is an art collector rich enough to rub elbows with the likes of the countess. He bankrolled the secret organization that trained Cynthia to assassinate terrorists. The possibility that Malcolm may have connected the dots from Paulson to the countess is disturbing.

"Never mind." Cynthia withholds her darkest suspicion while thinking things through. She recalls everything she heard last night—who said what, the door locking, how long Malcolm and Miranda had sex.

Cynthia has an *Aha* moment. Malcolm wasn't—

Wait! Her mind is galloping in the wrong direction. Malcolm's lie gives *her* an alibi. And he explained to Fist about the missing swimsuit.

Cynthia leaves a voice message for Lt. Fist, suggesting that he look behind the countess's personal artwork. She re-reads the same page of her John Grisham thriller ten times. Burning hot, she slips out of her shirt. She and Malcolm cool off in the pool, stroll the decks, and eat sushi for lunch, although Cynthia just picks. Every step is a chore, the magic long gone. Wherever they walk, she makes sure there are people around. For once, she doesn't want to be alone with Malcolm.

Fist approaches their lunch table, the same one where they ate breakfast. *Déjà-vu.*

"Miss James," Fist says, "I need to speak with you."

Her brows arch. "Did you search behind the countess's art?"

"Yes. And we found nothing amiss. However, we did find

something interesting in *your* cabin."

She pins a nugget of tuna between her chopsticks. *Stay cool.*

Fist sits next to her and sets her spy kit on the table. "We found this in your suitcase. Don't insult my intelligence by telling me it isn't yours."

"Then I won't." She pops the roll of tuna into her mouth and chews. Moist, but she tastes nothing.

"Don't be flip, Miss James. I'm this close to locking you up until we reach Fort Lauderdale."

She swallows. "Yes. It's mine. I told you: I'm Mr. Golden's bodyguard. It's tools of the trade."

"And this?" Fist runs a finger across a cell-phone-sized unit clipped to the side of the kit.

Cynthia, her throat dry as toast, sips iced tea.

"It's a tumbler-decoder," Fist says, "but you know that. For opening safes." Fist turns to Malcolm. "Did you know your bodyguard carried safe-cracking equipment?"

"No, I didn't."

Cynthia's heart stutters.

"But I bought the kit for her—all the spy gadgets," Malcolm adds. "I got her the deluxe package. That must have been part of it. Certainly, you can verify what's included."

Cynthia's pulse settles. Every time she fears the worst, Malcolm proves her wrong. "May we go back to our cabins now?" she asks Fist.

"The search is done, so yes. We left your two microphones in place." He stands. "We'll be in touch."

"What about the trash?" Cynthia asks.

"Still looking," Fisk says before leaving.

After Fist is out of sight, Malcolm says, "I hope we've seen the last of him."

"I doubt it."

"You know, Cyn…" He holds her eyes in his gaze. "I'm really sorry about last night. I'd like to make it up to you."

Shit, she thinks, I really want to believe him.

For Cynthia, the afternoon is a series of tedious distractions: A steel drum band plays calypso songs with over-amped guitars drowning out the island sound. Passengers show off their

Caribbean tans, although Francesca Goode has abdicated her sunbathing throne—probably pining over Brent Burns being suspected of grand theft. The cruise staff runs moronic swimming pool games, all the more frivolous in the wake of two murders.

With the Picasso stolen, Cynthia decides that it's okay for her and Malcolm to take their usual late afternoon run on the jogging track. After twenty laps without a word, Malcolm suggests a race over the final lap. Cynthia catches him halfway around the last turn and is pulling away when Malcolm slows, hopping on one leg, victim of another cramp. "Damn," he mutters, grinning. "Now we'll never know who was faster."

"Like there's any doubt," Cynthia says, but it occurs to her that he might have faked injury when he knew he would lose. A flood of misgivings melds into muddled theories.

At the staterooms, she does a lot of pivoting during a half-hearted security check—she's anxious whenever he stands behind her. Once Malcolm steps into his room, she closes the door... and breathes easier. After showering, she faces a clothing snafu. Both of her smart-casual pants were stained by spills, so she dons her only unworn outfit, a zebra-patterned turtleneck jumpsuit that seemed like a good idea during her expense-account shopping spree. The stripes are too flashy for her somber mood, but there's nothing else to wear. She knocks and opens the connecting door.

"Let's go," she says.

They take the stairs down to the Tehran Salon—the specific place doesn't matter as long as there are people. Malcolm orders two margaritas. Cynthia doesn't bother declining, but she doesn't touch her glass—not even a sip.

Dinner for two would be torture. Cynthia insists that they join people they don't know. The luck of the draw puts them with a self-absorbed French couple who prattle non-stop about their Riviera villa, but such drivel is preferable to more bullshit from Malcolm, who packs away food as if he hasn't eaten in weeks. Cynthia has no appetite.

After dinner, dancing is out of the question, so they opt for the closing night musical review, to which she pays little attention, despite the energy of Kitty, Raoul, and all the perky singers and dancers. She's thankful to be around people, including the Poindexters, sitting, as always, in the fifth row. Occasionally, she glances at Malcolm's profile, sometimes seeing the dark side of the Winter Prince.

It's 10:35 p.m. when they enter her stateroom. Malcolm asks, "So, Cyn, what does your gut say? Was the inside man Burns or Billingsley?"

Cynthia believes that the insider was Sophia, but she says, "I don't know." She chooses her next words carefully. "While Miranda was in your cabin, you did something that bothers me."

He stands up a bit straighter. "*Something?* You heard everything, didn't you? Your spy mikes? The neighbors must have heard some of it, too."

"But you *did* something suspicious."

"What's that?"

"You sent Miranda out *your* door."

"I was thinking of you, your privacy."

"Bullshit. You knew about the tape, so you knew that if she went out your door, there'd be no way to prove that you sneaked out earlier."

"What, you think *I* somehow killed Gorman?" Malcolm says with aristocratic insult. "I'm hurt. Our little lie is more beneficial to *you* than to me. That's why I manufactured it—for you. Do you want me to tell them the truth about which one of us wasn't in the room? I have Miranda to verify where *I* was."

"Your little pet. What hold do you have over—" Cynthia bites her lip, recalling the sequence of earlier conversations. She can think of no reason why Malcolm would voice the bedroom lie to Fist *before* hearing about Gorman's death... unless he already knew Gorman was dead. This revelation bleeds into queasiness.

Keep your wits, Cynthia tells herself. Don't tip your hand. Seek justice, not vengeance. Let the authorities take over. Encourage him to pack. Once he's in his room, lock the door and call Lt. Fist.

"We should probably pack," she says.

"Dinner was good tonight," Malcolm says, in no hurry to leave. He pats his belly and flashes a charming smile. But this time, she sees through him. Finally. And a belly is the proof—

Miranda's roll of belly fat. On Wednesday evening at the bar, the dieting girl told Cynthia that she was two kilos overweight. Last night, Cynthia heard Miranda say she was *five* kilos overweight. Nobody on a diet—and with Miranda's degree of motivation— *gains* six pounds in two days. *Last night's sex show was a recorded charade.*

Malcolm grimaces, raises his knee, clutches his foot— another cramp. Good, she thinks. That will hurry his departure. To look at him makes her sick. While Malcolm balances on one leg and massages his foot, she turns away to open the adjoining door—to give him the hint. It's another half-second before instinct warns her: the cramps are part of the charade. But she's a half-second too late.

Cynthia doesn't see the chopping kick that caves in her left knee. She hears a crunch—snapping ligaments—an instant before the pain, pain like a spike jabbed through her leg. His next move is exactly what she taught him—an elbow to her throat. Her hands have dropped toward the crippling pain, but she raises a shoulder and dips her chin in time to protect her neck. His elbow cracks her jaw and rattles her head into the jamb, but it doesn't crush her larynx. Off-balance and without use of one leg, she crumples like a discarded puppet, sliding down the jamb to a sitting position. He kicks her ribs, cracking several and knocking out her wind. He'll go for the throat again. She squeezes her chin to her chest and opens her eyes in time to see Malcolm's knee smash her face. Her nose snaps; she sees white as her skull explodes. Another knee disintegrates what was left of her nose. Blood streams onto her lips, tastes like copper. Gray clouds float into a black sky, then nothing as her torso topples sideways.

56

Malcolm Golden, II

Malcolm re-cocks his leg, but Cynthia lies motionless—a victim of moves she taught him: 1.) Stomp collapses the knee; 2.) Elbow crushes the larynx; 3.) Kick breaks the ribs; 4.) Knee knocks her out. He added a second knee to the head, just to be sure, and is poised to do more damage, although, looking at her beaten face, that appears impossible. He has squashed her. Easy as one-two-three-four.

Easy as lying.

Charm opens that avenue for a man—makes women believe him. Malcolm almost lost control twice. He lusted for Cynthia when he saw her naked in the shower—saw the second "80" branded on her ass—and he wanted her again after the dirty dancing, when she was drugged. But he resisted because the plan required control. Now, he, Malcolm Golden, II, owns Cynthia James.

He admires her mangled remains the way a lion savors a mauled carcass. Don't kill her yet, he reminds himself. In the unlikely event that her corpse is found, the autopsy must reveal either a broken neck—from her impending ten-story fall—or drowning as the cause of death. He sneers, proud of his work: the bloodied face, one leg cocked at a distorted angle.

Malcolm knew it would come to this. Cynthia's presence on the cruise was part of his plot to pin the theft and two murders on a scapegoat who won't be able to testify. He takes a moment to savor the execution of his plan, particularly the self-administered bruise in the men's room on St. Maartens, followed by a deft switch of belt buckles and quick removal of the pocket patch from his shirt. With his back to Cynthia, he dropped the patch and new buckle into a garbage bin—

Stop! No gloating. Be a closer. The world is full of people who don't close. He still has to finish strong. Only after Cynthia splashes into the Caribbean will everything be complete. One final task: disposal.

He drags her body to the balcony in a lurch-breath-lurch cadence. While pulling her arms, he thinks several moves ahead.

Malcolm will tell Fist that he lied at first about Cynthia being in the room with Miranda to cover for his bodyguard. He'll say that when he confronted Cynthia with his suspicions, she attacked him. He'll explain that he threw her off the balcony in self-defense. Fist will buy the story. After all, it's a masterpiece. Pliant Miranda will admit that she was facing away from Cynthia and the door. When the time's right, she'll be silenced.

Are there any loose ends? No. Malcolm removed the cash from Gorman's room. No money trail there. And no audio trail, either. The tape and player are at the bottom of the Caribbean along with the orange bikini and wig. The ship is a convenient place to commit crimes—so easy to dispose of evidence.

The authorities will hound everyone involved—especially him—looking for the painting. After tearing the ship apart, investigators will conclude the Picasso must have been hidden behind the Wyland. They will trace the package to New Jersey, but of course, there will be no Picasso behind the print mailed to Cynthia's address.

Whatever the authorities' suspicions might be, there will be no evidence with which to prosecute. After the furor dies, Malcolm will smuggle the Picasso home, where it will become part of his private collection, hidden behind an inner wall—next to his Vermeer—in a secret basement chamber. There is incredible intoxication in being the only person in the world who can savor such wonders. But first, Cynthia must take the fall— literally.

On the balcony, Malcolm hoists Cynthia's dead weight until she jackknifes on the railing, her head aimed at the sea. He catches his breath and grabs her thighs. One more heave, and she'll nose-dive to her burial at sea.

But black-and-white stripes flash past his eyes—her good leg cartwheels over the rail on its own. He clutches at her hip, then her top hand—too late. It slips away. She drops her grip to something lower and times a two-handed release with inward horizontal momentum, like a gymnast on the uneven bars. Both hands are gone. Her scream is louder than the crash.

For an instant, Malcolm isn't sure if she caught on the lower deck or bounced off. He listens for a distant splash. What he hears are cries of agony. Close. She's on the balcony one deck below. He leans out and looks down, sees the stripes of one leg. *Fuck!* Everything depends on speed; he must throw her overboard before she can get inside. Malcolm pivots on the rail at the waist, intending to get down the same way Cynthia did: feet first. After all, if a woman with a shattered knee and cracked ribs can do it, so can he.

There's a gutter at the base of the Pexiglas for his handhold. He ignores the sucking, black fear that pulls him toward the ocean. A slip is as good as plummeting from the Empire State Building. He clutches one hand on the gutter, then drops down, grabbing hold of the gutter with a double grip. His dangling feet grope for the railing. His hammering heart threatens to shake his hands loose.

Malcolm hangs, swinging, kicking with his feet. There, something solid. He finds the railing with a toe. One foot. Then both feet. Firm. Good. He's composing the story he'll tell the passengers in this stateroom. Cynthia is a deranged serial killer who murdered Sophia and Gorman. Malcolm will be protecting the passengers when he tosses Cynthia James off their balcony.

57

Last Act

Cynthia's pain is agonizing. It's hard to remember what actually happened. When she slumped to the floor in her cabin, flashes bleached her eyeballs so white that everything went black. Toppling sideways was the path of least resistance. Holding her eyes open was futile, so they closed. No coherent thoughts crystallized. Sweet surrender.

A yank on her arms revives her. The carpet burns her back. Too much pain to measure, too much to resist, but each violent tug makes her more alert.

By the time he lifts her onto the railing, Cynthia knows who she is, where she is; her only hope, the balcony below—with luck. If not, she'll bounce off the side of the ship and fall to her death. At least that will end the pain.

She waits until he gets her halfway over before she moves: left hand where her belly pivots, right hand on the gutter's lip. He starts her legs. She accelerates the motion. Lifting with the hips— up, out, and around—she flips with her good leg, the bad one trailing. It's like going over the fence to sneak into high school football games, but doing it blind, 100 feet up. She lets go with her high hand. For an instant, she's flying. Her left hand catches on the gutter next to the right. The jerk rips her chest. Stabs of agony. Ten fingers let go.

She times her release with a swinging, one-legged kick for the balcony below. One ankle bangs the railing, and she crashes face-first into a plastic chair.

Pain explodes inside her head and left knee. On her hands and right knee, she shakes out the cobwebs. There is no time to force open the slider, no hope of racing Malcolm on one leg. He's coming after her—he has to—over and down. If he makes it, she dies. There's no collapsible stiletto in her hair, no belt on her jumpsuit, no strength in a shattered leg.

But both arms work. Fighting through the pain, she pushes herself up onto one foot. There's enough light to see Malcolm's blurry legs as they steady on the railing. She flails her arm, hits something hard—a makeshift weapon. She grabs the plastic chair with both hands. She hops on the good leg and lunges, ramming the chair up into Malcolm's thighs. The blow rips his hands free from the gutter above. He clutches the chair as it shoves him out. She lets go—her abdomen catching on the rail—and watches him diminish into blackness. She sees a white blotch that bounces off a lower deck railing, deflecting out. Now, just a dot. He and the chair disappear—so far down that she doesn't hear a splash. A salvo of pain sinks her onto the good knee. Both hands clutch the rail.

Lights come on inside. The door slides open a few inches. A child's voice. "Who's there?... Mom! Dad! Wake up! There's someone on our balcony!"

Cynthia knows that voice. She turns her neck and sees a short fuzzy figure, wearing plaid pajamas. Pain obliterates visual recognition, but she hears.

"Maverick Lady?" Jake says. "How'd you get out there?"

"What is it?" Nora squeals from inside the room.

"It's the Spiderwoman lady! On the balcony! She musta flown in!"

"On her *web*! I *told* you: she *is* Spiderwoman!"

"Uh... better not come out here, Nora. Go next door and wake up Mom and Dad. Quick!" Jake doesn't move from the open slider. "What happened?" he says.

Cynthia could take the moral high ground and cry, "Man overboard." Instead, she hopes that the plastic chair sinks under the weight of evil. "Fell off my balcony," she mumbles. Adrenaline gives out, replaced by unbearable pain. Shock overwhelms her, and she blacks out.

Day 8 – Saturday

Ft. Lauderdale

58

Disembarkation

Cynthia's knee burns.... Something solid dams her nose.... She hears faint voices.... Two voices.... one Italian, one British.... The words are filtered through cotton in her ears.... There's more cotton in her mouth.... Definitely in her brain.... What she wouldn't give for something fluffy in her left leg, mangled by jagged machetes. The whole limb rips apart, over and over, in slow motion.

"I should really give her morphine." It's the Italian speaking.

"No," says the Brit. "Wait."

She knows that pompous voice. It's the security officer. Things are less muddy.... She's on the *Persian Prince*.... Her name is Cynthia James.... She's royally fucked up.

"But the pain will be excruciating," the Italian says.

It already is, thinks Cynthia. She moves her cracked lips to say just that, but there's too much cotton.

"Give me ten minutes," Fist says.

"She really needs the morphine *now*," the Italian says. A less familiar voice, but she knows it, too. It's the ship's doctor.

Cynthia forces out a muffled groan.

"Hear that?" Fist says. "Just give me five minutes. We have

to find out what happened before they take her to the hospital."

Cynthia opens her eyes, but a bright light forces them to slits. She's lying on her back in a white room with perforated tiles on the ceiling—must be sick bay. Her nose, stuffed with gauze, is three feet wide; her ribs ache, but it's the leg that'll be fatal. Her neck barely moves, braced by something she can't see, but her eyes flit from side to side. To her right is a man, standing, dressed all in white. To her left is another white man next to a raised tabletop upon which lie silver instruments and a bloody zebra skin.

She tries to say, "My fuckin' leg is killing me," but can't hear herself through the cotton. She tries to move her right arm. Her hand twitches, maybe an inch. She moves it higher.

"She's motioning you closer," the doctor says from the left.

"What happened last night?" Fist says, inches from her nose. His breath somehow penetrates the bandage, blowing pain up her nostrils.

"Give me..." Cynthia whispers, "the fuckin' morphine."

"Ah, she's alert," Fist says. "Allow me three minutes."

Cynthia can't live three *seconds*. "No," she spits, stronger. "The morphine. I need the fuckin' morphine. Now!"

"I really should give her the shot."

"Wait. *Two* minutes. A few questions while she's lucid."

"This is lucid?" the doctor says.

"Fuck," Cynthia moans. The pain has limited her vocabulary to various forms of the f-bomb. She tastes salty drops.... tears.

"Listen to me, Miss James," Fist says into her right ear. He holds her hand. His grip is strong. (It's a good sign that she can feel that over the pain, isn't it?) "What happened up there on the balcony?... Once you answer my questions, I'll let the doctor give you morphine. You want that, don't you?"

"This is illegal torture," she growls, grinding her teeth. "You can't fuckin' do this."

"Just relax, Miss James. Tell me what happened. Where's Golden?"

She remembers that Satan dropped into a cold, black hell. Her face contorts into a twisted smile. For a second, she actually feels better. "Dead, I hope," she grunts. "Maybe he'll wash ashore in Cuba."

"What happened?"

"It was him." Cynthia grimaces. "Everything. He had the other guy poison Sophia." She fights off a jab of pain, arches her back, stretches her neck. She can't breathe through the concrete in her nose.

"What other guy?" Fist asks. "Gorman?"

"Yeah," she huffs. "Little shit. Then he killed him, too. He kept me alive long enough to frame me. But first..."

"Go on."

"He and Sophia stole the painting.... Somehow.... She must have smuggled the fake onboard behind some other canvas.... Used the trick box to make the switch.... before she was killed.... That's why...." Cynthia sucks air. "It must be the Wyland..." Words slop in her mouth like sludge. The pain won't go away. She digs her nails into the back of Fist's hand. "Gimme the fuckin' morphine."

"You're doing great, Miss James. I promise you'll get the drugs. Just a few more questions."

"Fuck the questions! The guy faked his own shooting. Put a bullet in the buckle ahead of time. He had a wig like my hair, stole my clothes. He faked cramps. Fuckin' played me."

"*Played* you?"

"Set me up... He drugged me one night. That's when he stole my clothes. Must have. Then broke my knee.... my ribs... my nose... Tried to... throw me off the balcony...."

"Why?"

"He was gonna frame me for everything."

"Then what happened on the balcony?"

She grits her teeth. Tears stream down her cheeks, around her ear, down her neck. "I'm gonna fuckin' kill you."

"You can kill me in a minute," Fist coos.

"I'll fuckin' *do* it. I've done it before."

"What do you mean?"

She takes a breath that stabs her ribs. "He *picked* me... Must have found out I'd killed men.... So he could pin it all on me."

"What men?"

"Fuckin' terrorists... Never mind... He used me."

"What happened on the balcony?"

She squeezes his hand, digging nails toward bone. "I

dropped down a deck. Caught hold...." She grunts through a bolt of pain.

"Go on..."

"He had to come after me.... He had to kill me.... Then..."

"Then what?"

"He climbed down.... swung down like me.... While he was hanging, getting his feet on the rail, I pushed him off.... with a cheap...." She moans, exhausted by the relentless throbbing.

"With a cheap what?"

"Chair... shitty plastic chair...." She forces a guttural laugh. "*Now* can I get the fuckin' morphine?" She squeezes her eyes shut, but tears still leak.

"Yes, Miss James. You can have the morphine now." Fist's head moves away. "Doctor..."

She waits, feeling only the shredded tissue in her leg. "Hurry," she says. "It hurts so bad."

"I know," the doctor says. "But it'll be better soon."

"Hey, Fist," Cynthia says. "He used my bikini to kill Gorman... Then threw it overboard with the tape. Now can I get the shot?"

"You already got the shot," Fist says. Then, "What tape?"

"The tape of..." Soon is arriving—finally—with life-saving comfort. And warmth. The pain is dying. Her brain floats inside her skull. Everything turns Caribbean blue.

"What tape?" Fist is far away.

She licks her lips—dry as sand. "Sex," she mumbles. "Sex that... never... happened...."

"What never happened, Miss James?" He pats her hand. "Miss James?..."

"Something else," she slurs.

"What?"

Her eyes can't focus. Dreamland surrounds her. "One more thing."

"Yes?" Fist says.

Cynthia purrs.

"What is it? Don't nod off on me yet."

Cynthia's words are mere whispers between breaths. "Where did... you shoot... the zebra?"

Epilogue

The rehab session is a four-Advil pain-a-thon. Cynthia's left leg weighs a thousand pounds. Her left knee aches as if a locomotive ran over it. Dark circles of sweat stain her gray *Louisiana Lady* T-shirt—chest, back, and armpits. The stitched incision down the outside of her knee is a railroad track to agony.

She leans into the next leg lift and groans.

"Nine.... C'mon," Maria urges. "Ten.... Good. Two more for an even dozen."

"*You* do a dozen," Cynthia mutters. Her injured leg flops next to the good one. She slumps in the chair. Leg lifts are the last of eight exercises, her fourth set of the day. The physical therapist has told her to do three sets of ten reps with a 5-pound ankle weight. Cynthia made Maria strap on 7.5 pounds. Doing twelve reps was Maria's idea.

"That's okay," Maria says. "You did great. Does it hurt?"

Cynthia grimaces. "Very funny."

Maria shakes a prescription bottle. "Want the heavy-duty stuff?"

"No," Cynthia grunts. "Just these." She taps out three more Advils then washes them down with a drink from her water bottle.

The doorbell chimes.

"I'll get it," Maria says.

"Like, I'm getting out of the chair?" Don't get depressed, Cynthia reminds herself, you've only been home for two days. The nose splints come out tomorrow. Things get better when you can breathe.

She looks around her condo's living room—her rehab gym.

Colored ankle weights litter the floor; two crutches lean against the couch. A tumbling mat—borrowed from the studio—covers a plywood board atop box-springs, for the prone exercises.

Maria returns, dragging a package the shape of a flat-screen TV across the carpet. "UPS. From the FBI. Didn't know they were in the mail order business."

It's the framed prints, forgotten in the chaos of questioning, two operations, and rehab. Evidence. Murders. Grand theft. Has Cynthia blocked out everything to do with Golden? Not quite.

She focuses. "Those are the prints I told you about. The FBI seized them as part of the search. Open it. There should be two. One's a belated present for you."

Using a penknife, Maria slices open the carton. Inside are two picture frames.

"The larger one is yours," Cynthia says. "That's the dolphins. The Wyland. Golden bought it onboard and took it ashore on St. Thomas—as a gift for a friend. Turned out the friend had split, so he gave it to me to give to you. We mailed it from St. Thomas. The FBI tracked it down."

"You sure you want to keep it? I mean, anything from him?"

"You bet," Cynthia says. "Golden taught me one valid truth: nobody can take away my connection to art. Any art. I really like both these pieces, so we're keeping them."

"Okay." Maria pulls a large frame from the box. Cynthia points above the couch. "Take down that one and hang it up."

While Maria works, Cynthia says, "The feds thought Golden smuggled the Picasso off the ship hidden behind this Wyland. So did I."

Maria grunts while lifting a large abstract off its hangers. "And?"

"The Picasso wasn't there...obviously. They still haven't found it."

A few grunts later, the Wyland graces the wall above the couch.

"I love it!" Maria beams.

"I'm glad. It's a limited edition. One of only two hundred in the world. Or is it two thousand?" Cynthia laughs. Then it hits her—the missing puzzle-piece. She shakes her head like a kid waking up. "Take it down."

"Why?" Maria says. "I like it, too."

"Take it down and open up the back. Right now."

"Okay. Easy. I'll do it."

Cynthia watches Maria take down the picture and use a pen knife to slice open the brown paper covering the rear of the frame. Underneath, they find a thin piece of cardboard backing, the Wyland, and two layers of matting.

"Bingo," Cynthia says. "I know where the Picasso is. Get the phone—please—and get me my folder from the cruise. In the filing cabinet under *Vacations*. The number's in my—"

"Slow down."

"I've been a moron," Cynthia says. "Golden took me to a house on St. Thomas—rented a car so there'd be no taxi log or witness. Said the house was his friend's; found a key under a planter. He set the package—the Wyland—in a hall closet."

"Go on."

"He acted really pissed that his friend wasn't there. We talked about what he should do with the picture. He suggested giving it to you. He pulled the package out of the closet, locked up, and we drove to the post office. But he didn't put the key back."

"So?" Maria says.

"The house he took me to *wasn't* his friend's. It was a *different* house, and he had an identical package already stashed. He switched packages in the closet."

"Possible," Maria says "But that's a lot of planning."

"Jeez, the shit-head faked his own shooting! It was easy to buy a duplicate print and wrap it up in advance. And *he* re-taped the one on the ship after inspection so he could match the taping to the box in his closet."

Maria frowns. "A switch seems too simple, too low-tech. And too high-risk. He took you there. If you ever put two-and-two togeth—" Maria cups a palm over her mouth. "He was planning to kill you all along, wasn't he?"

"Yes. He just had to wait until after the second murder."

"So," Maria says. "A priceless Picasso is in a closet on St. Thomas wrapped up behind a print?"

"Not just any print. It's registered. Look at the corner of yours. There's the number. Write it down." Cynthia stands on one leg and hops toward her pocketbook. After two hops, she flops on the couch. "Hand me my phone. I have to call the ship's security officer."

"Not the FBI?"

"Need to double-check something."

Ten minutes later, alone in the kitchen, Cynthia takes Lt. Sebastian Fist's ship-to-shore return call. She sits on a rolling chair, her leg propped on a pillow atop a second chair. "Hello, Lt. Fist," she says. "Thanks for calling back. Do you have the auction records I asked for?"

"Right in front of me," Fist answers in his stuffy British accent. The connection flip-flops from weak to strong.

"I got the print from St. Thomas today," Cynthia says, her voice strengthening. "What's the registration number on the Wyland print that Golden bought at the auction?"

Fist reads the number. "Ninety-five."

"Not the same!" Cynthia's voice climbs a half-octave. "This one is *seventy*-five. Close enough so he could plead that someone mis-logged the number. He switched pictures in a house on St. Thomas. You can send someone—"

"Too late," Fist says. "We already checked Marcie Green's address. The house burned to the ground the day after you were there, so the Picasso is ashes."

"No!" Cynthia shouts. "That fire was arson, right?"

"How did you know?"

"He drove me to *another* house. I don't know the street name, but I can describe it. Windy, steep, near a hairpin turn. White stucco—"

"That's half the houses on St. Thomas."

"Number two-forty-something, I think. To the right of the door. The house is about two-thirds up the mountain, great view of the harbor." Cynthia rattles on. "The house is three doors up from a silk cotton tree. Golden said it was rare that high on the mountain. And Golden's house had a flowerpot on the front steps with bright flowers—blue and red. The painting will be in the hall closet."

"Not if an accomplice removed it."

"He wouldn't trust anyone else with his baby. He wouldn't

even let me help carry it. I'll bet he had plane reservations back to St. Thomas."

"We'll check that out." He pauses. "We've been all over every angle. He couldn't have gotten the Picasso out underneath the Wyland unless Burns was in on it, too. Burns says he took the damn frame apart before Golden took it off the ship."

"I know. I was there. But the cardboard backing was thicker for that picture than the one that came here. Sophia must have sealed the Picasso canvas inside backing material."

"Could be," Fisk says.

There is an awkward silence.

"By the way," Fist says, "Miranda came clean after Golden disappeared—about him leaving the cabin. Said she lied because he promised to get her a green card and pay for her family to come to America."

"How's she doing?" Cynthia asks.

"Pretty distraught—not eating. Her supervisor says that she made her weight, though, and qualified for a bonus."

"One silver lining," Cynthia says. "Now have somebody look for that house. When you find the house, you'll find the Picasso."

"We'll get people searching on the island today. I'll ring back if I need more information. And Miss James, thank you for calling. It will be a small saving grace if Empire Lines beats the FBI to the Picasso.... And if this pans out—"

"It will."

"I'll make sure the FBI returns your passport. You'll be in the clear." Fisk pauses. "I hope it pans out."

"Thanks. Now find the painting."

Nothing. For a moment, Cynthia thinks the connection is lost.

"How did Golden get Gorman to murder Sophia?" Fisk asks.

"I was wondering that, too. I think Golden brought the poisoned champagne on board and had Gorman deliver it in disguise, maybe as a prank. Maybe that's where he snuck off to the first night."

Fisk coughs. "But when Gorman found out Sophia was dead...?"

"Golden had him by the balls," Cynthia says. "Made it hard

to come forward and say he didn't know the bottle was poisoned."

"Perhaps," Fist says between *crackles*. The call is breaking up. "Oh, Miss James," he says. "I meant to ask: How's your recovery coming along?"

"Slow but sure. Thanks for asking. And, Lieutenant?"

"Yes?"

"Call me Cynthia, okay?"

"Sure. You take care of yourself, Cynthia. And thank you."

"You, too. Goodbye." Cynthia snaps her phone closed. She hobbles to her feet and crutches her way into the living room, enduring rib pain with every swing. Maria has unwrapped the second picture—Cynthia's fountain woman—and propped it on a chair.

"Sounded like good news," Maria says.

"Yeah." Cynthia drops into her exercise chair and admires the picture. The bond between her and the painting is eerie.

"I love it," Maria says with a chuckle. "It's so *you*."

Cynthia smiles at that not-so-understated truth. She sits forward, holding the crutches in one hand, rubbing her knee with the other. "It *is* a beautiful picture," she says, seeing something from a fresh angle, intuitively knowing why. The golden light in the painting isn't a sunset. It's a sunrise.

7535760R0

Made in the USA
Charleston, SC
15 March 2011